The Collected Jim Maitland, Adventurer

The Collected Jim Maitland, Adventurer

Jim Maitland
and
The Island of Terror

Sapper
(Herman Cyril McNeile)

LEONAUR

The Collected
Jim Maitland, Adventurer
Jim Maitland
and
The Island of Terror
by Sapper
(Herman Cyril McNeile)

FIRST EDITION

First published under the titles
Jim Maitland
and
The Island of Terror

Leonaur is an imprint
of Oakpast Ltd

ISBN: 978-1-78282-407-7 (hardcover)
ISBN: 978-1-78282-408-4 (softcover)

http://www.leonaur.com

Publisher's Notes

The views expressed in this book are not necessarily
those of the publisher.

Contents

Jim Maitland

The first time I heard Jim Maitland's name mentioned was in the bar of a P.&O. We were two days out of Colombo, going East, and when I confessed my complete ignorance of the man a sort of stupefied silence settled on the company.

"You don't know Jim?" murmured an Assam tea-planter. "I thought everyone knew Jim."

"Anyway, if you stay in these parts long you soon will," put in someone else. "And once known—never forgotten."

They fell into reminiscences of old times, and I was well content to listen. Ever and anon Maitland's name was mentioned, and gradually my curiosity was aroused. And when one by one they went off to turn in, leaving me alone with the tea-planter, I asked him point-blank for further details.

He smiled thoughtfully, and took a sip of his whisky-and-soda.

"Ever been in a brawl, Leyton, with ten men up against you, and only the couch keeping a fellow with a knife in the background from sticking it into your ribs? Well, that's Jim's heaven, though he'd prefer it to be twenty. Ever seen a man shoot the pip out of the ace of diamonds at ten paces? Jim cuts it out by shooting round it at twenty. He's long and thin, and he wears an eyeglass, and rumour has it that once some man laughed at that eyeglass." The tea-planter grinned. "Take my advice and don't—if you meet him. It's not safe. He's got his own peculiar code of morals, and they wouldn't wash with an Anglican bishop. He never forgives and he never forgets—but he'd sell the shirt off his back to help a pal. Who he is and what he is I can't tell you; whether it's his right name even I don't know. And I've never asked; Jim doesn't encourage curiosity."

7

"Yes—but what's he *do*?" I asked as he finished.

"Do?" echoed the tea-planter. "Why, man, he lives. He lives: he doesn't vegetate like nine out of ten of us have to."

With a short laugh he rose and finished his drink.

"Well—I'm turning in. That's what he does, Leyton—he lives."

The door closed behind him and for a while I sat on thinking. "He lives: he doesn't vegetate." The words were running in my head, the man to whom they had been applied was only a name to me. Nine out of ten! Ninety-nine out of a hundred would have been nearer the mark.

And since the doings of the one may be of passing interest to the ninety and nine, I have ventured to put on record these random recollections. For Fate decreed that I was to meet Jim Maitland, and eat with him, and drink with him, and fight with him. Fate decreed that the man who was only a name to me should become my greatest friend.

But for those who may read I have one word of warning. By the very nature of things, when a man is a wanderer on the face of the earth, the people he meets are here today and gone tomorrow. Maybe paths may touch again: more likely it is that they do not. The bunch with whom one drank at Shanghai and found good fellows one and all, disappear and are no more seen—just lives that crossed for an instant never to touch again. And so it must be in these pages. Across them will flit men and women—only to disappear as suddenly as they came. Today, as I write, they may be alive; they may be dead—I know not. MacAndrew, the Scotch trader at Tampico: Count von Tarnim of the Prussian Guard: Colette of the dancing hall in Valparaiso—where are they? How has life dealt with them? Has Captain James Kelly got his poultry farm in Dorset? No: by Jove! a U-boat got him in the war, and he went down with his flag flying having pot-shots with a rifle at the submarine commander who had shown himself on the conning-tower too soon. And does Jock Macgregor still wander in strange seas cursing the government for his inadequate pay? As I said before, I know not. Which is why those who may read will not know either.

1.—RAYMOND BLAIR—DRUNKARD

You probably do not know the Island of Tampico. I will go further and say you have probably never even heard of the Island of Tampico. And in many ways you are to be pitied. If ever there was a flawless jewel set in a sapphire sea Tampico is that jewel. And because flawless jewels are few and far between the loss is yours.

But on balance you win. For if ever there was a place where soul and body rotted more rapidly and more completely I have yet to find it. That beautiful island, a queen even amongst the glories of the South Seas, contained more vice to the square mile than did ever the slums of a great city. For in any city there is always work to be done; through a portion of the twenty-four hours at least, the human flotsam are given in labour. But in Tampico there was no work to be done, save by the very few who came for a space on business and departed in due course.

In Tampico, where fruit and enough food could be had for the asking, there was no struggle to survive. In fact, no one ever struggled in Tampico save for one thing—drink. Drink could not be had for the asking. Drink had to be paid for in hard cash. And hard cash was not plentiful amongst the derelicts who came to that island, and having come remained till death took them, and another false name was written roughly on a wooden cross to mark the event. Wood is cheap in Tampico, which is why the tombstones in the graveyard of the lost are monotonous to look at. After all, who could be expected to put, up the price of a perfectly good bottle of gin in order to erect some fool ornamental stone on the grave of a man who had died of *delirium tremens?*

It was out of the beaten track of the big liners by many hundred miles: only small boats ever called—boats principally engaged in the fruit trade, with passenger accommodation for six in the first class. For fruit was the particular trade of Tampico; fruit and various tropical products which grew so richly to hand that it was almost unnecessary to pick them. If you waited long enough they fell into your hands. And nobody ever did anything but wait in Tampico, which is why it is so utterly rotten. Even when a lump of ambergris comes ashore— fat and stinking and an Event with a capital E—the fortunate finder does not hurry. True, he may knife the man who tries to steal it, but otherwise his movements are placid. There is a dealer in the town, and ambergris means drink for weeks, or maybe days, according to the capacity for liquid of the finder. The scent upon your dressing-table, my lady, has ambergris in it, though the whale which supplied it is dead, and the man who found it is dead too.

The first time I saw Raymond Blair he had just found a lump of the stuff and was, in consequence, utterly and supremely happy. I'd heard, about him from MacAndrew the trader, and I watched him with the pitiful interest a sound man always feels for the down and outer.

"The most hopeless case of all," MacAndrew had said to me in the club the night before. "A brilliantly educated man—Balliol—he told me one evening just before he got insensible. He'll spout classics at you by the yard, and if he's in good form—not more than one bottle inside him—he'll keep a dinner-table in roars of laughter."

"He belongs to the club?" I said in some surprise. MacAndrew shrugged his shoulders.

"It's easier to belong to our club here than the Bachelors' in London. He's got money, you see—quite a bit of money. Comes out every month. And, he's educated—a gentleman. And he's a drunkard. Hopeless, helpless, unredeemable." He filled his pipe thoughtfully. "And though it's a strange thing to say, it's better to keep him drunk. It's all that keeps what little manhood is left in him alive. When he's sober he's dreadful.

"Towards the end of the month always, before the money comes—he isn't a man, he's a crawling, hideous thing. Anything, literally anything will he do to get drink. And there's a Dago swine here who torments him. He loathes him because one night Blair—who was drunk and therefore in good form—put it across the Dago in a battle of words, so that the whole club roared with laughter. And the Dago gets his revenge that way. Why, I've seen him, when Blair has been crawling on the floor—and that's not a figure of speech, mark you, I mean it—crawling on the floor for the price of a drink, make him stand up on a table and recite Humpty Dumpty,' and other nursery rhymes, and then give him a few coppers at the end as a reward. And he's Balliol."

"But can't anything be done?" I asked.

MacAndrew had laughed a little sadly.

"When you've been here a little longer, you won't ask that question."

I was sitting in the window of the club as Raymond Blair came in, and we had the room to ourselves. He had been pointed out to me a few days previously, but he had then been far too drunk to recognise anybody, and from the look he gave me as he crossed the room it was evident that he regarded me as a stranger. I took no notice of him, and after a while he came over and drew up a chair.

"A stranger I think, sir, to our island?"

His voice was cultivated, and he spoke with the faintest suspicion of a drawl.

10

"I arrived about a week ago," I answered a little abruptly. Somehow or other the thought of this English gentleman standing on a table reciting nursery rhymes at the command of a Dago stuck in my throat. It seemed so utterly despicable, and yet—poor devil, who was I to judge?

"And are you staying long?"

"Probably a month," I said. "It depends."

He nodded portentously, and it was then that I saw he was already drunk.

"A charming island," he remarked, and his hand went out to the bell-push. "We must really have a drink to celebrate your first visit."

"Thank you—not for me!" I answered briefly, and he gave a gentle, tolerant smile.

"As you like," he remarked, with a wave of his hand. "Most new arrivals refuse to drink with me, in a well-meant endeavour to save me from myself. But I'm glad to say it's quite useless—I passed that stage long ago. Such a fatiguing stage, too, when one is struggling uselessly. Far better to drift, my dear sir, far better."

He took a long gulp of the double whisky-and-soda which the native waiter, without even asking for orders, had placed beside him.

"I am only myself now," he continued gravely, "when I am drunk. I am supplied regularly with money from—er—a business source at home, and I am thereby enabled to be myself with comparative frequency."

It was then, I think, that I realised what an utterly hopeless case he was, but I said nothing and let him ramble on.

"I get it monthly." He was gazing dreamily out of the window, across the water to the white line of surf where the lazy Pacific swell lifted and beat on a great coral reef. "A most prosperous business, though this month the remittance has not arrived. Most strange; most peculiar. The boat came in as usual, but nothing for me. And so you can imagine my feelings of pleasure when I found yesterday afternoon a quite considerable lump of ambergris on the shore. The trouble is that the dealer is such a robber. A scandalous price, sir, he gave me—scandalous. Still, better than nothing. Though I am afraid my less fortunate confreres outside will have to suffer for his miserliness. Charity and liquor both begin at home. It is the one comfort of having the club, one can escape from them."

I glanced into the street, and there I saw his *confreres*. Five haggard, unshaven human derelicts clustered under the shade of a palm tree, eyeing the door of the club hungrily, wolfishly, waiting for this product of a university to share with them some of the proceeds of his find.

"As you see," he continued affably, "they are not quite qualified for election even to the Tampico club." He dismissed the thought of them with a wave of his hand. "Tell me, sir, does the Thames still glint like a silver-grey streak by Chelsea Bridge as the sun goes down? Do the barges still go chugging past Westminster? Do children still sail boats on the Round Pond back London way?"

And for the life of me I could not speak. Suddenly, with overwhelming force, the unutterable pathos of it all had me by the throat, so that I choked and muttered something about smoke going the wrong way. Hopeless, helpless, unredeemable, MacAndrew had said. Aye—but the tragedy of it; the ghastly, fierce tragedy. Back London way—

With wistful eyes he was staring once more over the wonderful blue of the sea, and he seemed to me as a man who saw visions and dreamed dreams. Dreams of the might have been; dreams of a dead past. And then he pulled himself together and ordered another whisky and soda. He was himself once more—Raymond Blair—drunkard and derelict; and as for me, the moment of overwhelming pity had passed.

I was in Tampico—and facts were facts. But it left its mark—that moment: through all that followed the memory of the haunting tragedy in his face stuck to me. Maybe it made me more tolerant than others were: more tolerant certainly than Jim Maitland. For it was in Tampico that I first met Jim, and Blair was the unwitting cause of it.

It must have been a month or five weeks later. The fortnightly boat had just come in, and I intended to leave Tampico in her next day. It was tea- time, and, as I turned into the club, I saw a stranger lounging on the veranda. And because in the outposts of Empire one does not wait for an introduction, I went up to him and spoke. He rose as I reached him, and I noticed that he was very tall.

"I'd better introduce myself," he said with a faint, rather pleasant drawl. "My name is Maitland—Jim Maitland."

I looked at him with suddenly awakened interest. So this was the man of whom the Assam tea-planter had spoken—the celebrated Jim Maitland who lived and didn't vegetate.

"My name is Leyton," I answered, "and I'm glad to meet you. Several strong men had to be helped to bed a few weeks ago after the shock they got when I said that not only had I never met you, but that I'd actually never heard of you."

He grinned—a slow, lazy grin—and then and there I took to him. And, strange to say, after all these years the memory of him which lives freshest in my mind is the memory of that first evening before I knew him at all.

If I shut my eyes, though it's fifteen years ago, I can still see that immaculately dressed figure—tall, lean and sinewy, the bronzed clean-cut face tanned with years of outdoor life—and clearest of all, the quite unnecessary eyeglass. Of the inward characteristics that went to make up Jim Maitland—of his charm, of his incredible lack of fear, of his great heart, I knew nothing at the time. That knowledge was to come later. On that afternoon in Tampico I saw only the outside man, and, in spite of the eyeglass, I pronounced him good.

"Yes—I know most of the odd corners out here," he said as we sat down, and I rang for a waiter. "Though funnily enough I've never been to Tampico before."

"What's yours?" I said as the waiter appeared.

"Whisky and soda, thanks," he answered, stretching out his long legs in front of him.

"Yes—as I say—I've never been here before. I've just arrived in the boat, and I want to get off in her again tomorrow rather particularly."

A peculiar look, half cynical, half amused, came into his eyes for a moment—a look to the meaning of which I had no clue. And then the amusement and the cynicism changed, I thought, to sadness, but, maybe, I was wrong, and it was only my imagination. Certainly his eyes were expressionless as they met mine over the top of his glass.

"Here's how," he said. "You know this place well?"

"Been here six weeks," I answered. "Going tomorrow myself."

"Six weeks should be enough for you to tell me what I want to know. I joined the *Moldavia* at Port Said, and struck up an acquaint-ance with a little woman on board. She was all by herself—extraordi-narily helpless, never-been-out-of-England-before type and all that—and she was coming here. In fact, she's come this afternoon by the boat to join her husband. I gather he's a fruit merchant in Tampico on rather a big scale. Well, when we berthed there was no sign of him on the landing. So I took her up to that shack of an hotel, and started to make inquiries. Couldn't find out anything, so I came along here." He put down his glass suddenly and rose. "Hullo! here she is."

I glanced up and saw a sweet-looking girl coming towards us along

13

the dusty street. Her age may have been about twenty-five, but her wonderful freshness was that of a girl of seventeen. And it seemed to me as if Tampico had vanished, and I was standing in an old English garden with the lilac in full bloom.

"Mr. Leyton," murmured Maitland, and I bowed.

She nodded at me charmingly, and then gave him the sweetest and most beseeching of smiles.

"I couldn't wait in the hotel, Jim," she said. "It's a horrible place."

"The Tampico hotel," I laughed, "is not an hotel but a sports club for the insect world."

She sat down daintily, and I thought of the few leather-skinned products of Tampico. And then—why, I know not—I glanced at Jim Maitland. And his eyes were fixed on the girl, with that same strange, baffling expression in them that I had noticed before—the expression that in years to come I was destined to see so often. But at the moment I remember thinking that it was, perhaps, as well that he was going by the boat next day. Strange things are apt to happen in the Tampicos of this world—things which are not ordained by the Law and the Prophets.

Then I realised he was speaking, and recalled my wandering attention to the question before the house.

"He can't have got your letter, Sheila. Or, perhaps, he may be away from the island on business."

"Well, I asked everyone at the hotel, after you went out, but they didn't seem to understand," she said a little tremulously.

The man turned to me.

"Mrs. Blair has lost or temporarily mislaid her husband," he remarked whimsically. "A large reward is offered information as to his whereabouts."

"Blair," I said, puzzled, my mind being busy with fruit merchants of the place. "Blair! I don't seem know the name."

"Raymond Blair," she cried, leaning forward. "Surely you must know him."

And for a moment it seemed to me as if the street behind her and everything within my vision turned black. How long I sat there staring at her foolishly I know not—perhaps but the fraction of a second. A kindly Providence has endowed me with a face which has enabled me to win more money at poker than I have lost, and when I heard myself speaking again in a voice I hardly recognised, her face still wore the same little eager, questioning smile.

"How stupid of me," I remarked steadily. "Raymond Blair! Why—of course. The last time I saw him he was going into the interior of the island, and he did say, if I remember aright, that he might be catching the boat which left a fortnight ago."

I felt the eye behind that eyeglass boring into me, and I wouldn't meet it. In an island where if a man sneezes the fact is known by the whole community in half an hour, the whereabouts of a leading member of society are not a matter of vague conjecture. But she didn't know it, poor child—with her English ideas. And I watched the smile fade from her face, to be replaced by a little pitiful questioning look which she turned on Jim Maitland.

"Perhaps I could go to his house," she said doubtfully. "If you could tell me where it is."

And now I was lying desperately, furiously.

"He was going to have it done up," I remarked. "I think, Mrs. Blair, that the best thing to do would be for you to go back to the hotel, while I make inquiries as to where your husband is. If he is away from the island, I think you had better put up with the chaplain's wife until—er—until he returns."

And it was at that moment that MacAndrew passed by to go into the club and nodded to me.

"Perhaps your friend might know," she hazarded. There was nothing for it, and I rose and caught MacAndrew by the arm. My grip was not gentle, and, as he swung round, my eyes blazed a message at him.

"Mrs. Blair has come out to join her husband, Mac," I said. "You know—Raymond Blair."

I heard him mutter "God in Heaven," under his breath, but MacAndrew was a poker player himself of no mean repute. "I have a sort of idea that he sailed on business by the last boat, didn't he?" I continued.

He took his cue.

"I believe he did," he said thoughtfully. "Yes—now you mention it—I believe he did."

And then Jim Maitland began to take a hand.

"I think you had better do what this gentleman suggested, Sheila. I'll take you back to the hotel, and I'll see you get a good room. Then you can lie down and rest for a bit, while we find out for certain where your husband is." He turned to us, and we knew he'd guessed something. "Shall I find you here when I've seen Mrs. Blair back to the hotel?"

"We'll be here," said MacAndrew quietly, and in silence we watched

15

them go up the street. In silence, too, did we wait for his return, save for a brief period when Mac cursed savagely and horribly with no vain repetitions.

"Where is he, Mac?" I said, as he finished.

"In Dutch Joe's gin hell," he answered. "And they're baiting him. He's got no money. Who is the fellow with the pane of glass in his eye?"

"Jim Maitland," I remarked briefly, and MacAndrew whistled.

"So that's Jim Maitland, is it?" he said slowly. "Well, if one-tenth of the yarns I've heard about him are true, there will be murder done tonight. He doesn't like Dagos, I've been told—and that swine who is baiting Blair is half drunk himself." He looked at me shrewdly. "How does Maitland stand with the girl?"

"Don't ask me," I answered. "I know no more than you. They both came in today's boat; that's all I can tell you. And, anyway, she's Blair's wife."

MacAndrew grunted, and relapsed once more into silence. Five minutes later Jim Maitland returned, and strode straight up to us.

"Mrs. Blair is a friend of mine. I don't know her husband from Adam, but I know her. You take me?"

His blue eyes, hard as steel, searched our faces.

"Well, gentlemen, I'm waiting. I don't know what the hell the game is, but your lies, sir"—and he turned on me—"wouldn't have deceived an unweaned child who knew these parts."

And strangely enough I felt no offence.

"I lied right enough," I said heavily. "I lied for her benefit, not yours."

"Why?" snapped Maitland.

"You'd better come and see for yourself," said MacAndrew.

"Then Raymond Blair is on the island," said Maitland slowly.

"He is," returned MacAndrew briefly. "Nothing on God's earth is quite as sure as that."

And in silence he led the way along the dusty street towards the native part of the little town. Once or twice I stole a glance at Jim Maitland's face as he strode along between us, and it was hard and set, almost as if he realised what was in front of him. But he spoke no word during the ten minutes it took us to reach Dutch Joe's gin hell; only a single long-drawn "Ah!" came from his lips when he realised our destination.

"Nothing on God's earth is quite as sure as that," repeated MacAndrew grimly, as he flung open the door and we stepped inside.

It came with almost as much of a shock to me as it must have to Jim Maitland. For since that day at the club I had not seen Blair again, and, if Blair drunk was a pitiful sight, Blair sober was a thousand times worse. Almost, in fact, did I fail to recognise him. He was crawling about the' floor like a dog and barking, and sometimes the spectators kicked him as he passed, and sometimes they threw him a copper which he clawed at wolfishly.

Leaning over the bar was Dutch Joe, his fat face oozing perspiration and geniality; while, seated at tables round the room, were a dozen or so of the sweepings of every nation—Greeks, English, Germans, Chinamen—temporarily united in the common bond of watching an ex-Balliol man giving an imitation of a dog at the order of a swarthy-looking Dago sitting at a table by himself. It was the Dago who noticed us first, and an ugly sneer appeared on his face. Baiting this drunken sot would prove more interesting in front of three of his own countrymen.

"Thank you, Mr. Blair," he remarked, affably. "A most excellent imitation of a pariah; but then, of course, you would be able to give a good one of such an animal. You will now please stand on the table and recite to us *Mary had a little lamb*. You will then get this nice shining dollar."

Amidst a shout of half-drunken laughter, Blair, his eyes fixed longingly on the silver coin which the Dago was holding loosely in his hand, proceeded to climb on to one of the tables. He was shaking and quivering; he was a dreadful, terrible sight, but he was spared that final indignity.

I had one brief vision of a man whose nostrils were white, and who wore that very unnecessary eyeglass, going in on that Dago, and then the fighting began. Mercifully for us, Blair, the temporary bond which had united the divers creeds and colours in the room, had subsided foolishly in a corner and was forgotten. The one thing they all understood—a gin-hell fight—had taken his place. And in a gin-hell fight you scrap with the nearest man to you whose nationality is not your own. Wherefore, out of the tail of my eye I saw no less than four fights going on in different parts of that bar, while Dutch Joe, no longer genial, cursed everyone impartially.

It was hot while it lasted, so hot that I had no chance see what an artist Jim Maitland was till quite the end. I was too busy myself with a greasy Portuguese who tried to knit me. But I got in on the point of his chin, and it was no indifferent blow. He slept, even as a child, and I had leis to watch the principal event. And I saw Jim do a thing had never seen before, or since. His Dago—the main Blair baiting Dago—had gone down twice and was snarling like mad dog. There was murder in his heart, and there would have been murder in that room if he had been fighting any one else.

Like a flash of light he flung a knife at Maitland, and I heard afterwards that he could skewer a card to the wall at ten paces five times out of six. It was then that Jim did this thing—so quick that my eye scarce followed it. He side-stepped and caught the knife in his right hand by the hilt, and, so it seemed to me, all in the same motion he flung it back. And the next moment it was quivering in the fleshy part of the right arm of that Dago, who was so astounded that he could do nothing save curse foolishly and pluck at it with his left hand.

"Get out of it," said Jim tersely; "I'll bring Blair."

I got MacAndrew, who was enjoying himself in his own way with an unpleasant-looking Teuton in a corner, and together we made our way to where Maitland had hauled Blair to his feet. We all got round him and then we rushed him through the door out into the sunny street. I was sweating and MacAndrew was breathing hard, but Jim hadn't turned a hair. His eyeglass was still in position, his clothes were as immaculate as ever, and his face wore a faint, satisfied smile.

"Not bad," he remarked quietly. "But it was time to leave. They'll be drawing guns soon."

And even as he spoke, there came the sudden, sharp crack of a revolver from Dutch Joe's gin hell.

With Jim on one side and me on the other, and MacAndrew pushing behind, we got Raymond Blair along, gibbering foolishly. We took him to MacAndrew's house, and we dropped him in a chair—and then we held a council of war.

"Merciful God!" said Jim, after he'd taken stock of the poor sodden wreck. "How can such things be? This thing—married to that divine girl."

He said the last sentence under his breath, but I heard it, and I saw the look in his eyes and certain vague suspicions of mine were confirmed.

"What are we going to do?" he continued. "She's come out here from England to join her husband whom she hasn't seen for two years. She thinks he's a prosperous fruit trader. And there he is. What are we going to do?"

18

"He's better when he's drunk," said MacAndrew. "He's almost normal then."

"But, good Lord, man!" cried Jim angrily, "do you propose that he should be kept permanently drunk by his wife?"

"There's the alternative," answered MacAndrew, quietly pointing to the chair.

For a while there was silence, broken only by the mutterings of Blair.

"Why on earth didn't you say he was dead?" Jim swung round on me, and I shrugged my shoulders.

"It might have been better, I admit," I answered. "But think of the complications. And at any moment he might have heaved in sight himself—normal, as MacAndrew says."

And once again there was silence in the room, while Jim Maitland paced up and down smoking furiously. Suddenly he stopped, and I saw he had come to a decision.

"There's only one thing for it," he said. "His wife must know: it's impossible to keep it from her. If we say he's gone on a voyage, she'll wait here till he comes back. If we say he's dead—well, even she will hardly swallow the yarn that we've only discovered the fact since we last saw her. Besides"—he frowned suddenly—"I can't say he's dead. There are reasons."

"Aye," said MacAndrew quietly. "Let's take that for granted."

"She's got to see him at his best, you understand. At his best. And then—if, well—if—" He was staring out of the window, and MacAndrew's eyes and mine met.

"Aye, lad," said the gruff Scotchman gently, "it's the only straight game."

He rose and crossed to a cupboard in the corner, and having opened it he took out a bottle of gin. Without a word he handed it to Blair, and then, signing to us to follow him, he left the room.

"There are things," he said, "on which it is best for a man not to look."

"Will one bottle be enough?" asked Jim Maitland.

"There's plenty more where it came from," answered MacAndrew, and with that we sat down to wait. Five minutes passed; ten—and then we heard the sounds of footsteps coming along the passage. They were comparatively steady, and Jim, who had been standing motionless staring out of the window, swung slowly round as the door opened and Raymond Blair came in. He was still shaky; his face was still grey and lined, but he was sane. He was a man again, as far as in him lay, and in his hand he held an empty bottle of gin.

"I thank you, MacAndrew," he said quietly. "It was badly needed."

And then he saw Jim Maitland, and paused as he realised there was a stranger present.

"Mr. Blair, I believe," remarked Jim in an expressionless voice.

"That is my name," returned the other.

"I have recently arrived from England, Mr. Blair," continued Jim, "and your wife was with me on the boat." Raymond Blair clutched at the table with a little shaking cry.

"She is at the hotel," went on Jim inexorably, "waiting to see her husband, whom she believes to be a prosperous fruit trader."

I couldn't help feeling sorry for the poor devil—his distress was too pitiful. Even Jim Maitland's eyes softened a little, as bit by bit the rambling, incoherent secrets and degradations of his soul came out.

We heard how he'd lied to her in his letters, writing glowing accounts of the success of his fictitious business: we heard how he'd on one excuse and another prevented her coming out to join him before. And we heard that the money which he'd received each month had not come from any business at home, but from her, out of the small private means she had. And he had pretended he was investing it for her in the island. All that and many other things did we hear as we sat in the darkening room—things which may not be written in black and white.

And then, gradually, a new note crept into his voice—the note of hope. The reason for the non-arrival of the usual remittance was clear now; she had come—his little Sheila. With her at his side he could make a new start; she would help him to fight against his craving. And then at last he fell silent, while MacAndrew lit the lamp on the table beside him. Jim's face, I remember, was in the shadow, but instinctively MacAndrew and I said nothing; it was for that tall, clean-living sportsman to speak first.

And at length we heard his voice quiet and assured.

"You had better come and see her at the hotel now, Mr. Blair. But on one thing I insist. You must tell her what you have told us here tonight, otherwise I shall tell her myself."

★★★★★★

And that was almost the last I ever saw of Raymond Blair. I saw him go to his wife in the hotel; I saw her welcome him with a glad little cry, though even then it seemed to me that her eyes went over his shoulder to Jim. And then, grey and shaking, he went to her room, while the man who had no right there turned on his heel and strode out into the night. And MacAndrew and I had a split whisky and soda, and discussed some futility, being made that way.

An hour later she came down the stairs, and her face made me catch my breath with the pity of it. But she came up to me quite steadily, and we both rose.

"Where is Mr. Maitland?" she said quietly, and at that moment he came in.

And from then on her eyes never left his face; as far as she was concerned MacAndrew and I were non-existent.

"Why did you give him that bottle of gin?" she asked, still in the same quiet voice. "Why did you send my husband to me drunk just after he had recovered from a dose of fever?"

I saw MacAndrew's jaw drop, but it was Jim Maitland I was staring at. After one sudden start of pure amazement, he gave no sign; he just stood there quietly, looking at her with grave, thoughtful eyes.

"I trusted you utterly," she went on. "You were good to me on the boat—and I thought you were my friend. And you presumed—you dared to presume—that you might become more than that. You thought, I suppose, that if I saw Raymond drunk I might leave him in disgust—and that you—Oh! how dared you do such a wicked, wicked thing?"

I opened my mouth to speak, and Jim Maitland's hand gripped my arm like a steel vice. And I saw that he was looking over her head—upstairs. For just a second I caught a glimpse of Raymond Blair, staring at him beseechingly—his hands locked together in agonised entreaty; then the vision vanished, and once more Jim was looking gravely at the girl with a strangely tender expression in his eyes.

For two or three minutes she continued—speaking with cold, biting scorn—and Jim never answered a word. As I said, she seemed to have forgotten our existence; her world consisted at the moment of the poor derelict upstairs and Jim Maitland—the man who had made him drunk. Once MacAndrew did stick in his oar to affirm that it was his gin, and she brushed the remark aside contemptuously. MacAndrew and I were nothing to her; only Jim Maitland counted.

"Have you anything to say—any excuse to make?" she asked at length, and he shook his head.

"You cur," she whispered very low. "Oh, you cur!" Then without a backward glance she went up to her room like a young queen and we heard the door close. And after a while he turned to us with a little twisted smile on his face.

"It's better so," he said gravely, "much better so."

But MacAndrew was not so easily appeased.. His sense of fair play was outraged, and he said as much to Maitland.

"He's lied—yonder swine," he growled. "He's lied to her after his promise to you. She should be told."

The smile vanished from Jim Maitland's lips, and he stared very straight at the Scotchman.

"The man who tells her," he said quietly, "answers for it to me."

And with that he swung out of the hotel.

★★★★★★

Thus ended my first meeting with Jim Maitland. We left in the boat next day, and I saw him leaning over the stern staring at the island till it was but a faint smudge on the horizon. Then he went to his cabin and I saw him no more till the following morning. He sat down at ten o'clock and played poker for six hours without a break: won a hundred and fifty pounds, and rose from the table with the concentrated weariness of all hell in his eyes. And two days later he left the boat.

It was six months before I saw him again. I was up in Nagasaki and he lounged into the bar just before dinner. He greeted me as if we had parted the day before—that was one of his peculiarities—and we took our cocktails outside. And after a while he looked at me with a faint smile.

"Been back to Tampico, Leyton?"

"No," I answered. "Have you?"

"Just come from there." He took out his pocket-book. "There's an additional ornament in the island."

He handed me a photograph, and I stared at it in silence. It was the cemetery with its rows of little wooden crosses. But in the centre rose a big white stone cross, and on the cross was written:

In Loving Memory
of
Raymond Blair

"How long ago did it happen?" I asked.

"He lasted three months—and he nearly broke her heart. But she stuck it—and she never complained. MacAndrew told me. And when it was over she went home to England."

"Why don't you go after her?" I said quietly, and Jim Maitland stared at the cherry tree opposite.

"You cur," he said below his breath. "Oh, you cur! Man, I can hear her now. And I'd have given my hopes of heaven for that girl."

"Then you're a fool," I answered. "Go back to her." But he shook his head.

"She wouldn't understand, old man; she wouldn't understand. No—I'm a wanderer born and bred: and I shall wander to the end. But it's a funny life sometimes—isn't it?—a damned funny life."

He glanced at his watch. "What about some dinner?"

And it was over the coffee that the conversation took a personal turn. The death of an uncle in England had made me independent, and I was at a loose end. I had half made up my mind to go back home by the States and buy a small property, and Maitland shrugged his shoulders as I said so.

"You'll be able to do all that when you're fifty," he remarked. "Why do it now?"

"What else is there?" I asked.

He looked at me thoughtfully.

"Care to join forces with me?" he said at length. "As I said before, I'm a wanderer, and I go whenever and wherever the spirit moves me. But I enjoy life."

It took me one second to decide.

"I'd like it immensely," I said, and he nodded as if pleased.

"Good," he remarked, holding out his hand. "We'll have some fun. There's a tramp going tomorrow for Colombo and the Mediterranean, and the skipper is a pal of mine. We might go in her."

"Where to?" I asked.

"Heaven knows," laughed Jim. "We'll get off when we feel inclined."

"Right you are," I said. "I'll get my kit sent down."

"How much have you got?" he demanded.

"A couple of trunks and a hand grip."

"I'd leave the two trunks and take the grip," he remarked. "A man can go round the world with a spare set of underclothes and a gun, you know."

I suppose I stared at him a little blankly, for he laughed suddenly.

"There's plenty of time for you still to take that property in England, old man."

That night the trunks were dispensed with.

2.—THE KILLING OF BARON STOCKMAR

We left that tramp at Alexandria—though Heaven knows why. Going up the Red Sea we fully made up our minds to go on in her as far as Gib., and pop over from there to Africa, where Jim assured me that trouble was brewing.

But going through the Canal we changed our minds—or rather Jim did.

"I want to go to Shepheard's," he announced, "and see all the tourists buying genuine Egyptian scarabs. I own shares in the factory that makes. them."

So we went to Shepheard's, and when the soul of the capitalist was satisfied with what he saw, we adjourned to the bar to find a chubby-faced youth eating salted almonds and consuming something that tinkled pleasantly in a glass. "Hullo, Pumpkin," cried Jim cheerfully from the door. "Order two more of the same."

"Jim!" shouted the drinker. "Jim! This is a direct answer from Providence. I would sooner see you at this moment than the shores of England."

"A fiver is the utmost I can manage," remarked Jim gravely. "And in the meantime let me introduce—Dick Leyton—Captain Peddleton—otherwise known as Pumpkin, owing to his extreme slenderness—a Bimbashi of repute."

Peddleton nodded to me, and we all three drew up to the bar.

"Jim," he said earnestly, "one of the Great Ones will be very glad to see you. Are you doing anything in the immediate future?"

"Nothing to write home about," said Jim. "I might take a tram and go out and see the Pyramids by moonlight."

"Dry up," laughed the other.

"My dear boy," answered Jim, "there's a fat woman in the lounge there, wearing five veils, who is going to do it tonight. Surely with such an example—"

"Jim," interrupted the other seriously, "I'm not joking." He lowered his voice to a whisper. "It's a little Secret Service job south of Khartoum. It won't take long, but you're one of the few men in the world who can do it."

Jim grunted non-committally.

"Will you come up and see the chief this afternoon?" continued the other, only to break off suddenly and stare at the door. "Good Heavens!" he muttered, "what have we here?"

Coming into the bar was the most unpleasant-looking individual

I have ever seen in my life. His height must have been at least six feet three, and he was broad in proportion. His face seemed set in a permanent scowl, which deepened to a look of positive fury as he saw us staring at him. He possessed a straggling black beard, which did not improve his appearance, and his great arms, abnormally long, terminated in two powerful hands which were so covered with black hair as to be positively repulsive. In short the man looked like a huge gorilla dressed in clothes.

Now, as luck would have it, Jim was nearest to him as he came up to the bar. He had his back turned, and was on the point of resuming his conversation with Peddleton, when the newcomer—either by accident or design—shoved into him heavily, so heavily that Jim, who was quite unprepared, lurched forward and spilt his drink. But for our subsequent discoveries of the gentleman's character, I would have been inclined to think it was accidental. In view of what we afterwards found out, however, I have not the slightest doubt that the thing was done deliberately. It appeared that he wanted the high stool which was just behind Jim, though there were several others vacant. In fact the bar was empty save for the four of us.

As I say, it was unfortunate, because I would sooner play tricks with a man-eating tiger than with Jim if he gets angry. His face went white and his eyes blazed ominously, then he turned round slowly. And the newcomer was about to sit down. He did, heavily—on the floor. It is an old trick for which I have distinct recollections of having been severely beaten at my preparatory school. Rumour has it that removing a chair just as a person is about to sit down on it is apt to damage that person's spine. And, judging by the way the floor shook, the damage in this case must have been considerable, though it certainly did not produce unconsciousness. In fact, I have witnessed many unpleasant scenes in my life, though the one that followed lives ever in my memory.

The man's face was purple as he got up from the floor, and for a moment or two he stood there plucking at his beard and swallowing hard. His lips were working as if he were trying to speak and could not: his great hairy hands kept clenching and unclenching. And quite motionless, sitting on the stool that had caused the trouble, Jim stared at him through his eyeglass. To all appearances he was as cool as a cucumber, but I noticed the danger signals were out. A little pulse was hammering in his temple, and he was white round the nostrils—a sure sign of trouble with Jim. In fact, in a few seconds the atmosphere that breeds murder had arisen in the bar at Shepheard's Hotel.

"Was it you who pulled my stool away?" asked the man at length in a guttural voice which shook so that we could scarcely hear what he said.

"Was it you who deliberately barged into my back, upset my drink, and failed to apologise?" retorted Jim icily.

And then the man broke loose. Every vestige of self-control left him. He cursed, he swore, he used the foulest language—and all the time Jim watched him unblinkingly. The barman with a terrified look on his face had beckoned to me when it started, and from him I found out the gorilla's name.

"It's Baron Stockmar," he whispered to me, "and he goes mad if he's crossed. For God's sake, sir, get your friend out of it! He ain't a man—the Baron; he's a devil in human form."

And assuredly there was a good deal of truth in what the barman said. This thick-voiced, foul-mouthed brute was not a man—he was a maniac. Many less dangerous cases have been locked up in madhouses for life; men whom no warder would dare to go and see alone. But as to removing Jim, I would as soon have tried to remove a leopard from its kill.

He had put down his drink on the bar beside him and was standing up. His breath was coming a little faster than usual, but his eyes never left the other's face. Not a word had he spoken; not a word did he speak even when the Baron gave up generalities and became personal. And it wasn't until the Baron admitted that it had been no accident but an intentional insult when he entered the bar, and launched into his private opinions of Englishmen in general and Jim in particular, that Jim did anything. Then like everything Jim did, it was clean and decisive, and showed the perfect fighting man that he was.

The Baron's great head was thrust forward, the last foul insult was not cold on his lips, and his two hands were coming up slowly towards Jim, when there came the sharp, crisp noise of two billiard balls meeting. With every atom of weight in his body behind the blow, Jim Maitland struck Baron Stockmar on the point of his jaw—and Jim, at one period of his life, had held the Amateur Heavyweight Championship of Great Britain. And the Baron crumpled up, like a horse that is shot through the brain, and toppled over backwards.

For a moment we stood there watching the heavily breathing, unconscious figure, and then for the first time we realised that an excited and terrified crowd of spectators had thronged in at the door.

"Get him out of here, Leyton," said Peddleton urgently in my ear. "There's going to be trouble over this, and we must get to the chief at once."

So one on each side of him we formed up, and Jim was grinning.

"I think," he murmured happily, "though I wouldn't swear to it, that I heard his jaw break."

"Come on, Jim, old man," said Peddleton insistently.

"There are reasons, very important reasons, which I'll explain as I go along. Oh! yes—you can come back afterwards and finish him off ... .Rather."

We dragged him through the crowd at the door, casting longing glances over his shoulder at the man who still lay prostrate on the floor—and we rushed him into the street.

"Confound you!" he said, stopping at the entrance to the hotel. "Why are you taking me away? That swine hasn't apologised yet."

"Doesn't matter, old man," laughed Peddleton. "For the next few hours he'll be too busy wondering whether a horse kicked him in the jaw or not to bother about apologising."

Still arguing and protesting he suffered us to pull him along, and not till we turned into the mess at Kasr-el-Nil, did Peddleton breathe freely again.

"Sit down, Jim," he said, "and get outside a whisky and soda. I want to talk to you for a moment, and then I'm going to take you straight up to the Chief. I didn't realise when that swine first came into the bar who he was. Then I heard what the barman told Leyton. He's a gentleman about whose coming we've been warned. We were told he had a peculiar temper; we were not told that he was a raving maniac. And there are diplomatic reasons, Jim, which render it a little unfortunate that you removed that seat just as he was going to sit down."

"Well, what the deuce did he want to barge me in the back for?" demanded Jim angrily.

"I know, old man—I know," said Peddleton soothingly. "Personally, I've never been so pleased in my life as when you laid the brute out. And from that point of view the chief will probably want to kiss you. But diplomatically, old man, it is unfortunate."

Peddleton's good-natured face was looking quite worried, and suddenly Jim leant across to him with his wonderful, understanding smile.

"Pumpkin, old boy," he said quietly, "I shall make it absolutely clear to the Chief that it was nothing whatever to do with you. But you wouldn't have had me not hit the blighter?"

"Heaven forbid!" answered the Pumpkin fervently. "I very nearly gave three cheers as you laid him out." He got to his feet. "Look here, Jim, come along and see the Chief, now. Leyton—you won't mind waiting here, will you? Shout for anything you want."

"Of course," I answered. "Don't worry about me. I shall probably stroll over to Ghezireh."

But though I went over to the Sporting Club, and tried to concentrate on a game of polo, I could not get the extraordinary scene at Shepheard's out of my mind. At the time it had all been so quick, had all seemed so naturally continuous, that one had had no time to wonder. But now, looking back on it at my leisure, the whole thing seemed like a dream—like one of those sudden desert sand storms which rise out of nothing, pass by and are gone.

In an instant murder—raging, hot-blooded murder—had been let loose in an hotel full of the most commonplace tourists. There had been murder in Baron Stockmar's eyes as his hands went out towards Jim; the difference between the blow that stunned him and a bullet through his heart had been small in motive. And the original cause—a push in the back. Intentional—true: a deliberate insult by a foul-mouthed bully. But knowing Jim, as I did, I couldn't disguise from myself the fact that even had it been an accident, the result would have been the same. He was not a man who took kindly to accidents, especially those for which no apology was rendered. And it was just before the last *chukka* finished, while I still felt as mentally confused as ever, that I saw Jim coming towards me.

"Can you leave for Khartoum with me tonight?" he remarked, as he came up.

"I can," I answered. Then my curiosity got the better of me. "What's happened?"

"The Pumpkin was right," he said, lighting a cigarette. "Unofficially the chief kissed me on both cheeks—so to speak; officially he cursed me into fourteen different heaps. There are certain things I can't tell you, old man—but our friend the gorilla is the accredited agent of a certain government. He has arrived, apparently, on some question of trade concessions in the Sudan, and he is not welcome even officially.

"Unofficially, I believe special prayers are now being offered that his jaw is broken in two places, and that he'll never eat again. He has not endeared himself to anyone in Cairo. But the funny thing is that the job the Pumpkin was actually speaking to me about before the swine came in this morning is concerned directly with the brute. It is to frustrate—this between ourselves—the very thing he has come out to do. And it must be done—unofficially. Hence—me. I have been told unofficially exactly what the chief wants officially—and I leave tonight." A lazy grin spread over his face. "I gather Baron Carl Stockmar proposes to visit Khartoum in the near future."

"Things become clearer," I murmured. "Jim—the man's mad."

He shrugged his shoulders.

"From quiet inquiries made, Dick—since our little episode in the bar, we have found out that the beggar had been drinking before he came in. And when he gets into the condition of 'drink-taken'—I gather he never gets drunk—he is a very ugly customer. He manhandled a sailor who annoyed him on his *dahabeah* the other night and nearly killed him. And his principal hatred is for the English. I trust most fervently that we shall renew our friendship in Khartoum."

And the grin had faded from his face.

★★★★★★

And now I come to the second and final act of the drama. It is the first time that the facts have been put on paper, though many shrewd guesses as to what occurred were made by officers of the Royal South Sussex who were quartered at Khartoum. They were interested in the matter—very interested, since it was in their mess that the insult took place. And I can still see that ring of brown-skinned alert men in mess-kit standing motionless in the ante-room, with blazing eyes and clenched fists: I can still hear the C.O.'s quiet word of warning—"Gentlemen."

But one thing I would say at the beginning, if by any chance these words should meet the eye of anyone who was present that night: there can't be many, for the battalion ceased to be a battalion at Festubert in '15, Von Tarnim of the 3rd Regiment of the Prussian Guard was a *sahib*. He was forced into an invidious position against his will, simply because he was a Prussian officer, and there was no one else to take his place.

But I am jumping ahead. Four weeks after we left Cairo—Jim and I—we returned to Khartoum. On the way through we had dined with the South Sussex, and at dinner Jim had hinted to the colonel the nature of his business.

The next day we went into the wilds, and of the next three weeks there is nothing to tell. Jim talked to many strange, dignified men in their own lingo—and every one of them seemed to know him as an old friend. They suggested sport; they promised us wonderful shooting; but Jim smiled and refused, and pushed on deeper into the desert.

And then came the day when we turned and retraced our steps. The job he had been sent to do was done; the results were locked in Jim's brain. He wasn't communicative, and I didn't ask questions—but there was a pleased twinkle in his eye, and I knew he was satisfied with his work. Only once did he allude to it, and that was the night before we reached Khartoum. "I think, old son," he remarked, "that we have euchred the dear baron."

Next evening we arrived, and dined quietly at the hotel. And after dinner we strolled over to the South Sussex mess. That the baron was dining there as an official guest we had no idea; that the baron had interviewed a tall, stately prince of the desert during the course of the day, and had met with a suave but perfectly firm refusal to certain propositions he had advanced, we had even less idea. It was the first fruits of Jim's mission, and the immediate result had been to throw the baron into a white heat of rage. The concessions had not gone a month ago, he roared furiously; how did it happen they had gone now? And the grave Bedouin had shrugged his shoulders and stalked from the room.

The immediate result also was that Baron Stockmar arrived at the South Sussex mess for dinner still in the same mood. From certain non-committal remarks made by the Arab during their interview, he had gathered that the same refusal would meet him from every quarter, and the baron was not the type of man to take such a thing lying down.

To have failed absolutely in what he had specially decided to do was an unusual experience for him, and his mood at dinner was one of smouldering passion. It was an official invitation, but he made no attempt at even ordinary politeness, and a general desire to sling the swine out of the mess became prevalent before the soup was finished. But one thing the baron did do with gusto, he punished the excellent South Sussex champagne till even the colonel—hospitable sportsman though he was—began to look uneasy.

Then came the first unpleasant episode. The cloths were removed; the wine had been passed round, and officers with their glasses untouched were waiting for the toast of "The King."

The colonel rose and addressed the vice-president. "Mr. Vice—the King."

"Gentlemen—the King."

Every officer rose—but not so the baron. I was told all this after by one of the subalterns. There were a few moments of icy silence, while the band-sergeant, his honest face the colour of a beetroot with rage, glared at the offender and kept his band silent. Then the colonel spoke quietly, and the second-in-command, an officer of choleric temper, plucked feverishly at his collar as if it were choking him.

"We are about to drink the health of our king, Baron Stockmar," said the colonel. "May I request you to stand up."

The baron rose. There was something in the ring of furious men who were staring at him that warned even his drink-bemused brain not to go too far. He rose, and the king was played—but the episode did not improve the harmony of the evening.

And it was into this atmosphere that in all ignorance Jim and I blundered later on. The baron was sitting with his back to us as we came in, drinking his third brandy and soda since dinner, and we neither of us noticed him. All we saw was a bunch of officers looking about as cheerful as a crowd of deaf mutes, and Jim looked at them in surprise.

"Why so merry and bright?" he cried cheerfully. "Having returned from a most successful trip in the wilds, and seen all my old pals—amongst 'em Mahomet Ali—we've come up to play hunt the slipper."

And Mahomet Ali was the man whom the baron had seen that afternoon.

He rose from his chair and turned round facing Jim. Whether or not he realised that it was Jim who had forestalled him, I do not know, but on his face was the look of a maniac. What vestige of restraint he had imposed on himself during the evening vanished; for the moment the man was mad. It was the first time he had seen Jim since the episode at Shepheard's, and he walked towards him swaying slightly.

"You struck me a little while ago," he said thickly. "Then you ran like a coward *and* an Englishman. Will this force you to give me the satisfaction one gentleman demands of another?"

And he flung the contents of his glass straight in Jim's face.

A suppressed murmur ran through the ante-room, and it was then that the colonel's quiet word "Gentlemen" came as a douche of cold water; for passion was running high and ugly, and even the *padre* was muttering unprintable things under his breath. In fact the only man in the room who seemed completely unmoved was Jim. With exaggerated nonchalance he mopped his face with his handkerchief, then he polished his eyeglass and replaced it.

"Dear me, Colonel," he remarked at length, "I wondered what had become of that gorilla I caught on my trip. But really I can't congratulate you on the manners you've taught it. I shall have to take the coarse brute in hand myself."

With a snarl like a beast the baron hurled himself at Jim, and for a moment my heart stood still. Immensely powerful though Jim was, at close quarters with this human monstrosity he could not have stood a chance. But once again I'd reckoned without my man. Even as he spoke he had been measuring the distance with his eye, and had moved back a couple of paces. And as Baron Stockmar rushed at him, Jim dived forward and tackled him below the knees. It was a perfect rugby tackle, and the baron's head in falling hit the edge of the piano. And they left him where he lay.

"That is the second time, sir," said Jim to the colonel. "The world is not big enough for this gentleman."

"Careful, Jim," said the colonel. "For God's sake don't get yourself into any trouble, old boy."

"You can't go having any fool tricks with revolvers, Jim," said the second-in-command. "Duelling ain't allowed in His Majesty's domain."

"Nevertheless, Tubby, old man," said Jim quietly, "I shall deal with him. Shall we leave it at that? I don't think you had better ask any questions."

And at that moment the baron staggered to his feet.

"You will hear further from me, sir," he said shakily.

"I should hate to think so," answered Jim coldly. "There's the door."

No one spoke till the sound of his swaying footsteps had died away; then the colonel again shook his head.

"Jim," he said earnestly, "do, I entreat of you, be careful. You'll put me in such an awful position if... if ..."

"Colonel," said Jim quietly, "did you hear what he said?—'Like a coward *and* an Englishman.' Here—in your mess." His voice shook a little; then he went on quietly:

"Unfortunately this place is so confoundedly civilised that one has got to be careful, as you say. So if he takes no further steps in the matter, and apologises before you all for his remark, I am prepared to let the matter drop. But otherwise—well, as I said before, you had better ask no questions."

And it was at that moment that the mess-sergeant flung open the door of the ante-room, and ushered in a tall, fair-haired man who held himself stiffly.

"Mr. Maitland," he said, standing by the door. "That's me," remarked Jim.

"I am Count von Tarnim of the 3rd Regiment of the Prussian Guard. I am here on behalf of Baron Stockmar. Is there any gentleman here who is acting for you, and to whom I can speak? I presume you have guessed my mission."

"I certainly have," said the colonel quietly. "And you must quite understand, Count, that anything in the nature of duelling is strictly forbidden under English law, and that I, as the senior military officer here, flatly forbid it." Count von Tarnim bowed.

"I understand, sir," he answered. "I am to give that message to my principal, am I, Mr. Maitland?"

"You are," said Jim. "And when you've given that message, Mr. Leyton here will be delighted to discuss with you the weather conditions and the prospects of sport a little further up the White Nile."

Count von Tarnim bowed again, and the suspicion of a smile hovered round his lips.

"I shall find Mr. Leyton—where?" he asked.

"At the hotel," I answered briefly, and with another stiff bow that included us all, he left the mess.

"Maitland," said the colonel sternly—and Jim grinned at him.

"There's a spot I know of, Colonel," he remarked, "where the lion shooting is excellent. I feel sure Baron Stockmar would like some to ease his ruffled temper."

And the colonel began to smile.

"Go away, confound you," he said, "I don't want to know anything about your shooting."

"But for goodness' sake hit the lion," piped the *padre*, and as we left the mess they were standing him on his head in the corner for being a bloodthirsty little man.

It was an hour later that Count von Tarnim came up to me in the hotel. Jim had told me his scheme; everything was cut and dried, and it only remained for me to put the details before the count. From the beginning I had done nothing to dissuade Jim; in the first place I knew it was useless, in the second—well, the scheme appealed to me. Judged by the standards of English country life it was not perhaps all it should have been; but England seemed very far away that night.

"My principal wishes to know when and where he may expect satisfaction," said the count abruptly.

"Precisely," I answered. "I am not well up in the etiquette of these matters, but I may say at once that my principal is only too ready to grant that satisfaction. But there are certain considerations which he has to bear in mind. As Colonel Latimer told you tonight, duelling is forbidden, and any infringement of the law against it would result not only in the survivor—should the duel end fatally—being hanged, but it would also involve Colonel Latimer in grave trouble.

"In those circumstances my principal has decided as follows. He has, I believe, the choice of weapons. He has chosen big-game rifles. He proposes that we should all go ostensibly after lions to some suitable place. He then proposes that your principal and he should take cover as directed by us, and at a given signal, each should regard the other as the lion. Each will proceed to stalk the other until a result takes place. Should that result prove fatal, the survivor, for his own sake, is not likely to talk about it. In addition, both you and I will be in a position to state that the one who loses was mauled and killed by a lion, and the vultures will do the rest. Do I make myself clear?"

"Perfectly," said von Tarnim, clicking his heels together. "I will acquaint my principal with what you have said."

With that he left me, to return in ten minutes with the information that the baron agreed. And then for a moment or two he stared at me irresolutely.

"It is most unorthodox, what I am going to say," he said, with a great deal of hesitation. "I am Baron Stockmar's second, and, therefore, his interests are mine. But he is a peculiar man; his reputation is notorious. And I think it only fair to tell you that he is probably the finest shot in Germany. Moreover, he is quite determined to kill your friend."

He was very stiff about it. I could see the man's decent nature struggling with his scandalised horror at his own breach of etiquette. And the next moment his horror deepened. Jim, who had come into the room unnoticed, smote him heavily on the back.

"Tell the baron, with my love," he said earnestly, "that I once slaughtered a sparrow with a catapult."

But though Jim laughed and was his usual self during the two days that we trekked south to the place we had decided on, there was an undercurrent of seriousness beneath his gaiety. He slept, as usual, like a child; I do not believe that for a single instant during the whole time did his pulse quicken by one beat. But he gave me in full the report which I was to render to the chief in Cairo in case anything happened; also he gave me one or two private commissions to carry out.

And the night before the duel he was a little more silent than usual. I had fixed the final details with von Tarnim; the spot had been duly selected. And it was as I came back that Jim looked up with a lazy smile from oiling his rifle.

"What extraordinary blokes we are," he remarked thoughtfully. "I don't know that it affords me any pleasure to go out and try to kill this bird tomorrow. I *felt* like murdering him in the mess that night, but—now. . ."

He returned to his task and shortly after we turned in. And of the two of us I know who slept the worse. I don't think I closed my eyes the whole night.

Even the next morning Jim seemed bored. He told me afterwards that he'd lost interest in the affair and all the smouldering fury in Baron Stockmar's eyes failed to rouse him. He was as immaculate as ever; his eyeglass seemed even more conspicuous, and when I showed him the place we had selected for him, he lounged over as if he was looking for butterflies.

"He means business, Jim," I said urgently. "He's blind mad with rage still."

"Is he?" said Jim indifferently. "Make him shoot the worse."

They were to start when we fired a revolver, and von Tarnim gave the signal as soon as we were both satisfied they were ready. We were standing on a little sandy hummock above the scrub, whence we could see both men though they could not see one another. And then there began the grimmest, most exciting fight that it has ever been my fortune to witness. Von Tarnim beside me was smoking cigarette after cigarette; I was chewing an empty pipe.

Occasionally a shot rang out, but it seemed to me that Jim was taking things too easily. As a *shikar* his name was famous through three continents, but the baron, despite his bulk, was no mean performer. And once I saw a bullet flatten itself on a stone not an inch from Jim's head.

He was just underneath us at the moment and he drew back quickly. Then he looked at the stone very carefully and I saw his face change. Through my glasses I could see the look of boredom vanish and I breathed a sigh of relief. Something had roused him at last, and the man beside me realised it too, and whistled under his breath. Jim's lethargy had gone; something had happened which had turned him from a bored individual into a grim and ruthless man. At a quick lope he turned and vanished into the scrub. Every now and then we saw him listening intently; every now and then we saw the great figure of the baron squirming forward, with his head turning from side to side as he peered into the undergrowth. And then suddenly von Tarnim gripped my arm convulsively; the two men were not more than twenty yards apart. A big bush was between them, but we could see them both. And it seemed to us that at that moment each of them became aware of the other. Like a flash Jim was round the bush, and he fired standing, the fraction of a second before the other man. Then he spun round and sank on his knees, while von Tarnim and I raced towards them.

I raised Jim up in my arms; the baron had shot him through the shoulder. But it was a dreadful wound, and I stared at it in amazement. Even from such a short range the wound was almost incredible, and suddenly Jim opened his eyes and stared at me.

"He was using dum-dums," he said, and his voice was hard. "The swine was using dum-dums."

A shadow fell on me, and we looked up at Count von Tarnim. He had heard Jim's remark, and his face was stern.

"I apologise in the name of my country," he said with quiet dignity. "My principal cannot."

For the first time I looked at the baron, and understood. Jim had shot him through the brain.

★★★★★★

And so we came back to Khartoum. It was Count von Tarnim who came with me to see Colonel Latimer the instant we had got Jim stowed in hospital.

"A regrettable accident has taken place, sir," he remarked, with stiff military precision. "Baron Carl Stockmar, while following a lion with Mr. Maitland, was turned on suddenly by the brute. He fired, unfortunately missing the lion and hitting Mr. Maitland in the shoulder. The lion killed him, Mr. Maitland being unable to give any assistance owing to his wound."

The colonel stared at him in thoughtful silence; the Adjutant stood stiffly by the side of his chair.

"Am I to understand, Count von Tarnim," he said at length, "that that is the information which will be conveyed to the baron's friends in Germany? Just what you have told me?"

"Exactly that, sir—and nothing more," said the count.

"Good," answered the colonel, rising from his chair, and holding out his hand. "The officers of my regiment and myself will be very pleased if you will dine with us tonight."

3.—A Game of Bluff

It was three months before Jim came out of hospital, and even then his arm was stiff. The expanding bullet had torn the ligaments badly, and for quite a time the doctor had looked grave.

"A long course of electric massage is essential," he said emphatically. "Otherwise I warn you seriously that your arm may remain like that permanently. There's a wonderful new man in Paris: give you his name if you like."

"We might do worse, Dick," remarked Jim. "They tell me that there are worse places."

"Confound you," I said. "What about those two trunks of perfectly good clothes I left in Nagasaki?"

"What about your perfectly good uncle," he laughed, "who has left you all his money? Besides, we shall probably never get as far as Paris—so nothing matters."

We started anyway, and, amazing to relate, in the fullness of time we got there. But we had a little contretemps en route which might have ended very unpleasantly but for Jim. And it bore out in a rather remarkable manner one of his theories on life.

Jim is the least dogmatic man in the world, but there are certain things on which he holds definite opinions—very definite. Some of those opinions are hardly suitable for propagation in a Sunday School: some are—though they are not down in the text books. But they are all worth listening to. And the particular one to which I am alluding is his theory on the matter of Bluff. Moreover, since you can't get through life without bluff, it may be worth while stating it, as I once heard Jim state it to a youngster who asked his advice.

"Bluff, my son, is winning an unlimited jackpot with a queen-high hand from a fellow with three aces, and upsetting the table before you can be asked to show your openers. Bluff, my lad, is getting a man with a gun pointed at the pit of your stomach to look the other way for just long enough to allow you to alter the target. Bluff, my boy, is, in short, the art of winning a game with losing cards, and the essence of that art is to play the hand right through as if you held winners without a thought of failure. Not a touch of hesitation, not a moment of doubt."

And if ever there was a case when a game was won with losing cards, the affair at Monte Carlo was it.

When we left Port Said in a home-going P. &O. we never intended going near the place. Paris was our destination *via* Marseilles, but you never can tell.

Incidentally the purser's humour had something to do with it, if such a great being as the purser has anything to do with arranging the menus. The Gulf of Lyons was at its worst, which means that food should be chosen with care. And to select pork chops for dinner simply shows a fiendish ingenuity not far short of diabolical. In tens and dozens weeping women and frenzied men lurched from the dining saloon, until but a bare score of hardened sinners were left endeavouring to conceal their unseemly mirth.

It was the uncontrolled joy of a very pretty girl sitting two tables away from us that principally attracted our attention. I had noticed an elderly man who had been sitting beside her rise suddenly and depart with a fixed and glassy stare in his eyes. And it being an ill wind in more senses than one, his place had immediately been taken by a boy who moved up from the other end of the table.

We knew the boy slightly—a great youngster by the name of Jack Rawson. He was in cotton at Alexandria—a junior member of one of the big firms, and he was returning to England on business. And after a while Jim turned to me with a faint smile and then looked across again at the pair of them.

"The only story in the world, old man," he remarked, "that is older than sea-sickness."

"Who is the girl?" I asked.

"An Australian, I think. Jack told me her name. Mother is at Nice, and I suppose the bird who fled from the crackling is Father."

We finished our dinner and went above. She was pitching very badly in a long following swell, and for an hour or so we strolled up and down the almost deserted deck. And it wasn't until we were thinking of a nightcap before turning in that we stumbled on Jack Rawson and the girl snugly ensconced in a sheltered corner. We tried to get away unnoticed, but the boy hailed Jim at once.

"Maitland," he cried, "I want to introduce you to Miss Melville, my *fiancée*."

Jim bowed gravely and smiled.

"My heartiest congratulations," he remarked. "A pork chop is sometimes a godsend, isn't it?"

"Poor old Daddy," said the girl with quick remorse. "I'd forgotten all about him. But I couldn't help laughing, because he always tells everyone he's never been sick in his life. I'd better go and see how he is."

"From my knowledge of the complaint," said Jim, "I don't think he'll thank you. Complete seclusion is generally the victim's one demand of life."

And so she stopped, and for a few minutes we talked. Young Jack, we gathered, was getting out at Marseilles, and going to meet her mother at Nice. Then he was going back overland so as to arrive in London at the same time as he would have done if he'd stuck to the boat. And then the question of his father would crop up. In fact, fathers loomed rather large on the horizon. For the engagement had only been fixed that night, and Mr. Melville was also in ignorance of the devastating effect of pork chops on the young and healthy. Which was where the trouble came in. Would he have sufficiently recovered by the following morning to make it advisable to spring the news on him? Or would he regard it as a mean advantage to have taken while he was otherwise employed? It was undoubtedly a point demanding careful consideration. So much depends on the way these matters are approached.

The girl was dubious. She was convinced that next morning would be fully occupied in listening to his explanations that it was not the rough sea which had caused his indisposition, but that his bit of fish at lunch had been slightly stale. The moment would not be opportune, she was sure. And that being the case, why should Jack suddenly alter his plan of going home by sea, and come to Nice? In fact, what was to be done? How could Jack come to Nice in an easy, natural manner, which should cause no suspicion on the part of her paternal parent, and at the same time allow the news of the engagement to be broken at a more favourable time?

We discussed the knotty point at some length, until Jim suddenly settled things in his usual direct way. He and I would also break our journey at Marseilles and go to Nice, or rather to Monte Carlo, and Jack would come with us. It was, as he remarked, part of every man's education to see the Casino, and more especially the people who frequented it, and since Jack had never seen it, it was high time he did so. If, when he got there, Jack was foolish enough to prefer going over to Nice and sitting in the sunshine with his girl rather than haunting a roulette table, it was a point which hardly arose at that stage of the proceedings.

And with that we left them, cutting short their thanks, and retired to the smoking-room. Half an hour later, as we turned in, I saw them still sitting in their secluded corner, dreaming God's great dream in a world of their own.

******

Somewhat needless to state, we did not see much of young Jack during the next three or four days. We lounged about the terrace, and had a mild flutter or two at the tables. But the place irked—irked terribly. It was so intensely, superlatively artificial. And Jim particularly sickened of it.

"By Jove, Dick," he said to me on the fourth night of our stay, "I've seen more primitive sin in my life than most of the people here put together, but I don't believe there's a place in the whole world where quite so much rottenness is concealed beneath a beautiful surface as in Monte."

A lovely French girl strolled by in the company of an elderly swain of puffy aspect, and glanced at Jim as she passed. He looked at her thoughtfully, and then turned to me with a faint shrug.

"I suppose she thinks it's worth it," he remarked. "But what a price to pay! I'm no moralist, but I like things big. Big virtues; big sins if you like. But in this place the only thing that is big is the price."

And then he fell silent and stared over my shoulder. "Hello!" he went on slowly, "here's Jack Rawson. And something has happened."

I turned round and saw the boy coming towards us. He was walking unevenly, and on his face was a look of hopeless despair.

"Well, young fellow," said Jim quietly as he came abreast of us, "what's the worry?"

Jack paused, and seemed to see us for the first time. Then, with a quick shake of his head, he made as if to pass on. But he had only gone a step or two when Jim's hand fell on his shoulder and spun him round.

"Let me go, confound you!" muttered the boy.

"All in good time, old man," said Jim in the same quiet voice. "Just at the moment I think a little talk will clear the air."

He forced Jack to a seat between us, and suddenly put his hand into the boy's coat pocket.

"This won't help, Jack," he said a little sternly, and I saw that he

40

had a small revolver in his hand. "That's never the way out, except for a coward."

And it was then that the boy broke down, and I caught Jim's eye over the shaking shoulders. It was savage and angry, as if he realised, even then, that we were in the presence of another of those rotten little tragedies which have their breeding ground in those few square miles. Jack pulled himself together after a few seconds and lit a cigarette while we waited in silence. And then bit by bit the whole sordid story came out—as old as the hills and yet perennially new in every fresh case.

The engagement was all right, we found out, as far as her father and mother were concerned. The only question had been one of money. Her father didn't think that Jack's income was sufficient to allow of matrimony yet; further, he thought that in view of the shortness of their acquaintance a little waiting would be a good thing from every point of view. He wouldn't go so far as to say that if Jack had actually had the money he would have insisted on a long engagement, but since he hadn't, he thought it was much the most satisfactory solution. And it was just after this interview with Mr. Melville that Jack met a very charming Frenchman in a bar at Nice. He was the Comte de St. Enogat, and they had entered into conversation.

It was at this stage of the disclosure that Jim's eye again met mine.

Apparently one cocktail had been followed by another; and then a third and fourth had joined their predecessors. And Jack, drawn on by his new friend's delightful and sympathetic manner, had taken the charming Comte de St. Enogat into his confidence. After four—or was it five?—cocktails the problem was a simple one. The girl's father—a silly old fool—insisted that he should have more money before he could marry his daughter. How was he to get that money quickly and certainly, because any idea of waiting was simply unthinkable? After five—or was it six?—cocktails the solution to the problem was even simpler.

The Comte de St. Enogat, touched to the very core of his French soul by such a wonderful tale of devotion and love, would do for this new friend of his what he had never before done for any human being. Locked in the *comte's* heart was a system—*the* system—the *only* system by which one could with absolute certainty make money gambling. If Jack would come with him that afternoon he would take him to a private gambling place where he guaranteed on his word as a member of the French nobility that Jack would win enough money to snap his fingers at the idiotic father of his lovely *fiancée*.

And Jim's eyes met mine for the third time.

He lunched at the expense of his new friend—lightly, with a bottle of champagne; and then proceeded in the *comte's* powerful Delage to a villa halfway between Nice and Monte Carlo. A charming villa, we gathered, where he was introduced to one or two of the *comte's* friends. And then after a short while the Comte suggested an adjournment for business. There was roulette in one room, and baccarat in another. *Petits-chevaux*, poker, and even fan-tan seemed to be legislated for each in their own separate room. But the great point over which Jack was most insistent was the singular charm of everyone he met.

"Quite so," cut in Jim shortly, as he paused. "I'm sure they were. But to come down to more prosaic details—which game did you patronise?"

"*Baccarat*," said the boy. "The *comte* advised it."

"Holy smoke!" muttered Jim. "Baccarat! Yes, I can quite imagine that he did advise it."

"He said it was the easiest to make money at by his system."

"Undoubtedly," answered Jim. "Quite the easiest to make money at—for him. Now, Jack, what did you lose?"

The boy hesitated.

"Out with it," said Jim. "You've been a triple-distilled young fool, but there's no good mincing things now."

"A hundred thousand *francs*," answered Jack, almost inaudibly, and leaning forward he buried his face in his hands.

Jim raised his eyebrows. A hundred thousand francs was four thousand pounds in those days before currencies went mad, and the same thought came to both of us. Where had young Jack Rawson found four thousand pounds to lose?

"Did you give them a cheque?" asked Jim quietly.

And then, slowly and hesitatingly, the real trouble came out. He hadn't given them a cheque; it wouldn't have been honoured if he had. But he had been entrusted with twenty thousand pounds' worth of bearer bonds in some Egyptian Government security to take home with him and hand over to the head office of the firm in London. Why the matter had been done that way we did not inquire; the mere bald fact stuck out and was sufficient.

Jack Rawson had lost four thousand pounds of money which belonged to his firm, playing baccarat. And since the actual loss was in bearer bonds, not even the replacing of the money could save him from detection. Nothing short of regaining the actual scrip could be of any use. And unless that was done it meant disgrace and ruin for the boy sitting miserably between us.

So much was clear on the face of it, and for a while we sat in silence staring over the bay. "I was a bit tight," he stammered miserably at length. "Otherwise I wouldn't have been such a darned fool. But he seemed such a good sort, and all I could think of was getting enough to marry Peggy."

And with that he broke down utterly; it meant losing his girl as well.

"When did it happen, Jack?" said Jim quietly.

"This afternoon," answered the boy.

"You'd know the house again?" pursued Jim.

"Only too well," muttered Jack, miserably throwing pebbles into a flowerbed opposite. And then suddenly he straightened up and gripped Jim by the arm.

"Look, Maitland," he cried excitedly, "there's the swine himself! There's the Comte de St. Enogat."

He half rose, but Jim pulled him back.

"Sit down," he said quietly. "Bend forward. Don't let him see you with us. It's that man, is it, in evening clothes, walking with the girl in the scarlet cloak?"

"Yes; that's the blighter," answered the boy.

We watched him as he ascended some steps a few yards to our left, and turned with his companion towards the casino. He looked, as Jack had said, a charming man—just a typical French aristocrat carrying himself with the assured ease of a man of the *haute monde* in Monte Carlo during the height of the season. The girl with him was laughing at some remark he had just made; he was bending towards her with just the right amount of deference. And after a few moments they both disappeared into the casino.

Jim thoughtfully lit a cigarette, and sat for a while in silence. Then, as if he had made up his mind, he rose to his feet and pitched his cigarette away.

"Go back to the hotel," he said curtly, "and turn in. I'll see what I can do."

It was typical of Jim that he added no word of reproach, and at once cut short the stammered thanks of the boy, in whose eyes hope was already beginning to dawn.

"Cut all that out," he remarked. "I don't promise that I'll be able to do anything, but I'll see. Oh! and remember one thing. Should you meet either Leyton or myself tomorrow or at any time with the Comte, you don't know either of us. Don't forget. Now clear off."

For a moment he laid his hands on the boy's shoulders, then he turned him round and pushed him towards the hotel.

"Silly young ass!" he said to me as Rawson disappeared round a corner. "But he's a good boy for all that—a real good boy. And she's a good girl."

"It's a bit of a tough proposition, Jim," I remarked dubiously.

"I don't deny it," he answered. "At the moment I haven't even the glimmering of an idea as to how to set about it. This place may be a sink of iniquity, but anything in the nature of gunwork would render one unpopular. No, it's got to be something more subtle than that, much more subtle. The first thing to do, however, is to cultivate the acquaintance of the Comte de St. Enogat; the second is to go to this house. I think we'd better separate for the time, old man, though we might join up later in the evening. I'll go on into the casino now— you come in in a few minutes. And then be guided by circumstances. We just know each other, that's all."

With a cheery grin he strolled away, that merry gleam in his eyes which was never absent if an adventure was on the cards. I watched him enter the Casino, and five minutes after I followed him.

I strolled round the rooms casually, but he seemed to have disappeared, and after a while I tried the bar. Sure enough there in a corner was Jim, with a dangerous-looking drink in front of him, the Comte de St. Enogat on one side and the charming girl in the scarlet cloak on the other. And the trio were in a convivial mood.

At least Jim was. Had I been asked to go into a court of law and give evidence on oath as to Jim's condition, I should have said that he was in that happy mood which comes from having drunk enough but not too much. And since Jim, if put to it, could put three hardened topers in succession under the table drinking them level, it was evident that the game had begun.

As soon as he saw me he hailed me cheerfully.

"Hullo! Leyton, old lad," he cried, "come and join us. A pal of mine, *Mademoiselle*—also from the ends of the earth." I bowed to the girl and sat down opposite Jim.

"I've just been telling the *comte*—oh! by the way, the Comte de St. Enogat—Mr. Leyton—that I can't stand these rooms here. Too crowded altogether. I like gambling high; I can afford to gamble high. I've

44

gambled in every corner of this little old globe, and there's not much I don't know about it. But I can't stand a crush. Hi! Francois—or whatever your name is—repeat the dose, my lad."

"And I have just been telling your friend, Mr. Leyton," said the *comte* with a charming smile, "that if he wants a quiet game, with stakes high or low, as he pleases—"

"High for me," interrupted Jim. "I'm not a curate playing halfpenny nap."

The *comte* bowed, and his smile broadened.

"No, Mr. Maitland, as a fair judge of men, I guessed that. Well, you can take it from me that you can play as high as you like, in perfect peace and quiet, and not with this crowd round you, if you care to come with Mademoiselle St. Quentin and myself to a villa a few kilometres on the road to Nice. Every form of game you can want is there, run for people exactly like yourself—people who prefer peace and quiet. You can play bridge if you like, or poker, or baccarat, or roulette."

Jim leant across the table to me.

"Leyton," he said, "did you hear that? These guys play poker. What about it?"

He winked deliberately, and the *comte* smiled again.

"There are two men there who play poker most nights and rather fancy themselves."

"The devil they do!" grunted Jim. "I'll come and play poker with them."

For a fleeting instant the *comte's* eyes met the girl's, then he rose.

"My car is at the door. Will Mr. Leyton come?"

"I'm with you," I said, finishing my drink. "But I warn you that I'm not a gambler like my friend."

"All tastes are catered for, Mr. Leyton," said the girl, speaking for the first time. But I noticed she was watching Jim, as he strolled with the Comte through the rooms towards t he entrance. "Is he very wealthy, your friend?"

"Rolls in it," I murmured.

"He looks a very determined sort of person," she remarked.

"He's as peaceful as a lamb," I answered. "A married man with four children."

"I hope he wins," she said. "It's high time those two men the *comte* was speaking of lost for a change."

With that we got into the car, and though I don't know about the

45

chauffeur, there were undoubtedly four stout-hearted liars that night who drove out along the road to Nice.

I had no inkling as to what Jim proposed to do; and, as he left me almost at once on arriving at the house and repaired to the poker room with the Comte, I had no opportunity of a private word with him. So I contented myself with a little mild roulette and kept my eyes open.

The whole thing was beautifully done, of that there was no doubt. The champagne was of a first-class vintage and unlimited; the furniture and the whole get-up of the house gave one the idea that everything had been done regardless of expense. There were some twenty people in the roulette room, and though play was high, I could see no suspicion of anything unfair. Nor for that matter at the baccarat table in another room, where I staked a few *louis* and won. In fact, it struck me that the whole place was what it professed to be—a first-class gambling-house where stakes were high and expenses were paid out of the five-*per-cent. cagnotte.*

My lady in the scarlet cloak, in the intervals of being very charming, pumped me discreetly over Jim, and I played up along the lines that he had started. It was quite obvious that I was regarded as the necessary encumbrance to the real quarry, and the idea was just what I wanted. Jim was rich, Jim was the gambler—Jim was the fish to be landed. And once or twice I almost laughed as I thought of the particular wolf who had strayed into the fold.

The sheep's clothing was still there two hours later when Jim appeared with the *comte*. A cheerful, but somewhat inane grin was on his face, and he stumbled once—very slightly. It was a magnificent imitation of a man who had drunk just a little too much, and once again I saw the Comte's eyes meet my companion's with a hint of triumph in them.

"Cleaned me out, Leyton," cried Jim, slapping the *comte* on the back. "Ten thousand *francs*, my boy—but that's only a bagatelle. Tomorrow afternoon we'll begin to play. Now, *Comte*—you'll lunch with me, and you too, Mademoiselle. I simply insist. Just the four of us, and afterwards we'll come back here. I'll show you tomorrow how poker should be played."

"You had infernal luck, Mr. Maitland," said the *comte* politely. "Tomorrow you will have your revenge. And lunch—at one?"

"One o'clock. I shall expect you both." He bowed over the girl's hand. "And you shall sit beside me, *Mademoiselle*, tomorrow afternoon and bring me luck."

The *comte* insisted on sending us home in his Delage, and all the way back Jim talked loudly for the benefit of the chauffeur.

It was not until we were in our rooms that the mask dropped, and he was himself again, cool and imperturbable.

"It's crooked, Dick," he said quietly. "They swindled me tonight. I saw 'em of course—the old trick of substituting a similar pack after the cut. They dealt me a flush, and the *comte* drew one to threes, and got four eights. I betted as if I hadn't noticed."

"The roulette and baccarat was perfectly straight as far as I could see," I said.

"Probably," he answered. "It's more than likely that for ninety *per cent*. of the time the thing is straight. It's only when they get hold of a plum that they risk the other. And mark you, it was well done. If I hadn't forgotten more about that sort of stunt than these fellows are ever likely to know, I wouldn't have noticed it."

He was pacing up and down the room thoughtfully, pulling hard at his pipe.

"I can't think what to do, Dick," he cried at length. "Gunwork is out of the question, and the mere statement that someone is cheating, even if you prove it then and there on the spot, is no use when you're up against a gang of them. Righteous indignation: the man would be ostensibly kicked out; one's losses would be refunded. Mark you, it wasn't the *comte* who cheated; he wasn't dealing. But the new pack was stacked so that he got the hand. They were all in it—all four of them. I can smell a thing like that better than a cat smells valerian. And it's going to be the same bunch tomorrow. The point is what to do."

He resumed his thoughtful pacing.

"Bluff! Some sort of bluff! But what? How can I bluff that bunch— how can I bluff the *comte* into disgorging those bonds?"

And then suddenly he stopped short in his tracks, his eyes blazing.

"I've got it," he almost shouted. "I've got the main idea. Go away, Dick—go to bed. I've got to work out the details."

With that he bundled me unceremoniously out of the room, and when I turned out my light I could still hear him pacing up and down next door. But when I went into his room next morning about half-past ten he had already gone out, and I didn't see him again until he came into the American bar twenty minutes before lunch.

He grinned at me and we sat down in a corner. "Got it worked out?" I asked.

47

"I think so, old man," he answered with a faint chuckle. "And it's best for you to know nothing about it until the time comes. But there's one thing you can do for me, with your well-known tact and discretion. If you get an opportunity, let it be known by *Mademoiselle* that though in normal circumstances I have the disposition necessary to run a babies' *crèche*, at the same time if I happen to get roused things happen. Hint, old son, at dark doings in strange corners of the globe: corpses littering up rooms—you know."

"Is this part of the plan?" I asked.

"A very necessary part," he answered quietly. "And here, if I mistake not, are our guests."

We met them in the lounge—the *comte* suave and *debonair*, the lady looking even prettier by day than by night—and adjourned at once in to lunch. It was a merry meal, during which Jim accounted for far more than his fair share of the bottle of Veuve Cliquot. I noticed that the *comte* drank sparingly, and his companion hardly at all. And they didn't talk very much either; Jim monopolised most of the conversation.

And since of all men in the world Jim talks less about himself than anyone I know, it soon became evident to me that there was some specific object in his mind. He was almost vulgar with his: "I've been there, of course,"—and "I've seen that and done this." But because he had been, and seen, and done, he was also extraordinarily interesting. Especially when he launched at length on to the question of snakes and rare native poisons. He might almost have made a study of them, so extensive was his knowledge, and Mademoiselle St. Quentin shivered audibly.

"You make me quite frightened, *Monsieur*," she said, taking a sip of champagne. "Just one teeny scratch, you say, and a horrible death. Ugh!"

Jim laughed, and ordered another bottle.

"Such things don't come your way in civilised parts, *Mademoiselle*," he cried. "It's only we who have lived at the back of beyond who run across them."

"You must have had an interesting life, Mr. Maitland," said the *comte*. "A life which many men would not have come through alive."

Jim laughed again.

"Because they don't know the secret of life, *Comte*."

"And that is?"

"Bluff." Jim drained his glass. "Bluff. Any man can win when he's holding winners, but success only comes to the man who wins with losers. And in life—as in poker—it's bluff that enables you to do that."

The *comte* smiled.

"*Mon Dieu!* Yvonne, we have a formidable opponent this afternoon. I think I had better go to the bank and get some more money."

And so in due course we came once more to the house set so charmingly on the high ground looking over the sea.

Without delay they went indoors, while I followed slowly. As a piece of acting it was superb; almost did he deceive me during the next hour. Not by the quiver of an eyelid did he deviate from the character he had set himself to play—the bluff Colonial with money to lose if necessary, but with money only secondary to the game. I played more as a matter of form than anything else; my whole attention was occupied in what I knew must be coming. And gradually excitement took hold of me till my hand grew a little unsteady and my mouth a trifle dry. If only I had known what to look out for—what to expect!

And then quite suddenly it came. I had noticed nothing, but in an instant the atmosphere of the room changed from quiet suavity to deadly fury. And dominating them all—more furious than any—was Jim.

With a single heave he jerked the dealer from his chair, and there on the seat was the pack of cards for which the stacked pack had just been substituted.

"The same trick as last night, you bunch of sharpers!" he snarled. "Do you think I didn't spot you?" He swung round on the *comte*, who, with a livid face, was backing towards the bell. "Stand still, you swine!" he roared, and he seemed to be lashing himself into a worse rage. "I'll show you how I deal with sharpers. You wretched fool—I came prepared for this!"

There was a sudden sharp whistling hiss and a long thornlike piece of wood hung quivering from the *comte's* cheek.

"Put away that gun," he sneered contemptuously, as the *comte* produced a revolver. "Don't you understand, you wretched cheat—you're a dead man now. Is it beginning to prick and smart, that cheek of yours? I told you I came from the East, didn't I? And do you know what this is?"

He held out a long wooden tube, and the *comte* stared at it fearfully.

49

"That is the *sumpitan*, or blow-pipe," roared Jim, "used by the Senangs in Malay. And that"—he pointed at the *comte's* cheek—"is a poisoned dart." He laughed contemptuously. "You scum—to dare to swindle me, as you swindled that unfortunate boy out of those Egyptian bonds." He plunged his hand into his pocket and produced a small bottle. "There is the antidote, my friend—don't move, or I smash it in the grate. It will add to my pleasure to see you die, watching the bottle that could save you all the time."

And now pandemonium broke loose. Two men dashed to the door, to find themselves looking down the barrel of Jim's revolver.

"I think not," he said pleasantly. "It will only be a quarter of an hour before our friend leaves us—for good. During that brief space we will all stop here."

And then the girl flung herself at me.

"Do something!" she screamed. "He is a savage—a monster! Beg him to save Pierre; he is my husband." But Jim only laughed.

"*Mon Dieu! Monsieur,*" she cried, going down on her knees to him, "I entreat of you to spare him. I love him—you understand; I love him!"

Jim grunted, and lowered his revolver as if in thought.

"He is your husband, is he? Well, get me those Egyptian bonds at once. Is it smarting, *Comte?* Then you have no time to lose, Madame. Hand me those bonds, and I will consider whether I will save this man."

He stood aside and she rushed from the room like a woman distraught. The *comte* was moaning in a corner with the two other men bending over him, and Jim caught my eye and winked. And so superb had been his acting, that it was only then, for the first time, that I began to wonder about the *sumpitan* and the poisoned dart. It occurred to me that it had looked much more like an ordinary long wooden cigarette holder.

But at that moment the girl returned. Feverishly she thrust the bonds into his hands, and with maddening deliberation Jim looked through them while she waited in an agony of impatience. At last he thrust them into his pocket, and produced the little bottle.

"Let this be a lesson to you," he snapped. "There is the antidote. See that he drinks it all—at once."

We waited just long enough to see the contents of that bottle go down the *comte's* throat; then, on a quick sign from him, we left.

And finding the Delage waiting outside the door, it seemed but fitting that we should use it to take us back to Monte Carlo. We did.

★★★★★

It was not till much later on that he consented to allay my curiosity. At intervals through the afternoon he had shaken with silent laughter until he had almost driven me insane.

I knew there had been an interview with Jack, and the girl had been there too; a girl who had left with eyes misty with joy and happiness, and a boy who had left almost dazed by his good fortune.

The girl came up to me as I sat reading the paper, and I rose with a smile.

"He's just the most wonderful man in the world, Mr. Leyton," she said, and her voice trembled a little.

"He is that," agreed Jack fervently.

And with that they were gone, and I sat on waiting for Jim.

He came at last, a quiet smile on his face, and we decided it was cocktail time.

"A good bluff that, Dick," he said thoughtfully.

"Darned good!" I agreed. "What had you got on the darts?"

"Some stuff the chemist made up. Quite harmless, but irritates abominably."

And then he started to choke with laughter.

"What's the jest?" I demanded.

"My dear old man," he spluttered, "you haven't got the plum—the supreme gem of the affair. That lies in the antidote."

I looked at him. "What the deuce was the antidote?"

"It came to me in the chemist's shop this morning," he murmured gravely. "All great ideas come suddenly like that. The antidote, Dick, was just half a pint of castor-oil."

4.—Colette

From Paris to Valparaiso is a long call, and what started us off in that direction for the life of me I can't remember. I know Jim's shoulder was a much longer job than we anticipated: I also have distinct recollections that Paris may have been partially responsible for the fact.

But that is neither here nor there: at Valparaiso we arrived one fine morning, and at Valparaiso we decided to stay. And in Valparaiso we ran into one of those adventures for which Jim seemed to have a special attraction. They came to him as a nail goes to a magnet, though he always swore he was the most peaceable of men. And, as a matter of fact, he never did look for trouble. It just came, and that saved him the bother.

It came this time right enough, and it nearly cost us both our lives. But since it didn't quite, and moreover was responsible for a magnificent work of art, all was well. It lies before me as I write—that work of art. It consists of a photo of a family group, taken by a local photographer down in Sussex and printed on a picture postcard. Sitting on a chair is a girl—a pretty girl with happiness written all over her face, and on her lap are two remarkably healthy-looking infants. Standing behind her is the proud father arrayed in his best clothes, with a collar half an inch too small and an inch and a half too high. The girl's arms are round her babies, and it's only when I look very close that I can notice the difference between those two arms. For the right one was splintered to pieces, and the splintering saved us from death, and the girl from a fate far worse. Though even now, maybe, she hardly realises it, which is just as well.

★★★★★★

The thing happened in MacTavert's bar. Incidentally, it was more than a mere bar; flamboyant notices and flaring lights in the street outside proclaimed it to be a dancing saloon. And even that fell short of the full truth, for Bully MacTavert knew—none better—the principal source of income from sailors just in from a voyage. When a man has taken forty days merely to get a wind-jammer round the Horn, on the top of the rest of the voyage, and has then beaten up the west coast of South America towards Valparaiso, it isn't only drink he wants. When the second officer, with a marlin-spike in his hand as an adjunct to speech, has discharged every possible member of the crew to save the wage-bill while unloading and loading, men are apt to run a bit wild. There's money to burn in their pockets, and when it's finished a crew will be wanted for some other boat. Until then—there are women.

That was MacTavert's principal line. It means a quicker return for your money, and not such a rapid depreciation of stock. Not that MacTavert laid out much money to start with; there are quicker and surer ways into which it is perhaps better not to enter. And MacTavert was a past master in them all. All that may be said is that once a girl was there, God help her! for she was beyond human aid. She was MacTavert's property body and soul, and as such she did his bidding for the price of her keep.

For MacTavert was no believer in letting them have any money. Money makes for independence, and independence was the very last thing he wished to encourage. He fed them, he housed them, he bought them their tawdry finery, because that was a good investment. But money—no; that was his side of the contract. They could be bought like his drink—no credit allowed—and MacTavert pocketed the cash.

Not often does one find a man so completely dead to every sense of human decency as he was. Originally, as his name implied, he was a Scotsman. Just about forty-eight years ago he had first seen the light of day in a Glasgow slum. There may be kind-hearted people who will say that he never had a chance; maybe he didn't. Born and nurtured in the gutter, at ten years old he was a man in vice, or at any rate, in his knowledge of it. At fifteen he went to sea in the three-masted ship *Celandine*, and Glasgow saw him no more. At thirty he decided that he could do better for himself than seafaring, and, helped by a strong will, an utterly unscrupulous character, and an intimate knowledge of what seamen wanted when they came ashore, he started on his own in Valparaiso.

He began small; perhaps the only Scotch trace left to him save his name was an unusual canniness over money. During those fifteen years while he roamed the seven seas from Newfoundland to Australia, from China to Suez, he managed to save a little out of his pay, which he had banked here and there all over the globe. And when he finally gave up the life and decided on Valparaiso as the scene of his future operations, he found that he had quite a respectable sum he could draw on for capital. He chose Valparaiso because the majority of shipping there is American, and the American sailor gets paid higher. Trifles like that told with MacTavert.

And now, eighteen years later, the small, stuffy saloon in which he had started had grown into a big garish dancing hall, while its owner, heavy-jowled and gross, looked on his creation with beady eyes and found it good. His *clientèle* remained the same, but many more could be accommodated. And, further, a very lucrative side-show had developed gradually during the last few years. Tourists, anxious, as they put it, to see the sights, were apt to be escorted there by specially-selected touts of his own—people who paid anything up to ten times the regular tariff without a murmur. And MacTavert himself would welcome the poor fools with an expansive smile, which displayed his yellow teeth to the full advantage.

It was one of these touts who approached Jim and me before dinner. We neither of us knew Valparaiso, and we were at a loose end, but that tout had "tout" written altogether too largely all over him. So

Jim, with commendable brevity, consigned him to his undoubted future destination, and we turned back towards our hotel for a cocktail before dinner.

And then there occurred one of those things which a man ignores or does not ignore, according to the particular brand he is. When a woman gives a little cry for help, it is as often as not advisable to continue one's stroll and leave matters to the proper authorities to deal with. Ulterior motives have been known to be behind such cries.

Not, however, for Jim. He was perfectly capable of dealing with ulterior motives should they arise, and, until they arose, he was of the brand who emphatically does not ignore. He swung round, and the next instant I was standing alone. And when I came up with him again, the tout who had recently accosted us was struggling impotently in his grasp, and Jim was staring over his head at a girl who was standing on the pavement beyond. She was a pretty little thing, but what struck me most was the look of terror in her eyes as she glanced at the man whom Jim was holding.

"Can I help you in any way?" said Jim, in Spanish. "I thought I heard you call out."

She looked at Jim, and her mouth drooped.

"It doesn't matter," she said, despairingly. "I thought you were English."

Jim smiled.

"I most certainly am," he answered, and the girl's face lit up once more. "I must blame the bad light for failing to see you were too."

And then he looked at the man who was still struggling in his grasp.

"That being the case," he continued, "how comes it that a Dago made you cry out for help? Dagos who do anything so foolish as to molest English girls are simply asking for trouble, aren't they, you repulsive little beast?"

The Dago squirmed and twisted in his hands, and Jim smiled placidly. Then he took him by the collar and the seat of his trousers and fairly slung him across the road. He lay for a moment where he fell; then, with a look of venomous hate on his face, he vanished down the road, and Jim turned back to the girl.

"Now, what can I do for you?"

She was gazing at him in admiration, and then she clapped her hands together.

"Oh, but you're strong!" she said, and her eyes were shining. "That little brute ought to be killed. He's one of MacTavert's men."

"So I gathered," said Jim quietly. "In fact, a little while ago he was suggesting to my friend and me that we should go to MacTavert's place this evening."

The girl shuddered, and once again the look of terror came into her eyes. She began to speak a little breathlessly, touching Jim's arm every now and then with her hand.

"It's an awful place—a ghastly place. And when I saw you, somehow I knew you were English, and I followed you. I thought perhaps you might be able to help me. That's why that little brute tried to interfere and prevent me speaking to you."

"But why should he object to you speaking to us?" said Jim, looking a trifle puzzled. "What has he got to do with you, anyway?"

"I'm in the most dreadful trouble," said the girl, and her lips were trembling. "You see, I'm at MacTavert's."

"You're at MacTavert's?" repeated Jim slowly. "But I don't understand. Why are you at such a place?"

"I was told to go there last night. I had no money, and I met a woman who said she could give me a room, and it didn't matter about paying her. And then I found that it was at this awful dancing saloon."

It was all a little incoherent, and Jim looked at her gravely.

"Then why not go away?" he said at length. "Surely there must be a British chaplain here, or somebody to whom you could apply."

"But I can't find my box, or any of my things." The girl was on the verge of tears. "They've taken them away and hidden them. And I don't know anyone in this horrible town, and I can't speak Spanish."

"I see," said Jim quietly, and his eyes were very gentle. "I see. Well, what do you want me to do?"

"If only I could tell you my story!" she cried. "But it's getting late, and I haven't got time now. I must get back, or that brute will find out I've gone, and get in a rage. You see, he told me I wasn't to go out unless he said I might. Oh, if you could come to the place tonight, and tell MacTavert you want to dance with me—That's what I have to do, you see: dance with anyone who wants me to. And then I could tell you. And perhaps you could help me."

She was looking up at Jim through eyes that were swimming with tears, and Jim smiled at her reassuringly.

"All right, kid," he said quietly. "We'll come, and you shall tell us all about it. And then we'll see what we can do."

"Oh, thank you a thousand times!" cried the girl, dabbing at her eyes with a handkerchief. "I think I should have drowned myself if I hadn't seen you passing by. You know where it is, don't you? Just down the road there."

"We'll find it," said Jim. "Now you trot along. By the way, what is your name?"

"Colette," said the girl simply, and she gave Jim a look such as a dog gives its master. And then she was gone, flitting like a shadow, through the trees that lined the road.

For a few moments Jim watched her: then he turned to me.

"I may be several sorts of a fool, Dick," he remarked, "but I'll take my oath that wasn't a put-up job. In fact, I'm thinking we may be just in time to prevent a tragedy."

"You'll probably find MacTavert a fairly tough customer," I said, as we strolled back towards the hotel.

Jim grinned. "I like 'em tough. Let's dine."

He was silent during dinner, and it was not until we had nearly finished that he spoke.

"If it's what I think it is, Dick, Mr. MacTavert and I will have words tonight."

And his voice was savage.

★★★★★★

MacTavert's dancing saloon took very little finding. As we entered the doors, the strains of an automatic piano grinding out a waltz met our ears, and for a moment or two we stood just inside watching the scene. It was typical of scores of similar places to be met with in seaports all over the world. A little larger perhaps than the average—apart from that there was nothing to distinguish it from a hundred others. A general reek of perspiring humanity and stale spirits filled the air: the thick haze of tobacco smoke made it almost impossible to see across the room. In the centre, where a space had been left, five or six couples were dancing; around the walls, seated at little tables, were men of every nationality drinking. Every now and then one of them would seize some woman by the waist and solemnly gyrate round the floor in the centre to the strains of the piano. Then the pair would sit down again, and more drink would be ordered; MacTavert expected his girls to increase the liquor consumption.

"Good heavens, Jim!" I muttered in disgust, "what a horrible spot!"

And it was as I spoke that we saw Colette. She was dancing with a big Dago, and her eyes lit up as she saw us.

Jim smiled at her, and at that moment MacTavert himself approached. His shrewd eyes had soon discerned two toffs standing by the door, and he had no intention of letting them escape if he could help it. He bowed obsequiously, showing his tobacco-stained teeth in an ingratiating smile, and Jim regarded him in silence.

"And what can I do for you gentlemen?" said MacTavert. "There is a good table unoccupied at the other end of the room, and I think I may say that my whisky is good. Or champagne, if you prefer it," he added, hopefully.

"Show us the table," said Jim curtly, and we followed MacTavert across the room.

"Now bring me some whisky," he continued, when we were seated.

"Certainly, sir," returned the other. "And if there is any lady," he continued, with an odious leer, "who takes your fancy—you have merely got to mention the matter to me."

"There is," said Jim quietly. "That girl over there dancing with that Dago. Tell her that my friend and I will be honoured if she will join us at our table."

MacTavert rubbed his hands together; things were progressing altogether to his fancy. Just as there was a special tariff for wines when consumed by visitors like ourselves, so also there was a special tariff for girls.

"Leave it all to me," he remarked, confidentially. "And if"—his voice sank to a whisper—"you would care to smoke a pipe, or possibly—" He paused meaningly.

"I don't go in for opium or coke or any other rotten dope," said Jim shortly. "Get my whisky."

For a moment MacTavert's eyes gleamed angrily; he was not used to being spoken to in such a way. But a second glance at Jim's face decided him that speech on his part would be not only superfluous but unwise, and with a further bow he left us.

We saw him approach the table where Colette was sitting, and speak to her. She rose instantly and followed MacTavert across the room, leaving her late dancing partner scowling furiously. But he said nothing: it was pretty evident that what MacTavert said went in that place. He spoke to her with a kind of savage intensity as she tripped along at his side, and I thought she answered him back. Anyway, a sudden snarl showed on MacTavert's face, and he caught her roughly by the arm, only to pull himself together at once and regain his oily obsequiousness as he reached our table.

"This is Colette, sir," he said, pinching the girl's cheek playfully, and she promptly smacked his face.

"Splendid!" said Jim lazily. "Do it again."

For a moment I thought MacTavert would murder the girl. His great hands shot out towards her, and she shrank back terrified. And then Jim spoke again.

"I ordered whisky, barman."

MacTavert swung round.

"Who the hell are you calling barman?" he snarled. "I'm the owner."

"Are you?" drawled Jim. "How fearfully jolly for all concerned! But it doesn't alter the fact that I ordered whisky."

The veins stood out on MacTavert's neck like whipcord, and his face turned to an ugly red. There was no mistaking the utter contempt in Jim's voice, and MacTavert was not accustomed to contempt. But he found, as others had found before him, that there was something about this tall, perfectly-dressed individual, with his quite unnecessary eyeglass, which lent force to the old saw concerning discretion being the better part of valour. And after a moment or two he swung round on his heel and slouched over to the bar to get the required drink, while Colette sat down, and Jim laughed.

"He wanted me to make you order champagne," she said, "and I wouldn't. Oh, thank God you've come! It terrifies me, this place— more and more every moment."

With a scowl on his face, MacTavert lurched over to the table and banged down the whisky.

"Four dollars," he grunted.

"Think again," said Jim quietly. "I'm not buying your beastly saloon: merely two glasses of whisky."

"If you don't like the price you can clear out," snarled MacTavert.

"I shall clear out exactly when I please," returned Jim. "In the meantime, there's a dollar for the whisky. And if you don't like the price you can take your poison away and throw it down the sink."

And once again MacTavert retired muttering, with, the dollar bill in his great mottled hand. He was being beaten all along the line, and he knew it. He was up against something he couldn't understand— something that left him vaguely frightened, though no power on earth would have extracted such an admission from him.

Drunken sailors, mere strength in any form, he could cope with—had coped with successfully for the whole of his life. But in Jim he had encountered something new, and like most ill-educated men, anything new made him uneasy. It was outside his experience to be calmly and superciliously browbeaten in his own saloon. He relapsed into dark mutterings behind his bar, assuring himself with frequent repetition that if he had any further lip from this damned toff he personally would throw him into the street.

And in the meantime the toff was smiling across the table at a very frightened girl into whose face the colour was slowly coming back.

"My name is Jim," he said quietly, "and his is Dick. So now we all know one another, Colette. And what we want to know is how you came into this unpleasant place. Then, after we've heard that, we must see how we can get you out."

The girl looked at him with shining eyes; to her he seemed the most wonderful man she had ever seen.

"You'll think me such a little fool when I tell you," she whispered miserably; and Jim smiled again.

"We've all of us made idiots of ourselves at one time or another. Tell me, Colette—you're not French, are you—like your name?"

The girl laughed. "No; I'm English." Her voice faltered for a moment. "I come from Sussex; from a little village lying under the South Downs."

Her eyes had filled with tears, and suddenly Jim leant across the table.

"Steady, kid, don't cry. I want to talk to you about that little village. I want to find out how you came to leave it."

And then, little by little, we heard the whole pitiful tale—not new to those who listen, but bitterly, tragically new to each one who tells. And as we heard it, told falteringly with many a pause, my only coherent wish was to have the throats of some of the men involved between my hands. I left MacTavert to Jim, who was staring at that gentleman with smouldering eyes.

She had run away from home, had the girl who was called Colette. It was dull, and a gentleman had assured her that she would be able to earn big money in London. On the stage, he said—pretty clothes, and jewels and lots of dancing and amusement. So she'd stolen out of the house one night, and gone up to London to an address he had told her of. She had never seen her mother and father again—and for a time, as she came to that part of her story, she fell silent. The automatic

59

piano thumped on in MacTavert's bar, the haze of tobacco smoke grew denser, but all Colette could see was a little cottage, way back in Sussex, with honeysuckle climbing round the windows and a kitchen spotlessly clean. Just home—that's all. . .

The *dago* she had been dancing with lurched by with a snarl, which effaced itself as he caught Jim's eyes fixed on him, and with a little start Colette came back to reality. She was telling us her story—that new and original story—little dreaming how well we knew every line before she spoke it. For the main theme is always the same—only the details differ.

The address in London to which she had gone so hopefully turned out to be a theatrical agency. And there an oily gentleman had taken stock of her, and offered her a job on the spot with a company that was to go on tour in South America. He had assured her that all she required was experience, and that on her return he, personally, would get her an engagement at a West-End theatre. And she swallowed it whole, as hundreds of other unfortunate girls have swallowed it.

Then came the awakening. The company had played for a week in a fifth- rate hall in Valparaiso to find last Saturday night that the manager had decamped with what money there was. They were stranded—penniless, or practically so in a foreign town, with not a soul to turn to for assistance. The rest we knew already; the woman with the kindly offer of assistance—the woman in MacTavert's pay.

"She seemed so nice," said Colette, miserably, "and then I found myself here."

Once again the poor child's eyes filled with tears; she was paying a big price for her one mistake of foolish vanity in England. And Jim's eyes were very gentle as he looked at her.

"I see, Colette," he said quietly. "I understand. I'm thinking it was very lucky you saw us today."

For a moment he looked at me; how lucky it was I don't think the girl quite realised. A good deal of the innocence of that little Sussex village still remained to Colette.

"And so now," continued Jill cheerfully, "the only thing that remains is to get you away. I don't think we'll bother about your box and things tonight; I'll fix up about them tomorrow morning. We'll just walk out, and I'll find you a room at some hotel."

He smiled as he saw the look of amazed hope on the girl's face—a look which faded almost as quickly as it had come.

"Well—what's troubling you now?" he said.

"I can't, Jim," she cried. "It's wonderful of you to have thought of it—but I can't."

"Why not?" His voice was a little stern.

"There was a missionary here last night," she said, at length. "And he took one of the girls away. And that brute MacTavert's got two men he keeps here. And they threw him into the docks and nearly drowned him."

For a moment Jim look puzzled; then with ostentatious deliberation he lit a cigarette.

"And you're afraid, Colette, that they will do that to me?" She nodded. "I couldn't have you hurt for me," she answered. "I'm not worth it."

And Jim was polishing his eyeglass, which had suddenly become a bit misty.

"Thank you, little girl," he said quietly, after a while. "That's awfully sweet of you. But you needn't worry about it, I promise you. Somehow or other, I don't, think MacTavert and his pals will throw me or Dick into any dock. And if they do," he went on, with a sudden grin, "I'll guarantee that they will come in with us."

He pushed back his chair and rose to his feet.

"Come along; we'll go now."

He led the way towards the door, and after a moment's hesitation the girl followed him. And they had got halfway when MacTavert saw them. With a shout of anger he rushed out from behind the bar, and reached the door just ahead of Jim.

"Where are you taking that gel to?" he demanded, barring the way.

Instantly a silence settled on the room; everyone craned forward with zest to see what was going to happen. And Colette, her breath coming in little frightened gasps, cowered close to me, while her eyes were fixed on the tall figure of Jim just in front of her.

"In England, MacTavert," he remarked, and every word cut like a knife through the room, "in England you would be flogged with the cat for your method of living. Unfortunately, we are not in England, and so I propose to take the law into my own hands. If you don't get out of my way I shall hit you."

And MacTavert laughed, or rather he bared his yellow teeth in what was intended to be a grin. At last this man was talking the language that he understood, and when that language was talked MacTavert, to do him justice, was no coward.

"You'll hit me, Percy, will you?" he mimicked. "Sure, you frighten me, darling."

A burst of laughter went round the room, which died away in a gasp of astonishment. At one moment MacTavert was standing there leering at Jim—the next he had disappeared. And only the drumming of his feet, which stuck out from under a table that he had overturned in his fall, indicated his position. Not till the drumming ceased did Jim turn and contemplate the room.

"When he takes interest again," he remarked pleasantly, to no one in particular, "you can remind him that I gave him fair warning."

He passed through the door and we followed—no one lifting a finger to prevent us.

"Easy money," said Jim, grinning, "but I think we'll get a move on now. When MacTavert wakes up he won't be full of brotherly love."

We walked quickly away up the street, the girl between us, and as we turned the corner that hid the flaring notice out of sight, I looked back. As far as I could see the street was deserted, and I breathed more freely. At last we reached a small and respectable-looking hotel, and after a brief survey Jim decided it would do. A room was available, and he engaged it for Colette.

"I'll be round in the morning," he said, cutting short her thanks with a smile. "Until then you go to bed and sleep."

We watched her go up the stairs before we left. At the top she turned and waved her hand, and Jim waved back.

"Poor little kid," he said, as we went out into the street. "Thank heaven we were here, and she saw us! Otherwise. . ."

He paused suddenly, gripping my arm, and stared across the road.

"Under that tree, Dick," he whispered. "Do you see anything?"

And it seemed to me there was a shadow on the path such as a man might throw. But when we got there and looked about there was nothing. The road was deserted, and at last we turned and retraced our steps towards our own hotel.

★★★★★★

It was eleven o'clock next morning that we returned to the hotel where we had left Colette. And we found she'd gone!

The clerk, in the intervals of picking his teeth, informed us dispassionately that a message had come round for her to the effect that the gentleman with the eyeglass wished her to come at once to his hotel—the Grand. And she'd gone. Apparently her bill had been paid, and he could tell us nothing more. A car had been waiting and she had got in. With which he returned to his teeth, while Jim cursed with marvellous fluency under his breath.

"What a fool I was, Dick! We ought to have taken her to the Grand." We were standing in the sunny street outside the hotel. "That swine MacTavert has got her back."

"What about going to the police?" I suggested.

"Man, we've got no proof," he cried. "And even if we had, the police in a place like this are no more use than a sick headache. We've got to handle this thing ourselves, Dick. Are you on?"

"Of course," I said briefly. "What's the first move?"

"A further conversation with MacTavert," he remarked. "And at once."

The dancing saloon was empty as we turned into it. The reek of stale smoke and spirits was worse than the night before, but it was evidently too early for the *habitués* to arrive.

"So much the better," said Jim grimly. "It gives us a clear field."

He gave a shout of "Bar!" and after a moment or two MacTavert's evil face appeared through a door. He stared at us for a time in silence; then he pressed an electric bell twice.

"This bar don't open till midday," he remarked at length.

"That's very fortunate," said Jim placidly. "It gives us an hour to break it up in. How is the face this morning?"

"Get out of it!" roared MacTavert, completely losing control of himself.

"Certainly," answered Jim. "The instant that you produce Colette I shall be delighted to go."

But the scoundrel wasn't going to give himself away.

"So you've lost her, have you?" he sneered. "She fooled you nicely last night, didn't she?"

He was leaning over the bar, shaking with laughter.

"You dear little mother's innocent, with your little pane of glass in your eye! I admit you can hit, but you've a lot to learn yet, Percy. Sling him out, boys," he snarled suddenly, "and half-murder him!"

I swung round to see two men creeping on Jim from behind—two men who had entered noiselessly while MacTavert was talking. They were great, powerful brutes, in better condition than MacTavert, and they thought they had a soft thing on. Slinging out a toff with an eyeglass was just pure pleasure—better even than half-drowning a missionary.

It was then I discovered what a wonderful weapon a bottle of

French vermouth can be if used skilfully. So did the leading tough. He crashed like a log, with vermouth dripping from his head, and Jim returned the broken bottle to MacTavert.

"A poor fighter," he murmured placidly, though his eyes were very bright and watchful. "Is your other friend going to sling me out?"

But the second man showed no signs of attempting to do anything of the sort. He was muttering to MacTavert behind the bar, and suddenly the latter began to grin.

"There's something up, Jim," I whispered, and he nodded without speaking.

"Well, Percy," said MacTavert, at length, "we've kind of come to the conclusion that you must be powerful fond of that little girl. So out of the kindness of my heart I guess you may take her—if you can. She is through that door there and up the stairs. The room on the right is hers. And, as I say, you may take her—if you can."

The leer had deepened on his face, and Jim was watching him narrowly.

"Not afraid, are you?" sneered MacTavert. "I'll come with you and show you the way."

He slouched over to the door, and we followed him. Jim had his hand in his pocket, and I could see the outline of his gun, but if MacTavert saw it he gave no sign. He led the way up the stairs, and paused at the top waiting for us. And it was then I noticed that the other man had left the bar. It was empty save for the unconscious scoundrel on the floor.

"Here's the room," remarked MacTavert, flinging open the door and leading the way in.

"You infernal swine!" roared Jim, as we saw the terrified girl. She was lashed to a chair and gagged, and in an instant he was beside her undoing the rope, and Colette was free!

"Cover him, Dick!" he ordered briefly, and my gun went into MacTavert's waistcoat. His great, coarse face was within a few inches of mine, but it was the look of triumph in his eyes that warned me of the trap. He was staring at something over my shoulder, and suddenly he gave a great shout of "Now!"

I swung round, like the fool I was, and the next moment he'd knocked my revolver away, and his hands were round my throat. Out of the corner of my eye I saw Jim fighting desperately with two men who had sprung through the door, but it wasn't there that the trap lay; it wasn't that which had caused the sudden shout of "Now!"

Coming towards the window from the outside along a flat piece of roof was the man who had been talking to MacTavert downstairs. He had a revolver in his hand, and he was covering Jim through the window—Jim, who was all unconscious of the danger. I strove to shout—to warn him, but MacTavert had got my throat, and it was all I could do to hold my own. And all the time the triumph deepened in MacTavert's eyes.

The two men were being flung all over the place by Jim, but they hung on to him. And steadily they manoeuvred him nearer and nearer to the window. He had his back towards it, and once the man outside raised his revolver, only to drop it again as the three of them spun round, spoiling his shot.

But it couldn't last long, and I put forth one supreme effort to get the better of MacTavert. We crashed, both of us rolling over and over on the floor. And so I didn't see the actual deed by which Colette saved our lives. All I knew was that suddenly we were fighting in darkness, MacTavert and I. I heard dimly the crashing of the window, and the splintering of wooden shutters. Then two shots rang out quite quickly, and the room was light again.

Instinctively MacTavert and I loosened our hold on one another, and got dazedly to our feet. And, save for our heavy breathing and a little sobbing whimper from that wonderful girl, there was silence in the room.

"She closed those wooden shutters," said Jim at length, and his voice was a little dazed. "She closed those wooden butters, and put her arm where the bar ought to be that bolts them. She hadn't time, I guess, for the bar. And he broke her arm for her."

He looked at the man who had done it—the man who had smashed through the shutters, and fired at him—and he was lying motionless on his face. He looked at Colette, and she had fainted. And then he looked at MacTavert, and his face was terrible to see.

"Get out!" snarled Jim to the two men whom he had been fighting. He slipped his own revolver back in his pocket. "Get out—or I might shoot you, as I shot him."

And the men slunk out, leaving MacTavert alone. For a moment Jim stared at him, and his eyes were hard and merciless. Then without a word he sprang on him, and MacTavert gave a hoarse cry for help. But there was no one to answer it, and Jim laughed gently.

He could have done it by himself, for MacTavert was like a child in his hands. But since I was there to help him it took less time. We lashed him to the bed face down.

"The cat is the proper weapon for MacTavert," Jim remarked, "as I think I told you last night. But since I haven't got one a leather strap must do instead."

And he flogged MacTavert with his leather belt till MacTavert fainted, even as Colette had fainted. Then, with the tenderness of a woman, he picked the girl up in his arms, and carried her down the stairs to the saloon below. It was still empty, and we chartered a passing cab, and got in. It was on the way to a doctor that Colette opened her eyes and looked at him.

"He didn't hurt you, Jim?" she whispered.

And Jim bent and kissed her. I don't think he could quite trust his voice.

We fixed up a passage for her, and as I said before she has two little Colettes of her own now. But I wonder if she realises. . .

5.—The Fight at Bull Mine Creek

We first heard the rumour at Sydney three months later, from a man in our hotel. And two nights after, he confirmed it: gold had been found at a place called Bull Mine Creek. The wildest stories were flying around: it was going to be a second Klondike.

There was gold in the river, masses of it. And since easily worked placers are nearly all exhausted, thousands of the old-time miners arrived in force. Deep placer deposits, requiring shaft sinking and therefore capital, are today the source of almost all the gold in the world, and the gold-mining industry is a highly organised affair. The wild rushes of the last century are things of the past, though occasionally they still occur. And Bull Mine Creek was one of them.

Exactly why Jim and I went there I don't know. Novelty, perhaps—a new experience; and new experiences were the wine of life to him. We didn't much mind if we made a fortune or not, though we should neither of us have refused it if we had. Incidentally we didn't, and what we did net after expenses had been paid, we handed over to One-eyed Mike, an old scoundrel of repulsive aspect, who had lost his left eye in circumstances we never fully got to the bottom of. He was a remarkable character, was Mike. His nationality varied according to his company—with us he was English, and he appeared to have been in every mining rush during the last thirty years. I think he robbed us right and left, though like the Chinese servant, he took care that nobody else did. And he knew everything there was to know about the game.

He talked about sluice-boxes and riffles in the intervals of telling the most lurid stories I have ever listened to, and for six weeks we camped out by our claim some fifteen miles from the town of Bull Mine Creek.

The town consisted of a few shanties, a store and the hotel. Before the rush it must have been a fairly pleasant little place; within a week of the boom it became a miniature hell on earth. Gambling saloons were opened, and the place was invaded by a horde of blackguards whose sole aim in life was to see that the miner and his gold were soon parted. And in many cases it wasn't a difficult proposition. Unlimited drink, gold to chuck about, and crooked gambling after the drink had taken effect, generally produced the desired result, after which the miner returned to his claim with an empty "poke" and a bursting head.

★★★★★★

It was One-eyed Mike who insisted on going down to the town for Christmas. And since he had been going teetotal—or rather confining himself to only one bottle of whisky a day—for some weeks, we felt he deserved a respite. So Jim gave him his share of all the proceeds up to date, and on Christmas Eve we all drove into Bull Mine Creek.

Outside the door of the hotel was a buggy drawn by two fine Arabs, around which stood a ring of loungers contemplatively spitting. The horses were tied up to the rail of the veranda, and Jim glanced at them as we drove past.

"A nice pair of cattle," he remarked. "I wonder whom they belong to."

The next moment our own horse stopped suddenly, and then gave a sudden plunge forward. She was not used to having her head nearly pulled off unexpectedly, and Jim was certainly not accustomed to treat an animal in such a way. In some surprise I looked at him, and the expression on his face amazed me. It also decided me against making any comment.

Instead, I looked back and made a further inspection of the owner of the two Arabs, whose sudden appearance had so upset my companion. He was a tall, good-looking man whose age I put at about thirty. He had a small, fair moustache, and was rather of the pink-and-white type. So much I saw before we turned the corner and were out of sight. My last glimpse of him was leading his two horses towards the back of the hotel while the ring of loungers still contemplatively spat.

Jim drove on in silence to the shanty where we were putting up. He was frowning thoughtfully, and underneath the beard which he had allowed to grow during the past two months his mouth was set in a straight line. But he said nothing, even after we had put the mare up; and he only nodded curtly at One-eyed Mike's earnest hope that we would raise the roof with him that night. So Mike, fully capable of performing the operation on his own, departed to the hotel to lay the foundation for a forty-eight-hour jag.

"Did you see that fellow, Dick?" said Jim at length. "The fellow at the hotel with those two greys?"

"I did," I answered. "Who is he?"

Jim smiled a little grimly.

"He is John James Hildebrand, fifteenth Marquis of Sussex, the eldest son of the Duke of Plumpton."

"All that, is he?" I said. "One rather wonders what John James Hildebrand is doing at Bull Mine Creek."

"One does," agreed Jim. "Excessively so."

And with that he swung on his heel, and I saw him no more for some hours. I wrote two or three long overdue letters, and then having nothing better to do, I strolled along the dusty road to the hotel to get a drink. The place was filling up with the crowd who had come in for Christmas, and the first man I saw was One-eyed Mike. He beckoned to me joyously and I went over to his table.

"There's going to be some fun here tonight, boy!" he cried as I sat down. "There's a dude that calls himself Hildebrand wandering around, and the boys are just crazy to know him better. They want to know if he's real."

So the fifteenth Marquis of Sussex had decided not to advertise the fact.

"What's he doing here, Mike?" I asked.

"Come out to look at some property he's got, so he told the boss here. Taken a room, and wants his dinner served upstairs." Mike began to chuckle again. "Look out; here he is."

★★★★★★

John James Hildebrand had just entered the room from the other end, and I watched him curiously. There was no doubt that Mike's prophecy was going to be fulfilled; the fun had started already. Following close at his heels came half a dozen miners, all gazing at him in rapt awe and admiration. The baiting of John James had begun in earnest.

He halted by the bar, and the miners instantly came to a standstill.

"Boys," shouted the leader, "let us have silence! Mr. Hildebrand is about to consume some liquid refreshment. And the slightest sound might interfere with Mr. Hildebrand's enjoyment."

A dead silence settled on the room, and I wondered how he was going to take it.

"Quite right," he remarked, with a faint, rather pleasant drawl. "Which is why I don't ask you to join me. Six of you—all drinking—would fairly put the lid on."

The leader roared with laughter, and I grinned gently. Quite obviously John James had the right stuff in him.

"I'm dashed if you drink alone, Mr. Hildebrand," cried the leader, coming up to the counter. "You drink with me right here."

He shouted for a round, and they formed up on each side of John James.

"I'm not so certain that you are going to have your fun, Mike," I remarked, when suddenly he leant forward and stared at the door which had just swung open.

"Holy Moses!" he muttered. "Here's Pete Cornish. I didn't know he was up these parts."

A sudden cessation of conversation took place as the man who had just come in moved up to the bar. As if he had noticed it, and attributed it to his sudden entry, a faint smile hovered round his lips. His face was almost bloodless, and a great red scar across his right cheek emphasised the pallor. But the most noticeable feature of the man's face was a pair of very light blue eyes which seemed to stare unwinkingly from under his big forehead at the object of his scrutiny. He stooped a little, but even with the stoop he measured over six feet. And the depth of his chest betokened his immense strength.

"Steer clear of him, boy," muttered Mike to me. "I haven't seen him for six years, but I guess he hasn't changed. And he's the devil incarnate, is Pete Cornish. I once saw him break a man's back with his hands alone—across his knees. He's spent fifteen years of his life in prison as it is."

But I wasn't paying attention to Mike's reminiscences. I was watching Pete Cornish. He came to a standstill just behind John James, and for a moment or two he stood there in silence. It was the miner who had called for drinks who' first saw him, and he turned round with a somewhat sickly smile.

"Hullo, Pete!" he said, "will you join us?"

"I will," answered Cornish quietly. "And who is your friend?"

"Hildebrand," returned the other. "This is Pete Cornish."

"Pleased to meet you, Mr. Hildebrand," said Cornish. "And what might you be doing? Prospecting?"

"I've come out to see a property of mine," answered Hildebrand briefly.

The blue eyes never left his face for an instant, even when their owner raised his glass to his lips. There was something baleful in their unblinking intensity, something almost terrifying which the quiet voice and general immobility seemed only to enhance. The man never moved; he merely stared until after a while the other fidgeted a little and turned away. And the faintest flicker of a smile appeared on Cornish's lips.

"I seem to recognise your face, Mr. Hildebrand," he remarked as he put down his empty glass. "In fact, I am sure I do. And so, you will drink with me."

It was not a question; it was a statement, and Hildebrand flushed slightly.

"Thank you, no," he answered. "I don't want anything more to drink at present."

"I said, Mr. Hildebrand, that you would drink with me," said the other gently, and it was then I noticed that five of the original six miners who had lined up at the bar had slipped unostentatiously away. Only the leader remained, and he was shuffling his feet.

"The guy is all right, Pete," he muttered awkwardly. "Guess he may not have the head for our whisky."

The blue eyes temporarily transferred their gaze to the last speaker.

"I'm not quite clear how you come into this matter," remarked Cornish. "I wasn't aware that you were even in the picture."

The miner turned and stammered out something, but Cornish simply ignored his existence.

"Now, Mr. Hildebrand, you will drink a little toast with me," he continued, pushing a glass towards him.

"I have already said that I will not have another, thank you," returned the other icily. "I drink when I like, and with whom I like."

He nodded briefly and turned to leave the bar. But before he had taken two steps Cornish had stretched out a hand and caught him by

70

the arm.

"Will you kindly leave go of my arm?" said Hildebrand quietly, though two ugly red spots had appeared on his face.

"When you have drunk my toast, Mr. Hildebrand; not before."

For a moment John James, fifteenth Marquis of Sussex, stood very still. He was no fool, and he knew that if it came to a scrap he might with luck last exactly one second with the man who held his arm. At the same time he came of a stock to whom the meaning of the word fear was unknown.

"And what is your toast?" he asked at length.

"Damnation to the English—especially their aristocracy," answered the other mildly. "Your glass, Mr. Hildebrand."

The Marquis of Sussex smiled faintly, as he took the glass in his right hand. "Do you play cricket, Mr. Cornish?" he asked.

"I do not," returned the other, looking slightly surprised. "Because if you had ever fielded at cover point, you would realise that this is a very good return to the wicket keeper."

It was done in one movement like a flash of light, and the heavy glass broke in pieces on Cornish's face. He staggered back a step with a curse, letting go of the other's arm, and without undue hurry, but also without undue pause, John James Hildebrand left the room. For a moment or two I expected Cornish to rush after him, but he didn't. He stood in the centre of the room wiping the whisky from his face. Then, without a word, he too turned and left the bar by the door which led into the street.

★★★★★★

It was the miner by the counter who broke the silence.

"Good for the youngster!" he cried ecstatically. "But, my word, boys! Pete will kill him for that!"

A murmur of assent went round the room, which was stilled by the sudden reappearance of Hildebrand. He stood by the door, and glanced about him; then he smiled.

"Oh! he's gone, has he?" he said cheerfully. "It struck me after I got upstairs that I had left a bit quickly, and that he might think I was afraid of him. But you see, gentlemen—my wife is with me, and one doesn't want to get mixed up in a scrap."

The miner at the counter took a couple of steps forward.

"See here, Mr. Hildebrand," he said earnestly, "you've proved your-self. You've got guts; you've got nerve, and I want to apologise here and now for ragging you. But for God's sake, man, get away out of this! I know Pete Cornish, and I know his reputation, and I tell you straight he'll pretty near kill you for bunging that glass in his face. He ain't a man; he's a blind, mad, roaring devil when he gets going. Get away now—with your wife. Them greys of yours are good for another fifty miles. We'll get you into your trap, won't we, boys?"

A murmur of assent came from the others present, and the man by the door gave a quick smile.

"I thank you, gentlemen," he said, quietly. "But if you imagine that my wife and I are going a fifty-mile drive, or for that matter a fifty-yard one, because some renegade Irishman gets gay, you misunderstand the situation. And while I am at it I must apologise for a small deceit I have practised on you. I'm really Lord Sussex. Hildebrand is a sort of family name."

With another smile he was gone, and a sort of sigh went round the room. And it struck me that the general feeling was voiced by One-eyed Mike as he pessimistically finished the whisky.

"I don't know nothing about Sussex—nor family names," he remarked. "But what I do know is that there's going to be dirty work here tonight, and I guess he's going to be the dirt."

I found Jim at the shanty when I got back. He had shaved, and changed his clothes, and with his feet on the mantelpiece he was reading a month-old newspaper. He glanced up as I came in, and dropped the paper on the floor.

"Anything doing?" he asked.

"Quite a lot," I answered. "Your friend John James Hildebrand has quite distinguished himself."

He listened while I told him what had occurred, and a faint look of surprise crossed his face.

"I didn't know he had it in him," he remarked thoughtfully. "In fact, I have always been under the impression that his principal claim to notoriety lay in the fact that being his father's eldest son, he would in the fullness of time become a duke."

And for, I think, the first time in our friendship I saw Jim Maitland sneer.

"What of it, Jim?" I said. "Why the sarcasm?"

"Nothing, old man," he answered. "At any rate nothing that I care to go into. It's an old story anyway, and I thought it had died in my mind years ago. Only seeing him unexpectedly this evening brought it back—that's all."

"Well, from what I gathered there is every possibility of trouble tonight," I said. "I must say that that man Cornish is quite the ugliest-looking customer I've ever seen. And I didn't like the absolute silence in which he left the bar. If he'd sworn or made a fuss it would have been more natural."

Jim shrugged his shoulders.

"John James must fight his own battles."

"He seems quite capable of it," I answered shortly. "But I wish his wife weren't there."

"His wife?" said Jim very slowly. "His wife, did you say?"

"Certainly. Stopping at the hotel with him."

He was staring at me almost dazedly.

"Ruth—at that hotel? Good Heavens! man—she can't be!"

I made no comment on his use of her Christian name.

"He told us so," I answered, "at the same time as he announced who he was."

And now Jim was pacing up and down the room with his hands in his pockets. He was frowning deeply, and every now and then he paused and stared out of the window.

Already some of the boys had begun their celebrations, and occasional shouts of half-drunken laughter came from the street outside.

"The fellow must be mad!" exploded Jim suddenly. "Stark, staring mad to bring her to a place like this on Christmas Eve. Confound it! has he left his nurse in England?"

"It's not the boys I'm worried about, Jim," I said gravely. "They won't hurt a woman even if they are a bit tight. And, anyway, presumably she will stop in her room. It's that man Cornish who frightens me. I tell you the men at that bar dried up like so many frightened puppies as he came in. And he means murder."

Jim laughed contemptuously.

"You've got Cornish on the brain, Dick."

And even as he spoke the door was flung open and One-eyed Mike came in. He had been running and he spoke in gasps.

"Cornish!" he cried. "Pete Cornish! He's raving mad up in the hotel. He's got that Lord fellow who threw the liquor in his face, and he's got his wife, and he's doing trick-firing with a couple of revolvers."

And as he finished I realised we were alone: Jim was, racing up the darkening street towards the hotel.

I heard six shots ring out like bullets from a machine-gun; as I followed him, and just ten seconds behind Jim I turned, into the bar I had so recently left. It was an amazing' scene, and that first impression of it is photographed indelibly on my brain. Huddled in small groups sat some twenty miners, and even the drunkest of them seemed to have sobered up. In the centre of the room and hanging from a beam swung a smoking naphtha lamp. Underneath it stood Pete Cornish, holding in one arm a girl, whose look of frozen horror failed to hide her loveliness.

Seated on a chair against the wall was the fifteenth Marquis of Sussex, and like a halo round his head there was a row of holes in the wall. As Mike said, Pete Cornish was trick-firing.

The man on the chair was sitting bolt upright, while his knuckles gleamed like ivory where his hands gripped the seat. His face was white, but with rage—not fear: and his blazing eyes met those staring blue ones without a quiver.

"Don't move, my darling," said Cornish with an ugly snarl. "You might spoil my aim. And that would be a dreadful thing for your dear husband, wouldn't it?"

Again the six shots rang out, and the wood round the seated man's head splintered anew. The girl moaned piteously, and her husband cursed and stirred in his chair.

"My other gun," said Cornish thoughtfully, and a horrible-looking brute came forward with a freshly loaded six-shooter. And at that John James Hildebrand sprang. It was his only chance, but it was pitiful to watch. As well might a Pekinese spring at a bull-terrier, if one may so insult a grand breed of dog by comparison with Pete Cornish.

He tried to get home with his fist, did John James—and Cornish hit him once. He hit him straight in the face with a grunt of passion, and the poor devil pitched forward and lay still.

"I still want my gun," said Cornish thoughtfully, and as he spoke one solitary shot rang out. The man who was holding the revolver cursed hideously as his hand was shattered, and Jim laughed gently. Slowly the blue eyes came round and fastened on him, staring unwinking; and for a moment or two there was silence—broken at length by a little gasping cry of "Jim!" from the girl.

"Did you fire that shot?" asked Cornish softly, dropping the girl and taking a step forward.

"I did," answered Jim, equally softly. "And I would suggest your standing very still, because I'm now going to fire five more. Stand away, Ruth,"—but the girl was on her knees beside her husband.

The five shots cut away a strip from Cornish's shirt, and they sounded almost continuous so incredibly quickly were they fired.

"I have also another gun," drawled Jim, "so that any attempt to pick up your own would be a little unwise. Dick, would you retrieve it?"

But Cornish never moved a muscle. The scar on his face showed red and angry, but the eyes, unwinking as ever, stared, and went on staring at Jim.

"Quite passable shooting," he said at length. "And what do you propose should be the next move? Or do we stand like this all night?"

"We do not," answered Jim. "I have been informed of the toast which you suggested Lord Sussex should drink, just before he wasted good liquor on your face, and it fails to appeal to me. So having given you a little of your own medicine in the shooting line, we will now try the second form of exercise. We will fight here and now to a finish with our fists."

A sudden gleam came into Cornish's eyes—merciless and triumphant; and an audible gasp ran round the room. Was this fellow with an eyeglass completely insane? But only One-eyed Mike said anything, and he was nearly frantic.

"For God's sake, sir," he whispered to Jim, "don't do it! He's been a professional, has Cornish—and he's a slaughterer even with gloves."

But Jim paid no attention. He was peeling off his shirt and giving me instructions.

"If he fights fair, Dick, do nothing. But if any of his pals get gay, I rely on you. I'm not under any delusions as to what I've taken on."

For a moment he glanced across the room to where the girl sat crouched on the floor with her unconscious husband's head pillowed on her lap, and he smiled whimsically.

"I'm over it now," he said, "but seven years ago I thought my world had finished when she turned me down for him. But he's a good boy, Dick—and if Cornish knocks me out—well, again I rely on you."

And just then the girl raised her head and looked full at Jim. In her eyes was a wonderful message, for the Marchioness of Sussex was merely a very primitive woman at that moment. Certainly it was the message Jim wanted, and he smiled at her reassuringly as he stepped into the circle of light thrown by the naphtha lamp.

★★★★★★

Men still talk about that fight on Christmas Eve in the hotel at Bull Mine Creek. And now as I write about it, it comes back to me as if it had taken place only yesterday. Word had flashed round the camp like lightning that a man was taking on Pete Cornish, bare fists, to a finish, and men came pouring in till the room was crammed almost to suffocation. They stood on the bar, they lined the windows, and very soon it was obvious which way their sympathies lay. Not one out of ten knew Jim, but there wasn't a soul in the room who did not know—and hate Pete Cornish. The betting it is true started at five to one on Cornish, for his form was known, and money is money; then the odds shortened and held steady at threes, when Jim, stripped to the waist, was sized up. But even before the first blow was struck there wasn't a soul who wouldn't willingly have lost his money to see Cornish down and out.

There was no time wasted on preliminaries, no introductions, no retinues of seconds. But one could feel the nerve-gripping tension as the two men faced one another, swaying slightly on their feet under the flaring lamp. Cornish, his blue staring eyes fixed unwinkingly on Jim, was a shade the bigger man of the two. As he stood, crouching a little forward, his huge depth of chest was more apparent than when he had had his clothes on, and a little feeling of sick anxiety got hold of me and made it difficult to swallow. Without doubt he was an amazingly powerful brute, and there was a look of implacable rage on his face that boded ill for Jim if the worst happened. And then I glanced at Jim; took in the glistening health of his skin, the clear, unconcerned eyes, and felt better. And in my own mind I sized up the position to find later that it was exactly how Jim had sized it up himself. Cornish was the stronger man of the two; Cornish was probably the better boxer; but Cornish was not in such good condition.

And then they closed, and a kind of sigh went round the packed spectators. Smack, smack and they were away again, with a jaw-jolting punch on Jim's jaw as Cornish's contribution, and a heavy body blow on the other side of the ledger which made Cornish draw in his breath with a hiss. Not quite such a spectacular punch perhaps, but as Jim said to me afterwards, it was that first blow that probably won him the fight. For it rather more than touched up Cornish's wind, and there lay his weakness. It was a case of bellows to mend, and inside a minute a sullen-looking purple patch was showing on his ribs.

But there was a long way to go yet, and a punishing way. Cornish was no fool; he knew his weakness, none better. And he started to force the fighting. A quick decision was his best hope, and for the next three minutes my heart was in my mouth. Savagely, but never wildly, he went for Jim, taking his own punishment without a sound. And at least two of his upper cuts, if they had got home, would have ended the fight there and then.

But they didn't. Coolly and warily Jim gave ground, letting the other man follow him round and round the room, and concentrating always on his one objective, Cornish's body. Twice, three times he landed—heavy punishing blows, and was away before the other had time to counter. He was bleeding from the mouth, and one eye was horribly swollen.

The room was deadly silent. The patter of their feet was the only sound; that, and the thing that was music to me, Cornish's laboured breathing. And then suddenly an angry roar burst out.

"Too low, Cornish—foul!"

With a snarl Cornish sprang back, but Jim was smiling now. An attempted foul right enough, but countered just in time, and Jim changed his tactics. Rightly he guessed that it was the other man's last throw—his breathing was becoming more and more painful. From the defensive he changed to the attack. He gave Cornish not one second's respite; he was here, there and everywhere waiting for the opportunity of a knock-out. Twice Cornish hit him, heavy stopping rib binders, but he was weakening perceptibly. His blue eyes, fixed and implacable, still stared at Jim from his swollen face, but he was getting slower and slower, while he sucked in air in great wheezing gasps. And then quite suddenly came the end. Jim feinted at his body, and as his guard dropped Jim hit him under the jaw. Feet, body, weight were exactly right, and the blow sounded like the dropping of a billiard ball on a wooden floor.

So came the finish. Cornish spun round, his knees sagging under him, and crumpled up on the floor. He lay there motionless and inert—knocked out, insensible, and Jim stood watching him and rubbing the knuckles of his right hand. For the blow that had knocked out Cornish, had also broken three of Jim's fingers.

There was one dazed moment while nobody spoke; then pandemonium broke loose. A seething, shouting crowd of miners thronged across the floor to where Jim stood, led by One-eyed Mike. For Mike was nearly speechless; he could only babble strange oaths in an almost inarticulate voice.

"Knocked out—Cornish knocked out," he kept on saying over and over again. "And he's my pard, you sons of a gun—don't you forget it!"

But Jim with a faint smile on his battered face pushed through the crowd to where his clothes lay.

"Tell 'em, Dick," he muttered to me, "to come to our shanty. They can't stop here."

With that he was gone, and I crossed the room to Lord Sussex and his wife. He was conscious again, but it was the girl I was looking at. And I had to deliver my message three times before she took it in. She was rubbing her hands gently together, and the expression on her face would have caused a positive sensation in a drawing-room. But then in a drawing-room, I am told, one rarely sees two heavy-weights fight to a finish without gloves.

★★★★★★

We found Jim, clothed and comparatively presentable, trying to cut the wire of a champagne bottle. And the Marchioness of Sussex walked straight up to him and kissed him.

"I hardly know you, Jim," she said, a little tremulously, "without your eyeglass."

Jim grinned. "I'm afraid we shall have to dispense with that for a day or two."

"Good Heavens!" shouted John James Hildebrand, "it's Jim Maitland!"

"Bright boy," said his wife, and it struck me she wasn't quite at her ease.

"I only came to when you were fighting," he went on, "and I never recognised you."

And then he too dried up a little awkwardly.

"By Gad, old man," he said steadily, after a moment, "I feel it horribly, that I couldn't fight my own battles for myself. It was fine of you to take that swine on—fine!"

Jim poured out the champagne.

"I don't profess that I'd have done it five years ago or even tonight if Ruth hadn't been there," he remarked quietly.

And then he smiled suddenly.

"Yes—I would. Your going for him as you did was a darned sight better than my show. We can't all be made big, old chap."

He held out his sound hand.

"John," he said, "shake. I haven't loved you much for the past seven years. In fact I haven't loved you at all. I thought—well, I thought lots of things at the time. But the years have healed, and—" He turned to the girl. "Is it well, Ruth, with you?"

"Yes, Jim, very well," she answered gently. "My dear, I'm sorry. But it was because you thought, and let me see you thought, that it was

78

owing to John being a duke one day, that I was annoyed."

Jim nodded thoughtfully.

"I was a fool," he said quietly. "Still," he added whimsically, "perhaps it was as well. I've had seven good years in the edge of beyond."

"You're very rude," laughed the girl. "We'll have to find you a wife now, Jim."

"You preferred your blessed old John James," Jim said, "and *she* thinks I'm a cur. She told me so."

"Then she must be mad," said Ruth indignantly. "Where is she, Jim?"

"In England somewhere."

"Then come home and stop with us and look for her."

Jim laughed. "I don't know about that, but if I come back I'll spend a few days at the ancestral seat if you'll have me."

"If you don't," cried John James, "you'll have to fight me, my boy. And in the meantime, Ruth, kiss him again."

"I was just going to," said his wife.

And she did.

"You'll come, Jim," she repeated. "And Mr. Leyton too."

"Shall we go back to England, Dick?" he said with a little laugh.

"The one sure thing," I remarked, "is that if we decide to, we shan't."

"You see our habits, Ruth," he said. "We're dreadful people to have about the house. Anyway I don't know what you think, Dick, but we might take the first step on the journey in the near future. My unalterable conviction is that gold mining at a hundred and ten in the shade is an overrated amusement."

And at that we left it.

6.—Pete Cornish's Revenge

It was the first time that the curtain had been lifted on the years before I met him. Even to me he had never talked. Jim wasn't made that way. But as he wished Lady Sussex a merry Christmas next morning I couldn't help wondering what would have happened if she had become Mrs. Maitland. And I think it must have been a close thing on her side as well as on his, though I've got no earthly right to say so. But as she said goodbye, it struck me that. . . .

Anyway—that's enough. This is no account of the love affairs of early youth.

We saw them off from the hotel, and stood in the road watching till the dust from their buggy had died away in the distance. And then we started to stroll back to our shanty.

"What I said last night, Dick," he said with a faint smile, "was perfectly right. If she hadn't married John James Hildebrand, she'd have married me. And I should have hunted and shot and fished in England; probably done a nice tour round the world chaperoned by Mr. Thomas Cook, and missed seven years of life."

He grinned ill-advisedly.

"Whew!" he cried, hurriedly composing his face, "don't let me laugh again. It hurts. Mr. Pete Cornish has got what you might describe as a fairly useful punch behind him."

"Once or twice last night, Jim, I thought he'd got you." Jim nodded briefly.

"So did I. Especially in that first minute. I don't mind telling you, Dick, that if that first smack he got me on the jaw had been half an inch lower, it would have been a knockout. It was his poor condition that did the trick."

We paused at the door of our shanty, as One-eyed Mike came down the steps to meet us. Judging from the torchlight appearance of that one eye, our friend and partner had celebrated Christmas Eve in his own fashion, but a broad smile adorned his face.

"A merry Christmas, boys!" he cried. And then he went into a fit of ecstatic chuckling. "To think of it: Pete Cornish knocked out with bare fists inside ten minutes. Why, man—I wouldn't have believed it possible. I just wouldn't have believed it possible! I guess I'd give every penny I possess in the world to see you do it again."

"You don't seem particularly fond of him, Mike," said Jim, as he went indoors.

"Fond of him," snarled the other. "Fond of that—swine. Eight years ago he swindled me out of the best claim I ever had, and when I taxed him with it, he and two of his pals waylaid me. That's where I lost this eye."

"A cheerful sort of customer," said Jim thoughtfully. "Well, you got a little bit of your own back last night anyway. And now that you're here, Mike, we might go into business. Dick and I are quitting: we're going back to England—perhaps. . ."

"Quitting?" There was genuine regret in One-eyed Mike's voice. "Boys, that's too bad. I guess you've got a real good claim up there."

"It's yours, Mike," said Jim. "We're handing it over to you, and the very best of luck, old man."

Speechless surprise showed in the one eye, and Mike's voice was a little husky as he answered.

"I guess I don't know what to say, sir," he remarked at length. "Sure Cornish didn't tap you on the head or anything last night?"

Jim laughed. "No, we're quite sane, Mike. But we're going back to England, to look for somebody."

"I hope you find her," said Mike, and then he strolled to the window and stood staring out down the dusty street. "I hope you find her," he repeated. "I reckon a woman—the right woman—is worth most other things put together. Though some of us don't have much luck that way." He paused and drummed on the window. "But Sandford's up early this morning. Moreover, pards, he's coming here, unless I'm greatly mistook."

We heard steps outside, and the next moment the door opened and the man in question entered. He held no official position in so far as the government was concerned, though his power was far greater than if he had. By common consent he had been elected boss, and sheriff, and general settler of disputes, and what he said at Bull Mine Creek went. He was a man of about fifty, with shrewd grey eyes and a reputation for impartial fairness in his decisions, which was just what was wanted in such a community.

"Morning, Bud," said Jim. "Take a seat."

Bud Sandford somewhat deliberately took a chair, and lit a cigar.

"Morning, boy," he remarked. "How's the face?"

Jim grinned. "Wants a week's rest, and it'll grow again."

Bud gazed out of the window.

"I saw your scrap last night," he remarked, "and I lost a tenner on the result. I may say that I'd willingly have lost two. I suppose you know it was a quarter of an hour before Cornish sat up and took notice?"

"As long as that?" said Jim. "I must have hit him harder than I thought."

"It's not to talk about that that I came around," went on Bud, "though as we're on the subject I'd like to say that it was the finest fight I've seen in thirty-five years. But it was to find out what you propose doing in the near future."

Jim looked a trifle surprised.

"Well, Bud," he said at length, "I guess there's no secret about it. I and my pal here are quitting, and our claim passes to Mike."

Bud grunted thoughtfully.

"When are you quitting?"

"We might push off today, or we might wait till tomorrow," answered Jim. "We haven't really thought about it yet."

"I guess I'd feel happier if you could make it today," said Bud.

"You seem almighty keen to be rid of us, Bud," said Jim. "What's the idea?"

Once again Bud's eyes travelled to the window.

"Just this, boy," he said. "Another twenty-four hours' rest and the effect of that blow on Pete Cornish's jaw will be wearing off, but the effect on his mind will be wearing in. Do you follow me?"

"Not frightfully clearly, Bud," remarked Jim ominously. "I fail to see any relation between Pete Cornish's jaw and my future plans."

Bud Sandford's grey eyes twinkled.

"I was afraid you mightn't," he confessed. "Though it seems powerful clear to me. Look here, son," he went on, leaning forward, and emphasising his remarks with his finger on Jim's knee, "this is how the land lies. You beat Pete Cornish last night in a fair, straight fight. You laid him out as stiff as a piece of frozen mutton, and everybody knows it. If you fought him again—fair, you'd do it again. And everybody knows that, too. But the next time you fight Pete Cornish you won't fight fair—because he won't let you.

"You see, I know Pete Cornish, and his reputation. He's been a devil in the past when he's been top-dog; now that you've beaten him he'll be a fiend incarnate. He'll stop at nothing till he's got his own back. And, though you're a plaguy fine fighter, boy, with your fists and with a revolver, you don't cut much ice against a man with a rifle hiding up an alley-way and shooting you in the back. And that's what Pete Cornish will do, or something like it, unless, so to speak, you pass out of the picture while he's still holding a raw rump-steak to his jaw."

The worthy Bud leant back in his chair exhausted, and Jim smiled.

"It's very good of you, Bud," he remarked quietly. "And I guess if it was possible I'd just love to take your advice. But since you've been talking I've come to the conclusion that my early religious training doesn't allow me to travel on Christmas Day."

"Early religious fiddlesticks!" Bud remarked. "What you imply, young fellah, is that you'll see me in a warmer place than this before anything would induce you to foot it from Bull Mine Creek until tomorrow."

"Or maybe the day after," murmured Jim. "We've got to do a bit of business, Bud: transferring our claim to Mike."

Bud rose, and flung his cigar through the window.

"Hell!" he remarked tersely. "And if I hadn't come around, you might have gone today. But I can promise you one thing, boy "—he paused by the door with a faint grin—"if we can get the smallest shadow of proof we'll hang him the same time as we bury you. And even if we can't, we'll hang him, I think. Pete Cornish has gone on too long."

The door closed behind him, only to open again as he popped his head round. "You'd better think out a good epitaph," he said genially. "Something snappy and original. The last one I made up won't apply, though it's good—mark you, good:

"Here lies Bill Soames, a funny sort of joker who held four aces, when he didn't deal at poker."

For the rest of Christmas Day nothing happened to justify Bud's forebodings. We squared up our few belongings—we'd left most of our kit in Sydney—and we carried out the short necessary formalities for re- registering our claim in One-eyed Mike's name. And, having done that, the only remaining occupation was killing time. If only Sandford had not come butting in, though he had done it with the best intentions, we should have cleared off that evening in the cool. As it was—Jim being Jim, we didn't.

We saw no signs of Cornish the whole of that day. In the hotel we gathered that he was lying up somewhere paying close and earnest attention to his jaw. And in the hotel we also gathered that the general feeling of the community agreed with Bud.

"Pete Cornish ain't finished yet, pard," said one of a group standing by the bar. "Pete Cornish won't never be finished till some public benefactor kills him. And that guy whose hand you shot last night is almost as bad—Yellow Sam."

The others growled assent, and 'Jim drained his glass with a smile.

"No, thank you, boys," he said, to the chorus of invitation which followed. "No more. I guess I'd better keep the old head cool if Cornish is all you say."

"You weren't here last night when he came to," went on the first speaker. "I was—and I watched him. He sat up, and stared around for a moment or two as if he didn't realise what had happened. Then he remembered. Them eyes of his—well, a sort of film came over them; and then they cleared, and he looked quite slowly and carefully all round the room. Reckon he was looking for you, but you'd gone. He never spoke; he just got up and walked out into the street, swaying a bit as he moved. And he passed me, so close I could have touched him. There was a look on his face such as I've never seen before not on any living man, and hopes I never shall again. And I tell you straight," his voice was very quiet and serious, "if he could catch you—if he could get you into his power by some dirty trick—God help you!"

Once again there was a growl of assent.

"There are stories told about Pete Cornish which aren't good to listen to. Do you remember—in '96 I think it was—way up there in Queensland, when that coach came trotting in without a driver? And inside they found two women and three children all murdered. The boys went out to look, and found Jake Harman, the driver, hanging side by side with his mate. There had been gold in the coach, but there was no one left to say what had happened. Only Cornish was in the neighbourhood, and people said lots. But there weren't no proof.

"That's just one story of many. There's another I remember, about a fellow in his gang who fell foul of him. He just disappeared, that's all—no one knew where. But months after a crazy black told a crazy story, as to how one night up by one of the smelting furnaces he'd heard someone screaming with fear. He'd crept a bit nearer, and a man with staring blue eyes had passed him in the dusk. The furnace was still alight when the black told his yarn—hadn't been let out for seven months—and there ain't much trace left after that time of anything or anybody that might have fallen in. Well—here's fortune, pard."

He lifted his glass and nodded to Jim.

"All I say to you is: Keep your gun handy as you drive over Lone Gully tomorrow. There's fifteen miles there where lots of things might happen."

With another nod and a quick handshake he turned and strolled out of the bar, and after a short while we followed him. We meant getting off early the next day, and we still had our final packing to do. And it was as we were walking down the street towards our shanty that I happened to glance up at a house we were passing. Whether it was purely accidental, or whether indeed some strange outside force was at work, I don't know. But in that momentary glance I saw quite distinctly a pair of light-blue eyes staring at us with a look of such malevolent hatred that I paused involuntarily. Then they disappeared, and I walked on at Jim's side. But I couldn't help wishing, as I blew out my candle that night, that civilisation in the shape of a railway train had extended to Bull Mine Creek. The prospect of driving over Lone Gully failed to appeal to me.

We were away by four next morning. One-eyed Mike—not at his best at that hour—was there to see us off, divided between real, genuine regret that we were going, and joy that he was now the sole and undisputed owner of our claim. Poor devil! he little knew that it was the last time he was going to see that pitiless sun rise: that before the end of the day he was to be shot without mercy by that cold-blooded murderer Cornish. Rough, honest sportsman—he came after Jim and me to save our lives, and in doing so he lost his own. But perhaps he knows that it wasn't altogether in vain: perhaps he knows that his murderer followed him not long after.

I'm getting on too fast. But sometimes even now I dream of that half-hour when death stared us in the face at the old mine-shaft in Lone Gully, and I wake—dripping with sweat. What Jim must have gone through is beyond my comprehension: in fact, he once confessed to me that if he ever had a nightmare it was always the same. He dreams that his hand—the one he had hurt the preceding night—failed him as he swung for over a minute, with certain death as the result if he let go.

But, as I said, I'm getting on too fast. Except for Mike there wasn't a soul stirring when, without much regret, we said farewell to Bull Mine Creek. Our idea was to push on till about ten o'clock, and then to call a halt until four that afternoon. We reckoned on reaching the beginning of the deserted stretch of country known as Lone Gully in the morning, and getting across it in the evening. And then the next day would see us on the railway. So we calculated, as we drove steadily along the flat, dusty road.

The sun was not too powerful, and Jim's jaw had sufficiently recovered to allow him to sing. The air was like wine, and after a while, under the influence of the, at any rate, powerful concert from the seat beside me, I forgot Pete Cornish. Certainly there had been no sign, of him or his pal that morning, and every mile between us and Bull Mine Creek seemed to render the likelihood of trouble less probable. If only I'd been able to get rid of the memory of those eyes as I'd seen them the previous evening, with their look of unwinking, implacable hatred. . .

★★★★★★

Half-past nine found us at the place where we had decided to stop for the midday halt, and it was none too soon. Already the sun was uncomfortably hot, and the buggy we were driving would not have won a prize for springing.

"Grub first," said Jim, "and then I think a little sleep, Dick. And perhaps, in view of everything, it would be as well if we took it in turns to watch."

We scanned the country in the direction from which we had come, but there was no sign of movement. The shimmering heat haze blurred and contorted the ground, but of life there seemed no sign.

"I can't help feeling sorry we've got no rifle," remarked Jim thoughtfully, a little later. "A revolver is all very well in its way, but it ain't much use against a man with a gun. However, I don't believe myself that we're going to have any trouble at all. They've made a bogy man of Mister Pete Cornish, and all the fellow is is just a low-down swine and bully."

And sure enough, when we harnessed up again at four o'clock, there had been no sign of him. Once about noon, while Jim was asleep, I thought I saw a little cloud of dust moving two or three miles away, but I had no field- glasses, and in the glare and haze it was quite possibly my imagination. And it very soon disappeared again.

The track began to rise almost at once towards Lone Gully, and assuredly the place deserved its name. On each side of the road there ran a line of low, broken hills covered with huge boulders and scrub, while here and there disused sheds and the remains of old furnaces showed the positions of worked-out mines. For gold had once been found in Lone Gully, but only in deep placer deposits, requiring shaft-sinking. And the venture had not been a success financially; the seams had proved poor and given out, and nearly five years previously the last of the mines had closed down.

But it wasn't of derelict mining ventures that either Jim were thinking, as the mare picked her leisurely way up the hill. And after a while he looked at me a trifle thoughtfully.

"I can't say I like it, Dick," he said. "If one deliberately set out to find a place suited for trouble, you couldn't beat this. We're simply two slow-travelling bull's-eyes for any man with a gun lying up hidden in that stuff."

He waved the whip at the monotonous expanse of rock and bush which stretched as far as the eye could see on each side of us, and in-voluntarily I thought of that little cloud of dust. What if my eyes had not deceived me? What if that cloud had been a man, or perhaps two, on horseback, making a detour to get in front of us? The idea was not a pleasant one. No man bent on lawful business would have travelled by any other track save the one we had come by. And no man bent on lawful business would have been likely to travel at all during the heat of the day.

I peered ahead, trying to see some sign of movement, but it was hopeless. An army could have hidden concealed in that country, and I soon gave it up. If my vague forebodings were correct, if that cloud of dust had indeed been a man—well, that man was in front of us by now. Somewhere in the fifteen miles we still had to go he could hide himself, so that it would be absolutely impossible to see him until— For the first time I told Jim about what I thought I had seen, and his face grew graver.

"I don't like it, Dick," he repeated, "not one little bit. And I'll never forgive myself, old man, if anything happens. We should have gone yesterday, and it was only my wretched bravado that prevented it. Though, to tell you the truth, I'd really forgotten that this place was quite so unpleasant as it is."

We had reached the top of the rise as he spoke, and he whipped up the mare. For the next ten miles the road was level, running almost straight between the two lines of low hills on each side. We could see it stretching away like a long white ribbon into the distance, flanked on each side by that interminable grey-brown scrub. At the rate we were going, it would take us an hour and a half to get through to the descent the other side and safety. Jim's revolver lay on the seat beside him, while I held mine in my hand, though in our hearts we knew it was a perfectly useless precaution. A revolver is no good at a hundred yards, and we formed a sitting shot at two hundred to a man with a rifle.

We had been driving perhaps for a quarter of an hour when suddenly Jim stiffened in his seat, and then looked round over his shoulder.

"There's a horse galloping somewhere, Dick," he muttered.

The next instant we saw it. Away back along the dusty road we had just covered, a man was following us at full gallop.

"Seems a foolish way of doing the trick," said Jim, watching the approaching rider through narrowed eyes. "I think we'll dismount for a while, and await this gentleman on foot."

The mare stood placidly nibbling at some short rank grass by the road, while the horseman, still at the same furious rate, came nearer. And suddenly Jim, who had been holding his revolver in his hand, slipped it into his pocket with a surprised exclamation.

"The devil!" he cried. "It's One-eyed Mike—or I'll eat my hat!"

Mike it was sure enough, and I don't know which was sweating most—he or his horse. He flung himself off his saddle as he reached us, and his breath was coming in great gasps.

"Pete Cornish and Yellow Sam left Bull Mine Creek at ten this morning," he gasped out. "Riding all out. Said they were going up north. . .Started that way...But a kid at the house they was in told me she heard 'em talking last night. And they mentioned Prospect Mine. Prospect Mine is here—we're close to it—not a mile on. Their going north was a blind—they're after you. Get in your trap again, Jim—and gallop. Gallop like hell—even if you kill the mare." We got into the trap as he was speaking.

"They'll have to make a big round to get here, and maybe you'll get through before them."

And at that moment two shots rang out. The shooters were nowhere to be seen, but they could shoot. I saw Mike's horse crumple up quite slowly and lie still, and the next instant I pitched forward out of my seat. Our own gallant little mare had taken the second bullet, and in falling had broken both shafts. We scrambled out of the useless buggy a little bewildered by the suddenness of it all. But it wasn't in Jim's nature to remain undecided for long.

"Run like hares," he cried. "Don't run straight—dodge. Get into the scrub if you can."

And had we been able to do it all might have been well. Once amongst those rocks and bushes the advantage of a rifle over a revolver would have disappeared. But as luck would have it, at the particular spot where we had halted there was a stretch of about seventy yards of open ground to be covered before the protection of the low foothills could be reached. And we hadn't gone ten yards before another shot rang out and Mike gave' a cry of pain. He had been plugged through the shoulder and instinctively we stopped to help him.

It was then that we saw Cornish. He had risen from behind a boulder about eighty yards away, and his rifle was still up to his shoulder.

"Put up your hands, or I shall fire again."

His voice was perfectly quiet, without a trace of excitement or anger, and for a moment we hesitated. There was another sharp crack and once again Mike groaned and staggered. This time it was the other shoulder, and it became increasingly obvious that Pete Cornish with a gun was not a man to be played with. Our hands went up,

Jim's and mine—while Mike stood beside us helpless. And there we waited in a row while he leisurely approached us. He had been joined by Yellow Sam, and they both were holding their rifles ready for an immediate shot.

"Take their guns," ordered Cornish as he came up, and his companion disarmed us. "And now," he continued almost gently, but with his unwinking eyes fixed on Jim, "we will go for a little walk. And then, Mr. Maitland—I believe that is your name—we will have a little talk. And after that—who knows? You will keep your hands above your heads, and Sam and I will be behind you. Will you lead the way, Mr. Maitland?"

"Where do you propose that we should go to?" said Jim indifferently.

"To that old mine shaft you see there," answered Cornish, and we started off, Jim leading. A rough disused track marked the way up the hill, and after a few minutes' walking we reached a rotting wooden palisade erected in days gone by around the crushers and stamps and offices generally.

"Straight on, Mr. Maitland," came the quiet voice from behind us. "Through the gate, and then to the left. That's right, and now we will stop and have a little talk. Kindly stand there in a row and I will endeavour to entertain you."

His blue eyes, with a strange, almost filmy, look in them, never left Jim's face.

"Possibly you are unacquainted with deep placer mining," he began gently. "You are now standing at the top of probably one of the deepest shafts in the world. Not the main shaft, but a ventilation shaft. As you will see, there is no lift. But you will also note that this shaft has been used for lowering stores or something of that kind: timber perhaps—but the point is a small one. That pulley attached to the overhead beam, which I have carefully oiled this afternoon, Mr. Maitland, is, you will perceive, immediately over the centre of the shaft. Moreover, this very long coil of rope, which with some difficulty I passed over the pulley, is clearly intended to lower things to the bottom of the shaft. Considering how long it is since this mine was used, it seems in astonishingly good condition."

Fascinated, I stared at the rope as the whole plot became clear. Coil after coil of it lay on one side of the shaft, but one end passed over the central pulley and was loosely tied to a stake beside Cornish.

"I hope my intentions are clear," he continued gently. "I shall request you to take hold of this end that you see attached to this post, and then walk to the edge of the shaft. You will then step over the edge, and I shall lower you to the bottom. Shortly afterwards your friend will repeat the performance, after which the rope will be thrown down to keep you company. Of course," his voice was almost regretful, "should the rope prove unequal to the strain, or should it be too short, you will drop. And the length of the fall will decide whether you do it successfully or not. Oh! and while I think of it, lest you should doubt my words as to the depth." His eyes came round to Mike, who shivered. "We have met before, I think. Just step forward a little. I don't quite know why you have intruded yourself, but since you have——"

It was over in a second. As calmly as if he was eating his dinner Cornish shot Mike through the heart. He had been standing near the edge of the shaft, and he spun round and toppled over backwards.

"You cold-blooded murderer," howled Jim, springing forward, to stop as Cornish's revolver covered him.

"Just listen," said Cornish gently, and with a sick feeling of helpless rage we stood there waiting. And at last it came—a dreadful noise, which echoed faintly, and then died away.

"I should say nearly a quarter of a minute to reach the bottom," he said mildly. "I always believe, you know, in removing all traces of these little affairs, and he's not much loss. So now if you're ready, Mr. Maitland. . ."

"And what if I refuse?" said Jim steadily.

"Then your hands will be lashed behind you, and your feet will be attached to the rope, and you will be lowered head first. Or, failing that—you will be shot here and now. I give you five seconds to decide."

For a second or two Jim hesitated. Then he stepped forward and took the rope in his hands. He knew as well as I did that Cornish would do what he said, and it seemed the only possibility. If he did reach the bottom in safety there might still be a bare chance of getting out somewhere. At any rate it was the only hope.

"Sorry, Dick, old man," he said, as he passed me. "It's my fault."

He grinned at me, that wonderful careless grin of his, and without another word, he crossed to the edge of the shaft. And there he stared at Cornish. "Now, you chickenhearted coward!" he said contemptuously; "carry on."

But Cornish showed no sign of resenting the insult; his face was quite expressionless.

"I am quite ready, Mr. Maitland," he remarked, picking up the rope.

And Jim swung off into space. Not a vestige of hesitation—not a trace of fear, though he told me after that he fully expected Cornish to leave go the rope and let him drop. And what was really in Cornish's mind must remain an unsolved enigma. Whether he actually did intend to do exactly what he said, or whether he intended to let the rope slip when Jim was half-way down, will never be known.

Certain it is that quietly and steadily he went on paying out the rope—coil after coil, leaning back to take the weight with his feet braced against the shoring at the edge of the shaft—while I watched fascinated and Yellow Sam covered me with his gun.

And then suddenly came the idea. Old memories of mathematics, perhaps, problems on pulleys done in days gone by—but like a flash it came. The coils beside Cornish were getting fewer and fewer, and it had to be done at once.

"Good Lord! Look there!" I shouted, and Yellow Sam turned for a second. There was an iron bar at my feet, and by the mercy of Allah I hit him in the right place. And now came the second awful risk—would Cornish let go? His blue eyes were staring at me over his shoulder, but for just that fraction of time which meant life or death he didn't realise what I was going to do. He held on to the rope, and as I sprang at him he straightened up instinctively. And with all my force I pushed him in the back.

It was enough. He was off his balance, and with a fearful curse, still clinging on to the rope, he swung out himself over the shaft.

"Hold on, Jim!" I roared. "Hold on!"

For I saw at once that luck had held—Cornish was a heavier man than Jim. For a perceptible time he hung there swaying, his blue eyes almost frenzied in their animal rage and the scar on his face a livid purple. Then slowly but steadily his weight told, and he began to sink down and down. And with every foot he fell Jim came up. For a while Cornish tried to climb, but he could make no headway. And Jim was climbing, too, and getting the double advantage. And then I think it crossed Cornish's mind to cut the rope on Jim's side, until he realised that once the counter weight was gone he must fall himself. They passed two hundred odd feet below the level of the ground, and Cornish tried to grab Jim's leg. But he kicked himself free, coming up quicker and quicker as the acceleration increased. And then suddenly I heard his voice shouting, urgently:

"Check the rope, Dick—check it somehow!"

For a moment I couldn't understand his reason, but I scrambled out along the beam to the pulley. I used a piece of wood as a brake, and then I saw Jim's plan. He was still fifty feet below me, swaying dizzily, but as the rope checked with the brake and finally stopped, he got the part of it on Cornish's side of the pulley with one hand. Gradually he got both ropes into that hand—shifting his legs to help the strain. And then with his free hand he got out his clasp-knife.

He opened it with his teeth, and Cornish from the depths below realised what was happening. He started frenziedly shooting up the shaft, heedless now of whether he died or not, provided he got Jim too. But he was swaying too much, and the end was quick. Jim cut the rope on Cornish's side below the place where he had both returns gripped in his other hand. And once again there came that dreadful dull noise which echoed faintly and then died away.

Half a minute later, using the two ends of the rope as one, Jim reached the pulley beam, and scrambled into safety. And then, for the first time in his life, Jim Maitland fainted.

******

Later on we walked to the next township, with Yellow Sam in front of us carrying our bags. We gave him to the inhabitants, with our love, and I believe they hanged him, though the point is not of great importance. The man who had called himself Pete Cornish was more dangerous than twenty Yellow Sams, and in his case the hangman had been saved the trouble. Who he really was is a mystery, for the man talked and spoke like a gentleman. There were some who said that he had been the illegitimate son of a well-known peer famed in his day for wild living and enormous strength. Others there were who maintained that he was the direct descendant of a famous pirate who had ended his days in Botany Bay, after a career of unbelievable ferocity. Who knows? But whatever may be the truth, the one unforgettable picture of him that lives in my mind is just two staring implacable light-blue eyes swinging backwards and forwards and then gradually sinking to the death he had planned for us.

7.—The Madman at Corn Reef Lighthouse

If you lie on the close-clipped turf that stretches between Beachy Head and Biding Gap, not too far from the edge of the white chalk cliffs, you will see below you the lighthouse. It stands out in the sea some two hundred yards from the base of the cliff, and every few seconds with monotonous regularity, once dusk has fallen, the beam from the revolving light will shine on you and then pass on, sweeping over the grey water below. A dangerous part of the coast, that one-time haunt of smugglers, till the lighthouse made it safe.

There are treacherous currents and shoals; but the worst is when the sea wrack comes gently drifting over the Downs and lies like a great grey blanket over the sea below. Then that sweeping light is useless, and every two or three minutes comes the sound of a maroon from the lighthouse—a sound which is answered by the mournful wailing of sirens out to sea, as vessels creep slowly through the fog. Like great monsters out of the depths they wail dismally at one another and pass unseen, their sirens growing fainter and fainter in the distance.

Only the roar of the maroons from the lighthouse goes on unchanged, while the grey fog eddies gently by, making fantastic figures as it drifts. Implacable and silent, it seems to mock such paltry man-made efforts to fight it, and yet there are amazingly few accidents, even in that crowded shipping area. The effort may be man-made, but it is successful.

It depends, however, for its success upon the man. Elaborate your mechanical devices as you will, introduce the most complicated automatic machinery to control the regular sweep of the light and the monotonous explosion of the maroons, it all comes back finally to the man who lives in that tall, slender building rising out of the water. A dreary life to which not many men are suited; a life where strange thoughts and fancies might come drifting into one's brain—drifting as gently and slowly as the grey wisps of fog outside. And after a while some might remain, even though outside the fog has gone, and the water shines blue again in the sunlight. It is that way that danger lies. In the crowded waterways where inspectors are many and inspections numerous, the risk is small. Moreover, in the crowded waterways the loneliness is not so great.

But there are others where from month's end to month's end a man will see no soul save the other fellow who lives with him; where save for the occasional visit of a boat with supplies there is nothing to break the deadly monotony. Sometimes even there is no other fellow; the man is alone. And strange things may happen if then those drifting thoughts and fancies come and take root. When faces float past, pressing for a moment against the glass, and then are gone; when voices unheard by the other man come clearly out of the night; when strange shapes materialise and gibber mockingly—there is danger ahead. The step between sanity and madness is not a great one, and once it has been taken there is no safe return.

And Corn Reef was one of those others.

******

We were drifting homewards, though we neither of us admitted it in so many words, but we were drifting in our own way. Not for Jim the conventional P. & O.; his tastes, as always, were for the small coasting boat which called at unknown islands and dealt in strange cargoes. One went as far as one liked in her and then stopped and waited for something else. Which takes time, but has its advantages undreamt of by the occupants of the millionaire suites in big liners.

And so it happened that one day in the following spring we came back to Tampico, that island where I had first met him—that island which held the grave of the husband of the only woman who mattered to Jim. We took rooms in the hotel, and almost as if the words had been spoken aloud I heard again her voice bitter with unmeasured contempt: "Oh! you cur!" I think Jim heard it too, for suddenly he smiled at me a little bitterly.

"Is it much use going home, Dick?"

He didn't wait for my answer, but turned away with a shrug of his shoulders and went upstairs while I strolled down the street towards the club. Nothing had changed; nothing ever will change at Tampico. Each drunken derelict who dies is replaced sooner or later by another, which can hardly be accounted as change. And as for the club, I might have left it the day before instead of two years previously.

It was unoccupied save for one man, who glanced up as I came in, and then continued reading the letter he held in his hand. Every now and then he gave a little frown, and I looked at him covertly as I ordered a drink. There was that nameless something about him which marked him instantly as one of those thousands of Britishers who spend their lives in God-forsaken quarters of the globe carrying on the little job of Empire. They generally die of some disease, unknown and unthanked, or else they return to England in the fullness of time and sink into utter obscurity in some suburb of that Empire's capital. But while they're in harness they live, and when the harness drops off they don't mind dying. So perhaps it doesn't matter very much.

The native waiter brought me my drink, and with a three-months-old illustrated paper in my hand, I sat down and forgot about him. He did not seem disposed for conversation, and, to tell the truth, no more was I. The club house at Tampico was the starting-point of many memories, and I was feeling lazy. Chiefly they centred round Jim, and it wasn't until I heard his voice behind me cheerfully greeting the stranger that I realised I was holding the paper upside down.

"Why, it's MacGregor," I heard him say. "The last time I saw you was in Singapore. How are you, my dear fellow?"

"Jim Maitland, by all that's wonderful!" The stranger got up and seized Jim's hand, and just then Jim caught sight of me.

"Come over here, Dick," he cried. "This is Jock MacGregor, and a partially-demented Government pays him a salary for cruising up and down outlandish waters and seeing that no one has walked off with a lighthouse or two. If they only knew what he did with his salary when he gets ashore they'd halve it in the interests of public morals."

"Salary!" snorted MacGregor. "Call my beggarly pittance a salary! And now the blighters have put a survey job on to my shoulders as well. Think I haven't enough work to do, I suppose."

"But what brings you here, Jock?" asked Jim. "Tampico is a bit out of your beaten track, isn't it?"

MacGregor nodded abruptly and the frown appeared once more.

"The supply-boat for the lighthouse at Corn Reef goes from here," he said. "It starts tomorrow, and I'm going with it."

"Visit of inspection?" said Jim.

"Yes and no," returned the other. "In all probability I shall stay there for a week or so."

Jim raised his eyebrows.

"Since when has the great Pooh Bah stayed at particular lighthouses?" he inquired. "I thought you merely looked in to see that the occupant hadn't been frying sausages on the lamps, and then passed gracefully on."

Jock MacGregor grinned, and then grew serious again.

"That's why I said yes and no. This isn't an ordinary inspection." He hesitated a moment, and then leant forward in his chair. "Care to hear the story, Jim?"

"Get it right off your chest, Jock," he said, beckoning to the waiter for drinks.

★★★★★★

"Well, if it won't bore you, I will," began MacGregor. "Only I'll have to go back a bit. When we last met, I had nothing to do with this area at all. Bill Lambert had it, and mine was farther north. I don't know if you ever met Bill, but he took to seeing things that weren't there, from the usual cause, and has recently gone on permanent sick leave. They said they'd send a successor, as they always do say, but so far there's been no sign of him. And until his arrival Mr. MacGregor was to carry on with both areas—and no increase of pay. Bless their hearts! However, I didn't mind, and to do them justice, in normal circumstances it would have made no odds to me. If you've twice the area to cover, you do half the number of inspections, and it comes to the same thing in the end. It's just a matter of form and routine as you can guess—in normal circumstances."

He emphasised the last three words, and Jim glanced at him.

"One gathers that Corn Reef is not quite normal?" he remarked.

"I'm coming to that," said MacGregor, putting down his glass. "I don't know whether you know the part or not—personally, I only know it from the map. Corn Reef sticks out from a smallish island, called Taba Island, which I believe is inhabited by a few natives. It stretches about half way across a deep-water channel towards the next of the group, which is uninhabited. Beyond that again come other small islands and reefs, and in fact the only method of navigating the belt is through the other half of the deep-water channel I have told you about—one half of which is blocked by Corn Reef.

"The lighthouse stands on the end of the reef, midway across the channel. At low water it can be reached from the island on foot; at high water the reef is covered. So much for the locality; now for the personal details. Six months ago, as I said, I took over from Bill Lambert. It was an informal sort of taking over, as he had delirium tremens pretty badly, and I got no information out of him. But it didn't worry me much, as I'd no idea then that there was anything peculiar in his area. And it wasn't till a month ago, when I received a communication from the keeper at Corn Reef lighthouse, that I began to look into things. His name is David Temple, and the communication was brief and to the point. It stated that his assistant, when attending to the bell, had fallen into the sea and been drowned, and could another be sent."

"Bell?" interrupted Jim. "I don't quite follow."

"Sorry," said MacGregor. "I forgot that point. Apparently at certain times you get a thick belt of fog across the reef and the channel, and stretching right along the belt of islands. Probably it's some form of heavy ground mist. When that comes down they have as a warning for ships a huge bell, which is tolled mechanically. It is built out on a sort of platform below the level of the light, and as far as I can make out from the plans, it seems a pretty antiquated sort of arrangement.

However, there it is, and as long as it functions you won't get them to spend any money in having it replaced by anything more up-to-date.

"Well, when I got Temple's letter I began looking up the files. And to my amazement I found that about three months before Bill Lambert had gone a precisely similar letter had reached *him*. At first I thought that the second was merely a reminder, and that Bill had forgotten all about it. So I made inquiries, only to discover the somewhat sinister fact that it was far from a reminder. Bill *had* sent a man, and I was therefore confronted with the situation that within some nine months two men, when attending to the bell at Corn Reef lighthouse, had fallen into the sea and been drowned. Which seemed to show that there was something radically wrong with the bell arrangements generally: something"—and MacGregor paused—"something, Jim, which I utterly failed to get at from the plans. I'm not denying that the whole idea is antiquated; but, granting the plans and sections are correct, it is perfectly safe. And I could see no reason whatever—short of a desire to commit suicide—why two men should fall into the sea."

"And even granting that, why of necessity they should be drowned?" said Jim quietly.

MacGregor shrugged his shoulders.

"The place is alive with sharks, of course," he remarked. "But I've not quite finished yet. Another unpleasant fact was brought to my notice shortly after I received this letter from Temple. I ran into the skipper of some craft or other in the club at Singapore, and he was looking for Bill Lambert's blood. And when he heard I was doing Bill's job he turned his wrath on me. And his accusation amounted to this: that on the morning of February 24th he was on the bridge of his ship nosing her gently through a thick mist. Suddenly there came a bellow from the look-out man, and to his horror he saw looming out of the mist on the starboard side—Corn Reef lighthouse.

"'My God, man!' he said to me. 'I could have spat an orange pip at it, and hit it; I could almost have touched it with my hand. In thirty years I've never had such an escape. Another foot—another six inches—and we'd have been on that reef.'

"But wasn't the bell ringing? I demanded.

"'Not a sound!' he roared. 'Not a sound. You can hear that bell for fifteen miles—and there wasn't a sound. Only as I passed by— damn it, why, the platform on which the bell is built nearly grazed my wireless—I looked up. Man! I tell you the bell was ringing right enough—I could see it through the fog—but no sound came. Only above the beat of the engine, I thought I heard a steady thud, thud, thud in time with the beat of the bell. But maybe it was my imagination.'"

★★★★★★

Jock MacGregor paused and drained his drink.

"So that is the rather peculiar situation I'm up against."

"And how do you propose to deal with it?" asked Jim.

"Temple asked for an assistant," said MacGregor briefly, "and he's going to have one. He's going to have me." He lit a cigarette, and leant back in his chair. "There's something wrong, Jim," he continued after a moment, "something very wrong out there. That merchant skipper was as hard-headed a customer as you could meet, and if he saw that bell moving—it was moving. Then why was there no sound? And then two men drowned in nine months! I guess I'm not going to send a third till I've, had a look round myself. This man, David Temple, doesn't know me, hasn't ever seen me, so there won't be any difficulty in passing myself off as his new assistant."

Jim was looking thoughtfully out of the window.

"How long has Temple been there?" he said at length.

"Years as far as I can make out," answered MacGregor. "There was one paper in the file—the usual routine paper with regard to an exchange—dated five years ago. He'd refused, or rather had requested to be allowed to stay on. And since I gather there is no vast rush for Corn Reef, I suppose Bill Lambert was only too glad to let him."

Jim shook his head.

"Five years is a long time, Jock," he said gravely. "A very long time. It's far too long for a man to spend in a place like that."

"You think I may find Temple a bit queer?" said MacGregor slowly.

Jim shrugged his shoulders.

"Jock," he said, "I've got a proposal to make to you. Temple doesn't know you, and he doesn't know me. You go as his assistant as you have already decided. I'll go as your new boss who has just taken Lambert's place. Dick can come as a pal of mine. If everything seems all right, well, we shall all have had a very pleasant little trip, and Temple will be none the worse. If, on the other hand, things are not all right—three heads are better than one, Jock."

"Do you mean it, Jim?" said MacGregor. "Will you both come?"

"I do," answered Jim. "And as for Dick—"

"Count me in," I said at once.

98

"Then I accept your suggestion with the greatest pleasure," said MacGregor. "And to tell you the strict truth, I might add with the greatest relief."

★★★★★★

At dawn next morning we started in the supply boat, and of the run to Taba Island I shall say nothing. The first part of it was uninteresting, and the last few miles was so inconceivably beautiful as to defy description. In front of us stretched the belt of islands, with the lighthouse standing up slim and clear-cut straight ahead. On our left lay Taba Island, a riot of tropical vegetation and glorious flowers which reached right down to the water's edge, broken here and there by stretches of golden sand almost dazzling in its brightness.

Between the lighthouse and the island was a line of surf marking Corn Reef; while to the right of the lighthouse lay the deep-water channel of unbroken blue. And as we got nearer we could see the strange structure which marked the position of the bell. It was built out from the side, and it reminded one of those mediaeval galleries which jut out from the walls of old castles into which the defenders used to go to pour burning oil on the gentlemen below. And this bell jutted out in just such a manner on the deep- water channel side of the lighthouse.

"Great Scott!" said Jim, who had been examining it through his field-glasses; "even allowing for pictorial effect, if that fellow passed close enough to see that bell in a fog, I don't wonder he wanted somebody's blood."

And now we were near enough to see the details with the naked eye. On a rough landing-stage at the foot of the lighthouse a man was standing gazing at us fixedly through a telescope, and as we came close he shut it up and awaited us with folded arms. He was dressed in white, and as the boat made fast he might have been carved out of stone: so motionless did he stand. Then he took a step forward, and spoke in a curiously harsh voice.

"Which is my new assistant?"

He was tall and gaunt, with a coarse, straggling beard, and as I looked at him I could conceive no more awful fate than being condemned to spend month after month alone with him.

It was Jim who answered as we had arranged.

"Here is your new assistant—MacGregor," he said, stepping ashore. "And I am your new inspector in place of Mr. Lambert."

"You will find everything in good order, sir," he said quietly, but it was at Jock MacGregor he was staring.

"How comes it that two men have been drowned within such a short time, Temple?" demanded Jim sternly. "There must have been gross carelessness somewhere."

"It is the bell, sir," answered the man, still in the same quiet voice. "When the mist comes down and presses round one's head with soft, clammy fingers it is sometimes difficult to see."

Jim grunted, and eyed the man narrowly.

"Then the bell must be removed," he said, and Temple started violently.

"It is only carelessness, sir, on their parts," he cried. "The bell has never hurt me."

"Well, I will inspect everything," said Jim curtly. "I shall stay here until the supply boat returns the day after tomorrow."

I saw Temple shoot a quick, suspicious glance at him, but he merely nodded and said, "Very good, sir."

Then he glanced towards Taba Island and nodded as if satisfied.

"There will be fog tonight, sir," he remarked. "When the Queen of the Island is crowned in mist at this time of day there is always fog. So you will hear the bell."

He went off to superintend the disposal of his stores, and Jim turned to MacGregor.

"What the devil is he talking about, Jock?" he muttered.

"The queen of the island is that hill, old man," answered MacGregor. "I remember seeing it marked on the map."

"He seems a strange sort of bird," said Jim thoughtfully, and MacGregor nodded.

"You're right, Jim," he said. "Though I'm bound to admit that at present he doesn't strike me as anything out of the way. You meet some queer morose customers on this game, you know."

And certainly during the next hour or so there seemed nothing peculiar about Temple. Jim, carefully primed by MacGregor, asked a few leading questions, but for the most part he said nothing and let the other man talk. We examined the mirrors and reflectors; we examined the lamps; but most of all we examined Temple himself. And then we came to the bell.

If it had looked big as we came towards the lighthouse it looked enormous from close to. Built out from the side, it was carried on a steel cantilever arm, while underneath it, about eight feet below, a narrow wooden platform jutted out over the water—a platform some eighteen inches wide. It was but little more than a single plank ten feet long, and as one walked out on it, though the railing on each side made it perfectly safe, it gave one almost a feeling of dizziness.

Above one's head the bell with its motionless clapper; below one's feet the water; and poised between the two the narrow platform—all too narrow for my liking.

"Now was it from here that the two men fell?" demanded Jim, still in his role of inspector.

"Yes, sir," said Temple quietly. "Though I did not see it happen myself. I was inside attending to the mechanism that works the bell."

"And did you make no effort to save them?"

For answer Temple peered over the side for a moment or two—then he pointed downwards without a word. And while I looked I counted three evil shapes glide by in the clear blue depths.

"And when did the last man fall over?" went on Jim. "On what date?"

"On February 24th, sir," said Temple, and MacGregor caught his breath. "In the early morning when the fog was thick. It is entered in my log book."

"Was the bell ringing at the time?" demanded Jim sharply.

"The bell always rings when there is a fog, sir," answered Temple, and Jim glanced at MacGregor, who shook his head imperceptibly. "Would you care to hear it now, and see how it works?"

"Yes," said Jim, "I should."

"There is a heavy weight inside, sir," said Temple, "inside the lighthouse I mean, which works the bell by means of cogged wheels. On the principle, sir, of the weights in a grandfather's clock." His tone was that of a man who is patiently explaining something to a child. "If you will come inside, I will start it."

We followed him in, and he pressed down a lever. Almost', at once the bell began to oscillate, slightly at first, but gradually and steadily increasing in swing, until at length the first deep note rang out as it struck the clapper. The notes came deeper and more resonant, though irregularly for a time, till at last both clapper and bell settled down to a rhythmic swing. Like a huge pendulum the clapper passed backwards and forwards over the platform outside, while the bell swung down to meet it first on one side and then on the other. And the deep, booming note ringing out every two or three seconds seemed to fill the whole universe with one vast volume of sound. It deadened one's brain; it stunned one; it made one gasp for breath.

Suddenly I felt Jim grip my arm. Speech was impossible, but I followed the direction of his eyes. He was looking at David Temple, and so was Jock MacGregor. For the lighthouse keeper was staring at the Queen of the Island with blazing eyes. His hands were locked together, and he was muttering something, for we could see his lips moving, while the sweat glistened on his forehead. He seemed to have forgotten our existence, and when Jim touched him on the shoulder he swung round with a hideous snarl.

"Stop the bell," shouted Jim, and the snarl vanished. He was the disciplined subordinate again, though in his eyes there was a look of sly cunning.

He pressed another lever, and after what seemed an interminable time the bell gradually ceased. Not at once, for it went on swinging under its own momentum for a while, but at length the noise died away; beat after beat was missed till at last it swung in silence, save for a faint creaking.

"Is that satisfactory, sir?" asked Temple quietly. "Because I would like to stow away my stores as soon as possible. Afterwards I will go through my log with you."

Jim nodded. "All right, Temple. Go and attend to your stores."

The man went out, and we stared at one another thoughtfully.

"February 24th," said MacGregor. "Did you note that, Jim?"

"I noted it right enough," answered Jim. "Jock, the man's queer. Did you see his face while that infernal bell was ringing, and he was staring at the mountain yonder?"

MacGregor had strolled over to the window himself, and suddenly he beckoned to us with his hand.

"Come here," he muttered. "Look at him now."

Below, on the landing-stage, knelt David Temple with his arms flung out towards the mist-crowned mountain. For half a minute he stayed there motionless; then he rose and came inside the lighthouse.

"He's worse than queer," said MacGregor. "He's mad."

★★★★★★

And now I come to the final chapter, and the thing that happened when the mist came down on Corn Reef. Jim and I had spent the night—I cannot say we had slept very much—in the room normally used by the assistant, while Jock MacGregor had stopped in the other room to take his turn with the lamp. At the faintest sign of trouble he was to call us, and to make doubly sure, Jim and I had taken it in turns to lie down on the bed and sleep while the others remained awake.

There was no good in letting Temple see that we suspected anything, since no steps could be taken till the return of the supply boat. Then Jock MacGregor had decided that Temple was to go back in it while he remained in the lighthouse till a relief was sent.

During the evening Temple had been quiet and perfectly rational, though I had caught him once or twice eyeing MacGregor with a curiously furtive expression. He had lit the light and explained the simple mechanism quite normally, and then had stood with us while we watched the beam sweep round the water below. It was a glorious night, such as can only be seen in the tropics, without a trace of fog, and for a time our suspicions were lulled. It seemed impossible that anything could happen in such an atmosphere of peace and beauty. Only once did a stray remark of Temple's bring back our doubts, and then it was more owing to our previous suspicions than to the remark itself.

"The queen is angry tonight," he said, staring at the island. "She demands a sacrifice."

"What do you mean by such rot, Temple?" said Jim sternly.

"When she veils her head, sir," he answered quietly, "her subjects must appease her. Otherwise she will be revenged."

He left the room with a word of apology, and we heard him going downstairs.

"Native superstition," grunted MacGregor.

"Perhaps," said Jim. "But once native superstition gets hold of a white man, Jock, it's the devil."

And that is all that had happened before we turned in: little enough to prepare us for the thing that was to come later. It must have been about three o'clock when Jim roused me, and prepared to take my place on the bed. And as we were changing round we heard a ship's siren wail in the distance. And then we heard it a second time. For a moment or two it made no impression on our minds, and then the same thought struck us both simultaneously.

We dashed to the window and looked out—looked out into a thick mist that drifted slowly past, blotting out everything. No water could be seen, no star—just dense, clammy vapour. The fog had come down on Corn Reef, and the bell which had deafened us only that afternoon was silent.

Once again the siren wailed mournfully, and then, as we listened, we heard a steady creaking such as the bell had made as it had gradually come to rest the day before. And every now and then a strange, dull thudding noise—*creak, thud! creak, thud!*

Jim sprang to the door, and turned the handle; but the door refused to budge. We had been locked in, and outside Jock MacGregor was alone with a madman. And even as we realised it there came through the open window a faint shout of "Help!"

It took six shots to shatter that bolt, and by the mercy of heaven there wasn't a second. And then we dashed up the short flight of stairs into the room above, to halt somewhat abruptly as we entered. For confronting us was David Temple with an iron bar in his hands, and his face was the face of a maniac. But it wasn't at him we were look-ing—it was beyond him to the place where the platform stretched out into the mist. For the door was open, and we could see the great bell swinging to and fro. And lashed loosely to the end of the clapper and clinging to it desperately, was Jock MacGregor.

"The queen demands a sacrifice," roared the madman. "Two she has had, and now she requires a third. Stand back!"

There was no time for half-measures. MacGregor's voice, breath-less and gasping, came to us faintly: "For God's sake, hurry!" And out of the mist, much louder and nearer wailed the siren.

So Jim shot the poor devil through each arm, and the crowbar crashed to the floor. Even then he tried to stop us, till a blow on the point of the jaw put him to sleep. And then it became a desperate race against time. Outside the siren was going continuously, seem-ing almost on top of us, while standing on the platform we tried to catch MacGregor as he swung past us. But the bell was heavy, and it seemed an age before we could check the clapper sufficiently to cut him down. And every moment we expected to hear the dreadful grinding crunch of a ship striking rock. But at last we had him down, and Jim darted to the lever to restart the bell.

The first deep boom rang out, and in the silence that followed be-fore the swing became regular we heard a sudden agonised shout, and the thrashing of a propeller. Then the bell tolled again, and then again. All outside sound was obliterated; only the bell swung on, crashing out its message of warning. And so three sweating men sat and waited for the mist to lift off Corn Reef, while in a corner, David Temple, sometime lighthouse keeper, smiled happily to himself, nodding his head in time with the bell. He had put a drug, we discovered, in Jock MacGregor's coffee, and the next thing MacGregor knew was when he found himself swinging violently through space, to stop even more violently as he hit the side of the bell. How even a madman had had

104

the strength to lift a full-grown man and lash him to the clapper was a mystery till we discovered some rough steps of the housemaid variety, and even with them the strength required was prodigious. But he'd done it right enough, and for ten minutes MacGregor had swung backwards and forwards, dazed and half-stunned, while the madman had crouched below him with his arms flung out towards the queen of the island.

At seven o'clock the mist lifted, and we stopped that accursed bell. Out to sea lay a steamer, and a boat was being lowered. Through glasses we saw an officer get in, and then the boat was pulled to the lighthouse.

★★★★★★

I have met angry men in my life, but for sheer speechless fury the skipper of the good ship *Floriana*, one thousand five hundred tons and of mixed cargo, wins in a canter. I don't blame him; when the first clang of the bell rang out he was to all intents and purposes on the reef. He'd gone full speed astern with a second to spare, and his eyes still held the look of a badly-frightened man.

So we told him the story, and Temple smiled placidly in his corner. And after a while, when he'd grunted his amazement, he apologised handsomely. He went out to look at the bell, and for a while we stood on the platform. And then that skipper leant forward, peering at the inside of the bell. In silence he pointed to two dull stains—stains we had not noticed. They were just where the clapper hit the bell—one on each side, and they were a rusty red.

"Two assistants, you say?" he grunted. "God! What a death!"

I looked over, down into the blue water. Three more evil shapes were there, shapes which glided by and disappeared. And then I looked at Taba Island. Clear and beautiful in the morning sun the Queen of the Island rose to the sky. Her crown had disappeared.

8.—THE SEVEN MISSIONARIES

It never really got much beyond the rumour stage—Captain James Kelly, of the s.s. *Andaman*, saw to that. It wouldn't have done him any good nor his line, and since England was troubled with railway strikes and war scares at Agadir, things which happened on the other side of the globe were apt to be crowded out of the newspapers.

But he couldn't stop the rumour, and "Our Special Correspondent" in Colombo made out quite a fair story for his paper at home. It didn't appear: seemingly the editor thought the poor devil had taken to drink and was raving. In fact, all that did appear in the papers were two short and apparently disconnected notices. The first ran somewhat as follows, and was found under the shipping intelligence:

The s.s. *Andaman* arrived yesterday at Colombo. She remained to carry out repairs to her wireless, and will leave tomorrow for Plymouth.

And the second appeared some two or three months later.

No news has yet been heard of the s.y. *Firefly*, which left Colombo some months ago for an extensive cruise in the Indian Ocean. It is feared that she may have foundered with all hands in one of the recent gales.

But she didn't—the sea was as calm as the proverbial duck-pond when the s.y. *Firefly* went down in the thousand fathoms of water not far from the Cocos Islands. And but for the grace of heaven and Jim Maitland that fate would have overtaken the good ship *Andaman* instead.

The s.s. *Andaman* was a vessel of some three thousand tons. She was in reality a cargo boat carrying passengers, in that passengers were the secondary consideration. There was only one class, and the accommodation was sufficient for about thirty people. Twelve knots was her maximum speed, and she quivered like a jelly if you tried to get more out of her. And last, but not least, Captain James Kelly had been her skipper for ten years, and loved her with the love only given by men who go down to the sea in ships.

When Jim and I went on board she was taking in cargo, and Kelly was busy. He was apparently having words with the harbour master over something, and the argument had reached the dangerous stage of politeness. But Jim had sailed in her before, and a minute or two later a delighted chief steward was shaking him warmly by the hand.

"This is great, sir!" he cried. "We got a wireless about the berths, but we had no idea it was from you."

"You can fix us up, Bury?" asked Jim.

"Sure thing, Mr. Maitland," answered the other. "We've only got twelve on board—two Yanks, a coloured gentleman, two ladies and a missionary bunch."

We had followed him below, and he was showing us our cabins.

"Seven of 'em, sir," he went on, "with two crates of Bibles and Prayer Books, all complete. Maybe you saw them sitting around on deck as you came on board?"

"Can't say I did, Bury," said Jim indifferently.

"They never go ashore, sir," continued the steward. "We've been making all the usual calls, and you'd have thought they'd have liked to go ashore and stretch their legs, but devil a bit. There they sit from morning till night, reading and praying, till they fairly give you the hump."

"It doesn't sound like one long scream of excitement," said Jim. "But if they're happy, that's all that matters. Come on, Dick, let's go up and see if old man Kelly is still being polite."

We went on deck to find that the argument was finished, and with a shout of delight the skipper recognised Jim. Jim went forward to meet him, and for a moment or two I stood where I was, idly watching the scene on the quay. And then quite distinctly I heard a voice from behind me say, "By God, it's Jim Maitland!" Now, as a remark it was so ordinary, so completely expected when Jim was about, that I never gave it a thought. In those parts of the world one heard it or its equivalent whenever one entered an hotel or even a railway carriage. And so, as I say, I didn't give it a thought for a moment or two, till Jim's voice hailed me, and I turned round to go and be introduced to the skipper.

It was then that I noticed two benevolent-looking clergymen seated close to me in two deck-chairs. Their eyes were fixed on the skipper and on Jim, while two open Bibles adorned their knees. Not another soul was in sight: there was not the slightest doubt in my mind that it was one of them who had spoken. And as I stood talking with the skipper and Jim my mind was subconsciously working.

There was no reason, to be sure, why a missionary should not recognise Jim, but somehow or other one does not expect a devout man with a Bible lying open on his knee to invoke the name of the Almighty quite so glibly. If he had said "Dear me!" or "Good gracious!" it would have been different. But the other came as almost a shock. However, the matter was a small one, and I should probably have dismissed it from my mind, but for the sequel a minute or so later. The skipper was called away on some matter, and Jim and I strolled back past the two parsons. They both looked up at us with mild interest as we passed, but neither of them gave the faintest sign of recognition.

Now that *did* strike me as strange. A clergyman may swear if he likes—in fact, I am given to understand that they frequently do; but why in the name of fortune he should utterly ignore a man whom he evidently knew was beyond me.

"Come and lean over the side, Jim," I said when we were out of earshot. "There's something a little funny I want to tell you. Only don't look round."

He listened in silence, and when I had finished he shrugged his shoulders.

"More people know Tom Fool, old boy, than Tom Fool knows. I certainly don't know either of those two sportsmen, but it's more than likely they know me, at any rate by sight. And wouldn't you swear if you had to wear a dog collar in this heat?"

Evidently Jim was inclined to dismiss the episode as trifling, and after a time I came round to the same view. Even at lunch that day, when the skipper was formally introducing us and the clergyman still gave no sign of claiming any previous acquaintance with Jim, I thought no more about it. Possibly to substantiate that claim he might have had to admit his presence in some place which would take a bit of explaining away to his little flock. For the man whose voice I had heard was evidently the shining light of the bunch.

He turned out to be the Reverend Samuel Longfellow, and his destination, as that of all the others, was Colombo. They were going to open a missionary house somewhere in the interior of Ceylon and run it on novel lines of their own. Apparently no such place existed belonging to their particular denomination, but at that point Jim and I got out of our depths and the conversation languished. However, they seemed very decent fellows, even if they did fail somewhat signally to add to the general gaiety.

★★★★★★

The voyage pursued its quiet normal course for the first four or five days. The two Americans and the skipper made up the necessary numbers for a game of poker; the two ladies—mother and daughter they were, by the name of Armstrong—knitted; the seven parsons prayed; and the coloured gentleman effaced himself. The weather was perfect; the sea like a mill-pond, with every prospect of continuing so for some time. And so we lazed along at our twelve knots, making a couple of final calls before starting on the two-thousand mile run to Colombo. It was the first night out on the last stage that Jim and I were sitting talking with the skipper on the bridge. Being a privileged person, Jim was allowed there and the skipper's private whisky was a better commodity than that sold below. Occasionally the sharp, hissing crackle of the wireless installation broke the silence, and we could see the operator in his shirt-sleeves through the open door of his cabin.

"I guess it's hard to begin to estimate what we sailor men owe to Marconi for that invention," said Kelly thoughtfully. "Now that we've got it, it seems almost incredible to think how we got along without it. And what can I do for you, sir?"

An abrupt change in his tone made me look round to see the Reverend Samuel Longfellow standing diffidently behind us. He evidently felt he was trespassing, for his voice was almost apologetic.

"Is it possible, Captain," he asked, "to send a message by your wireless?"

"Of course it is," answered Kelly. "You can hand in any message you like to the operator, and he'll send it for you."

"You see, I've never sent a message by wireless before," said the parson mildly, "and I wasn't quite sure what to do. Can you get an answer quickly?"

"Depends whom you are sending it to and where he is."

"He's on a yacht somewhere in this neighbourhood," answered the clergyman. "He is a missionary like myself whose health has broken down, and a kind philanthropist is taking him for a cruise to help him recover. I felt it would be so nice if I could speak to him, so to say, and hear from him, perhaps, how he is getting on."

"Quite," agreed the skipper gravely. "Well, Mr. Longfellow, there is nothing to prevent your speaking to him as much as you like. You just hand in your message to the operator whenever you want to, and he'll send down the answer to you as soon as he receives it."

"Oh, thank you, Captain Kelly," said the parson gratefully. "I suppose there's no way of saying where I am?" he continued hesitatingly. "I mean, on shore when one sends a wire the person who gets it can look up where you are on the map, and it makes it so much more interesting for him."

The skipper knocked out his pipe.

"I'm afraid, Mr. Longfellow," he remarked at length in a stifled voice, "that you can't quite do that at sea. Of course, the position of the ship will be given on the message in terms of latitude and longitude. So if your friend goes to the navigating officer of his yacht, he'll be able to show him with a pin exactly where you were in the Indian Ocean when the message was sent."

"I see," said the clergyman. "How interesting! And then, if I tell him that we are moving straight towards Colombo at twelve knots an hour, my dear friend will be able to follow me in spirit all the way on the map?"

The skipper choked slightly.

"Precisely, Mr. Longfellow. But I wouldn't call it twelve knots an hour if I were you. Just say, twelve knots."

The Reverend Samuel looked a little bewildered.

"Twelve knots. I see. Thank you so much. I'm afraid I don't know much about the sea. May I—may I go now to the gentleman who sends the messages?"

"By all manner of means," said Kelly, and Jim's shoulders shook. "Give the operator your message, and you shall have the answer as soon as it arrives."

Again murmuring his thanks, the missionary departed, and shortly afterwards we saw him in earnest converse with the wireless operator. And that worthy, having read the message and scratched his head, stared a little dazedly at the Reverend Samuel Longfellow, obviously feeling some doubts as to his sanity. To be asked to dispatch to the world at large a message beginning "Dear brother," and finishing "Yours in the Church," struck him as being one of those things which a self-respecting wireless operator should not be asked to do.

★★★★★★

"Poor little bird!" said the skipper thoughtfully, as the missionary went aft to join his companions. "I'm glad for his sake that he doesn't know what the bulk of our cargo is this trip. He wouldn't be able to sleep at nights for fear of being made to walk the plank by pirates."

Jim looked up lazily.

"Why, what have you got on board, old man?" The skipper lowered his voice.

"I haven't shouted about it, Jim, and as a matter of fact, I don't think the crew know. Don't pass it on, but we've got over half a million in gold below, to say nothing of a consignment of pearls worth certainly another quarter."

Jim whistled. "By Jove! it would be a nice haul for someone. Bit out of your line, isn't it, James, carrying specie?"

"Yes, it is," agreed the other. "It generally goes on the bigger boats, but there was some hitch this time. It's just as safe with me as it is with them. That has made it safe." He pointed to the wireless operator busily sending out the message from 'Yours in the Church.' "That has made piracy a thing of the past. And, incidentally, as you can imagine, Jim, it's a big feather in my cap getting away with this consignment. It's going to make the trip worth six ordinary ones to the firm, and—er—

to me. And, with any luck, if things go all right, as, humanly speaking, they will do, I have hopes that in the future it will no longer be out of our line. We might get a share of that traffic, and I'll be able to buy that chicken farm in Dorsetshire earlier than I thought."

Jim laughed. "You old humbug, James! You'll never give up the sea."

The skipper sighed and stretched himself.

"Maybe not, lad; maybe not. Not till she gives me up, anyway. But chickens are nice companionable birds, they tell me, and Dorset is England."

We stopped on talking for a few minutes longer, when a sudden and frenzied explosion of mirth came from the wireless operator. I had noticed him taking down a message, which he was now reading over to himself, and after a moment or two of unrestrained joy, he came out on deck.

"What is it, Jenkins?" said the skipper.

"Message for the parson, sir," answered the operator. "There is a duplicate on the table."

He saluted, and went aft to find the Reverend Samuel.

"I think," murmured the skipper, with a twinkling in his eye, "that I will now inspect the wireless installation. Would you care to come with me?"

And this is what we, most reprehensibly, read:

"Dear Brother how lovely the gentleman who guides our ship tells me we pass quite close about midday the day after tomorrow will lean over railings and wave pocket-handkerchief.—Ferdinand."

"My sainted aunt!" spluttered the skipper. "Lean over railings and wave pocket-handkerchief!"

"I think I prefer the gentleman who guides our ship," said Jim gravely. "Anyway, James, I shall borrow your telescope as we come abreast of Ferdinand. I'd just hate to miss him. 'Goodnight,' old man. I don't think anyone could blame you if you had that message framed."

✶✶✶✶✶✶

It was about half an hour later that the door of my cabin opened and Jim entered abruptly. I was lying in my bunk smoking a final cigarette, and I looked at him in mild surprise. He was fully dressed, though I had seen him start to take off his clothes twenty minutes before, and he was looking grave.

"You pay attention, Dick," he said quietly, sitting down on the other bunk. "I'd just got my coat off when I remembered I'd left my cigar-case in a niche up on deck. I went up to get it, and as I was putting it in my pocket I heard my own name mentioned. Somewhat naturally I stopped and listened. And I distinctly heard this sentence: 'Don't forget—you are absolutely responsible for Maitland.' I listened, but I couldn't catch anything else except a few disconnected words here and there, such as 'wireless', 'midday', though I must have stood there for five minutes. Then there was a general pushing-back of deck-chairs, and those seven black-coated blighters trooped off to bed. They didn't see me; they were on the other side of the funnel—but it made me think. You remember that remark you heard as we came on board? Well, why the deuce is this bunch of parsons so infernally interested in me? I don't like it, Dick." He looked at me hard through his eyeglass. "Do you think they are parsons?"

I sat up in bed with a jerk.

"What do you mean—do I think they're parsons? Of course they're parsons. Why shouldn't they be parsons?" But I suddenly felt very wide awake.

Jim thoughtfully lit a cigar.

"Quite—why shouldn't they be?" At the same time he paused, and blew out a cloud of smoke. "Dick, I suppose I'm a suspicious bird, but this interest—this peculiar interest—in me is strange, to say the least of it. Of course, it may be that they regard me as a particularly black soul to be plucked from the burning, in which case I ought to feel duly flattered. On the other hand, let us suppose for a second that they are not parsons. Well, I don't think I am being unduly conceited if I say that I have a fairly well-known reputation as a tough customer if trouble occurs."

And now all thoughts of sleep had left me.

"Just exactly what do you mean, Jim?" I demanded. He answered my question by another.

"Don't you think, Dick, that that radiograph was just a lit-tle *too* damn foolish to be quite genuine?"

"Well, it was genuine right enough. Jenkins took it down in front of our eyes."

"Oh, it was sent—I'm not denying that. And it was sent as he received it and as we read it. But was it sent by a genuine parson, cruising in a genuine yacht for his health? If so, my opinion of the brains of the Church drops below par. But if"—he drew deeply at his cigar—"if, Dick, it was not sent by a genuine parson, but by someone who wished to pose as the drivelling idiot curate of fiction—why, my opinion of the brains of the Church remains at par."

"Look here," I said, lighting a cigarette. "I may be several sorts of ass, but I can't get you. Granting your latter supposition, why should anyone not only want to pose as a parson when he wasn't one, but also take the trouble to send fool messages round the universe?"

"Has it occurred to you," said Jim quietly, "that two very useful pieces of information have been included in those two fool messages? First, our exact position at a given moment, and our course, and our speed. Secondly, the approximate time when the convalescing curate in the yacht belonging to the kind friend will impinge on that course. And the third fact—not contained in either message, but which may possibly have a bearing on things, is that on board this boat there is half a million in gold specie and a quarter of a million in pearls."

"Good heavens!" I muttered, staring at him foolishly.

"Mark you, Dick, I may have stumbled into a real first-class mare's nest. The Reverend Samuel and his pals may be all that they say and more, but I don't like this tender solicitude for my salvation."

"Are you going to say anything to the skipper?" I asked.

"Yes," he answered. "I think I shall tell James. But he's a pig-headed fellow, and he'll probably be darned rude about it. I should if I were him. They aren't worrying over *his* salvation."

And with that he went to bed, leaving me thinking fairly acutely. Could there be anything in it? Could it be possible that anyone would attempt piracy in the twentieth century, especially when the ship, as the skipper had pointed out, was equipped with wireless? It was ridiculous, and the next morning I went round to Jim's cabin to tell him so. It was empty, and there was a note lying on the bed addressed to me. It was brief and to the point.

"I am ill in bed with a sharp dose of fever. Pass the good news on.—Jim."

I did so, at breakfast, and I thought I detected a shade of relief pass over the face of the Reverend Samuel, though he inquired most solicitously about the sufferer, and even went so far as to wish to give him some patent remedy of his own. But I assured him that quinine and quiet were all that were required, coupled with a starvation diet, and with that the matter dropped.

And then there began a time for me of irritating suspense. Not a sign of Jim did I see for the whole of that day and the following night. His door had been locked since I went in before breakfast, and I didn't even know if he was inside or not. All I did know was that something was doing, and there are few things more annoying than being out of a game you know is being played. Afterwards I realised that it was unavoidable: at the time I cursed inwardly and often.

And the strange thing is that when the thing did occur it came with almost as much of a shock to me as if I had had no previous suspicions. It was the suddenness of it, I think—the suddenness and the absolute absence of any fuss or shouting. Naturally, I didn't see the whole thing in its entirety; my outlook was limited to what happened to me and in my own vicinity.

I suppose it was about half-past eleven, and I was strolling up and down the deck. Midday had been the time mentioned, and I was feeling excited and restless. Mrs. Armstrong and her daughter were seated in their usual place, and I stopped and spoke a few words to them. Usually Mrs. Armstrong was the talker of the two—a big, gaunt woman with yellow spectacles, but pleasant and homely. This morning, however, the daughter answered, and her mother, who had put on a veil in addition to her spectacles, sat silently beside her.

"Poor mother has got such a headache from the glare that she has had to put on a veil," she said. "I hope Mr. Maitland is better."

I murmured something about his being the same, just as two of the parsons strolled past, and I wondered why the girl gave a little laugh. Then suddenly she sat up with a cry of admiration.

"Oh! look at that lovely yacht!"

I swung round quickly, and there, sure enough, about a hundred yards from us, and just coming into sight round the awning, was a small steam yacht, the one presumably from which Ferdinand was to wave. And at that moment the shorter of the two parsons put a revolver within an inch of my face, while the other ran his hands over my pockets. It was so unexpected that I gaped at him foolishly, and even when I saw my Colt flung overboard I hardly realised that the big hold-up had begun.

Then there came a heavy thud from just above us, and I saw Jenkins, the wireless man, pitched forward on his face half in and half out of his cabin door. He lay there sprawling while another of the parsons proceeded to wreck his instruments with the iron bar which he had used to stun the operator. It was then, with a squawk of terror like an anguished hen, that Mrs. Armstrong rose to her feet, and with her pink parasol in one hand and her rug in the other fled towards the bows of the ship. She looked so irresistibly funny, this large, hysterical woman, that I couldn't help it, I laughed. And even the two parsons smiled, though not for long.

"Go below," said one of them to Miss Armstrong. "Remain in your cabin. And you"—he turned to me—"go aft where the others are."

"You scoundrel!" I shouted, "what are you playing at?"

"Don't argue, or I'll blow out your brains," he said quietly. "And get a move on."

I found the two Americans and the coloured gentleman standing in a bunch with a few of the deck hands, and everyone seemed equally dazed. One of the so-called parsons stood near with a revolver in each hand, but it was really an unnecessary precaution: we were none of us in a position to do anything. And suddenly one of the Americans gripped my arm.

"Gee! look at the two guns on that yacht."

Sure enough, mounted fore and aft and trained directly on us were two guns that looked to me to be of about three-inch calibre, and behind each of them stood two men.

"What's the game, anyway?" he went on excitedly, as two boats shot away from the yacht. For the first time I noticed that the engines had stopped, and that we were lying motionless on the calm oily sea. But my principal thoughts were centred on Jim. Where was he? What was he doing? Had these blackguards done away with him, or was he lying up somewhere—hidden away? And even if he were what could he do? Those two guns had an unpleasant appearance.

★★★★★★

A bunch of armed men came pouring over the side, and then disappeared below, only to come up again in a few minutes carrying a number of wooden boxes, which they lowered into the boats alongside. They worked with the efficiency of well-trained sailors, and I found myself cursing aloud. For I knew what was inside those boxes, and one was so utterly helpless to do anything. And yet I couldn't help feeling a sort of unwilling admiration; the thing was so perfectly organised. It might have been a well-rehearsed drill instead of a unique and gigantic piece of piracy.

I stepped back a few paces, and looked up at the bridge. The skipper was there and his three officers—covered by another of the parsons. And the fifth member of the party was the Reverend Samuel Longfellow. He was smiling gently to himself, and as the last of the boxes was lowered over the side he came to the edge of the bridge and addressed us.

"We are now going to leave you," he remarked suavely. "You are all unarmed, and I wish to give you a word of advice. Should either of the gunners on my yacht see anyone move, however innocent the reason, before we are on board, he or both of them will open fire. So do not, Captain Kelly, be tempted to have a shot at me, because it will be the last shot you ever have. You will now join your crew, if you please."

In silence the skipper and his officers came down from the bridge, and the speaker followed them. For a moment or two he stood facing us with an ironical smile on his face.

"Your brother in the Church," he remarked, "thanks you for your little gift to his offertory box." Then he turned to one of the other parsons beside him. "Is it set?" he asked briefly.

"Yes," said the other. "We'd better hurry. What about that woman up there?"

"Confound the woman!" answered the Reverend Samuel. "A pleasant journey, Captain Kelly."

He stepped down the gangway into the second boat, and pulled away towards the yacht.

And then for the first time I remembered Mrs. Armstrong. She was cowering down with her hands over her ears, the picture of abject terror. But now curiosity overcame her fright and she knelt up and stared at the yacht. Her pink parasol was clutched in her hands, and tragic though the situation was, I could not help smiling.

A mocking shout from the yacht made me look away again. The scoundrel who called himself the Reverend Samuel Longfellow was standing beside the boxes of gold and pearls which had been stacked on the deck. He was waving his hand and bowing ironically, with the six other blackguards beside him, when the last amazing development took place.

Literally before our eyes they vanished in a great sheet of flame. I had a momentary glimpse of the yacht apparently splitting in two, and then the roar of a gigantic explosion nearly deafened me.

"Get under cover!" yelled the skipper, and there was a general stampede, as bits of metal and wood began falling into the sea all round us. Then there came another smaller explosion as the sea rushed into the yacht's engine- room, a great column of water shot up, and when it subsided the yacht had disappeared.

"What in heaven's name happened?" said one of the Americans dazedly.

I said nothing; I felt too dazed myself. And unconsciously I looked towards the bows. Mrs. Armstrong had disappeared.

The skipper sent away a boat, but it was useless. There was a mass of floating wreckage, but no trace of any survivor.

I met Mrs. Armstrong on deck half an hour afterwards. "Dreadful! Terrible!" she cried. "How more than thankful I am I didn't see it!"

I stared at her.

"You didn't see it?" I said. "But surely—"

And then I heard Jim's voice behind me.

"Mrs. Armstrong, I have a dreadful confession to make. Mrs. Armstrong, Dick, was good enough to lend me some clothes this morning, so that we could have a rag when crossing the Line, and I've gone and dropped her parasol overboard."

"We're nowhere near the Line," I remarked, but fortunately the good lady paid no attention.

"What does it matter, Mr. Maitland?" she cried. "To think of anything of that sort in face of this awful tragedy!"

She walked away like an agitated hen, and Jim smiled grimly.

"Poor old soul!" he said, "let's hope she never gets an idea of the truth."

"So it was you up in the bows," I remarked.

He nodded. "Didn't you guess, Dick? Let's go and have a drink, and I'll put you wise."

"I went and saw Kelly that night," he began, when we were comfortably settled, "and at first he laughed as I thought he would. Then after a while he didn't laugh quite so much, and presently I made a suggestion. If these men were what they said they were, the two big chests below would prove their case. Let us examine these two chests and see. So finally we went below to where the passengers' luggage is stored. There were the two cases, and there and then we opened one. It was packed—not with Bibles—but with nitro-glycerine."

Jim paused and took a drink.

"I don't think," he went on gravely, "that I have ever seen a man in quite such a dreadful rage as Kelly. There was a clockwork mechanism which could be started by turning a screw on the outside of each box, and the whole diabolical plan was as clear as daylight. There was enough stuff there to sink a fleet of battleships, and when they had cleared off in the yacht with the gold we should suddenly have split in two and gone down with every soul on board."

He smiled grimly.

"I had no small difficulty in preventing James putting the whole bunch in irons on the spot, but finally I got him to agree to a plan of mine. We changed the cargo round—he and I. Their chests containing nitro-glycerine we filled with gold, and the specie boxes we filled with nitro-glycerine and some lead and iron as a make-weight. And then we let the plan proceed. We banked on the fact that they wouldn't fool around with an hysterical old woman or a man in the throes of fever. Good girl, Miss Armstrong; she kept her mother below all the morning. And that, I think, is all."

"I'm hanged if it is!" I cried. "What made that stuff blow up, if it had been taken out of the prepared boxes?" Jim drained his glass.

"Well, old Dick," he said, "it may be that the Reverend Samuel dropped his Corona inadvertently. Or maybe something hit one of those boxes very hard—perhaps a bullet from a gun fired from this ship. Come down to my cabin."

I followed him, and he shut the door. On the bed was lying Mrs. Armstrong's pink parasol. Through a hole that had been split in the silk near the ferrule stuck out the muzzle of an Express rifle. Jim took it out and cleaned, it carefully, then he looked at the parasol.

"Beyond repair, old man. And since I told the old dear I'd dropped her gamp overboard, well—"

He rolled it up loosely, and threw it far out through the porthole.

9.—THE ROTTENNESS OF LADY HOUNSLOW

And now, in order to keep things in their correct chronological order, I must put down the story Jim told us himself only a month ago. It was news to me, and it happened while I was otherwise occupied in Cairo. Of which—more later.

But before I give his story I must mention quite briefly the circumstances which led up to it.

★★★★★★

Lady Hounslow, wife of Sir George Hounslow, is a very wonderful woman, as is only right and proper in the wife of a Cabinet Minister. She has the gift, as all the world knows, of giving just the right dinner-parties to just the right people. She also has the gift of flirting so mildly that not even the most censorious can really call it flirting; and she does it with just the right man. Private secretaries adore her—she is so impartially charming to them all; under-secretaries ask her advice, and not infrequently take it. And, of course, her labours on

118

behalf of charity are too well known to need description.

In fact, it was only the other day that she came down to open the new wing of the hospital in the village near Jim Maitland's house. A local deputation, with cinematograph operator complete, met her at the station, and she flashed her well-known smile on all those waiting on the platform as she stood for a moment framed in the carriage door. Then she entered the waiting motor-car: the band delivered itself of a noise, and the ceremony proper started.

It was a ghastly performance, as such ceremonies invariably are, and why Jim insisted on attending it defeated us all. But he would give no reason beyond an inscrutable smile, and when the actual opening was over, we found ourselves sitting in the second row in the village school waiting for the speeches.

Lady Hounslow specialised in little brief speeches—charming little speeches in which she said just the right thing. And if each charming little speech brought a peerage for her husband one step closer—well, surely the labourer is worthy of her hire.

And that afternoon was no exception. She listened prettily to the perspiring effort of the mayor; then, when the cheering had subsided, she rose to her feet. Just three minutes—no more, was her invariable rule. And for two minutes she rippled on, her theme being the sacred cause of devoting one's energy, one's time and one's money to the sick.

"Was it possible," she asked, "for us, who were in the full possession of our health, who were endowed, perhaps, a little more than some others with this world's goods—though in these days of this dreadful Income Tax it was only very little—was it possible to do too much for the sick and suffering?"

Her sweet, pathetic smile as she said it drew a sympathetic response from her audience, which changed suddenly to a little murmur of alarm. For with amazing suddenness the sweet smile faded from her lips, to be replaced by what was almost a look of terror. There was a hunted expression in her eyes, and her cheeks showed blotchy through her makeup. There were lines in a face grown strangely haggard, and she faltered and swayed towards her chair. And she was staring at Jim Maitland.

In an instant a doctor was beside her, and the reporter sitting below the chair heard her murmur something about the heat. Not surprising, of course; opening hospitals is tiring work for frail and delicate women. But it ended the meeting, and in the general confusion we departed. And it was as we got to the door that Jim stopped and deliberately turned round. Over the heads of the people he stared at the platform, and after a moment or two their eyes met. And in hers terror had been replaced by defiance: one could almost hear a spoken message.

Then Jim swung on his heel and we left. For a while he strode along in silence: then, as the band started again behind us, he stopped suddenly and laughed.

"Wife of a Cabinet Minister," he remarked thoughtfully. "A leader of philanthropic work in this country: probably a future peeress of the realm. And rotten—utterly rotten to the core. You don't mean to say you've forgotten her, Dick?"

Now, as she had stepped on to the platform, some vague chord of memory had stirred in my mind, but it had remained at that.

"Of course, you didn't see her as much as I did," went on Jim. "And it's some time ago. But don't you remember Mrs. Dallas in Cairo?"

"But you don't mean to say—!" I cried, and Jim grinned.

"But I do mean to say," he said. "Mrs. Dallas and Lady Hounslow are one and the same person. And with Mrs. Dallas I travelled for a month right up the White Nile. She did what she wanted, and she found what she wanted, and she proved herself to be what I said she was—a rotten woman, rotten to the core."

★★★★★★

And now memory was stirring in earnest. Still on our homeward journey, we had left the *Andaman* at Port Said. And the first person we ran into was a dark-skinned man in European clothes who halted dead in his tracks as he saw Jim. Then without a word he turned away down a side street and Jim followed him.

"Wait for me at the hotel," he said curtly, and there was a gleam in his eyes that had not been there a moment before.

It was an hour before he rejoined me, and the gleam was more pronounced than ever. "Dick," he said, "I'm going on in the *Andaman* as far as Malta. Wonderful sea-bathing in Malta in August and September. I'm going to spend all day and every day bathing. Care to come? You'll probably get some polo at the Marsa."

"Somewhat sudden," I murmured mildly. "What's the game?"

"It's *the* game, Dick: the Great Game. The only game in the world worth playing. Sometimes I've been tempted to chuck up roving and take to it permanently. Do you know who that fellow was that I followed?"

"Some Egyptian of sorts, I suppose."

"That was Victor Head, of the Loamshires, temporarily seconded for service with the Government. He's officially A.D.C., I believe, to some General, and he's been on leave of absence for a year." Jim grinned. "That's the sort of General to have."

And suddenly it dawned on me.

"Secret service work!" I cried.

Jim lifted a deprecating hand.

"Let us call it research work amongst the native population," he murmured. "You don't suppose, do you, old man, that the British Government runs five hundred million black men here and in India by distributing tracts to 'em?"

"But why Malta?" I cried, harking back. "What about Alexandria; there's excellent bathing there. And it's a hole of an island at this time of year."

"One doesn't get that wonderful goat smell here," he remarked, and his eyes were twinkling. "I know the actual rock, Dick, where one can lie and bask in the sun. Coming?"

It was an unnecessary question, and three days later found us in Valetta. A *sirocco* was blowing, and of all the foul winds that blow upon this universe the sirocco in Malta during the hot months has many strong claims to be considered the most foul. But Jim was in irrepressible spirits, and departed at once to commune with a certain staff officer. I went with him to be officially introduced, and then I faded out of the picture. For they spoke in a strange cryptic jargon, and when the staff officer had wiped the *sirocco* sweat from his eyes, I saw they were gleaming even as Jim's.

To one who has played the game himself the call of it is always there. But it wasn't a long interview, and it ended with the officer giving orders that a "Tent, bell, G.S., one, complete with pole," should be placed at our disposal for as long as we needed it. And an hour later we left the Union Club in a *carozzi* with our bell tent and drove away towards the west. We passed St. Paul's Bay, where the celebrated adventure with the viper is duly commemorated, and at last we came to the end of the island.

Below us lay a little bay with the water gleaming gold in the setting sun. We scrambled down the cliff, and we put up our tent on a patch of sand.

"There is the very spot I used last time, Dick," said Jim, pointing to a great sand-stone rock jutting out into the sea. "And let us pray to

Allah that there are rather fewer mixed bathing parties for our present effort. They always come in the hottest part of the day, and I reckoned that they made me take a week longer than I anticipated to cook."

He laughed at my look of mystification.

"That's what we've come here for, old man. I've got to cook in the sun, and you can take it from me that I turn into the choicest mahogany you've ever seen. But the red blistery stage is painful, and it's dull cooking alone. So if you don't mind keeping me company, and doing the grub side of the business, I shall be eternally grateful."

They're pretty thorough—the men who play that game. When there aren't any rules, and a slip may mean a singularly unpleasant death, they have to be. And Jim was taking no chances. A stain I gathered was all right for a one or two day show, but when it came to a question of weeks there was nothing like the permanent stain of the sun. And so like a chicken on a spit did Jim rotate on that rock, only ceasing when the sound of feminine voices announced the arrival of a bathing party. Then with horrible maledictions he would retire into the tent until they departed.

It took four weeks before he was satisfied, and I certainly would never have thought such a result possible. His skin had turned the dark brown of the typical Berber, and when he walked with the superb dignity of those sons of the desert it was difficult to believe that he was an Englishman at all.

And then one day he disappeared. Mysteriously from somewhere had arrived the necessary clothes; as I have said there was a staff officer in Valetta who had played the game himself. And to him I went for further information. But they're an uncommunicative lot—the players, and beyond a vague allusion to Tripoli the staff officer was noncommittal.

"The season will be beginning soon in Cairo," he remarked. "A P. & O. is calling tomorrow. Why not go and wait there?"

"Have you any idea how long he will be?" I asked.

"Two months: six! Who knows? You might return the bell tent to Ordnance, will you?"

******

And so I went back to Cairo and waited. It was then that I had met Mrs. Dallas. Little by little she came back to me—a charming, attractive widow with subalterns buzzing round her like flies round a jampot. And it was there, of course, that she must have met Hounslow: he was out there at the time on some Government investigation. But that

122

was all I ever knew, and I told Jim so as we sat in the garden having tea after the incident of the opening of the hospital.

Jim grinned, and proceeded to fill his pipe.

"Well, on the understanding that it goes no farther, I'll gratify your vulgar curiosity," he remarked. "After all, it's ancient history now, but there's no good stirring up mud, even if it were possible to do so. Presumably Sir George Hounslow is satisfied with his bargain, and it would be a pity to disillusion him. Though had he known at the time what I knew, infatuated though he was, I think that he would have thought twice about marrying her. I debated in my mind whether I'd tell him, and finally decided not to. There's quite enough trouble in this world already without making more, and anyway he wouldn't have believed me.

"You know, of course, what the situation was at that time. No? I thought it was pretty widely discussed by the Army out there. Well, in brief, though this point has nothing to do with Mrs. Dallas as she then was, the Germans had begun their tricks. They were working tooth and nail for a *Jehad* to take place in August 1914. A general revolt of Islam to coincide with the world war was their idea, and it is significant that one of their agents mentioned the actual date to me, eighteen months before. He thought he was talking to a fanatical Mahomedan and he became a little indiscreet.

"However, my job when I left you in Malta was a general contreespionage one. To find out just how widespread the influence was and feel the pulse of the natives. There were ten of us on it, and between us we got in eight reports. Not bad going, especially as the two who were murdered were not really up to the standard required—poor devils. But that's another story altogether; let's get down to my Lady Hounslow.

"He was known as No. 10—the man who lived many days' journey up the White Nile. Who he was exactly, no one knew; at least if anyone did it was not shouted abroad. Officially his name was Brown, and he was new to me. But I found that everyone else who was on the game knew him, and I also found that headquarters in Cairo placed great reliance on him.

"Three years previously he had suddenly appeared on the scenes out of the blue, and there he had remained ever since—buried. With the help of a little quinine and a few simple medicines he had established a big reputation as a doctor amongst the natives. And the Powers That Be kept him supplied with those medicines—because a reputation of that sort amongst the natives is a valuable asset when it is held by the right man.

"It was Victor Head, I think, who first discovered that he was the right sort of man. He ran across him by accident, and got from him some information which at first sight seemed to be not only unlikely but absurd. And it turned out to be correct. Then another fellow sampled him, and once again he put up the goods. Certain inquiries were made, and in due course he became Number 10. I confess I was a little anxious to see him. He was quite a young man, I gathered, and it seemed strange for a young man to bury himself in such a way, however much he might be actuated by a desire to serve his country.

"And so, in due course, I met him. He was doctoring a couple of natives at the time, and having given him the usual Arab greeting, and the sign by which those in the game can recognise one another, I sat down on the ground and studied him. I placed him at about five and thirty—a thin, wiry, sunburnt man. To all outward appearance he seemed fit and healthy, but there was something about him—it was his eyes, I think—that made me wonder whether the man called Brown would have been accepted by an insurance company as a first-class life.

"The natives departed in due course, and having gone through the customary formalities of meeting for the benefit of possible onlookers, I rose and followed him into his house.

"'You're new,' he said when we were alone.

"'New to you,' I answered, 'but not to the game, though I haven't been on it for some years.'

"And for a while we discussed matters irrelevant to this story. It was not until he had completed his self-imposed job that Number 10 allowed himself to turn to matters personal.

"'Are you going back to Cairo direct?' he asked, and when I told him I was he began walking up and down the room with quick, excited steps.

"'Will you do something for me? he cried.

"'Of course,' I answered. What is it?'

"'There's a girl in Cairo,' he said, and his voice was shaking a little. 'Her name is Dallas—Mrs. Dallas—and I've just heard that she arrived there a month ago. Will you find her for me, and say to her, "Jack is waiting. It is quite safe."'

"Then he paused suddenly and stared at me.

"'They are pleased with me, aren't they, at headquarters? I've done pretty well?'

"'Very,' I answered, feeling a little puzzled at what all the mystery was about. As far as I know they're delighted with your work.'

"'I mean, I'm useful to them. They—they won't let me be taken away.'

"'Who is there to take you away?' I asked, staring at him. The perspiration was glistening on his face, and his hands were trembling. 'It strikes me, Brown,' I went on quietly, 'that you're not too fit. You dish out medicine to these natives, when somebody ought to be doing the same to you.'

"'It's nothing,' he cried. 'I'm all right. If only I didn't get these awful night sweats.'

"Then suddenly he started to cough, and I didn't need to be a doctor to tell what was the matter with him. He'd got consumption—and he'd got it badly.

"'I want you to tell her,' he gasped when he'd recovered from the paroxysm, that it is quite safe. Impress it on her—that there's no danger. She will understand what you mean.'

"'All right,' I said. 'I will certainly do what you ask.'

"'You see,' he said quietly, 'she is my wife.'

"I sat up and stared at him.

"'Your wife?' I echoed. 'Then why the deuce don't you go to Cairo yourself, my dear fellow?'

"'I can't,' he answered; 'I daren't. But when she knows it's safe—impress that on her, don't forget—she'll come here. I suppose,' he went on diffidently, 'you couldn't help her over arrangements for the journey, could you?'

"I assured him that I would do everything I could to assist the lady, and the poor devil was pathetically grateful. After all it was none of my business. There are quite a number of men called Brown dotted about in odd corners, whose wives if they possessed one would not answer the name. I stayed on with him as long as I could, consistently with my role of Arab, and I let him talk. He could think of nothing except his wife, and in view of the fact that he hadn't seen her for four years it was hardly surprising. Once or twice I tried to mention his health, but he waved the matter aside. A bit of a cough—that was all, and everything was going to be perfect when his wife arrived. And his parting injunction to me was a repetition of the fact that there was no danger.

"'She ought to be here in a month,' were his last words, and I left him to his dreams—the man who called himself Brown.'"

Jim paused and knocked out his pipe.

"I was back in Cairo in about a fortnight, and the first thing I did, of course, was to give in my report. It was to Toby Bretherton I made it, and when I'd finished I got down to the other matter.

"'Mrs. Dallas,' he cried. 'Do I know her? My dear fellow, there's not a man in Cairo who doesn't. She takes very good care of that. Why do you ask?'

"But I wasn't there to gratify Toby's curiosity, and I put him off with some non-committal reply.

"'She's a widow,' he went on. 'A distinctly good-looking filly: a high stepper and a rapid mover. But excessively discreet, Jim—very excessively discreet.'

"'You don't appear mad about the lady,' I remarked.

"He shrugged his shoulders. 'I am not one of the privileged many. But from what I can see and from what I've been told she has altogether too shrewd an eye for the main chance to be particularly attractive. Her present quarry I believe is that ass Hounslow. Some minor official out from England,' he went on in answer to my look of inquiry. 'Conducting some statistical investigation. And I am told that the air of Cairo and the lady's charms have seriously interfered with the great man's work.'

"I left him soon after, and as you can imagine I was thinking pretty hard. For Toby Bretherton's description of the lady hardly fitted in with the one given me by the man called Brown. In fact I didn't quite see her rushing with outflung arms to the back of beyond up the White Nile. And when I finally met the lady the following afternoon I saw her doing it still less. I was still disguised as an Arab, and I took stock of her without much difficulty. She was surrounded by a bunch of men, and they were watching some flying out at Heliopolis. And Mr. Hounslow, as he then was, was watching her."

★★★★★★

"There was a fancydress ball that night at the Semiramis, and to that ball I repaired. I was determined to lay up for her, and I did—though it took some time. As Toby had said, she was excessively discreet, and the subalterns cajoled her to go with them to dark corners of the grounds in vain. But at last Mr. Hounslow, not being a subaltern, but a very much bigger fish, persuaded her to brave the rigours of the night air with him. She yielded with becoming reluctance, and allowed herself to be led to a discreet *carla jugga* in the grounds.

"And there I regret to say that the statistical expert's feelings so overcame him that he kissed her. And Mrs. Dallas murmured 'George—dear.' He kissed her again, and shortly afterwards Mrs. Dallas agreed to become Mrs. Hounslow. And then because Mr. Hounslow was a Public Man and had duty dances with the wives of other Public Men he left her. She would not come in for a while, she said: she would sit and dream. Even as the man called Brown was sitting and dreaming many moons away up the White Nile.

"It was the chance I had been waiting for, and I stepped into the *carla jugga*. She gave a little cry, as I bowed deeply before her.

"'Who are you? What do you want?'

"'My name is Ibrahim, lady,' I said, 'and I bring you a message. It is from an Englishman, and it is as follows: "Jack is waiting. It is quite safe."'

"I thought she was going to faint. In the semi-darkness I could see that every vestige of colour had left her face, and her breath was coming in great gasps.

"'But it isn't true,' she muttered after a time. 'It can't be true, I tell you. Jack is dead: I know he's dead.'

"'He is waiting for you,' I went on impassively. 'And he told me to impress on you that there was no danger.'

"'Where is he?' she cried. 'Tell me where he is.'

"And now she was clutching my arm feverishly.

"'Many days' march away up the White Nile,' I answered gravely. 'You will go to him?'

"'But don't you see it's impossible,' she almost screamed.

"And then what little pity I had for her went. As long as she had believed her husband was dead—and to do the woman justice I have no doubt that she really had believed it—I had nothing to say on the matter. The mere fact that I fully shared Toby Bretherton's opinion of her was beside the point: we don't all think alike. But now the thing was on a different footing altogether.

"'Why is it impossible,' I demanded, 'for a woman to go to her lord and husband?'

"She literally sprang at me.

"'You're not to say that,' she hissed. 'You're not to mention that word.'

"'It is the truth,' I answered, and she began pacing up and down like a caged tigress.

"'How am I to get to him?' she cried, snatching at the straw.

"But I wasn't going to let her off that way.

"'I will take you to him,' I answered.

"There came the sound of approaching footsteps, and she seized my arm.

"'Where can I see you again?' she whispered. 'I must have time to think.'

"I arranged a meeting place out beyond Mena House for the following day, and then I disappeared to make room for dear George."

Jim smiled a little grimly.

"I don't profess to know what she said to him, or how she accounted for her sudden determination to go up the White Nile. As I said before, she was a rotten woman, and she was an unscrupulous woman—but she certainly was not a fool. And whatever may have been the secret which had caused the man called Brown to bury himself—at the time, of course, I didn't know it—his charming lady-wife was not unacquainted with the law on bigamy. She had to go, and she knew it: and she had to go without arousing dear George's suspicions. She certainly succeeded: the poor boob was eating out of her hand when I met them near the Sphinx the next day."

★★★★★★

"It appeared that Toby Bretherton had been consulted as to my reliability, and I smiled inwardly as I wondered what he had thought about the matter. But true to the instincts of all those who play the game, he had not given me away. And to Mr. George Hounslow and his *fiancée* I was still Ibrahim—a thoroughly reliable Arab.

"The next day we started by train for Khartoum. There I got the necessary boys, and a fortnight later we came to the place where the man called Brown was awaiting his wife. Throughout the whole journey she had hardly spoken to me, save to ask how much farther it was. To her I was just an Arab guide, and when we arrived that was all I was to the man. I don't think he even recognised me: he had eyes for no one but his wife. She—this wonderful woman—had not failed him: his dreams had come true. And with his arms outstretched he went to her, heedless of everyone else.

"'Oh! my dear,' I heard him say, 'I can hardly believe that it's true.'"

Jim paused.

"Ever seen a dog jump up suddenly to welcome his master, and get a biff over the head for his pains? Ever seen a child run up to kiss someone and get rebuffed? Of course you have. And you've seen the light—the love-light die out of their eyes? Just so did the light die out of the eyes of the man who called himself Brown. You'd have thought that she might have acted a bit—Lord knows, she was a good, enough actress when it suited her book. You'd have thought that she might have had the common decency to pretend she was glad to see the poor devil, even though her plans had been knocked on the head. But I suppose it wasn't worth her while to act in front of a bunch of Arabs: she reserved her histrionic abilities for dear George and the callow subalterns of Cairo.

"'What on earth have you done this for?' she snapped a him. 'They told me you were dead a year ago.'

"There was no mistaking her tone of voice, and the man called Brown looked as if someone had hit him hard between the eyes.

"'But, my dear,' he stammered, and then suddenly he began to cough. A dreadful, tearing cough, which shook him from head to foot; a cough which stained his handkerchief with scarlet. And into the eyes of the woman there came a look of shrinking fear, to be replaced almost at once by something very different. Her husband, doubled up in his paroxysm, saw nothing, and a bunch of mere natives didn't count. Hope, triumph, the way out, replaced fear in her eyes: she knew the poor brute who had been waiting for her for four years was dying. Her path was clear—or would be very soon.

"'Jack—you're ill,' she said solicitously as the attack spent itself, and he looked pathetically grateful for the change of tone. He snatched at it—the one crumb of comfort he'd had, and putting his hand through her arm he led her towards his bungalow. He didn't see the hand away from his clenched rigidly: he didn't sense the strained tension of her whole body as she tried not to let him draw her too close: he didn't notice the horror which had come into her eyes again."

Jim laughed savagely.

"'Was it possible to do too much for the sick and suffering?'" he mimicked. "Great heavens! Dick, I tell you that woman was wild with terror at the thought of getting infected herself. She knew it was consumption: no one could help knowing it. And, as I say, the soul of the philanthropic lady who opened our hospital this afternoon was sick with fear.

"Then they disappeared—she and the man called Brown. What happened at that interview I cannot tell you, but it lasted about an hour. And then she came out of the bungalow alone, and came towards me.

"'Ibrahim,' she said, 'we will start back tomorrow.'

"Then she went to her tent, which the boys had just erected. I waited till she had disappeared: then I walked across to the bungalow. And the man sitting at the table, with a face grown suddenly old, stared at me for a while uncomprehendingly. Then he recognised me, and his shoulders shook a little.

"'Thank you for all you've done,' he said, and his voice was dead. 'I'm sorry to have troubled you uselessly.'

"'Why uselessly?' I asked.

"'It would have been better if I had left her to think I was dead,' he went on. 'I shall be pretty soon: and I realise now that I was asking too much of any woman. It's exposing her to too great a risk: it was selfish of me—damned selfish. But, you see, it was for her sake that I de-frauded the firm I was employed with in London of several thousand pounds, and I thought, somehow, that—' He broke off, and buried his face in his hands. 'Oh, God! Maitland—what that woman has meant to me through these four years! I got away—out of the country: I bur-ied myself here. And I used just to picture the time when she would join me. When I saw her arrive today, I thought I'd go mad with joy.' He raised his face and stared at me sombrely. 'Of course, I ought to have known better. Her coming here would inevitably lead to ques-tions. And besides—there's my health.'

"'And what does Mrs. Dallas propose?' I inquired curtly.

"He looked at me with a strange smile.

"'She proposes to join me,' he remarked quietly, 'as soon as I am well again—in some other country, under some other name. So if you would be good enough to escort her back to Cairo tomorrow we will await that happy day.'

"I looked at him quickly, but his face was inscrutable.

"'There comes a time, my friend,' he went on, when one ceases to see through a glass darkly.'

"And that time had come to the man called Brown. At the mo-ment I didn't realise the full meaning to him of the quotation—later I did. For I hadn't gone ten steps from his bungalow when I heard the crack of a revolver in the room behind me. It's not much good waiting to die of consumption in the back of beyond when the woman you've built your life on turns out rotten to the core.

"I took her to see him," went on Jim, after a while. "I dragged her there—whimpering: and I held her there while she looked on the man who had blown his brains out. He'd done it with a big-calibre service revolver, and she stood it for about five seconds. Then she fainted."

Jim Maitland gave a short laugh.

"Which is very near the end of the story—but not quite. I have sometimes wondered whether I would have told Hounslow if I hadn't gone down with fever at Khartoum. If I'd gone straight back to Cairo with her—well, I might have, and I might not. The situation, in parliamentary parlance, did not arise. It only arose considerably later, when Ibrahim the Arab emerged from hospital in European clothes, with eyeglass complete. Astonishing how quickly the colour fades away when you're indoors; astonishing how an eyeglass alters a man. So Ibrahim went in with fever, and yours very truly came out—a little sunburnt perhaps, but otherwise much as usual. And yours very truly went back to Cairo."

Once again Jim laughed.

"I went to see Toby Bretherton as soon as I arrived, and the first thing he said to me was, 'Pity you had your trip in vain, old man.'

"I grunted non-committally.

"'Dashed plucky thing on her part, going off to see her brother like that.'

"'Dashed plucky,' I agreed.

"'And then to find he'd blown his brains out. Bad show. Glad you were there, Jim. By the same token—you kept your identity pretty dark. She has no idea who you are. Why not come and dine tonight, and I'll ask her and Hounslow. She's going tomorrow. It will be rather interesting to see if she recognises you.'

"'It undoubtedly will,' I remarked. 'Eight o'clock?'

"She didn't recognise me; as I say, a boiled shirt and an eyeglass alter a man. But she was very charming and very sweet, and quite delightfully modest when Hounslow told me of her trip at great length.

"'It was nothing,' she said. Ibrahim—the wonderful Ibrahim had made everything easy. And she would rather not talk about it: it was all too horrible.

"'I do hope he's better, Major Bretherton,' she said gently. 'He looked so ill when he went into hospital at Khartoum. If only I wasn't going tomorrow I would have so liked to thank him again.'

"Toby Bretherton smiled.

"'You can thank him tonight, Mrs. Dallas,' he remarked, and she gave a little gasp and stared at him.

"'You surely don't suppose, do you,' he went on, 'that I would ever have allowed you—quite ignorant of the country as you are—to go a long trip like that alone with an Arab?'

"His smile expanded; it really was a devilish good joke. It was such a good joke in fact that her tortoiseshell cigarette-holder snapped in two in her hand.

"'There is your Ibrahim.' He waved his hand at me, and positively laughed.

"Even George was tickled to death and remarked, 'Well, I'm blowed!'

"As a situation it had its dramatic possibilities, you'll admit, and I've sometimes wondered how one would have ended it if one had been writing a story. The actual truth was almost banal. George had turned to speak to a man passing the table; Toby was giving an order to the waiter. She leant across to me and spoke.

"'What are you going to do?'

"And my answer was, 'George is waiting. It is quite safe. And may God help George!'

"I haven't seen her from that day till this afternoon."

10.—The Pool of the Sacred Crocodile

So much for Jim's doings on his own while I kicked my heels in Cairo and waited for him. As for mine during that period, sufficient let it be said that I met She who must be Obeyed. And the rest of these chronicles are concerned with her, and that other She who completed Jim's half-section.

By rights, I suppose, with the advent of the ladies the course of our lives should have at once developed a certain tranquillity. Only things don't always happen according to order. Certain it is that the narrowest shave of all we had occurred through my She: a shave when for a brief space the curtain was lifted on dark and horrible things—things it is better to forget, though, once seen, they are unforgettable.

I know that to the man who catches the 8.30 train every morning and spends the day in his office in the City, the mere mention of such a thing as Black Magic is a cause for contemptuous laughter.

It is as well that he should think thus. And yet, surely to even the most prosaic of train-catchers, motoring maybe over Salisbury Plain, there must come some faint stirring of imagination as he sees the vast dead monument of Stonehenge. Can he not see that ancient temple peopled with vast crowds of fierce savages waiting in silence for the first rays of the rising sun to touch the altar? And then the wild-eyed priests; the human sacrifice; the propitiation of strange gods?

Thus it was in England two thousand years ago; thus it is today in places beyond the ken of England's train-catchers. Stamped out where possible, retreating always before advancing civilisation, there are still men who practise strange and dreadful rites in secret places.

Moreover, it is not good for a white man to dabble in those ceremonies. For they are utterly foul and evil. They are without every law, moral and social—and those who have dealings with them must pay a terrible price, even as Professor John Gainsford paid—Gainsford the celebrated Egyptologist.

Most people by now have forgotten his name, though at the time the case aroused great interest. It may be remembered that, as the result of information given to them, the authorities raided a certain house on the right bank of the Nile about halfway between Cairo and Luxor. They found it empty and deserted, but possessed of one very strange feature. In the centre of the house was a large pool—almost the size of a small swimming-bath. It was filled with slimy, stagnant water which stank. And when they had drained the water away they made a very sinister discovery. On the bottom of the pool, partially hidden in the filthy ooze, was a pair of spectacles. And the spectacles were identified as belonging to Professor Gainsford.

No other trace of that eminent savant was ever found, and finally his death was presumed.

We let it rest at that—for, you see, we knew. We talked it over, Jim and Molly Tremayne, the professor's niece, and, rightly or wrongly, we made our decision. Molly insists that it was just a sudden phase of dreadful madness; Jim maintains that Professor John Gainsford was of all vile murderers the vilest, and that the fact that he didn't succeed in his coldblooded crime, but died himself, was no more than just retribution.

Be that as it may, I will put down now for the first time the real truth of what happened on that ghastly night. For Molly Tremayne is my She who was Obeyed then, and is now.

Professor Gainsford was the last man whom one would have considered capable of evil. His mutton-chop whiskers alone gave him an air of paternal benevolence, which was enhanced by the mild, blue eyes continually blinking behind his spectacles. At Shepheard's Hotel he was a familiar figure with his coat-tails flapping behind him whenever he moved, and a silk pocket-handkerchief hanging out of his pocket.

It was one night at dinner that the professor first mentioned the subject. He had omitted to put on his tie, I remember, and Molly had driven him upstairs again to remedy the defect. I was dining at their table—it was not an unusual occurrence—and we started to pull his leg about it. As a general rule he used to take our chaffing in the mildest way, blinking amiably at us from behind his spectacles.

But on this particular night the professor seemed strangely preoccupied, and our conversation grew a little desultory. He kept shooting little bird-like glances at Molly, and was, in fact, so unlike his usual self that once or twice we looked at one another in surprise.

It was towards the end of the meal that we found out the reason of his peculiar manner.

"I have had," he remarked suddenly, "an almost unbelievable stroke of luck this afternoon."

"Discovered a new beetle, Uncle John?" asked Molly with a smile.

"I have discovered," he answered solemnly, "that a secret cult thought by every Egyptologist to have become extinct centuries ago is still in existence. If it should prove to be the case, if this cult, which, as far as we know, came into being about the eighteenth dynasty, still lives, and has carried on intact from generation to generation the hidden secrets of the ages, then I shall have made a discovery of staggering magnitude."

"But how did you find out about it, Uncle?" said Molly.

"By sheer accident," he remarked. "I was in the bazaar this afternoon haggling with that arch-robber Yussuf over a scarab, when there strode into the shop a native who was evidently not a Cairene. Being engrossed in the scarab, I paid no attention to him until suddenly I happened to glance up. And I saw him make a sign to Yussuf which instantly made me forget everything else. I could hardly believe my eyes, for the sign he made was the secret sign of the highest adepts of this almost forgotten cult.

"A glance at Yussuf confirmed my opinion that I was in the presence of an adept. He was cringing—positively cringing—and my excitement became intense, though needless to say no trace of it showed in my manner. Outwardly I remained perfectly calm."

I caught Molly's eye, and smothered a smile. The professor's outward calmness when he thought he had made a find was strongly reminiscent of that of a wire-haired terrier confronted by a rat.

"And what did you do then, Uncle John?" asked Molly gravely.

"I waited until he left Yussuf's shop, and then I followed him. There was a risk, of course, that he might refuse to say anything. At first, in fact, he would say nothing, but gradually as he realised that I knew as much if not more than he did about the history of his sect, he grew more communicative."

The professor's hands were shaking with excitement.

"There seems not the slightest doubt," he continued, "that there has been no break whatever in the priesthood for over three thousand years. Through all these centuries the cult has been kept alive. It is— What is it, child? What are you looking at?"

I swung round quickly. Molly was staring into the darkness beyond the tables with frightened eyes.

"What is it, Molly?" I asked.

"A man," she said, "a horrible-looking native, was glaring at me with the most dreadful look in his eyes. He's gone now, but he looked awful."

"I'll go and see," I cried, getting up, but the professor waved me back.

"Tut, tut!" he said irritably. "The man hasn't done anything."

But it seemed to me that there was a nervous apprehension in the glance he threw at his niece.

"Sorry to be so stupid," she said. "Go on, Uncle John; tell us about your cult."

But I'm afraid I didn't pay much attention to what he said. I was too occupied in watching Molly, and a little later we rose and went into the lounge.

There was a small dance in the hotel that evening, and when the professor, true to his usual custom, had retired to his room, Molly and I took the floor.

"I can't tell you what that man's face was like, Dick," she said. "His eyes seemed to bore right into my brain, and I felt as if he were dragging me towards him."

However, I soothed her fears, and after a while she forgot him. So did I, and the professor's new cult, and most other things. Have I not said that Molly was She who must be Obeyed, and the idiocy of the irreparably landed fish had been my portion for some days. And it was not until much later that I remembered him again.

I had gone to bed, when suddenly there came an agitated knocking on my door, and I heard her voice:

135

"Dick! Dick!"

In an instant I had opened it, to find Molly outside. She was trembling all over, and before I knew what had happened she was in my arms.

"What is it, darling?" I cried. "What has frightened you?"

"That man—that awful native," she gasped. "He's in the hotel. Oh! Dick—I'm terrified. I'd just got into bed, when something made me get up and go to the door. I simply had to; I felt as if my legs weren't my own. I opened it, and there, standing in the passage just outside, was the man. I can't tell you the look in his eyes." She shuddered violently. "It was dreadful—horrible. He seemed to be gloating over me, and then all of a sudden he seemed to vanish."

"Vanish!" I said. "My darling—you've been dreaming. You've had a nightmare."

"But it wasn't a nightmare," she cried. "I tell you he was standing there in the passage."

I soothed her as best I could, and then I had to be firm. I admit that nothing would have pleased me better than to remain there with her in my arms for two or three hours or so. But this world is a censorious place, and the hour was well past midnight. So very gently I insisted that she must either go back to her room, or else spend the night with some woman friend in the hotel.

As luck would have it, the room of a little widow who was a pal of hers was almost opposite mine, and she had no objection to Molly sleeping with her. And to her Molly went, having first driven every coherent thought out of my mind by kissing me.

"When men call me darling," she murmured, "I always kiss them."

"How many men?" I began furiously.

And then the widow's door shut.

★★★★★★

I mentioned the matter to the professor next morning, and, somewhat to my surprise, he took it quite seriously, shaking his head when I said I thought it was merely a dream.

"Possibly, Leyton," he remarked, peering at me thoughtfully, "possibly not. But from what you say Molly seems to have been very upset. I think a change will do her good. What do you say to us all three going to investigate what I was talking to you about last night at dinner? This cult—this ancient religion—let us all start today and go to the place—the secret place—where it still flourishes."

"Have you any idea where it is, Professor?" I asked.

"Between here and Luxor," he answered. "We will take a *dahabeah*, and the exact place will be shown to me by the man I met in the bazaar yesterday."

"Nothing would give me greater pleasure, Professor," I said. "But do you think," I said, "that even if we find the place the priests will let you see anything?"

"Once we get to the Pool of the Sacred Crocodile," he answered, and his blue eyes were staring at me with almost uncanny brightness, "we shall have no difficulty. But Molly must come—you must see to that."

"I expect your niece would like the trip," I answered. "Anyway, here she is now."

And it was while he was outlining the plan to Molly that I looked up to see Jim Maitland strolling across the lounge.

"Hullo! Dick," came his cheerful voice. "I heard you were stopping here. How goes it?"

I murmured an excuse and followed him to a table a little distance away.

"Who's the girl, old man?" he asked. "She's a corker for looks."

"She's a corker in every way, Jim," I answered.

He grinned suddenly.

"So that's how it lies, is it?" he said. "My congratulations, old Dick. Or is it a little premature?

"It's not actually fixed yet," I said, a bit sheepishly, "but I'm hoping it will be very soon. We're going off today—if we can fix up a *dahabeah*—with the old bird. He's her uncle, and he's sane on all points except Egyptology. Come and be introduced."

I took him over to the professor and Molly, and we sat down.

"I think it sounds a lovely trip, don't you, Mr. Maitland? My uncle wants to find some place with a most romantic name. It's called the Pool of the Sacred Crocodile."

Jim stared at her for a moment or two in silence; then, with a slight frown, he turned to the Professor.

"What on earth do you want to go there for, sir?" he asked quietly.

"Do you know it, Mr. Maitland?" cried the professor eagerly.

"I know of it," said Jim. "I know of it as the headquarters of one of the most secret and abominable cults handed down from ancient Egypt. And I can assure you, Professor," he went on after a little pause, "that you will be wasting your time if you go there." I frowned at him horribly, but, strangely enough, Jim seemed very serious, and paid no attention. "No white man would ever be allowed inside their temple."

The professor was blinking so fast that his glasses nearly fell off.

"I think I shall be able to arrange it, Mr. Maitland," he said, rubbing his hands together. "You see, I am acquainted with one or two points concerning the ancient history of the cult of which even one of their leading adepts seemed in ignorance. In return for—for what I can give them I am to be allowed to have a copy of the ritual which has been handed down intact for three thousand years."

"Well," said Jim grimly, "all I can say, Professor, is this: If one-tenth of the rumours I have heard is true, the best thing you can do will be to burn the book unread."

But the professor seemed not to hear. His little, blinking eyes were fixed on Molly, and he was smiling gently to himself.

For a while the conversation became general, and it wasn't until an hour or two later that I was able to ask Jim what he had meant.

"You darned tactless blighter," I said, pushing a Martini in his direction. "What did you try and put the old man off for?"

"Dick," he answered quietly, "you know me pretty well by this time. You know that there aren't many things on two legs or four that I'm frightened of. But I tell you that no power on this earth would induce me willingly to have anything to do with the sect whose secret temple is at the Pool of the Sacred Crocodile. There are stories of unbelievable things which the natives whisper to one another; stories of black magic and devil worship which make one pinch oneself to see if one's awake. There are stories of human sacrifice carried out with the most appalling rites." I stared at him in amazement.

"But, good Lord, old man," I cried, "do you believe them?"

He didn't answer; he was looking over my shoulder.

"Something has happened to Miss Tremayne," he said quietly, and the next instant Molly was beside me.

"Dick," she almost whispered, "he's in the hotel. That native. He was standing outside the door of my room again—just now—as I was packing. I looked out into the passage, and there he was, staring, just the same as last night."

"I'll go and see if I can find the scoundrel," I cried, and dashed upstairs.

But the passage was empty. And I was just going down again, when the door of the professor's room opened and he peered out.

"Hullo!" I said. "I thought you were out making arrangements for a *dahabeah*."

"I have made them," he answered curtly. "We start this afternoon."

He shut the door again abruptly, and I went down to the bar feeling very thoughtful. For over the professor's head, reflected in a mirror on the other side of the room, I had seen a native. For a moment our eyes had met, then he had vanished. And a vague fear took possession of me. I felt as if I were moving in deep waters, and a sudden distaste for the proposed trip filled my mind.

It was just before we left that Jim took me on one side.

"Whatever you do, Dick," he said gravely, "don't let Miss Tremayne out of either your sight or her uncle's once you get to your destination. One of you must always be with her."

"What on earth are you frightened of, Jim?" I demanded. "I don't know, old man," he answered. "That's the devil of it—I don't know."

The boat was a comfortable one, and for two days we went slowly towards Luxor, tying up at night. We hardly saw the professor, except at meals, and then he barely spoke. He sat sunk in thought, shooting strange little bird-like glances at Molly until she got quite annoyed with him.

"Uncle John, I do wish you wouldn't keep looking at me like that," she cried. "I feel as if you were a canary, and I was a bit of bird-seed."

There was no disguising the fact that the professor was in a very queer mood. It was towards the evening of the second day that he appeared on deck with a pair of field-glasses. His hands were trembling with excitement as he searched the left bank of the river.

"We are there," he shouted. "We have arrived."

He gave a frenzied order to the captain, who swung his helm over and steered towards a small landing-stage. Behind it the outlines of a house could be seen partially screened by a small orange grove, and on the landing-stage itself there stood a native, motionless as if carved out of bronze.

I suppose we must have been still a hundred yards away when we heard a frantic commotion amongst the crew. They were jabbering wildly together, and seemed to be in a state of the utmost terror. In fact, we bumped that landing-stage badly, as the men, huddled together forward, refused to use a boat-hook or make her fast. It was left to the captain and me to tie her up, and it struck me that the captain himself had no liking for his berthing place.

His eyes continually came round to the tall native who had stepped on board the instant we came alongside. A few yards away the Professor and the native were talking earnestly together, and Molly slipped her hand through my arm.

"Dick," she whispered, "I'm frightened. Don't leave me. That man has been looking at me just like that brute did at Shepheard's. I wish we'd never come."

I soothed her, though I didn't feel too happy in my own mind. Suddenly the professor came over to me.

"We are in luck," he said, and his eyes were gleaming. "We are to be allowed to see the sacred crocodile at once." Molly drew back.

"I don't think I want to, Uncle John," she said. "You go—and stop here with Dick."

"Don't be ridiculous, child," he snapped. "It is what we have come here for. You will see a sight that no white woman has seen for a thousand years; the inner temple of one of the sister cults of Ammon Ra. Come at once."

He led the way, and after a moment's hesitation Molly followed.

"We'd better humour him, Dick," she whispered.

The native who had awaited us on the landing led the way towards the house half hidden in the trees, with the professor shaking with excitement just behind him, and Molly and I bringing up the rear. She was still clinging to my arm, and I could feel that she was trembling.

Our guide stalked slowly on towards the house. He knocked three times on the door and it swung open, slowly, of its own accord and he stood aside to let us enter. In front lay a long stone passage, lit with innumerable lamps and hung with tapestries which even to my inexperienced eye were literally without price.

Braziers sent forth choking clouds of incense which almost stifled one, but in spite of the overpowering fumes there was another smell which assailed one—a cloying, horrible smell. At first I couldn't place it: then I realised that it was the odour of musk.

Our guide stalked slowly on, while the professor darted from side to side staring at the hangings on the walls. And then another door opened slowly, and Molly and I stopped with a gasp of disgust.

For in an instant the smell of musk had become an overpowering stench. And once again the guide stood on one side to let us pass through. It was the actual pool itself that lay in front.

It was hewn out of a sort of sandstone rock. A gallery some two yards wide stretched right round the walls at the same level as we were standing; while directly opposite us, on the other side of the pool, a heavy curtain concealed what appeared to be another door.

In each corner there sat a motionless priest, cross-legged, in front of a burning brazier; and swinging from the centre of the roof was a marvellous old lamp which provided the only light. Cut into the walls were various Egyptian designs, which roused the professor to the verge of frenzy in his excitement. And, finally, just in front of us there stuck out over the pool a thing that looked like a diving-board. It shone yellow in the light, and with a sort of dull amazement I realised that it was solid gold.

"The actual platform of death," whispered the professor in my ear. "Thousands of victims have stepped off that into the pool. And to think that we are the first white people to see it."

"Good God!" I muttered. "Human sacrifice."

But the professor was engrossed in some hieroglyphics on the wall. And the next instant I heard Molly give a shuddering gasp beside me.

"Look, Dick, look! Over there in the corner."

Just rising above the surface was a thing that looked like a motionless baulk of wood. Suddenly, clear and distinct, a bell chimed out. As if in answer to a signal there was a swirl in the black, oily liquid of the pool, a vast head and snout showed for a moment above the surface, and I had a glimpse of the most enormous crocodile I have ever seen. And the baulk of wood was no longer there.

With an effort I took my eyes away from the pool and looked up. The curtain opposite had been pulled aside, and a man was standing there staring at Molly. He was clad in some gorgeous garment, but it was not at his clothes that I was looking, it was at the sinister, evil face.

And as I looked I heard Molly's voice as if from a distance. "Take me away, Dick, take me away! There's that awful native again, who haunted me at Shepheard's."

And it was also the native whom I had seen reflected in the mirror in Professor John Gainsford's room.

He disappeared as suddenly as he had come and Molly gave a sigh of relief.

"Let's get out, Dick, for goodness' sake," she said urgently.

I was only too glad to agree. The door behind us was open, and through it we went, intent only on escaping into God's fresh air. Not until we were clear of the entrance door, with the scent of the orange trees around us, did we breathe freely again.

"Dick—what an awful house!" said Molly, drawing in great gulps of fresh air.

"It was pretty fierce," I agreed. "By the way, where is the professor?"

Molly laughed.

"It would take more than a bad smell to get him away. But nothing on this earth would induce me to go inside again—nothing. Did you see that man, Dick—the one on the other side of the pool?"

"I saw him," I answered briefly.

"What was he doing in Cairo? And why is he here dressed like that?" She gave a little shudder, and stared across the Nile. "Dick, you may think it fanciful of me and silly, but inside that house just now I felt as if I were in the presence of something incredibly evil. I felt it before that man came in—but I felt it a thousand times more as he stood there."

I nodded gravely.

"If half the rumours I've heard, dear, are true, I'm not surprised. Personally, I couldn't get beyond the smell, but some pretty dreadful things have happened in that house. You saw that gold inlaid board in front of you stretching out over the pool? Well, that is the identical board, according to your uncle, from which human victims have been sacrificed to the crocodile."

"Dick—it can't be true," she whispered, her eyes dilating with horror.

"Incredible as it may seem, darling, I believe it is true." She shuddered again and I slipped my arm round her waist.

"Don't worry your head about it any more, sweetheart," I said gently. "Let's go on board and get something to wash this filthy taste out of our mouths."

We walked down to the little landing-stage and stepped on to the *dahabeah*. The boat seemed strangely quiet and deserted, but it was only after I had pressed the bell in the little dining-room three times without any result that I began to feel uneasy. I went into the pantry and kitchen, and there was no sign of either cook or steward. I went on deck again to find the Captain, and his cabin was empty. Finally I went to the crew's quarters and peered in; there was not a soul to be seen. The crew had deserted the boat, lock, stock, and barrel.

A step behind me on the deck made me look round. Molly was coming towards me with a letter in her hand.

"It was on the sideboard, Dick," she said. "Addressed to you."

I glanced at it; to my amazement the handwriting was Jim's. And the note inside was laconic and to the point:

"Get out of this at once. Don't spend the night here on any account."

"What is it, Dick?" she asked, looking at me steadily.

I handed her the slip of paper without comment.

"It's from Jim Maitland," I said, when she had read it. "And when Jim tells you to do something, there is generally a pretty good reason for doing it. Unfortunately, the whole crew—including the precious Captain—have chosen this moment to depart."

Molly heard the news without turning a hair.

"I wonder where Mr. Maitland is," she said thoughtfully. "He must be somewhere about to have left that note. What are we going to do, Dick?"

"That's just the point, darling; what are we going to do? Your uncle will never. . ."

The same thought occurred to both of us simultaneously.

"I'll go and look for him, darling," I said, with a great deal more assurance than I really felt. "He's probably forgotten that we even exist."

"Then I'm coming too," she said quietly, and nothing I could say would dissuade her.

But this time our fears proved groundless. Hardly had we entered the orange grove on the way to the house, when we saw the Professor coming towards us. He was muttering to himself, and under his arm he carried a large book.

"We thought you were lost, Professor," I said, as he came up to us.

He peered at us vaguely, as if he hardly recognised who we were. Then, without even answering, he went past us, and we saw him go below. And in the still evening air we heard the sound of a door shutting.

"'You were right, Dick," said Molly. "We simply don't exist at the moment."

"I'm afraid we've got to," I said gravely. "I can't help it if I do incur your uncle's wrath, my dear, but he must be told about the state of affairs. I'm going to have it out with him."

I went below to his cabin and knocked at the door.

"Professor," I cried, "I must have a talk with you. A very serious thing has happened."

143

I heard him muttering to himself inside, and after a while the door opened about two inches and he peered out. "Go away," he said irritably. "I'm busy."

"Then it's got to wait," I said sternly, and put my foot behind the door to prevent his shutting it. "You've got the rest of your life in which to study that book; but what the duration will amount to unless you listen to me, I can't say."

I intended to frighten him, and apparently I succeeded, for he opened the door and I stepped into his cabin. "What do you mean?" he said nervously.

"Well, in the first place, the whole of the crew and the Captain have deserted."

"Oh! I know—I know," he cried peevishly. "They'll all come back tomorrow."

"How did you know?" I said, staring at him in surprise. He blinked at me for a second or two, and then he looked away.

"One of the priests told me that they had gone," he said at length.

In an instant all my worst fears came crowding back into my mind.

"Now, look here, Professor," I said quietly, "please pay attention to me, and very close attention. But you've got to remember that we have on board here a girl who is your niece, and who is going to be my wife. Now I have the best of reasons for believing that the very gravest danger threatens us tonight. I believe that the desertion of the crew is all part of a deep-laid scheme concocted by the priests up in that house to keep us here tonight. I suggest, therefore, that we should cast off, and drift down stream. We shall go aground sooner or later; but, at any rate, we shan't be sitting at these people's front door."

"Quite impossible, Leyton," he cried angrily. "Out of the question. I'm amazed that you should even suggest such a thing. The most ancient ritual of the cult is being given tonight for my special benefit. Do you suppose"—and he lashed himself into almost a fury— "that I have gone to the expense of hiring a *dahabeah*, and coming all the way from Cairo, just to let the boat drift on to a sandbank? What danger are you frightened of? You talk like an hysterical girl."

And Jim's words spoken in Cairo came back to me.

"I don't know, old man. That's the devil of it; I don't know."

And now, confronted by the excited little man, I felt the most infernal fool. If only I had had one definite thing to go on. But I hadn't—with the solitary exception of the crew's desertion. That, and

Jim's roughly scrawled note. And to both of them the professor turned a deaf ear.

"Ridiculous," he snorted. "The captain was allowed ashore to attend the celebrations which always accompany this ceremonial, and the crew have taken French leave and, gone too." And then suddenly his manner changed, and he smiled almost benevolently. "Believe me, my dear fellow—you exaggerate tremendously. Do you think for one moment that I would allow my dear niece to run into any danger? There is no suggestion that she should come tonight—or you. You can stay with her and guard her against any possible harm."

He dug me playfully in the ribs.

"That ought not to be an unpleasant task, my boy," he chuckled. "And now, off you go, and let me study this book of ritual. Time is all too short as it is."

And with that I had to be content. I heard him lock his door behind me, and then I joined Molly on deck. Night, had come down, and the faint scent of the orange trees filled the air. Briefly I told her what her uncle had said, and when' I had finished she slipped her hand into mine.

"Don't let's worry, Dick," she whispered. "Let him go to his old crocodile, while we sit and watch the sun rise over the desert."

And after a while I forgot my fear, I forgot Jim's warning, I forgot everything except—

However, there is no prize for the correct answer.

And now I come to the thing that happened that night at the Pool of the Sacred Crocodile.

It was just as Molly and I were beginning to think about dinner, and had decided to go and forage for ourselves, that Abdullah, the steward, suddenly appeared in front of us and announced that it was ready.

"Where the devil have you been?" I cried angrily. "I searched all over the place for you an hour or so ago."

He was profuse in his apologies and explanations, and though I was far from satisfied there was nothing to be done about it. Dinner was ready and we sat down to it.

"What about Uncle John?" said Molly.

It appeared that he had given strict orders not to be disturbed, and so we waited no longer. The cook, Abdullah's brother, was a good cook, and in spite of his absence earlier in the evening he had prepared a good dinner. In fact, by the time we had reached the Turkish coffee stage I was feeling quite at peace with the world. Turkish coffee was our cook's speciality, and on that particular night he excelled himself. Even Molly remarked on it as Abdullah refilled her cup.

Of course it was in my coffee—the particular drug they used. What it was I don't know, though it must have been practically tasteless. Whatever it was they put it in my coffee, and not in Molly's. And as long as I live I shall never forget the supreme mental agony of those few seconds after the realisation of what had happened came to me.

Molly was staring out of the open doors into the wonderful desert night. I could see her sweet profile; I could see a sudden little tender smile hover round her lips. And then I made a desperate effort to stand up. I stood there for a second or two clutching the table, making inarticulate attempts to speak. And then I crashed back in my chair, dragging the tablecloth with me.

"Dick, Dick! What's the matter?"

I heard her voice crying from a great distance, and I made another futile effort to speak. But it was useless; she was getting hazier and hazier, though I could still see her like a badly focused photograph. And then suddenly she gave a little scream, and shrank back against the side of the saloon. She was no longer looking at me but into the darkness outside.

"Uncle John!" she screamed. "Uncle John! Save me!"

And then she rushed to me and clung to my chair. Oh God! the agony of that moment, when I realised I couldn't protect her—that I was just a useless drugged log. Hazily, through the fumes of the dope, I realised what was coming: I knew whom she had seen coming to her out of the night. And I was right—only there were three of them this time. They stood on the other side of the table—the man who had been in Cairo in the centre, the man who had met us on the landing-stage on his right, and one I had not seen on his left. They were all three dressed in similar gorgeous robes to that which the leader had worn that afternoon when we had seen him for a few seconds on the other side of the sacred pool, and they all three stood motionless staring at Molly.

I heard her terrified whisper—"Dick! Help me, Dick," and I lay there sprawling, helpless. And still they stood there—staring at my adored girl. Hypnotism, of course—I realised that after. They were hypnotising her in front of my eyes, and, poor child, it didn't take long. Even though time is jumbled in my mind, just as it is in a dream, it cannot have been more than a minute before I saw her—my Molly—

walking towards them round the table with little, short, jerky steps. I could see her hands clenched rigidly at her sides; I could see her dear eyes fixed on the central man with a dreadful glassy stare.

As she advanced they backed away—step by step—till they passed out of the range of vision. A moment or two later she, too, vanished. I heard her footsteps on the deck—then silence. She had gone—without anyone to help her—gone to that devilish house. And even as wave after wave of the drug surged over me it seemed to me that I gave one desperate shout.

"Jim—save her! Save Molly!"

Maybe I did; maybe it was only mental. But my last coherent thought was a prayer to the man who had never failed me yet. And then I slept.

The lamp was smoking and guttering in its final gasp when I opened my eyes again. For a moment or two I remembered nothing; I felt as if I had just woken from some awful nightmare. And then the table-cloth, which still covered me, the broken coffee-cups, the debris on the floor brought me to my feet with a dreadful terror clutching at my heart. I pulled out my watch; it showed a quarter-past twelve. And we had sat down to dinner at half-past eight. For more than three hours Molly had been in the hands of those devils.

I slipped my hand into my pocket and cursed foolishly. Someone had taken my revolver, and at that moment with a final splutter the lamp went out. But there was no time to look for any weapon; there was no time for anything except to get to Molly at once.

And was there even time for that? As I raced through the orange grove towards the house the thought hammered at my brain. Was I too late?

I had made no plan. I had no clear idea of anything except getting to Molly. What would happen when I got there—how I, unarmed and alone, was going to help her was beside the point.

A man sprang at me as I reached the door, and I hit him on the point of the jaw with all my weight behind the blow. He went straight down like a log, and I felt a little better. Then I flung open the door and dashed into the passage, to pause for a moment in sheer amazement at the spectacle.

The braziers still poured forth their choking clouds of incense; the innumerable lamps were lit as they had been that afternoon. But now the passage was not empty, it was crowded with natives. And one and all were bleeding from self-inflicted wounds.

They lay about on the floor in varying degrees of consciousness. Some were in a state of coma; others writhed in a condition of frenzied madness. And suddenly quivering in the air came the deep note of a drum, It was the signal for a wild outburst. They became as maniacs—stabbing themselves in the legs and arms, tearing out handfuls of hair till they ran with blood and looked like devils. And once again the deep note came quivering through the stifling air and died away.

Drum madness: that strange phenomenon of Africa. A sickening, horrible scene—and in my mind the sickening, horrible thought that for three hours my Molly had been in this ghastly house—alone.

Dodging between the writhing men, I rushed to the second door. It opened without difficulty—so that I stumbled forward on my face. And the next moment half a dozen men had hurled themselves on top of me. I fought wildly with the strength of despair; I even bit—but it was no good. They got me up and they held me—two of them to each arm, and what I saw almost snapped my reason.

Facing me were the three natives who had come to the *dahabeah* that night. They were on the other side of the pool—clad now in robes even more gorgeous than before. Behind them was the drum beater, rocking to and fro in a sort of ecstasy, and ranged on each side of them were other natives intoning a monotonous dirge. It rose and fell in a strange cadence, culminating each time with the beat of the drum. And at each beat I could feel the men holding me shiver in their excitement.

Below, in the pool, swirl after swirl of the stinking black water showed that the crocodile was waiting for the culmination of the ceremony. But the foul brute knew what that culmination was—even as the fouler brutes opposite knew—even as I knew. For standing on the platform, with her eyes still fixed on the leading native in that same glassy stare, was Molly—my Molly.

In a frenzy of madness I screamed her name. She took no notice, and once again I struggled desperately. If only I could get to her—pull her back—save her somehow. But they held me—there were six of them now—and when I shouted at her again one of them jammed my handkerchief into my mouth.

Suddenly the leader raised his hand, and Molly took another faltering step forward. One step more along the platform of death; one step nearer the end—the end where there would be no more board for her feet but only the pool below.

The drum became more insistent; the singers' voices rose to a harsh screaming.

And then it happened. Jim—Jim the superb, Jim the incomparable—was there on the other side of the pool. Jim with a jagged wound on his cheek, and his clothes in tatters. Jim with his eye- glass—and such cold, devilish fury in his face as I have never seen in any man's before or since.

I heard the dull smash of breaking bone as he hit the drum beater, and then I went mad with the sheer, tense excitement of it, for Jim had gone berserk. With a great shout he seized the centre native—the leader—and with one stupendous heave he lifted him above his head. And there for a moment he stood holding the struggling native at the full extent of his arms, while the others watched in stupefied silence. Then with cries of fury they closed in on him, only to stop as his voice rang out, speaking their own language.

"If anyone touches me, this man goes into the pool!"

He threw back his head and laughed, and the natives watched him, snarling and impotent.

"Go to her, Dick," he cried, and the next instant Molly was in my arms—a dazed, hypnotised Molly who didn't know me—but still Molly. I dragged her off that damnable platform; I took her to the door—and then I looked back at Jim.

The sweat was gleaming on his forehead; the strain of holding that full- grown native was taxing even his great strength. But once again he laughed—that wonderful cheery laugh of his.

"To the boat, old Dick. Good luck."

And in his heart of hearts that great-souled sportsman thought it was good-bye. Once—years after—he told me that he never thought he would see me again: that the odds would be too great. For even now, heedless of his threat, the natives were closing in on him from each side, and suddenly one of them seized his arm.

"So be it," he roared, and with a mighty heave he threw the leader of that cult into the pool below. There was one frenzied shriek of agonised terror; a dreadful swirling rush through the water: the snap of great jaws. And suddenly the blackness of the pool was stained a vivid crimson. To the crocodile it mattered not whether it was priest or victim.

I waited no longer. Taking advantage of the momentary stupefaction, Jim had vanished, and the next instant I was rushing Molly along the passage outside. With the cessation of the drum the natives there had become quieter, and none interfered with us. We reached the outer door and, half dragging, half carrying Molly, I ran on towards the boat. Behind us I could hear a frenzied babel of cursing and shrieking, but it seemed to come from the other side of the house. They were after Jim—the whole pack of them—and gradually the noise grew fainter and fainter. He was leading them away from us, which was just what Jim would do.

I darted on board to find the captain and two of the crew standing there.

"Quick, sir," he cried, and I realised the engine was going, Already he was casting off, and I shouted to him to stop. Once Molly was safe I had to go back to help Jim.

I took her below and laid her on the berth in her cabin. Then I rushed on deck again to find that we were in midstream.

"Orders, sir," said the captain, coming up to me as I cursed him. "Orders from the Englishman with the eyeglass."

I looked ashore: the bank was alive with lights. The shouting had died away: the devils were running mute, searching for him. And then suddenly I heard the most welcome sound I have ever heard in my life—a great, hearty laugh—Jim's laugh.

"Stop the old tub, Dick," came his voice. "I'm damned if I'm going to swim to Cairo after you."

And then I saw him—swimming out towards us—saw his head reflected in the light from the bank. We went full speed astern, and half a minute later he swarmed up the side on a rope.

"Not a healthy spot, old Dick," he said with his hands on my shoulders. "Is the girl all right?"

"I think so, old man," I answered. "Thanks to you. But I feel all dazed still. How did you get there?"

"All in good time," he laughed. "At the moment a large whisky-and-soda is indicated."

We went into the saloon, and it was as my hand was on the siphon that a sudden awful thought struck me.

"Good God! Jim," I muttered. "The professor. I'd forgotten all about him."

Jim's face grew very stern.

"You needn't worry about the professor," he remarked grimly. "The gentleman I threw to the crocodile was not its first meal tonight."

"You mean they've killed him?" I said, staring at him foolishly.

"Yes, they've killed him," he answered. "And I can think of no white man who more richly deserved to die."

And as the boat chugged steadily on through the soft Egyptian night, Jim filled in the gaps of the story.

"I got the wind up, as you know," he began, "right from the very start. Of course I hadn't an inkling of the real truth when you left Cairo—but I was darned uneasy in my mind. And after you'd gone off in' this barge I started making a few inquiries."

He paused a minute and refilled his glass.

"Didn't it strike you, old man, that you got this *dahabeah* with exceptional promptitude?"

"Now you mention it—I suppose we did. It hadn't struck me before."

"The gentleman I put into the pool tonight fixed it, as he could fix most things when he put his mind to it. And on this occasion he fixed it as the result of the most diabolical bargain with Professor Gainsford which it is conceivable to think of a man making.

"Mark you, I didn't find it out in Cairo—but I heard enough to send me off by train. I got out at Minieh, and then the game began. It's a good trek from the railway station, and with every mile the reticence and secrecy grew more profound.

"But I got hold of a certain amount which confirmed what I'd heard in Cairo. A great event was portending—some huge *tamasha*: you know how these things get about amongst the natives.

"Then you arrived, and I came on board to see you and make you clear out. But you were none of you here, and the boat was deserted."

"We were up in the house itself," I explained.

He nodded. "I know. So I sat down to wait, as I knew there was no danger till later. And then, old Dick, they caught me napping. A native came to the bank and told me he'd tell me everything: that he'd just found out the truth. So I scribbled that note, and I followed him. He took me with great secrecy into the house, where someone promptly sandbagged me."

Jim laughed. "Me—at my age—sandbagged by a damned native! And when I came to I found myself trussed up like a fowl, occupying the next place to the skipper of this craft. He's not a bad little man—this skipper, and it was he who told me the truth.

"At first I could scarcely believe it—the bargain made between Professor Gainsford and the native he met in the bazaar. For the professor had wished to obtain possession of some book of ritual belonging to this sect—a book unique in the world. And the native had agreed—at a price. The price was the sacrifice of your girl."

"What?" I roared. "You mean that that murderer brought Molly here knowing all along what was going to happen?"

"That is exactly what I mean," said Jim gravely. "Afterwards—well, I don't know if he worried much about afterwards. You were to be drugged—and for the rest the native guaranteed silence.

"That's what the professor thought; unfortunately for him the native's mind is tortuous. The sacrifice of a white girl was his object, and he didn't mind what he promised to achieve the result. And having, as he thought, achieved it when you arrived, he changed his mind about the book of ritual. Which was unfortunate for the professor."

He broke off suddenly and stared over my shoulder. Molly was standing in the door: Molly—sane and herself again—but with a look of terror in her eyes.

"Dick," she said, "I've had the most awful dream. It must have been seeing that crocodile yesterday. I dreamed that I was standing where we stood, and there were natives all round. And suddenly Uncle John appeared. He was screaming—and they dragged him in and pushed him over into the pool."

Jim and I looked at one another, and after a while he spoke.

"I'm afraid, Miss Tremayne," he said gently, "that it wasn't a dream. Professor Gainsford is dead."

She swayed to a chair and sat down weakly.

"Oh! the brutes—the brutes. Dick—why did we ever come here?" And then she stared at me with puzzled eyes. "But if it wasn't a dream—why, how did I see it? You don't mean to say—you can't mean that it wasn't a dream. That I was there, and saw it: that—that the rest of it was true as well. Dick! I can see you now, lying in that chair: those natives—and you, Mr. Maitland. My God! it hasn't really happened, has it?"

With dilated eyes she stared from one to the other of us, and after a while I went and knelt beside her.

"Yes, darling," I said gently, "it's all true. It's really happened. And but for Jim—" I looked across at him: there are things which no man can put into words.

"Rot," he cried cheerfully. "Utter rot, Dick. Though I admit it was touch and go till I found a sharp stone to cut through my ropes with. And now I think I'll leave you two for a bit."

He beckoned me to follow him on deck.

"I wouldn't tell her the truth, old man, about her uncle. At least—

not yet."

In the light of the dawn I saw his face, and it was very wistful.

"She's a great girl, that—old Dick—great. You lucky, lucky devil."

And with that Jim turned on his heel and went forrard.

11.—An Experiment in Electricity

Which might have been the end of it as far as we were concerned, only it wasn't. There was a sequel, and the sequel took place in Berkeley Square of all places.

Jim kept every hint of the possibility of such a thing to himself while we were still in Egypt: it was not till we were on board that he mentioned it to me. For Molly and I were going home to be married, and he was to be our best man. In another fortnight—a boiled shirt; a tail coat; London—

For me, at any rate, the days of wandering were over, and just as I was wondering how I'd like the change—a man can't help his *thoughts*—Jim, who was standing beside me, straightened himself up with a little sigh of relief.

We had been watching the last belated sightseers hurrying across the gangway after a frenzied dash round Port Said, and now the first faint throb of the propellers heralded the final lap of the journey.

Slowly the gap between us and the shore widened; the native boats, with their chattering owners busily counting the proceeds of their robberies, fell away. And suddenly Jim turned to me with a grin.

"This is the identical boat, old man, in which I first left England. From a glimpse into the smoking-room, the barman is also identical. Moreover, the sun is over the yardarm."

"Your return to respectability has made you very silent," I said with a laugh. "That's your first remark for half an hour."

He looked at me thoughtfully while the barman produced something that tinkled pleasantly in a long glass.

"Your girl all right, old man?"

"Molly!" I stared at him in some surprise. "Why—yes. I saw her being piloted to her cabin with that eminently worthy parson's wife. What makes you ask?"

"Well, I don't mind telling you now what I didn't tell you in Cairo," said Jim quietly. "To be quite candid, I've been distinctly uneasy these last two days."

"But what on earth about?" I asked.

"Our late friends at the Pool of the Sacred Crocodile. Oh! I know what you're going to say—that the place was empty and all that when we went back, and that the birds had flown. But when you know as much about the native as I do, old man, you'll realise that that means nothing. Put it how you will, Miss Tremayne escaped, and one of their chief scoundrels died a nasty death in the process. And a sect of that sort doesn't forgive things like that. So that when I received in Cairo a letter containing a typewritten threat I wasn't altogether surprised."

"But why the devil didn't you tell me?" I cried. He shrugged his shoulders.

"You couldn't have done anything if I had. And I didn't want to run any risk of alarming your girl."

"What was the threat?"

"Terse and to the point," laughed Jim. "It merely stated that, in view of what had happened, all our lives were forfeit, and that they would be claimed in due course."

"How frightfully jolly!" I remarked a little blankly. "Do you think it need be taken seriously?"

Once again he shrugged his shoulders.

"I take it a great deal less seriously now that we've left the country," he answered. "I think that undoubtedly the principal danger has passed, but I wouldn't go so far as to say that we are out of the wood. It may have been merely an idle threat. The fact that absolutely nothing was tried on any of us in Cairo rather points that way. But with these devils you never know. Once you start monkeying with these fanatical sects you're asking for trouble."

He drained his glass and we strolled out on deck.

"However, there's nothing to be done. We can only wait and see if anything happens."

"It's possible," I said, "that the whole thing is designed to have a mental effect only. To make one nervous anticipating things which are never really coming."

"It is possible," agreed Jim gravely. "If so, they succeeded quite well with me for forty-eight hours. Anyway there's your girl, old Dick, and she is betraying no signs of nervousness anticipating you. I'll go down below and pass the time of day with the purser, and incidentally fix up seats for *tiffin*."

The boat was fairly empty, as a number of passengers had broken their journey at Port Said. And when Jim discovered that he knew the Captain it was a foregone conclusion that we should sit at his table. A cheerful fellow, that skipper: I remember that there was a story concerning him and Jim and a little episode at Shanghai which was never satisfactorily elucidated. And it was he who introduced us to Prince Selim.

"A charming man," he remarked, as Jim made some comment on the empty seat just opposite him at lunch. "Fabulously wealthy, and almost more of an Englishman than an Egyptian. Has a large house in London, and spends most of his time there. I wonder you didn't meet him in Cairo."

The prince came in at that moment, and it struck me that the captain's remarks as to his appearance were quite justified. His clothes were faultless with the indefinable hallmark of the West End tailor: his face, save that it was a trifle darker, was that of a European. He was wonderfully good-looking, and when he smiled he showed a row of the most perfect teeth. Moreover, he spoke English without a trace of accent. In fact, a charming man, with a most astounding range of knowledge on all sorts of subjects and a fascinating way of imparting it.

Jim and I both took to him at once. He had travelled all over the world, and travelled intelligently. Most of his life seemed to have been spent in wandering, which gave him a common meeting-ground with Jim. Yet in spite of his roving propensities he was—so I understood from the Captain—an authority on old china, an electrical expert, and a wonderful violinist.

"I happen to know of those three," said the skipper. "But from what I've seen of the prince, I shouldn't think they exhaust his repertoire by any means."

Strangely enough, Molly didn't take to him. He was unfailingly charming to her, but for some reason or other she didn't like him from the very first.

"I don't know why it is, Dick," she said to me one day, as we were strolling up and down the deck. "He's charming; he dances divinely and he hasn't said a word that I could object to. But—I don't like him. There's something—but I don't know what it is. Probably all imagination on my part, but there you are. And anyway it doesn't matter very much."

"Not a brass farthing, darling," I agreed. "The loss is entirely his. And in all probability we shall never see him again after we land at Plymouth."

The sea was like the proverbial mill-pond. And a voyage in good weather with the girl who is shortly to become your wife is no unpleasant operation. So it is hardly to be wondered at that by the time Gibraltar hove in sight, Jim and his forebodings were forgotten in pleasanter thoughts.

Wandering was all very well—but a little place somewhere in England with a bit of shooting, and fishing, and some hounds in the neighbourhood seemed very much better. In days to come, perhaps, Molly and I would wander again. Japan, Colombo—there were lots of places I wanted to show her. But for the next two or three years, England filled the bill admirably. And in four days we'd be there; we were in the straight for the run home. The Rock was out of sight behind us; life seemed very, very good.

It was just as I was in that comfortable frame of mind induced by life being good that I saw Jim coming along the deck towards me. And the instant I saw his face I knew that something had happened. He glanced round to see that no one was within earshot; then he went straight to the point.

"I found this reposing on the pillow of my bunk an hour after we left Gib."

He held out a sheet of paper, and with a sense of foreboding I glanced at it. There was only one sentence on it, written with a typewriter:

"Remember all your lives are forfeit."

The words danced before my eyes; so much for the quiet life.

"How did it get there?" I asked at length.

"I know no more than you," he answered gravely. "I sent for our *lascar* at once"—Jim and I were sharing a cabin—"and frightened his soul out. No good; I honestly believe that he knows nothing about it. I've made inquiries from one of the officers about the steerage passengers. He tells me definitely that there are no Arabs or Egyptians amongst them."

He lit a cigarette thoughtfully.

"How it got there," he continued after a moment, "is, comparatively speaking, a trifle. A Scorp may have brought it off at Gib, and given it to one of the lascars; or what is far more likely, it may have been handed to someone before we left Port Said with instructions to put it on my pillow when opportunity arose. And the bustle and excitement at Gib may have been the first chance. No, old man, it doesn't matter *how* it got there; why is what concerns me. Is it just the continuation of a stupid bluff—or is it something more serious?"

"Why not ask Selim?" I said. "His opinion ought to be worth having."

"Tell him the whole story," said Jim thoughtfully. "By Jove, Dick, that's a good idea! Let's go and find him."

We ran him to ground in the writing-room, and he rose from his table instantly on hearing we wanted his advice.

"My letter can wait," he said courteously. "It is not the least important. Let us go and have a whisky-and-soda, and for what it is worth my knowledge is at your disposal."

And so without any exaggeration, but at the same time with some fullness, Jim told Prince Selim exactly what had taken place in the Temple of the Sacred Crocodile. Some of the details I put in, but by the time we had both finished he had every fact in his possession.

"You actually threw this priest into the pool yourself?" he said, when we had finished.

"I did," said Jim grimly. "And if I'd had time I'd have thrown the rest. The point, Prince, is this. Are those letters bluff or not?"

"Most emphatically not," answered the prince promptly. "I, of course, have heard of that sect, and you may take it from me that you only encountered the outside fringe of it. But even so, you have been instrumental in killing a priest who is very highly placed. And that they will never forgive. Whether or not they will be able to carry out their purpose in England is a different matter; they will assuredly try."

"What—to kill the lot of us?" said Jim.

"Certainly," said the prince calmly. "And deeply as I regret to have to say so, my friend, I wouldn't be at all surprised if they succeeded."

Jim's jaw came out.

"We'll see about that," he remarked quietly. "And in the meantime, Prince, what do you suggest we should do?"

"There is nothing to do," he answered. "Sooner or later they will find you, wherever you hide yourselves; then it will be you or them."

"Hide! Hide ourselves!" Jim stared at him in amazement. "My dear fellow—what an extraordinary flight of fancy. What in the name of fortune should we hide ourselves for?"

The prince waved a deprecating hand.

"Possibly I expressed myself a little infelicitously," he murmured. "I assure you, my friend, I intended no reflection on your courage. That, so I understand from our most excellent captain, is beyond dispute. But, for all that—"

He broke off with a little characteristic movement of his shoulders, and carefully selected a cigarette from his gold case.

157

"You can take it from me, Prince," said Jim quietly, "that as far as I am concerned, I don't propose to go into seclusion. But with regard to Miss Tremayne, the matter is altogether different. And if you think her life is in danger we had better take some steps about it. Somewhat naturally, she knows nothing of these two warning letters, and one doesn't want to alarm her unnecessarily."

"Precisely," said the prince. "That is quite obvious." He leant back in his chair and blew out a long cloud of smoke, while we watched him a little anxiously.

"I will tell you what I suggest," he said at length. "It is possible that I may be wrong altogether, in which case there is no necessity to do anything. If, on the other hand, I am not wrong, and you become aware that they are after you, then come and see me. I will give you my address, and possibly I may be of assistance. But it is no use our attempting to evolve any scheme now, when we have no idea what to be on our guard against. Therefore, let us leave it until we have got an idea, and then—well, three heads are better than two."

"I call that devilish sporting of you, Prince," said Jim heartily. "And I'm quite sure that we accept your offer with gratitude—don't we, Dick?"

"Certainly," I agreed. "And in the meantime you don't think there is any need to alarm Miss Tremayne, or take any special precautions on her behalf?"

"I do not," said Prince Selim. "If the attempt is made at all, I feel tolerably certain that it will be made in London." A moment or two later he rose and left us.

"That was a brainwave of yours, Dick," said Jim, as we watched him sauntering back to the writing-room. "'Pon my soul, it's extraordinary good of the fellow. All we can do is to hope that we shan't have to avail ourselves of his kindness."

★★★★★★

It was just a week after we reached London that the blow fell. I, certainly, as day by day went by and nothing happened, had been lulled into a false sense of security. The half-naked priests of that foul pool in Egypt seemed so utterly incongruous in the crowded streets that sometimes I almost believed it had all been a dream. And once or twice with a feeling of inward amusement I wondered what would be the result if I told the story at my club. To Podgers, for choice, of the firm of Podgers & Podgers—a chartered accountant of blameless life. Great Scott! I could see his face as he listened.

And yet, in London itself, in a house in the middle of Mayfair there took place a thing more amazing, more horrible by the very reason of the surroundings, than anything that had happened by the Nile. There, at any rate, the setting was appropriate, but in London it appeared even at the time to be unreal and incredible. To me—for I was destined to fill the role of spectator—it seemed as if I were watching some Grand Guignol play. But it was no play; it was grim reality—a little too grim.

As I say, it was a week after we reached London that it happened. I had been out all the afternoon shopping with Molly. She and I were going to a theatre that night, and, after seeing her to her hotel, I had returned to my club to dress. And I found Jim waiting for me in a state of unconcealed impatience.

"I thought you were never coming, Dick," he cried as soon as he saw me. "Take me somewhere where we can talk."

I led the way to a small card-room which was luckily unoccupied.

"What is it?" I said. "Further developments?" He nodded.

"You know I gave Selim my address? Until this afternoon I'd heard nothing from him, and nothing had happened on our side to make me get in touch with him. In fact, I was beginning to think the whole thing was a leg-pull. An hour ago I was told that someone wanted me on the telephone, and it turned out to be the Prince." Jim stared at me gravely. "It's evidently no leg-pull, Dick."

"What did he say?" I asked.

"He started off with a bright, chatty little remark," said Jim grimly. "The first thing he said when he heard my voice was, 'Thank heaven you're still alive.'"

"'Never better,' I assured him.

"He didn't beat about the bush at all, but came straight to the point. 'You're in the most deadly peril,' he said, in the same sort of voice as you'd ask someone out to dinner. 'I've just received information,' he went on, 'from a source that is open to me, which it is absolutely imperative you should know at once. It is too long to tell you over the telephone even if I dared.'

"Well, that sounded a jolly sort of beginning, and I asked him what he suggested as the next move. He'd got everything cut and dried, and it boiled down to this.

"You and I are to go round to his house this evening at nine o'clock precisely. The time is important, as he will then arrange that his Arab butler is out. That little precaution is for *his* benefit. He told me it would be signing his own death sentence if it were known he was warning us. He will then tell us exactly what he has found out, and it will be up to us after that.

"Molly—because I immediately asked about her—is perfectly safe for the next twelve hours. He further asked if we would both be good enough to preserve absolute silence as to where we were going. That—also for his sake.

"In fact, he made no bones about it. By doing what he was going to do he was running a very grave risk, and, somewhat naturally, he wants that risk minimised as much as possible. Which is quite understandable, because, after all, there's really no call on the fellow to do anything at all for us."

"None whatever," I agreed. "However, I must go and ring Molly at once, and tell her I can't go tonight. And after that you'd better stop and have an early dinner with me."

All through that meal we discussed it fruitlessly. What could it be—this danger that threatened us? The whole thing seemed so fantastic in the comfortable dining-room of a London club. And then, just as we had advanced the sixth wild guess, I saw one of the page-boys coming towards me.

"There's a black man as wants to see you, sir, in the 'all."

I glanced at Jim; then rose and followed the boy.

"This man, sir," began the hall-porter, looking out of his window. He stared round foolishly for a moment or two: the hall was empty.

"Hey! boy—where's that Arab gone, wot wanted to see Mr. Leyton?"

But the page-boy didn't know, and the hall-porter didn't know, and the sergeant outside didn't know. One and all were positive that a dark-skinned man who looked like an Arab had entered the club, to inquire for me. After that the situation was obscure. He had arrived: he was no longer there. Therefore, presumably, he had left. But the staff were still arguing about it half an hour later when Jim and I were ready to go.

"They're on to us, Dick—that's evident," he said gravely. "That man merely came round to find out if you were in the club. And that being the case, I think it's only fair to Selim to throw any possible watchers off the scent if we can. Let us, therefore, announce in a loud tone outside the door that we are going to Hampstead. Then we can double back on our tracks in case we're being followed."

He gave an address in Eton Avenue, while I looked round. Not a soul, as far as I could see, was in sight—certainly no other vehicle, but we were taking no chances. So it wasn't until we were in Oxford Street that we gave the driver the real address we wanted in Berkeley Square. And even then we didn't give him the number of the house: we intended to walk the last few yards for greater safety.

"Have you got a gun, Dick?" said Jim suddenly.

"I haven't," I answered. "But we shan't want one tonight."

He laughed shortly. "No—I suppose not. But old habits die hard with me. I don't sort of feel dressed unless I've got one. By Jove! I wonder what this show is going to develop into."

"We shall know very soon," I said. "It's five to nine, and here is Berkeley Square."

The door was opened by the prince himself, and he immediately shut it again behind us. He was in evening clothes, and we murmured an apology for our own attire, which he waved aside.

"Follow me, please, gentlemen. There is not a moment to be lost."

He led the way through the hall to a heavy green-baize door at the farther end, and even in the one rapid glance I threw round me it was easy to see that money was no object. Down two flights of steps we hurried after him, till another door barred our progress. The prince produced a key from his pocket, and the next moment an exclamation of wonder broke from both our lips as we saw into the room beyond. In fact, for a while I forgot the real object of our visit in my amazement.

It was a big room divided in half by an ornamental grille. There was an opening in the centre, and the grille itself hardly obstructed one's view at all. But it was the beauty of the furniture and the wonderful lighting effect that riveted my attention: it seemed like a room out of a fairy story.

The general design was Oriental, and save for the perfect taste of everything the display of wealth would have been almost vulgar. Luxurious divans, with costly brocades: marvellous Persian rugs, with small inlaid tables of gold and silver: the sound of water trickling through the leaves of a great mass of tropical flowers: and over everything the soft glow of a thousand hidden lights. Such was my first impression of that room, and the prince, seeing my face, smiled faintly.

"A room on which I have expended a good deal of time and money," he remarked. "The general effect is, I think, not unpleasing. I use it a lot when I am in London. And I may say without undue pride

161

that some of the things in here are absolutely unique. For instance, that chair in which you are sitting, Mr. Leyton, is one that was used by the *Doges* of Venice. Now put your arms along the sides as you would do when sitting comfortably—oh! by the way, Maitland, there's a head through there that will interest you. A record specimen, I'm told."

"That's comfortable now," I said as Jim strolled into the other half of the room.

"Well, all I do," said the prince, "is to turn this little lever behind our head, and there you are."

"Well, I'm damned!" I exclaimed. "That's neat."

Two curved pieces of metal, which were normally parallel to the arms and quite unnoticeable, turned inwards through a right angle and pressed lightly on my wrists. But though the pressure was negligible, it was none the less effective. The curve of the metal prevented me from disengaging my hands by moving them inwards: my elbows, hard up against the back of the chair, prevented me moving my arms in that direction. And by no possible contortion could I reach the lever at the back of the chair. I was a prisoner.

"That's extraordinarily neat, Prince," I repeated. "So absurdly simple, too."

And at that moment there came a faint clang: the opening in the grille through which Jim had passed a moment or two before had shut.

"Absurdly so," agreed the prince pleasantly. "But then, my friend—so are you."

For a moment or two the silence was absolute. On the other side of the grille Jim swung round; then he took three quick steps to the place where be opening had been, and shook the grille. It refused to budge.

"Is this a game, Prince?" he asked quietly.

"I don't know whether you will find it so, Mr. Maitland. I have every intention of enjoying myself thoroughly, but you may not see the humour of it."

"So it was a trap, was it?" Jim said thoughtfully. "At the moment I confess I'm a little in the dark as to your intentions, but doubtless I shall not remain so for long."

"You will not," agreed the other. "In fact, I propose to enlighten you now. When you first went into that half of the room, it was just a normal room. You could have sat on any of the chairs, Mr. Maitland, with perfect impunity. You could have stretched yourself on either of the two sofas and been none the worse. You could have stood any-where on the floor, touched anything on the walls. That was when you first went in. Now I regret to state things are rather different."

He stretched himself out in an easy-chair and lit a cigarette.

"You may happen to have heard, Mr. Maitland, that I am some-what of an expert on electricity. And during the last week I have been very busy on a little electrifying scheme. Having been cheated by you of my excitement at the Pool of the Sacred Crocodile, I am sure you will agree with me that you owe me some reparation."

"So you were there, were you?" said Jim slowly. "You damned swine!"

"Certainly I was there," answered the prince. "And though I con-fess I was quite amused by the evening, it had not quite the same zest as if the charming Molly had gone into the pool."

"You foul blackguard," I roared, struggling impotently to free my arms.

"This room is sound-proof," murmured the prince. "So when I ask you to moderate your voice you will realise that I am merely con-sidering my own hearing, and nothing else. And don't please let any thought of Molly mar your enjoyment, Mr. Leyton. I will look after her with great pleasure when—er—you are unable to."

He turned once again to Jim, who had slipped his hand into his pocket.

"Take it out, and have a chat," said the prince with a faint smile.

"Confound it!" cried Jim furiously. "What's the matter with the gun? Who is tugging at my pocket?"

He swung round with his fists clenched, and an amazed look on his face. He was alone: there was no one there. And yet I could see the pocket that contained his revolver being dragged away from him, as if pulled by an invisible hand.

"I told you that I had carried out a small electrification scheme," went on the prince affably, and just then Jim managed to extricate his revolver. Simultaneously the Egyptian leant forward and pressed a button.

It looked as if the revolver was wrenched from Jim's hand. It crashed to the floor at his feet, while he stared at it bewildered: then he stooped to pick it up. It was resting on two small pillars which stuck up a few inches from the floor; it continued to rest there. He tugged at it with all his great strength, and he might have been a child trying to push a locomotive up a hill.

Once again the prince smiled faintly.

"Magnetism, my dear Maitland," he murmured. "Perfectly simple and saves such a lot of trouble."

I saw the beads of sweat beginning to gleam on Jim's forehead.

"What's all this leading to?" he said a little hoarsely, staring at the Egyptian through the grille.

"What I told you before—an evening's amusement for me."

And suddenly Jim lost his temper. He sprang at the gate in the centre and shook it wildly, only to give a shout of pain and jump backwards again.

"What the devil was that?" he muttered.

"A severe electric shock," said the prince genially. "Not enough to do you any real harm—but enough to prove to you that I am not romancing or bluffing—when I tell you of my little scheme. You know the principles of electricity, don't you?"

The prince lit another cigarette, and lay back luxuriously in his chair.

"You remember them doubtless from your school days—anyway those that count. For instance, you must certainly remember the method of getting a shock, by holding two terminals in your hands. That is what happened a moment ago, except that you were standing on one terminal, and holding the other."

"Suppose you quit fooling and get down to it," said Jim grimly.

"Certainly," said the prince pleasantly. "In the week since I last saw you I have occupied myself in fixing scores of similar terminals all over your half of the room. For instance—the chair just behind you. There are two there. And though you might sit in that chair for quite a time in perfect safety, some chance movement might make the connection. And then you'd get another shock."

"Am I to understand," snarled Jim, "that you propose to keep me here hopping round the room having electric shocks?"

He again took a step forward towards the grille, to stop abruptly at the prince's shout of warning.

"Good heavens! My dear fellow, not yet. I couldn't bear to lose you so soon."

"What do you mean?" said Jim.

"You see, when you shook the gate before only one-fiftieth of the current was switched on. And now it's all on. Why, you'd have been electrocuted far too soon. I should have had no fun at all."

The prince lay back as if appalled at such a narrow escape from disaster, and Jim stood very still.

"You see, they're all over the room," he explained. "For all you know, at this very moment you may be within an inch of death. And I mean that literally. Perhaps if you moved your right foot an inch, you would complete the circuit and be electrocuted. On the other hand, you may not be within a yard of it. That's the game. Just like hunt the thimble. Sometimes as you move about the room you'll be warm, and sometimes you'll be cold—and I wait and watch. How long will you last? It may be next minute; it may not be for an hour or more. Some of the death spots I know; some I do not. They were put in by another. And that makes it more exciting for me."

He pressed a button, and an Arab came swiftly in with champagne and caviar sandwiches, to depart again as noiselessly as he had entered. And still Jim stood there motionless, staring at the prince. Was it bluff or was it not? That was the thought in both our minds.

"You can, of course, continue standing exactly where you are with perfect impunity," continued the prince suavely. "And as a matter of fact—this being my first experiment of this nature—I am quite interested in the psychology of the thing. How long will you go on standing there? Four hours—five? The night is yet young. But sooner or later, my dear Maitland, you will have to move. Sleep will overcome you, and it will be dangerous to sleep, Maitland, very dangerous for you. But interesting for me."

"What's your object in doing this?" said Jim slowly, after a long pause.

"Amusement principally—amusement and revenge. How dared you, you miserable Englishman, profane our temple, and put the authorities on our track?"

With his teeth bared like a wolf's, the Egyptian rose and approached the grille. He stood there snarling, and Jim yawned.

"You murdered a man," went on the prince, and his voice was shaking with rage, "a man who had forgotten more of the mysteries of life than you and all your miserable countrymen put together will ever know. And the penalty for that is death, as I told you."

"So it was you who wrote those notes, was it?" said Jim in a bored voice. "You wretched little man."

In a frenzy of rage at the insult the Egyptian shook both his fists.

"Yes, it was I," he screamed. "And it was I who went round to your club this evening, and it was I who heard you order the car to go to Hampstead; and it is I who have bluffed you all through. It was considerate of you, Maitland, to tell the taxi-driver that. There are numbers of excellent places on the tube line out there where both your bodies can be found—electrocuted. And as I've told you before,"—he turned to me—"I will look after Molly."

With a great effort he recovered himself and sat down again to his interrupted meal. And once more silence reigned. Motionless as a statue, Jim still stood there, and his eyes never left the prince's face.

I sat there watching him helplessly. In my own mind I knew that this was not bluff; in my own mind I knew that in all his life of adventure Jim had never stood in such deadly peril as he did at that moment. And the thing was so diabolically ingenious. Sooner or later he *must* move and then with every step he ran the risk of sudden death. But the hand that held and lit his cigarette was steady as a rock.

He smoked it through calmly and quietly, while the Egyptian watched him as a cat watches a mouse. It couldn't go on; we all knew that. It had to finish, and as Jim flung the end away the Prince rose and approached the grille. On his face was a horrible look of anticipation; his sinewy hands were clenched tight.

"Well, old Dick," said Jim steadily, "this appears to be the end of a sporting course. I refuse to stand here any more for the amusement of that foul creature. So I propose to sit down. And in case I sit the wrong way—so long."

He turned and lounged towards the big chair. Then he sat down and polished his eye-glass, while the Egyptian clutched the grille and gloated. I could have told then if I hadn't known it before that it was no bluff—that he was waiting in an ecstasy of anticipation for Jim to die. Anyway, it would be sudden, but when—when?

"A poor chair this," said Jim mildly—and then it happened. Jim gave one dreadful convulsive leap and slithered to the floor, where he lay rigid and stiff. For a moment I was stunned; for a moment I forgot that it was my fate, too. I could only grasp that Jim was dead. Murdered by a madman—for there was madness in the eyes of Prince Selim, as I cursed him for a murderer.

"Your turn next," he snarled, "but first we will remove the body."

He pressed over a switch on the wall, and a great blue spark stabbed the air. Then he went to the central gate and pulled it back.

"Not much sport that time," he remarked. "Too quick. But, anyway, my dear Leyton, you will now know one place to avoid."

"Which is more than you do," came a terrible voice, and the Prince screamed. For Jim's hands were round his throat, and Jim's merciless eyes were boring into his brain.

"You're not the only person who can bluff."

The grip tightened, and the Egyptian struggled madly to free himself, until quite suddenly he grew limp, and Jim flung him into the chair, where he lay sprawling. Then, picking up his revolver, Jim came towards me.

"Touch and go that time, Dick," and there was a strained look in his eyes as he set me free.

"I thought you were done in, old man," I said hoarsely. "At first I put him down as bluffing, but afterwards I knew he wasn't. And when you doubled up like that—" I broke off as Jim crossed to the switch.

"I knew he wasn't bluffing," he answered. "I saw that in his eyes. Now we'll see how he likes it."

There came another vivid spark, and with a loud clang the gate closed in the grille, while the Egyptian still sprawled unconscious in the chair.

"So I took the only possible way as it seemed to me. If it failed—I died, and by the mercy of *Allah* it didn't! Oh! my God! look!"

His hand gripped my arm, and I swung round just in time to see it. I suppose he'd slipped in the chair or something, but Prince Selim's back was arched inwards in a semi-circle, and for a moment he seemed to stand on his head. Then he crashed forward on to the floor and lay still.

"No," repeated Jim, and his hand shook a little, "it wasn't bluff."

★★★★★★

I don't profess to account for it. Whether he was indeed mad, or whether he was merely the victim of some terrible form of mental abnormality, will never be known. Amazing stories of unbelievable debauches were hinted at by his servant during the inquest—debauches always carried out in this room.

Tales showing his appalling cruelty and his fiendish pleasure in witnessing pain in others were listened to by an astounded and open-mouthed jury. But one thing they did not hear—and that was of the presence of two white men in the house on the night preceding the finding of the prince's dead body. The Arab who had brought in the champagne was not quite a fool, and a verdict of accidental death saved complications.

12—MOLLY'S AUNT AT ANGMERING

And so I come to the finish. As I have said, Jim's half-section was made up, and he wasn't our best man after all, for we had a double wedding. As is only meet and proper, it caused the cessation of his wanderings and turned him into an orderly member of society. How long it will last is another thing altogether. Sometimes now there comes a gleam into his eyes not induced, I regret to say, by the intense excitement of English country life. And sometimes now, when Molly and I go to stay with them, the two men of the party are routed out by their indignant wives at two in the morning.

The whisky is low in the decanter; the atmosphere gives every excuse for paroxysms of feminine coughing as the door opens. And then the two men rise sheepishly from their chairs and basely pretend that they had no idea it was so late. It doesn't deceive their wives for an instant, but they are merciful and kindly souls who have even been known to brave the atmosphere and come and sit on the arms of their respective husbands' chairs.

For he found her—did Jim. He found his girl—the girl he had last seen in the hotel at Tampico. The Fate that juggles the pieces gave the wheel another twist—a kindly twist, and the harbour for which old Jim in his heart of hearts had been steering through long years hove in sight. And now there was Molly, bless her! at the helm.

Great happiness is apt to make one a bit selfish, I think, and somehow or other Jim and his, quest had slipped a little into the background of my mind. As he had said to me with a shrug of his shoulders and an apparent indifference which failed to deceive, what chance was there of finding her—that girl who was never absent for long from his mind? And even if he did find her—what then? She hated and despised him. And I had agreed: the odds against finding her were long. Also I had forgotten, for such is the way of a man in love himself.

And then suddenly one afternoon it happened. At first I could hardly believe my eyes: I said to myself that it was merely an astonishing likeness. But after a moment or two I knew that it was no mistake: the girl talking to Molly was Jim's girl.

It was a hat shop—Chez Bernie it was called: and Molly had taken me there for the purpose of disregarding my advice. It appeared that she often came to this shop. It was run by a lady who had built up the business herself. Moreover she was a dear: had struggled through a real bad time and now had made good. Sheila Bernie was her name, and from the corner to which I had retired I saw Sheila Bernie come out from an inner sanctum and greet Molly.

And Sheila Bernie was the girl I had known as Sheila Blair—the wife of Raymond Blair, drunken derelict.

Molly called me up to introduce me, and for a moment Jim's girl—in my mind I always called her that—stared at me with a puzzled frown.

"Surely," she said hesitatingly, "we have met somewhere?"

I bowed and took her hand.

"Tampico," I said. "In the South Seas."

I heard her catch her breath, and then I went on.

"Mr. Maitland and I landed in London about a month ago."

I knew that Molly was looking from one to the other of us, but she didn't make any fool remark about the world being small. And even when the girl went on, with her head thrown back in that queer little way that I remembered so well, Molly said nothing, being that manner of human who knows when to speak and when not to.

"Will you tell Mr. Maitland," said the girl quietly, "that I made a very grave mistake which I have never ceased regretting. I can quite understand that he will find it impossible to forgive me, but I had no method of communicating with him."

"I will certainly tell him," I assured her. "But is there any reason, Mrs. Blair, why you shouldn't tell him yourself?"

For a moment she hesitated.

Then: "I am here every day from nine till five."

She turned to Molly, but for the first and last time in her life Molly's interest in hats seemed to have waned. Tea was her sole thought, and she would come back again tomorrow when she had more time. So tea it was, and at tea came the inquisition.

"Tell me everything, Dick. Why did you call her Mrs. Blair? I've known her now for two years: I've stayed with her sometimes down in a little bungalow she's got down in Sussex. And she's never mentioned the fact that she was married."

"Her husband died some years ago," I said quietly, and my thoughts went back to that sun-drenched dusty street in Tampico.

"It's an amazing, an incredible coincidence running into her this afternoon. You see there has never been another woman in Jim's life since he met her. And I think he'd given up all hope of ever seeing her again."

And then I told her the whole story. I told her of Tampico, of its loneliness and its rottenness; I told her of the human derelicts who died their drink-sodden deaths in it. And I told her of Raymond Blair.

"In your life, Molly," I. said, "you've probably never come across such a case. You've seen men tight maybe, and on that you've based your ideas of drunkenness. Blair was a crawling, pitiful thing: he wasn't a man at all. When the drink was out of him there was no depth to which he wouldn't sink to get it: when the drink was in him—and this is the point I want to make clear—he was almost normal. In fact, he had got into the last and final stage of the drunkard."

"And that was Sheila's husband," said Molly, very low.

"That was her husband," I answered gravely. "She wasn't out there with him, and she thought he was a trader in a big way. In fact, she used to send out money to him every month to help him expand his business. How she got it I don't know—but it went down his throat right enough."

"What a brute!" cried Molly.

"When a man gets to that condition, my dear, he's dead to every sense of decency. And things might have gone on till he died without her ever finding out, but for the fact that she suddenly decided to come out herself and see her husband. She arrived with Jim—he looked after her on the way out. And that was when I met him first."

"And what was her husband doing?"

"Raymond Blair was in a saloon reciting nursery rhymes for the benefit of a bunch of Dagos, and crawling on the floor like a dog to get the nickels they flung at him in their contempt."

"How awful!" whispered Molly.

"You see the drink was out of him, and that was the problem."

And then I briefly sketched for her the fight in Dutch Joe's gin hall, and the council of war in MacAndrew's house.

"There he was—a gibbering, crawling thing: and waiting for him at the hotel was his wife, utterly unsuspecting—his wife, the woman Jim loved. Don't make any mistake about that point—Jim loved her, and she wasn't far off loving Jim. But she was straight, and she was white, and she had come out to join her husband.

"It was Jim who decided. He might have taken Blair to the hotel as he was, and then waited for the inevitable end that could not be long delayed. But he didn't: he gave the man a bottle of gin and turned him into something comparatively normal. You see, as I've told you before, with Blair the position of things was reversed. Blair drunk was normal: Blair sober was just a dreadful nightmare. And it seemed to Jim that it was the only way of playing the game. But you could hardly expect the girl to understand that.

"What Blair said to her I don't know. I suppose she found him peculiar and changed—I suppose he tried to make some pitiful excuse. At any rate she found out that he had just drunk a complete bottle of gin. He'd gone to the hotel with Jim, and it was Jim she blamed. She thought he'd deliberately gone out of his way to make her husband drunk. Which was no more than the truth, but not for the reason which she imagined.

"I suppose she knew Jim was in love with her, and thought he hoped by this method to blacken her husband in her eyes. So she called Jim a cur, and told him she never wished to see him again. And Jim never said a word nor would he let MacAndrew or me explain. He just stood there until she'd finished—and at the top of the stairs stood her husband with his hands shaking and his lips trembling and a look of pitiable entreaty in his eyes. One could almost hear him saying, 'Don't give me away.' And Jim didn't. He turned on his heel and went out into the night, and he's never seen her since that day. We went off together next morning on the boat."

"But it was big, Dick—big," said Molly, and her eyes were shining. "And she knows now, anyway."

"Yes—she knows now," I answered. "During the remaining six months of his life she must have seen him sober fairly often. And maybe MacAndrew put her wise later."

"So it's all come right after all," cried Molly. "You'll tell Jim, and he'll go round and they'll meet again."

"I shall tell Jim right enough," I answered. "But he's a queer, proud sort of blighter, you know, and—"

"You don't mean to say," interrupted Molly, "that you think he'll be such an ass as to stick in his toes and jib?"

"Dash it all!" I said rather feebly, "you must admit that it's a bit galling to a fellow to be abused like a pickpocket for doing one of the whitest things he could possibly have done."

"That was years ago," cried Molly scornfully. "He ought to have forgotten all about it by this time."

"Well, he hasn't," I said. "Besides, how do you know that she is in love with him?"

"Because I saw her face when you mentioned his name."

"You weren't looking at her: you were looking at me."

"My dear boy," said Molly kindly, "don't expose your limitations too much. These things are a little beyond you. I have definitely decided that Jim and Sheila Bernie—or Blair, whichever you prefer— are to be married on the same day as you and I. You will, therefore, tell him where she is to be found, and if necessary conduct him to her shop tomorrow morning personally. You will then leave them alone, and engage a table for four at the Ritz for lunch."

"*Bismillah!*" I murmured, and consumed a cup of cold tea. "Everything shall be as you say." And up to a point it was. I dined with Jim that night, and over the port I told him.

"I've some wonderful news for you, old man. Who do you think I saw this afternoon?"

He sat very still staring at me.

"She's running a hat shop down in Sloane Street. I was in there with Molly today. And she wants to see you, and apologise for the mistake she made that night in Tampico."

"You've seen her, Dick?" he said at length. "Tell me—how does she look?"

"Prettier than ever, as you'll see for yourself tomorrow morning."

For the life of me I couldn't keep my voice quite steady, there was such a wonderful look in old Jim's eyes.

"You're to go round," I went on gruffly, "and you are to bring her to lunch with Molly and me at the Ritz. It's all fixed up. You're to tell her to shut up her shop for the remainder of the day."

He gave a little whimsical smile, and laid his hand on my shoulder as we strolled out of the dining-room.

"Methinks I see the work of one Molly in that arrangement, Dick, my boy. Bless both your hearts! And in the meantime only the old brandy can do justice to the occasion."

And so we fell to yarning till the reproachful eye of the waiter woke us to the fact that the last member had left half an hour previously. They were good years to look back on, those we had spent together, and now he, as well as I, had the wonderful years to look forward to also. So we had one final one, and after that the absolute definite last, and then Jim came with me to the door. Just for a few moments we stood there, and instinctively our eyes went up to the star-studded sky of the soft May night.

"Fine weather, old Dick; fine weather in front. And happy days behind. Surely the world is good."

And with the grip of his hand still on mine I walked back to my own club.

******

Now what on earth more could I have done than that? I'd given him the address of the hat shop; I'd told him she wanted to see him, and short of taking him there in a taxi and pushing him through the door I fail to see that I deserved the withering contempt poured on me next day by Molly at the Ritz.

"I've got a table for four," I began brightly as I saw her.

"Then you can countermand it," she remarked, "and order one for two. Not that you deserve to have anyone at all to lunch with you, but since I'm hungry I don't mind."

"Good heavens!" I cried, "you don't mean to say they've gone and messed it up?"

Molly gurgled suddenly.

"When you see him you ask him why he doesn't buy his matches wholesale in future. It would save such a lot of time."

"When you've quite finished talking in riddles," I murmured resignedly, "perhaps you'll condescend to explain." Once again she gurgled.

"Oh, Dick, what an angel he is! We were both up in the workroom, watching—"

"What on earth were you doing there?"

"Buying hats, silly, and other things—and talking generally. Suddenly we saw him getting out of a taxi about fifty yards away. Dick—he'd got on a top hat, and he looked too beautiful. He glanced at the numbers of the houses, and then very slowly he started to walk towards the shop. He got slower and slower and finally he stopped altogether. I think the poor darling's collar was a little tight, judging by the way he was fingering it.

"At any rate, that was when he bought his first box of matches. Must have been, because he went into a tobacconist's. However, after about five minutes he emerged—'rapidly crossed the road, strode furiously down the other side as if no such place as Bernie's existed, and bought another box of matches from an old man selling them in the gutter.

"After that he went off for a little ta-ta by himself, because he was not seen for quite five minutes. Then he appeared on our side of the street again, only coming from the other way. My dear, how so many tobacconists pay I don't know. He went to ground in another one; more matches. And then the poor old thing lost his head completely. He rushed straight past the door of the shop, and vanished into the blue. I suppose he'd exhausted the tobacconists in the near neighbourhood.

"Anyway, it was a full quarter of an hour before he appeared again, looking thoroughly grim and determined. In one hand he held a large bunch of flowers which were not in their first youth, and armed with them he advanced to the door. Marie was below—she's the assistant, and she greeted him with her best shop manner.

"Poor lamb! it was too pathetic. We were both just out of sight, listening hard. Was Miss Bernie in? Marie believed so, but she would see. Did Monsieur wish to see her particularly, for at this hour Mademoiselle Bernie was generally busy. My dear, he clutched at it. Horrible coward! It didn't matter at all; he wouldn't dream of worrying *Mademoiselle* if she was busy. Another time would do just as well. Perhaps Marie would give her these flowers. Then he took out his handkerchief to wipe his forehead: boxes of matches flew in all directions, and he bolted like a maniac to return no more."

"But why didn't Mrs. Blair go out and speak to him?" I demanded indignantly.

"Why didn't she?" said Molly, and of a sudden there came into her eyes a look I had never seen in them before. "Because, my dear, she loves him. And no woman wants the man she loves to see her for the first time when her eyes are wet."

"Oh!" I grunted foolishly. "I see."

"Just tears of joy, Dick, the most wonderful tears in the world. But they're quite as bad for the complexion as the ordinary brand. So when she was sure he wasn't coming back, she just picked up the boxes of matches for a few minutes, and kissed the flowers and put them in water, and then shut up the shop for the day."

"And what happens now?" I asked.

"I shall take the matter in hand myself," she remarked casually. "Though if it wasn't for the fact that I have decided on a double wedding I would let things take their natural course. He richly deserves to be kept on tenterhooks for at least six months after his revolting display of cowardice this morning. But since time is getting short, something has got to be done at once."

She looked at me thoughtfully, and I preserved a discreet silence. I felt that the male sex was not at a premium at the moment.

"At once," repeated Molly, and her eyes were still pensive. "I think—yes, I think you had better take a little motor trip in Sussex, Dick. The car's still going, I suppose."

"I put on a new bit of stamp-paper last night," I said with dignity.

"Good," said Molly. "You will take a little trip in Sussex, and you will bring Jim with you. Take enough clothes for the week-end, and something to bathe in."

"And which particular portion of Sussex am I to go to?"

"It's close to a little place called Angmering," she said.

"A charming bungalow with a strip of garden running down to the sea. I shall be there, and—"

"Mrs. Blair's bungalow," I announced brightly.

"What wonderful brain power!" remarked Molly. "But 'you're not to tell Jim that, or he'll funk it again. Just you bring him down and arrive tomorrow afternoon. Say I'm stopping with my aunt. Now pay the bill and buzz off. You're to keep the patient amused today, but don't let him get feverish."

So I buzzed off to find Jim at his club displaying every symptom of profound melancholia.

"Well," I said, affecting not to notice his anguished expression. "How did you find Mrs. Blair?"

"She was too busy to see me, old boy," he said sheepishly. "She's always too busy in the morning, so I was told."

And then I laughed in his face.

"You confounded old liar!" I cried; "you know perfectly well that you ratted horribly. You were in a pea-green funk and all the traces still remain."

"It seemed so different this morning from when we were talking about it last night," he said in an abashed voice. "Do you think I ought to try again this afternoon, Dick?"

"She's gone out of London for the weekend," I remarked at once, and the look of the reprieved prisoner appeared on his face. "I thought I told you last night that she was going. So you can't do anything till Tuesday. And in the meantime Molly wants to know if you will motor down with me tomorrow to her aunt's bungalow for a couple of nights or so."

"Aunt?" cried Jim suspiciously.

"Yes—aunt. Either mother's sister or father's. I didn't ask which. But lots of people have one or two lying about the place."

"Is anybody else going to be there?" he demanded.

"Not that I'm aware of," I answered. "They particularly want you to make a four at bridge or ludo or something. It will fill in the time quite nicely till you can go round and see Mrs. Blair on Tuesday. And a quiet weekend by the sea may make your nerves a bit stronger."

And suddenly he grinned like a schoolboy.

"You're right, old Dick. I did rat this morning. I've never been in such a funk in my life. For all I know she may be engaged to someone else or even married again. And anyway she's probably forgotten all about me by now."

"More than likely," I agreed brutally. "But you'd better talk things over with Molly this week-end—or her aunt."

And so the following afternoon we arrived at the bungalow where the garden ran down to the sea. Molly was there, and her aunt, and I heard Jim give an audible gasp as he saw his portion for the week-end. His job was the aunt, as I told him on the way down in the car, and she was some portion. Grey hair that hung in wisps appeared below a cotton sun bonnet; a pair of large yellow spectacles concealed her eyes, and one dreadful black tooth hit one in the face whenever she smiled. But her particular charm lay in her voice, which was a cracked *falsetto*.

"I'm a little hard of hearing, Mr. Maitland," she said, producing an ear-trumpet. "But if you speak into this all the time I expect I shall hear you. You must tell me all your adventures in those heathenish parts while the two young people enjoy themselves."

"Delighted," boomed Jim, and his face looked a little strained.

"It's wonderful to be young," she went on. "Now, my dears, you two run away and have a little talk while Mr. Maitland amuses me."

I had one fleeting glimpse of her adjusting the ear trumpet, and Jim's look of fixed horror as of a bird that gazes at a snake from close quarters: I just heard her first remark, "Now tell me all about pirates and sharks and things," and then Molly and I collapsed into one another's arms.

"She's wonderful," I murmured weakly. "How long is the punishment to last?"

"It depends," said Molly. "We'll give 'em half an hour at any rate."

We did, and when we got back Jim was a shattered wreck. "I can't stand it any more." He had seized my arm and took me on one side. "Much will I do for you, Dick—but not that. I don't want to be rude about Molly's relative, but the woman should be put under restraint. Are you aware that she's just asked me if I've ever eaten anybody? Said Molly had told her I had become a cannibal."

"Courage, *mon brave*!" I muttered in a shaking voice. "I'll do the same for you some day. Think how you're amusing the old pet! And after tea we're going to bathe."

"Not the elderly trout," he gasped. "Great heavens! my dear fellow, you can't tell me that she's going to bathe. I simply couldn't bear it."

"Auntie swims very well," said Molly, who had joined us unperceived. "But sometimes she gets cramp, Jim, and if she does you must be at hand to help her."

"Merciful *Allah!*" said Jim under his breath, and Molly turned away with suspicious abruptness.

And sure enough auntie appeared after tea completely enveloped in a bath robe. We were waiting for her in the garden and as she passed us only her shrill falsetto, summoning Jim, proclaimed who she was.

"You and I will swim together, Mr. Maitland," she announced. "And my right knee has been cracking dreadfully, so you mustn't leave me in case I get cramp. There's a lovely pool here with a diving-board, and then we'll swim out to sea."

"For heaven's sake get a boat and follow," croaked Jim to me. "If the old woman gets cramp we're lost. And surely she's not going to dive—"

The words died away on his lips, and of a sudden he stood very still. Silhouetted on the end of the diving-board was the lovely figure of a girl. Gone were the spectacles and the grey hair—gone was the ear trumpet. And for one second she looked back at him as he stood there speechless.

"Come with me, won't you—just in case I get cramp?"

Then she was gone, and only a little swirling eddy marked the perfect dive. And Molly, being a girl, slipped her hand through my arm and cried a little and laughed a little as we watched Jim's dark head pursuing the elusive scarlet cap in front of him.

"The dear fool!" she whispered at length. "But he deserved it, didn't he?"

And it seemed to me that just at that moment dark head caught scarlet cap. And whether it was cramp or not I don't know, but I saw her arms go round his neck. For you may kiss in the water just as you may kiss on land, and both methods were in use at that moment.

The Island of Terror

Chapter 1

Jim Maitland tilted his top-hat a little farther back on his head, and lit a cigarette. In front of him twinkled the myriad lights of London; behind the door he had just closed twinkled the few candles that had not yet guttered out. The Bright Young Things liked candles stuck in empty bottles as their illuminations.

The hour was two of a summer's morning; the scene—somewhere in Hampstead. And as he walked down the steps into the drive he pondered for the twentieth time on the asininity of man—himself in particular. Why on earth had he ever allowed that superlative idiot Percy to drag him to such a fool performance?

Percy was his cousin, a point he endeavoured unsuccessfully to forget. In fact the only thing to be said in favour of Percy's continued existence was that since he embodied in his person every known form of fatuitousness, he might be regarded as doing duty for the rest of the family.

He had seen Percy afar off in the club before dinner, and with a strangled grunt of terror had fled into the cloak-room only to realise a moment later that he had delivered himself bound hand and foot into the enemy's hands. For the cloak-room was a *cul-de-sac*, and already a strange bleating cry could be heard outside the entrance. Percy had spotted him, and relinquishing the idea of burying himself in the dirty towel basket he prepared to meet his fate.

"Jim, my dear old friend and relative, you are the very bird I want. When did you return to the village?"

He gazed dispassionately at his cousin through his eyeglass, and a slight shudder shook him.

"Hullo! Percy," he remarked. "I hoped you hadn't seen me. Are you still as impossibly awful as you were when I last met you?"

179

"Worse, far worse, old lad. We dine together—what?"

Another shudder shook him; short of physical violence all hope was gone. He was in the clutches of this throw back to the tail period.

"But for the fact that I adore your dear mother nothing would induce me to dine anywhere near you," he answered. "As it is I happen to be free, so I will."

"Splendid. And afterwards I shall take you to a gathering of the chaps."

"What chaps?"

"You'll love 'em, old fruit. We have one once a month. Starts about midnight. Just a rag, don't you know. We're meeting this time in a cellar up in Hampstead. Beer and bones. Or perhaps scrambled eggs. Or even kippers. Except that kippers whiff a bit in a cellar, don't they?"

He suffered Percy to lead him to the dining-room, and as he looked round the familiar room it seemed impossible that it was more than five years since he had last been in it. A new face or two amongst the waiters—though not amongst the senior ones, they were all there; a few new faces, of course, amongst the members; otherwise it might have been yesterday that he was dining there with Terence Ogilvy and Teddy Burchaps preparatory to their departure for the interior of Brazil. And of the three of them only he had returned . . .

"You're looking very fit, sir."

He glanced up to find the wine steward standing by the table.

"Thank you, Soames, I am. And you?"

"Much the same, sir. There is still some of the Lafite vintage wine left."

Good old Soames! Remembering that after five years. And yet—why not? That was life; to him a member's taste in wine was a thing of paramount importance. Especially, though he did not add this mentally, when the member was Jim Maitland.

That he was a sort of legendary hero in the club, was a fact of which Jim was completely ignorant. And had anyone hinted at it he would either have been annoyed or else roared with laughter. To him a journey to the interior of Turkestan came as naturally as one to Brighton comes to the ordinary man. He had been born with wanderlust in his bones; and being sufficiently endowed with this world's goods to avoid the necessity of working for a living, he had followed his bent ever since he left Oxford.

And the result, had he known it, would have surprised him. For it was not only in the club that a glamour lay round his name, but in a hundred odd places fringing the seven seas. Anywhere, in fact, where the men who do things are gathered together, you will sooner or later hear his name mentioned. And if some of the stories grow in the telling it is hardly to be wondered at, though in all conscience the originals are good enough without any embroidery.

Talk to deep-sea sailors from Shanghai to Valparaiso; talk to cattlemen on the *estancias* of the Argentine and after a while, casually introduce his name. Then you will know what I mean.

"Jim Maitland! The guy with a pane of glass in his eye. But if you take my advice, stranger, you won't mention it to him. Sight! his sight is better'n yourn or mine. I reckons he keeps that window there so that he can just find trouble when he's bored. He's got a left like a steam hammer, and he can shoot the pip out of the ace of diamonds at twenty yards. A dangerous man, son, to run up against, but I'd sooner have him on my side than any other three I've yet met."

Thus do they speak of him in the lands that lie off the beaten track, the man with a taste for Château Lafite. And as he sat sipping his wine, warmed to the exact temperature by the paragon Soames, there came the glint of a smile into his eyes. Dimly he was aware that near at hand the impossible Percy was drivelling on, but it seemed as far removed from him as the buzzing of an insect outside a mosquito curtain. White tie, white waistcoat, boiled shirt—and six weeks ago...London: the solidity, the respectability of his club—and six weeks ago.

"Have you ever hit a man on the base of the skull with a full bottle of French vermouth, Percy?" he said suddenly. "I suppose you haven't. You'd wait for an introduction, wouldn't you, before taking such a liberty?"

"I don't believe you've heard a word I've said, Jim," answered his cousin plaintively.

"I haven't, thank God! I heard a continuous droning noise somewhere: was that you?"

"Are you coming tonight?"

"Coming where?"

"I knew you hadn't been listening. To this meeting of the chaps in Hampstead."

"Nothing would induce me to. I don't want to see them, and they don't want to see me."

"But they do, dear old lad. I've told 'em about you, and they're all simply crazy to meet you."

"What have you told 'em about me?"

"All sorts of things. You see, I sort of swore I'd bring you along the first possible chance I had, and what could be fairer than this?"

And in the end Jim Maitland had allowed himself to be persuaded. Though he ragged him unmercifully for the good of his soul, he was really quite fond of his cousin: moreover, he was possessed of a genuine curiosity to gaze upon the post-war young in bulk. Since 1918 he had spent exactly seven months in England, so that his knowledge of the genus was confined to what he had read in books.

Presumably they were much the same as the young have ever been *au fond*. Only conditions today afforded them so much more freedom. Certainly the lad Percy could drive a motor-car all right, he reflected. He had one of the big Bentleys. Providence in the shape of a defunct aunt of doubtful sanity endowed him with more money than he knew what to do with. But he drove it magnificently, and Jim Maitland was a man who loathed inefficiency.

The traffic was thinning as they spun across Oxford Street, and Percy who had been silent for nearly five minutes began to give tongue again. He rattled off a string of names—the blokes, as he called them, who would probably be there. And then he paused suddenly.

"By Jove! That reminds me. I wonder if she'll roll up. The last of these shows I went to," he explained, "a girl beetled in who was a new one on me. Came with Pamela Greystone and her bunch. And I happened to be talking about you at the time. Well, as soon as this wench heard that you knew something about South America she was all over it."

"I should think there must be quite a number of people who know something about South America," said Jim, mildly sarcastic.

"Yes, but I was telling 'em, you see, that you knew all about the interior."

"All about the interior!" Jim laughed. "My dear old Percy, draw it mild."

"Anyway, she's damned keen to meet you. Got a brother out there or something."

"As long as she doesn't feel certain that I must have met him as we were both out there at the same time, I can bear it. What's her name, by the way?"

"Haven't an earthly, old lad. As far as I remember, Pamela called her Judy. But I'm not even certain about that. Here we are!"

They drew up in front of a largish house standing in its own grounds. Half a dozen other cars were already there, and two more were in the drive. A large notice board proclaimed that the place was for sale, and Jim remarked on it to his cousin.

"Been for sale for months, old lad. Belongs to the father of one of our push, and he lets us use it. Let's get in: there's most of 'em here already."

He approached the front door and knocked twice, upon which the top of the letterbox was lifted.

"Pink Gin with guest," said Percy.

"Pass Pink Gin and guest," answered a voice, and the door opened.

"To prevent gate crashing," explained Percy solemnly. "We have a different password each time, and it's always the name of some drink."

"I see," said Jim gravely. "A most necessary precaution. What do we do now?"

"Go below to the cellar and drink beer."

"Excellent," remarked Jim. "But why the cellar?"

"My dear old lad, why not?"

With which unanswerable remark Percy led the way.

The cellar was a big room, and Jim looked round him curiously. Some thirty people were there, and every one of them seemed to be talking at the top of their voices. The air was blue with cigarette smoke, and a strong aroma of kipper smote the nostrils.

"That's the filly I was telling you about, Jim," said Percy in his ear. "The girl in grey over there in the corner."

She was talking to two men, one of whom was evidently a licensed buffoon; and Jim glanced at her idly. Then once again his gaze travelled round the room. It all seemed very harmless, and very uncomfortable, and rather stupid. Why a large number of presumably wealthy young people should elect to sit in a cellar in Hampstead and drink beer, when they could have done so in comfort anywhere else they liked, defeated him.

He realised that Percy was introducing him to various girls, and he grinned amiably. Now that he had come he had better make the best of it. And then suddenly he found himself looking into a pair of level blue eyes—eyes with a faintly mocking challenge in them. The buffoon had drifted away: for the moment the girl in grey and he were alone.

"And what," she remarked, "brings the celebrated Jim Maitland into this galaxy?"

"Curiosity," he answered simply. "But why, in Heaven's name, celebrated?"

"Our little Percy has insisted so long and so often that you are, that we've got to believe him in common politeness. Well—what do you think of it?"

"Frankly, I think it's all rather childish," he said. "Does it really amuse you?"

She shrugged her shoulders.

"It's a change," she answered. "Let's go into that corner and sit down. I want to talk to you. Rescue some cushions from somewhere."

He studied her thoughtfully as she sat down with legs tucked under her. A slightly tip-tilted nose; a complexion, unaided as far as he could see, that only the word Perfect could do justice to: a slim, delicious figure. Her hands were capable but beautifully kept: her hair clung tightly to a boyish head.

"Well," she said calmly, "do you approve?"

He smiled: said as she said it the remark rang natural.

"Entirely," he answered. "But before we go any further, has it occurred to you that the egregious Percy has omitted the small formality of telling me your name."

"Draycott. Judy Draycott."

She took a cigarette from her case, and Jim held a match for her.

"Tell me, Mr. Maitland, are we very different to the pre-war vintage?"

"That's rather a poser," he said, sitting down beside her. "You see, I've been so little in England since the war that I'm not a very good judge."

"But—this." She waved her hand at the room.

"Good Lord!" he laughed, "what has this got to do with it? This is nothing: a tiny symptom in a tiny set."

"You know you are of what I always call the lost generation," she said. "What Daddy would call the senior subaltern brand."

He stared at her in silence, a little nonplussed by her serious tone.

"You were our age just before the war," she went on, "and you're still young enough to play. But there are so few of you left."

"True," he said gravely. "I suppose my contemporaries took it worst."

"There are the old people, and there are us. But the connecting link has gone—you and yours."

"The lost generation," he repeated slowly. "A nice idea—that."

"And that's why I asked you what you thought of us," she said. "You are one of the few who are qualified to judge."

He lit another cigarette before replying.

"Am I? I wonder. One can see changes—naturally, but who am I to say whether they are for the better or for the worse. This show, for instance. Frankly, I can't quite see this happening twenty years ago. Nor did everyone call everyone else 'darling' on sight."

"Trifles," she said impatiently. "Just trifles. What about the big things?"

"I should say," he answered without hesitation, "no change. Different methods, perhaps: different ways of doing them—but, in the end, the same."

"You don't think we're softer than you were?"

"I think this age is more comfort loving, undoubtedly, if that's what you mean. But that, I suppose, is only natural in view of the advance of science. Then one hacked to a meet—now one goes in a car."

"But are we as keen on adventure?"

Jim laughed.

"Adventure! Where is adventure to be found these days?"

"You ought to know," she said, "if half the stories I've heard about you are true."

"I'm afraid I'm a hard-bitten case," he answered. "But I can assure you that even I have noticed the difference in the last few years. Everything is getting far too quiet."

"Even in South America?" she asked.

South America! Percy's remark came back to him, and he wondered what was coming next. This, apparently, was what she had been leading up to.

"You can get a bit of fun out there at times," he said lightly. "But then if one looked for it I dare say one could get it in London."

"What sort of people are they?"

He laughed again.

"My dear Miss Draycott," he said, "they vary as much as the inhabitants of Europe. But by your question I assume you mean the brand that we generally lump together as *dagos*. Well—just like every other breed, you will find all sorts and conditions. I have excellent—very excellent friends amongst them. But they are people who require careful handling. For instance, there is one thing you must never do to a *dago*, unless you know him extremely well. Never pull his leg. He doesn't understand it: he takes it as an insult. There's another thing too. You stick a knife into one—or shoot him up—and he'll understand it. You hit him with your fist on the jaw and he'll never forgive you."

"Are they very quick with a knife?" she asked.

"Very—and with a gun. Moreover, they will shoot on the smallest provocation. You'll understand, of course, that I'm not talking about the vast majority of them, who are perfectly harmless people. But to show you what I mean about the minority I'll tell you a thing I saw with my own eyes. It was in Buenos Aires about seven years ago, and a *festa* was in progress. Streets crammed with people and cars: the whole place *en fête*. I was on the side walk, and a motorcar alongside me was being held up by a man who was standing just in front of the mud-guard. So the driver sang out to him to move. He didn't, and after a while the driver very slowly drove forward, and hit the man a glancing blow on the leg. Now it was a blow that wouldn't have hurt a fly: it didn't even make the man stumble. But what happened next? As the driver came abreast of the man, he calmly stepped on to the running-board, drew his gun and blew out the driver's brains. And this, mark you, with the wife in the back of the car."

"But didn't they arrest the murderer?" cried the girl.

"Not a hope," said Jim. "He just vanished into the crowd. No—they want watching, especially if they've got a drop too much liquor on board."

He pressed out his cigarette.

"Is it permitted to ask why you are so interested in South America?"

For a moment or two she hesitated, staring in front of her. Then she turned to him.

"I am almost tempted to use that stereotyped beginning, Mr. Maitland, and ask you not to laugh at me."

"Then I'll make the stereotyped reply and assure you that I shan't," he said quietly.

"I've got a brother," she went on, "a twin brother. Arthur is his name. And for the past two years he's been knocking about in South America. Brazil, Uruguay, and the Argentine. Now I know that must seem very small beer to you—I mean I don't think he's been much off the beaten track. But at any rate he's been out there, cutting away from this."

"Has he been on a job?" asked Jim.

"He went out there to start with for a big oil firm. Quite a good salary. And of course Daddy allows him something. But after two or three months he found he couldn't stick it—his manager was a swine—so he chucked it. Since then he's been drifting about."

"I see," said Jim quietly. Only too many youngsters had he met drifting about on something allowed by Daddy, and the brand did not inspire him with confidence. Then feeling that his remark had been a little too curt, he added—"It's difficult to get jobs out there—jobs that are any good, that is—unless a man is an expert. And it's a devilish expensive place to drift in."

"I know it is," she answered. "Arthur often wrote me to say how fearfully difficult he found it. At any rate he managed to carry on, until he had the most amazing piece of luck about six months ago. And now I'm coming to where I'm afraid you may laugh."

"Risk it," said Jim with a smile.

"If I'd known you were coming this evening I'd have brought his letter, but I think I can remember all that matters. It seems that he did some kindness to a broken-down sailor in Monte Video—an Englishman. And this sailor on his deathbed told him some wonderful story of buried treasure."

Jim's face remained expressionless, though this was worse than he had expected.

"I hope he didn't part with any money for it," he said quietly.

"I thought you'd take it that way," she cried. "I did myself when I first read it. But he didn't pay anything: the sailor gave him the whole secret. And, anyway, he'd only got his allowance: he had no capital to give away."

"What is the secret?" he enquired.

"That I don't know," she said. "He wrote something about a map, and fitting out an expedition, and from that moment I never heard another word till three weeks ago when I got a letter saying he was coming home by the next boat. He also said that if anything should happen to him I should find a letter addressed to me at my bank."

"If anything happened to him," repeated Jim thoughtfully. "Have you been to the bank to enquire?"

"Yes. I was actually in there this morning, and there was nothing."

"Then everything seems plain sailing, Miss Draycott. Presumably nothing has happened to him, and if you got his letter three weeks ago he ought to be in England by now. And as soon as you see him you'll be able to get the whole story."

"I know. But it is there that I wondered if you could help."

187

She looked at him appealingly.

"Me! I shall be delighted. But how?"

"By going into the whole thing with him, and telling him what you think. You know so much more than he does, Mr. Maitland, and if there's anything in it, it would be wonderful if we could have your advice."

For a while he hesitated: then he looked her straight in the face.

"I'm going to be perfectly frank, Miss Draycott," he said. "The story, as you've told it to me, is, not to mince words, as old as the hills. From time immemorial drunken seamen have babbled in their cups of treasure trove—gold ingots, diamonds, and all the rest of the paraphernalia. Generally, too, they have a roughly-scrawled map, with, as often as not, a skull and cross bones in the corner to make it more realistic. In fact the one point in which this story differs from the others is that he did not apparently touch your brother for money. Had he done that I should have advised you to dismiss the whole thing from your mind at once."

"You don't think there is anything in it, then," she said despondently.

"I don't want to be brutal," he answered with a smile, "but I fear that is my opinion. I'm not going to deny that there must be treasure—probably priceless treasure—hidden away in odd parts of the globe: relics of the old pirate days. I'm not going to deny that the Spanish Main, and the coast of South America are very likely localities for the hiding-places. But what I do feel doubtful about is the likelihood of a down-and-out seaman in Monte Video knowing anything about it, or getting the clue to its whereabouts."

"But as you said yourself he took no money," she persisted.

"I know that," he agreed. "And I think it is quite possible that the sailor *genuinely* believed what he was saying—they're the most gullible brand of men on earth. I think it is more than likely that when your brother befriended him he really intended to do him a good turn. What I'm doubtful of is the value of the information. Certainly I would say one thing. Unless your brother, when you see him, has something very much more definite to go on than the ramblings of a seaman on his last legs, and this map he was given it would be nothing short of madness to sink any money in an attempt to discover it."

"I quite see your point," she said. "But would it be too much to ask you to hear what he's got to say? And then give us your advice."

"Of course not," cried Jim. "I shall be only too delighted. The

Dorchester Club always finds me when I'm in London, and I shall be very interested to hear what he has to tell us. I know that country better than most men, and if I can be of any assistance—count me in. But for Heaven's sake—don't build any false hopes on it."

A sudden surge of Bright Young Things bearing kippers and beer descended on them, and carried her away, leaving Jim with an intense female who shook him to the marrow on sight. He suffered her for five minutes, at the end of which period, to his inexpressible relief, Percy bore down on him.

"I never thought I should be glad to see you, Percy," he said, as the female drifted away, "but that woman is a menace to society."

"She is pretty grim," agreed his cousin. "What price the other girl? I saw you with your noses touching for about half an hour!"

"A nice little soul," said Jim. "Do you know anything about her?"

"Just been asking Pamela. Her father is a retired General: got a house down in Sussex."

"Has he got any money?"

"Hullo! Hullo! Hullo!" Percy dug him in the ribs. "So that's how the land lies, does it?"

"Don't be such a damned fool," said Jim curtly. "To say nothing of being infernally offensive."

"Sorry, old man. I but spoke in jest. As a matter of fact, I think not. In fact Pamela said he was darned hard up. There's a pretty useless waster of a son, I gather. Out in South America somewhere."

Jim glanced at his watch: the time was two o'clock.

"Not going yet, old lad, are you?" cried Percy. "We're only just beginning."

"You needn't come," said Jim. "I shall walk. This terrific excitement is too much for me. Do I have to whisper some mystic counter-sign to get out of the place?"

"No, just open the front door and beetle away. Sure you don't want me to take you in the bus?"

"Quite," said Jim, and beetled.

Thus did we find him, top-hat tilted, pondering on things in general with the lights of London in front of him. He strolled slowly along drawing in great lungsful of fresh air. Lord! what an atmosphere there had been in that cellar. And what a damned-fool performance. Yet, in a way he was glad he had gone: the girl in grey was rather a dear. Stupid of him not to have asked her address: probably get it when this young brother of hers rolled up.

He grinned to himself: the hidden treasure yarn had whiskers on it even when compared to the old Spanish prisoner chestnut. No less than four times had it been put up to him—vouched for chapter and verse. Still he was sorry for the girl, especially as there was not much money. Probably been building on it a bit: only natural that she should. But the brother must be a fool as well as a waster to be taken in by it.

A belated taxi homeward bound hailed him, but he shook his head. He was not in the least sleepy, and the combined reek of smoke and kipper still clung to him. Young asses! He tried to picture what any of them would do in a really tight corner. That fellow who had been thumping the piano for instance, and thumping it damned well, to do him justice. But imagine him in a bar in Valparaiso, for instance, when a rough house started.

He threw away his cigarette: was he being quite fair? After all, none of them had had any experience of such a show. And maybe if they did do the wrong thing it would be from lack of knowledge, not from lack of guts. It wasn't given to many to have the opportunities he had had, even if the desire to have them was there.

Men had often told him that he looked for trouble, but that was not quite the case. There was no need for him to look: it came of its own accord. True, he never went out of his way to avoid it: he would even admit that he welcomed it with both hands. Something out of the ordinary, off the beaten track: something with a spice of danger in it—that was all he asked of life. And up-to-date life had given him full measure, pressed down and running over.

He glanced up at the houses he was passing: solid lumps of respectability, symbolic of everything that he was not. In them reposed lawyers, stock-brokers, city magnates—men who formed the backbone of the Medes and Persians. Not there was adventure in London to be found: the mere thought of it was an outrage. In Dockland, perhaps, but that was cheap: the glamour of Limehouse exists only in the imagination of the novelist. No—though he had told the girl that it could be found he was wrong: it could not be found anywhere these days. . . .

And at that moment, clear and distinct in the still, night air, there rang out the sharp crack of a revolver shot.

CHAPTER 2

Jim Maitland stopped dead in his tracks, and then with the instinct bred of many years he sought the cover of a neighbouring tree. In the country he had just come from he would not have given the matter a second thought—gun work was part of the ordinary day's round. But in London, especially in this part of London, it was a very different affair. The sound had come from the house in front of him—a house very similar to the one he had just left, save that it was not for sale. It was in darkness, but some kind of subconscious instinct told him that there had been a light in one of the upper windows a few seconds previously.

He glanced up and down the road: not a soul was in sight. He looked at the two neighbouring houses: there was no sign of movement. And then, as was his way, he summed up the situation. He was unarmed: whoever had fired the shot obviously was not. Short of breaking in there was no way in which he could get into the house. And finally it was no earthly business of his. Wherefore, by three very good reasons to *nil* he should have continued his leisurely walk towards home. Which was quite sufficient to decide him to do nothing of the sort. He would give it a few minutes at any rate to see if anything further happened.

He turned the collar of his evening overcoat up so as to cover the white patch of dress shirt. Then motionless as a statue he seemed to merge himself into the trees in front of him. For a while nothing happened: then from one of the windows there came a gleam of light. It was extinguished almost at once, only to appear in the one just below it and then go out again. Someone was coming down the stairs. It shone for a second over the front door, and then the door itself opened, and two men came out.

Jim realised they would have to pass within a few feet of him, and pressed himself still closer against the trees. He could hear their voices—one furiously angry, the other seemingly apologetic—though as yet he could not make out their actual words. One was a big man, the other a head shorter, and it was the big man who was in a rage.

"You damned, blithering fool, Ernesto."

The words suddenly rang out clearly as they approached the gate. "You've wrecked the whole thing."

The latch clicked, and Jim waited for the smaller man's reply.

"He should not have struck me," he said. "I do not like to be struck."

The two men stood peering up and down the road.

"Not a cursed thing in sight," growled the big man. "However, perhaps it is as well. No one heard. We'll walk. But we've got to get a move on."

They strode off, and Jim waited till their voices died away in the distance. The big man was obviously English: the other from his accent and name seemed Spanish. Or possibly South American. And it struck him that it was a queer coincidence that he should have been mentioning that characteristic of the dago to the girl only a little time previously—their hatred of being hit.

He came out from behind the tree, and began to size things up. In the house in front of him was a man who had been shot. He might be dead: he might only be wounded. The great point was—was there anyone else inside? If there were servants, some of them at any rate would have been roused by the noise of the shot, and lights would have been turned on. But the house was still in darkness. On balance therefore he decided against servants.

What about the owner of the house? Was it the big man himself? That seemed quite probable, and if so what was he going to do? To leave a dead man, or even a seriously-wounded man lying about the place would prove an awkward matter. He recalled his last words about getting a move on. What had he meant? And putting himself in his place Jim decided that the only possible course would be to take the body away and dump it elsewhere. It would be unsafe even to leave it till the following night, since any doctor would know that the man had been dead some time, and it would be most improbable for a corpse to lie through the day in the open undiscovered.... It would therefore give a strong pointer to the police that the body had been moved *after* death, whereas if it was done at once they might be deceived. So it boiled down to the fact that if he was going to do anything at all, it must be done at once. He crossed the pavement rapidly, opened the gate and skirted up the short drive keeping in the shadow of the bushes.

That he was proposing to break into somebody else's house disturbed him not at all. His position, even if he was discovered, was a far stronger one than the owners who would have to explain the presence of a dead or wounded man on his premises. But he had no intention of being discovered. Amongst other attributes possessed by Jim Maitland was an almost catlike gift for silent moving at night, and he proposed to utilise it to the full.

He glided up the steps like a dark shadow, only to find as he had expected that the door was locked. Yale latch-key: no hope there. Then keeping close to the walls he made a circuit of the house. There was a basement and with any luck he hoped to find a window open, or at any rate one he could force easily. There was just sufficient light for him to see without having to strike matches, and suddenly he gave a little exclamation. There, straight in front of him, was a broken pane of glass. He reached down, unfastened the bolt, and a moment later he was inside.

The darkness now was far more intense, and after taking two or three cautious steps forward he struck a match. It was a risk, but the window by which he had entered was at the back of the house, so the light could not be seen from the road. He held it above his head, and as he peered round a puzzled frown came over his face. The shortcomings of modern servants he had been told about, but the filth of the room called for some further explanation than that.

The dust was thick on the table and on the floor: clearly the place had not been touched for months. And when he opened the door and continued his exploration he found it was the same everywhere. Kitchen, scullery, and larder were all in like condition: the basement evidently was not used. Where, then, did they do the cooking?

A flight of stairs led to the next floor, and he went up them noiselessly. Luckily the door at the top was not locked. He opened it, and at once became aware of a strong odour of stale tobacco smoke. Directly facing him a faint light filtered in through the fan-light over the front door: he was in the hall.

He stood motionless, listening intently: the house was absolutely silent.

The smokers, whoever they had been, were there no longer. Then, step by step, he felt his way forward. And the first thing that struck him was that the condition of the basement was certainly not duplicated on this floor. His feet almost sank into the carpet, so rich was the pile, and a match carefully screened by his hand showed him that the whole place was furnished *de luxe*.

He found the staircase, and began to ascend on a carpet as thick as that in the hall. The second storey was his goal, and if he realised that every step he took now materially increased his danger his pulse beat no quicker. Every third or fourth stair he paused and listened: still the same deathly silence.

The smell of stale smoke seemed to be growing stronger the higher he mounted, till it reached a maximum on the first landing. His eyes were growing accustomed to it now, and in the very faint light that filtered in from a window at the end of the passage, he saw an open door just beside him. He stepped through it, and realised that he had found the origin of the smell of smoke.

Here the darkness was absolute, and after a moment's hesitation he struck another match. And by its feeble glimmer he solved one, at any rate, of his problems. A single glance showed him what he had stumbled into, and the mystery of the dirty basement was explained.

The place was a private gambling den, and as soon as he realised the fact, he realised also that much of the need for caution was gone. The house was empty: he would not be disturbed until the two men returned, if they returned at all. He shut the door and switched on the light.

Heavy black curtains covered the windows, and the room which ran the whole depth of the house was sumptuously furnished. At one end stood a cold buffet, with the remains of many plates of sandwiches on the table. Empty champagne bottles galore littered the floor behind it: the spread was in keeping with the furniture. In the centre of the room was a roulette board: on each side of it all the usual paraphernalia for baccarat and *chemin de fer* lay scattered on two tables.

No servants kept, he reflected: provisions ordered in from a caterer. And in his satisfaction at having settled one point, for a while he forgot that there was a second far more important one to be enquired into. Moreover, that time was getting on.

He could move more freely now, and having switched off he went boldly up to the next landing. If he had been right about the light in the window just before the shot, the room would be one facing the road. That narrowed the choice to two, and for a while he hesitated, wondering which to try first. Both doors were shut: it was a toss up. Finally he took a chance, and as luck would have it he was right.

A big roll-top desk stood in the centre of the room, which was furnished like an office. Two or three leather chairs: a few books of reference in which *Who's Who* and *Burkes* figured prominently: some sporting prints on the walls, and a big safe in one corner comprised the rest of the stuff. Except for a pair of legs that stuck out beyond the desk. . . .

He had turned on the light as he entered, and before examining the body he crossed to the window and drew the curtains closer together. Then he returned to the desk and stared down at the man lying on the floor. His face was in shadow but a glance was sufficient to show that he was dead. He was in evening clothes, and in the centre of his white shirt was a dark-red stain. One arm was thrown up as if to ward off the shot: the other, with fist clenched, lay outstretched along the carpet. He had been plugged through the heart.

There was no stain on the carpet, which proved that the bullet was still inside him. And in that curiously-detached mood which is experienced by some men when the circumstances are dangerous or unusual Jim found himself commenting mentally on what a very fortunate fact it was for the murderers, if they intended, as he assumed they did, to put the body elsewhere. The bleeding had ceased, and even the most bovine policeman would smell a rat if there was a wound in a dead man's back and no blood on the ground underneath it.

He was far too accustomed to battle, murder, and sudden death to feel particularly upset about the matter. What had happened seemed fairly clear. There had been some row below, and the three of them had come up to the office to settle it. The dead man had lost his temper, hit the *dago* and the *dago* had shot him. So much seemed obvious. The point was—what was his next move?

In certain countries the answer would have been one word—nothing. But in England things were different. It was perfectly true that if he now walked out of the house as he had walked in, no one would be any the wiser. But he felt a strange disinclination to let the matter drop. A telephone was on the desk, and for a while he stared at it. Should he ring up the police? And then it struck him he didn't even know the name of the house. It was absurd to state that he was in an unknown house with a dead man on the floor beside him. Almost equally absurd to ask the Exchange where he was. To find out he would have to go down and look outside the gates. Even then it might only be a number, and as he was also ignorant of the name of the road, he would be no better off.

At the same time it seemed equally fatuous to remain where he was. If the two men returned he knew that one of them, at least, had a gun which he did not scruple to use. And if there was one thing more than any other that he disliked, it was a balance debit in the matter of firearms. If they did not return it would be daylight in less than an hour, and he might be seen leaving the house, which would prove awkward.

Suddenly it struck him that as yet he had not examined the dead man's face. The eyes were wide open and staring: the teeth were set in a snarl: the expression, in fact, was just what he would have expected in a man killed instantaneously in the middle of a quarrel. And so it was not that that caused him some few seconds later to rise to his feet with a look of incredulous amazement on his face. The thing was impossible; frankly impossible. And yet there was no mistaking the likeness of the murdered man to the girl he had been talking to that evening.

Jim Maitland had none of the popular disbelief in coincidence. He had met so many amazing ones in his life that he took them as a matter of course. So that it was not so much the strangeness of the affair that worried him, but how this new development affected his course of action. If this was Judy Draycott's brother—and in view of the likeness he felt but little doubt on the fact—the whole thing became very much more personal. He liked what little he had seen of her immensely, and here he was confronted with the dead body of her twin brother, knowing full well that the murderer was a *dago* whose Christian name was Ernesto.

His course of action was obvious. Ring up the Exchange: explain briefly what had occurred, and ask them to tell the police to come round. With the clues he could give them it should prove a very easy matter to lay hands on the man who had done it. Moreover he realised that if he did not take that course of action, and it should ever transpire that he had been mixed up in it the girl would never forgive him. And yet he hesitated. Twice did his hand go out to pick up the receiver: twice did he refrain.

It was certainly not due to any desire to shield the murderer. Even if the dead man had been a bit of a waster that was no excuse for a *dago* plugging him. His hesitation came from a very different cause. The instant the police came into the matter he automatically went out. And he was not sure he wanted to go out. The coincidence of the thing, and the strangeness of the whole episode had intrigued his curiosity.

When talking to the girl he had poured cold water on her tale about buried treasure, but now he found himself wondering. Was it possible that this was not a mere gambling quarrel, but something bigger? After all, no one would come home after a long absence abroad and spend his first night playing *chemin de fer* without even letting his people know he had returned. And clearly the girl had no idea that her brother was back.

A liner had berthed that morning: the dead man then had been in London well over twelve hours. Surely he would under normal circumstances have got in touch with his relatives.

Jim realised that the reasoning was thin, but it afforded him just sufficient excuse not to do his plain duty and use the telephone. Which was negative, not positive: to decide what you are not going to do is easier than deciding what you are.

If his supposition was right: if this youngster had been talking out of his turn with regard to some genuine proposition in South America one thing was vitally important. He must have a closer look at the two men who had been responsible for the murder. The girl would be coming into it, and he could help her far more by spotting the enemy unknown to them than by handing one of them over to the police. And it was as he arrived at this satisfactory, if somewhat unmoral, conclusion that he suddenly straightened up with every nerve taut. From outside had come the unmistakable sound of a door opening. . . .

He looked into the passage, and realised he was a sitting target for a man with a gun: the only hope was to tackle him as he came in. And in one bound he was beside the door, pressed against the wall.

A board creaked close by, and Jim waited tensely. Then there stepped into the room a strange figure. It was that of a small man hardly more than five feet high, clad in a silk dressing-gown. His head, covered with a skullcap, moved quickly from side to side like that of a bird: his hands were stretched out gropingly in front of him. And suddenly Jim understood: the man was blind.

"Monty: is that you?"

The voice was querulous, and high pitched—almost like a woman's, and a feeling of repugnance almost akin to nausea gripped Jim Maitland. He felt an overwhelming temptation to seize this little monstrosity by the throat and throttle him, and in the days that were to come he often recalled the fact. What a lot of trouble would have been saved if he had yielded to the impulse.

"Monty: where are you?"

It was almost a hiss, and the blind man's head gradually moved slower and slower until at length it became stationary with the sightless eyes staring at Jim. With that strange sixth sense given to those who cannot see he had located the stranger in the room. With a feeling of unreality Jim stared at him: the whole thing seemed like a dream. There was something so hideously abnormal about the little man apart altogether from his blindness. The hands were huge but beautifully made: the shoulders had that great depth and width which showed strength far above the average. But the incongruous thing was the look of almost devilish malignity on the face, instead of the gentle peacefulness generally seen on the features of the blind.

Suddenly the man spoke again in a voice barely above a whisper.

"Who are you, and what do you want?"

197

Jim thought quickly. Should he say he was a policeman, and demand details of the crime? If he did he would have to carry the bluff through; an impossible thing if the others returned. And evidently the blind man was expecting them back, or at any rate someone called Monty. Better not: he would find out more if he kept silent. There would be no difficulty in eluding this little devil if it became necessary, or, should the worst come to the worst, in knocking him out. And then came the thing he had not expected. There was a click, and the room was in darkness.

For a moment he did not realise the significance of the move: then low breathing close beside him put him wise. The absence of light made no difference to his adversary, but it made all the difference to him. He stepped quickly backwards, and the other man chuckled gently. A hand touched his shirt front, and the chuckle was repeated.

"Evening clothes," came a whisper. "You foolish fellow."

Again Jim backed, but all the time he knew the other was following him. And suddenly there came to him a feeling he had experienced so rarely in his life that he refused to acknowledge it—fear. He had an almost irresistible desire to blunder about wildly: to hit out with all his force into the black, impenetrable wall around him. There was something abnormal about this squat, misshapen form which he knew was close beside him—invisible and yet so real.

He forced his nerves into control, and listened intently. Was that the sound of breathing behind his left shoulder? He swung his fist round, and cursed under his breath as he hit the wall. And once again came that odious chuckle from somewhere in the centre of the room.

A new idea came to him which steadied his nerves at once. With the room lit up he would have had the greatest compunction in hitting a blind man: it would have offended his sense of fair play. But now in the darkness things were different. The advantage was quite definitely on the side of his adversary. Superior strength was a legitimate weapon to use provided the other conditions were on an equality. He would lay the little swine out, gather what further information he could, and then clear out. And even as he arrived at this conclusion he heard the gentle click of a drawer shutting: the blind man was by the desk.

He took a step forward, and promptly blundered into a chair. Where the devil was he: he didn't remember any chair in that part of the room at all. He had lost his bearings completely: he did not even know in which direction the door lay. Or the switch. And with the thought of the switch he gave a sudden, short laugh. Assuredly the flesh pots of London had atrophied his brain. He had actually forgotten that in his pocket was a box of perfectly good matches. He fumbled in his coat, and it was then that, too late, he realised the folly of having laughed. It all happened with incredible swiftness. He had hardly felt that hands were touching him behind before they were on his shoulders. Then came a heave, and the legs of the blind man were gripping him by the waist, whilst two arms were flung round his neck. And in the pitch blackness the fight began.

From the beginning it was a foregone conclusion, but the only feeling he was conscious of was one of rage at having been such a fool. Immensely powerful though he was, he knew at once that as far as strength in the arms was concerned the blind man was his match. Moreover he was fighting under the most disadvantageous conditions possible. To dislodge even a comparative weakling from such a position is no easy matter: to get rid of an abnormal monstrosity was an impossibility. And he knew it.

With every ounce of strength he possessed put forward he tried to release the iron grip round his neck: then he went for the legs. And for the third time the chuckle was repeated. He blundered round the room till he bumped into a wall: then with his back towards it he crashed his burden against it time after time. If only he could wind the little brute there would still be a chance. But beyond a grunt of rage at each bump it was useless: the grip merely tightened round his throat.

He was weakening, and the knowledge drove him wild. He began staggering haphazard about the room, whilst the roaring in his ears increased. Once he hit the desk and nearly fell, only recovering himself with a vast effort. But it was his last kick: there was a limit to what even he could stand. His lungs were bursting: the veins on his forehead were standing out like whipcord. Hazily he realised that the room had suddenly been flooded with light, and that two men were standing by the door. Then with a crash he pitched forward on his face and knew no more. . . .

He awoke to find himself in a small, bare room. The walls were whitewashed: the furniture non-existent save for the very hard apology for a bed on which he was lying. The door had a singularly solid look: the window was barred. And for a while he stared round trying to pull himself together.

Gradually recollection returned. The blind dwarf: the dead man: the gambling den. And now where the devil was he? He sat up: his shoes had been removed. And into his still bemused brain came a sudden light. He was in the cell of a police station.

In his mouth was a foul taste, the significance of which he realised only too well. Once, in his extreme youth, he had been shanghaied out east, and the after-taste of a drug can never be mistaken for anything else. After he had been throttled into insensibility, dope of sorts had been forced down his throat: so much was obvious.

He glanced at the window: the sun was streaming in. Then he looked for his watch only to find it had been taken away.

"Awake, are you? What we might describe as some blind—what?"

The man's tone was good-humoured and Jim staggered to his feet.

"Then the description would be wrong, sergeant," he said shortly. "Doped, my boy: drugged. At my age, too, by the Lord Harry! For the love of Pete, give me some water. I've got a mouth like a volcano in eruption."

The sergeant shouted an order, and then looked at Jim curiously.

"Drugged, were you? Are you sure?"

"Am I sure? Of course I'm sure."

He took a long gulp of water from the glass that a constable had brought.

"If you'd got a head like hell with the lid off, and a mouth like a refuse heap, you'd be sure."

"I'm not denying," said the sergeant, "that I had some suspicions of it myself. At the same time nothing seemed to have been taken from you. We have"—he consulted a piece of paper he took out of his pocket—"a gold watch, a gold and platinum cigarette-case, and twenty-six pounds, five shillings, and four pence in cash. Now, sir, you say you were drugged. Who by, and where?"

"I can't tell you the name of the gentleman," said Jim grimly, "though I propose to find it out at the earliest possible moment. Nor can I tell you the exact locality. The nearest I can get to that is that it was somewhere in Hampstead."

"Hampstead!" ejaculated the sergeant. "Hampstead!"

"Why not?" said Jim irritably.

"Well, you know where you are now, don't you?"

"Not an earthly. How the devil should I?"

"You are in Streatham, sir. You were found on Streatham Common by the policeman on duty at seven o'clock this morning."

"What is the time now?" demanded Jim.

"Just after half-past three. You've been insensible for nearly eight hours."

For a time Jim stared at the officer without replying. His brain was beginning to work again normally and it was evident that he must do some pretty quick thinking. What had happened was, up to a point, clear. Having drugged him, they had put him in a car and dropped him as far as possible from the house where the thing had taken place. The two men he had seen just before he finally lost consciousness must have done it. But the immediate point to be decided was the important one. Should he tell the sergeant the whole story or should he not?

Reduced to the baldest terms the story sounded a bit thin. In a house—name unknown, situated in a road—name also unknown, somewhere in Hampstead he had found a dead man. He had then been attacked by a blind dwarf and doped. If he told it and stuck to it the police would be forced to investigate it which would mean pub-licity. And he did not want publicity. He was very angry, and his defi-nite intention was to deal with the matter himself. At the same time he realised that he was now in England, and that if he said nothing about the murder he was—if the facts came out—bringing himself quite definitely within the scope of the law as being an accessory to the crime. What, then, was to be done? The sergeant was beginning to look suspicious at his silence, and something had to be said. He decided to compromise.

"Do you people know of a private gambling den in Hampstead?" he asked.

"We certainly shouldn't know it here, sir, and I can't tell you what information they have up there. Whereabouts in Hampstead?"

"I don't know," said Jim. "I could probably identify the road, but with regard to the house I'm not so sure."

"Then it was the first time you'd been there?"

"It was."

"But if you don't know the house or the road how did you get in?"

"I was taken there by a man I met," said Jim. "He was a stranger to me, but he seemed a decent sort of fellow."

"Surely you know his name, sir?"

"Sorry, sergeant: I'm afraid I don't. I like a gamble, and he assured me this place was run on the straight. It wasn't: and that's all there is to it. I started throwing my weight about, and got my liquor doped for my pains."

"You'd know this man again if you saw him?"

"If I saw him—certainly," agreed Jim. "And you can take it from me I propose to look for him."

The sergeant shook his head disapprovingly.

"Well, sir, all I can say is that it serves you right. A gentleman of your age ought to know better than to run your head into a fool trap like that."

"Exactly, sergeant," said Jim mildly.

"I'll get on the 'phone to Hampstead and find out if they know anything, but unless you can be a bit more explicit it looks pretty hopeless."

"Would you at the same time, sergeant, get on to 3B Half Moon Street—Grosvenor 3X21—and tell my man Brooke to bring my clothes here at once. I don't want to drive through London in this rig. By the way," he added with a grin, "am I going to be charged with being drunk and disorderly or anything?"

"We'll let you off this time," said the other. "But if you take my advice you'll steer clear of that sort of thing in future."

The worthy officer departed closing the door, and Jim sat down on the bed. Save for a stiff neck, and a splitting headache he felt none the worse for the performance. At the small cost of appearing a fool in the sergeant's eyes he had accounted for his condition, and now he was left as a free agent to carry things on in his own way.

To say that he was angry would be to express it mildly. Jim Maitland was furious. That he should have been outed in Hampstead of all places, got the better of, fooled completely, made him wild. But since he never made the mistake of belittling an adversary he admitted to himself that no matter where it was, the blind man, given the tactical advantage he had possessed last night, would always do him in. Therefore he must never be allowed to obtain such a position again.

It was the question of the other two that worried him. It was possible but not probable that he might recognise their voices if he heard them again, but that was all. Outside it had been too dark to see their faces: inside he had been too far gone to notice anything except that two men were there. They might not even have been the same. But the annoying fact remained that two of the opponents knew him by sight, whereas he did not know them. Which started him at a grave disadvantage.

His property had been returned to him and he lit a cigarette. Percy would be able to tell him the name of the road, and he felt fairly confident that he could spot the house again. But even if he did, was it going to do any good? Was there anything further to be found out there? It would please him immensely to slog the blind man good and hearty, but it would not advance things much if he did. That they had left the body there was most improbable: if not, what had they done with it?

He opened the door, and hailed the sergeant.

"Got an evening paper there by any chance?" he cried.

An *Evening News* was forthcoming, and he scanned the headlines. There was no mention of the discovery of any dead body. To question the man was obviously absurd, so he returned it with a word of thanks.

"Hampstead knows nothing about any gambling den, sir," remarked the officer. "They'd be glad of any information you can give them. And your man is coming along at once with your clothes."

Jim returned to his cell and lit another cigarette. A faint smile flickered round his lips as he pictured Brooke's face on finding him in his present position. Then he grew serious again: now that he had definitely committed himself by his story to the sergeant he began to doubt whether he had been wise. After all, the probability of there being anything further in it than a mere gambling quarrel was small. And if that was all, he had played straight into the murderer's hands. It was impossible for him to alter his story now.

"Your clothes, sir."

He looked up: Brooke, a suitcase in his hand, was standing stiffly in the doorway with an expression worthy of an early Christian martyr.

"And this note, sir, was left by hand this morning."

He took the letter and glanced at it: the writing was unfamiliar. Inside was a half sheet of paper, on which some words were written in block capitals.

LAST NIGHT YOU DREAMED: TODAY YOU AWOKE. SHOULD YOU DREAM AGAIN YOU MAY NOT BE SO FORTUNATE.

"Who left this?" said Jim curtly.

"A messenger boy, sir. About ten o'clock this morning."

"Is there any letter in my evening coat, Brooke?"

"Only this, sir."

It was an invitation to a public dinner addressed to him at Half Moon Street, which he had slipped into his pocket meaning to send

203

a reply from his club. So that was how they had traced him. Assuredly the dice were loaded pretty heavily in their favour. They knew him by sight: they knew his name: they knew his address. But his face was quite impassive as he continued dressing. The bigger the odds, the better the sport. Moreover, the other side had committed, had they but known it, the one irreparable error. For a threat to Jim Maitland was even as a strawberry ice is to a greedy child.

Chapter 3

After a further admonition from the sergeant to be careful of the company he kept in future they parted on excellent terms. The necessity for a long drink and a strong drink was urgent: unfortunately a misguided legislation decreed that such a thing could not be at that hour. So sending Brooke on in the taxi he went for the most important thing—a shave.

The effects of the drug had very nearly worn off, and the need for formulating some plan of campaign was evident. And the first thing to do was to put himself in the enemy's position. Their assumption, it seemed to him, would be that he would most certainly tell the police. It would be the obvious thing that ninety-nine men out of a hundred would do in similar circumstances. In fact he would have done it himself but for the extraordinary coincidence of his previous conversation with the girl—a conversation about which they could know nothing. Taking that as a basis—what next? They would anticipate a visit of inspection from the police very shortly after he recovered consciousness. They could not know that he was blissfully ignorant even of the name of the road.

The strong probability therefore was that by now all traces of their occupation of the house would have disappeared. They had no time to lose: even the roulette and *baccarat* tables would involve them in unpleasant notoriety if discovered by the authorities. The point would have to be confirmed, of course, but it seemed to him that that was the obvious starting-point from which to begin. And if so, the problem became a simple one to propound, but a difficult one to solve. How was he to get in touch with them again?

The crude and stupid threat had presumably been written on the assumption that he would not receive it until after he had communicated with the police, and led them, apparently, to a mare's nest. They hoped that it would catch him in a mood of irritation and annoyance at having not only been made a fool of himself, but also for having made a fool of the police. And it was not hard to imagine what the police would have said if he had taken them to an empty and harmless house, on the plea that it was a gambling den where a man had been murdered. In fact with some men the threat might have fulfilled its object, and made them drop the whole thing. That he was not in that category was neither here nor there. Was it a sound move to let them think that he was?

He told the barber to give him a couple of hot towels, and under their soothing influence he followed up that line of thought. They would soon find out that he had not told the police: what would they deduce from that? Surely it would be confirmatory evidence that he was only too anxious to let the matter drop altogether. They might think he was a business man unwilling to be mixed up in any scandal. And the more he sized up the situation, the better it seemed to him to give them that impression.

The only point against it was that if he left them alone, they would certainly do the same to him. The last thing they wanted was to be interfered with. Between them they would have to account for a murder, and even if they succeeded in bringing home the actual deed to the man called Ernesto, they would all be guilty of complicity. So what chance was there of getting any further with it, unless he carried the war into the enemy's country?

A big point, certainly—almost a vital one. To let the matter really drop was unthinkable, but what was he to do? At the moment he was at a hopeless disadvantage. If only, while apparently letting things go by the board, he could get hold of some pieces of evidence which would give him a clue as to their whereabouts. If only, unknown to them, he could start all square knowing them even as they knew him. He was under no delusions: it would be sheer luck if he did it. But Jim Maitland was a believer in luck, and it was a hopeful portent that as he entered his club the clock showed half-past five. No longer did the law interfere with the consumption of alcohol.

The first person he ran into was Percy, who looked at him in some surprise.

"By Jove! dear old lad," he burbled, "you look a bit under the weather—what! The right eye resembles a poached egg: the general bearing hardly of that martial order which is the hallmark of our family."

"Dry up," said Jim. "It's the result of that devastating performance of yours. Look here, young Percy, what is the name of the road in which that house is? Where you drove me last night."

"Haven't an earthly, old fruit. I mean, who could be expected to know the name of a road in Hampstead?"

"But you've often been there, you blithering ass."

"I absolutely agree, dear heart. Absolutely. Times and again, and then some. I could find my way there in the dark with my eyes shut, but I couldn't tell you the name of the bally road to save my life."

Jim regarded him dispassionately.

"Your claim to continual existence grows more microscopic daily," he remarked at length. "However, it is you who will suffer. At eleven o'clock tonight you will call for me here in your car. You will then drive me to the scene of your ridiculous entertainment last night. After that you can go and play by yourself."

"But, my dear man," spluttered Percy, "what the deuce do you want me to do that for? None of the birds will be there this evening."

"A fact for which one can but give pious thanks to high heaven," said Jim, lighting a cigarette.

"Then why do you want me to drive you there?" persisted his cousin.

"So that I may mark it in my mind as a spot to avoid in the future," said Jim.

"Cut it out, old lad," cried Percy. "Joking apart, what is the blinking game?"

Jim Maitland stared at him thoughtfully. And after a while an idea, engendered perhaps by his conversation with Judy Draycott, began to take root in his mind. Here in the shape of his cousin was a test case. What lay behind that vacuous exterior? Supposing things did begin to move, how would Percy behave in a tight corner? And moved by a sudden impulse he signed to him to come closer.

"I am about to order you a drink, young feller," he said, "and while you put your nose in it I am going to tell you a little story. But before I begin I want your word of honour that what I say to you goes no further without my permission."

"You have it," said Percy quietly.

"After I left you last night, whilst strolling along to get the foul smell of those kippers out of my nostrils, I heard a revolver shot. It came from a house I was passing. Impelled by my usual curiosity I broke into the house, which I found to be a gambling den. Amongst other odds and ends I found a murdered man lying about: he'd been shot through the heart. Shortly afterwards I was doped, and I've spent today in Streatham police station."

"Go to blazes," laughed his cousin. "If that's your idea of a leg pull it is pretty poor, laddie."

"It happens to be the truth, Percy," said Jim gravely. "Now listen to me."

Without embroidery he told his cousin the whole story, omitting only one point—his strong suspicion that the murdered man was Judy Draycott's brother. That and all the implications that might follow with it, was not at the moment a thing he wanted to pass on to anyone. And by the time he had finished Percy's eyes were nearly goggling out of his head.

"But how perfectly priceless," he spluttered ecstatically. "Of course, old lad, you can count me in. Your idea is to go and have another look at the house tonight. Do a bit of amateur detective work. And, by Jove! that reminds me. There is a gambling place up in those parts: I've heard of it myself. Bloke in the club here told me about it—Teddy d'Acres."

He hailed a passing waiter.

"Is Lord d'Acres in the club?" he demanded.

"His lordship is playing cards, sir," said the man.

"I'll get hold of him, Jim," cried Percy, getting up.

"Not a word, don't forget," said the older man. "Just get the details of the place: nothing more."

"You leave it to me, laddie."

He rushed off to return in a couple of minutes with the information that Teddy was just finishing a rubber and would join them at once.

"Tell him," said Jim, "that I'm on the look out for a gamble, and want a straight place."

"It's a pity," opined his lordship, a few moments later, "that I didn't meet you last night. I was playing myself and I could have taken you along. And tonight I'm afraid I'm booked up three deep."

"What's the name of the house?" demanded Percy.

"Damned if I know, old boy," said the other. "It's a number, I think. But the road is Oakleigh Avenue."

"That's it," cried Percy, turning to Jim, "I remember now. That's where we met last night."

"As a matter of fact," went on d'Acres, "it's perhaps as well you weren't there. A poor evening. We generally carry on till three or four, but this morning we broke up about one."

Jim looked at him thoughtfully.

"Any particular reason?" he asked.

"Bloke there half screwed, who was asking for trouble. Began swearing he'd been cheated, which was all tripe. I've been to the damned place for months, and it's run absolutely square. Then he swore he'd get the police, which seemed to little Willie the moment to quit."

"Did he get the police?" asked Jim casually.

"Ask me another," said d'Acres. "I got to bed at a respectable hour for once."

"I wonder if he was the fellow I met at dinner," continued Jim, catching Percy's eye for a second. "Distinctly elevated even then, and asking everyone if they could tell him where to get a game. Big fellow and fat, with fair hair."

d'Acres shook his head.

"Not guilty. This was a slight, dark bird. Haven't an earthly what his name was, but he'd just come from South America, where according to him gambling was gambling, and not messing about with chicken food."

Not too good, reflected Jim. The evidence as far as it went at present seemed to point to nothing bigger than an ordinary gambling row as the cause of the shooting. And if so it would have been far better if he had telephoned the police from the house, for all interest would have left the situation as far as he was concerned.

"Who runs the place?" he asked.

"A syndicate, I believe. *Cagnotte* of five *per cent*—drinks and sandwiches chucked in."

He rose.

"Let me know any time you want to go," he remarked. "But give me a bit of warning, because I'm pretty full up. And if I can't manage it—you must be introduced the first time by someone who is known—I'll get old Monty to take you. He's always there: believe he's one of the syndicate, as a matter of fact. From all I hear, the old lad needs every penny of boodle he can lay his hands on."

Not a muscle of Jim's face twitched: his expression was one of polite interest.

"Monty," he murmured. "Monty who?"

"Monty Barnet," said the other. "Thought everyone knew old Monty. Well—so long: you just let me know when you feel like a flutter."

He lounged away, and Jim turned to his cousin.

"Who the devil is Monty Barnet when he's at home?"

"Good Lord! man—it can't be him your blind friend meant. He's Sir Montague Barnet, umpteenth Bart. Got a big place not far from Crowborough."

"At the moment I don't give a hoot where his place is," remarked Jim. "What sort of a man is he to look at?"

"Great big fellow with a small, dark moustache. Rather red in the face."

Jim Maitland lit a cigarette with some deliberation.

"If that is so, Percy," he said quietly, "the betting is just about five to one on your umpteenth Bart being one of the birds I want. Your description fits, and we have it from your pal d'Acres that he uses the place considerably. It may, of course, be only a very strange coincidence, but as a basis to work on I propose to start with the assumption as correct."

"But what are you going to do?" demanded Percy. "You can't go and accuse the bloke of murder."

"There are moments, little man," said Jim kindly, "when the thought that the same blood runs in our veins drives me to thoughts of suicide. Run away now, and play, and return at eleven o'clock in a dark suiting bringing an electric torch in your pocket."

He glanced at his watch: it was just on six. With luck he would have time to catch the man he wanted before he left his office. The firm of Henley Bros.—fifty pounds to ten thousand advanced on note of hand alone—kept late hours.

"And don't forget," he gave a final warning, "not a word to a soul, or I'll break your darned neck."

He penetrated the holy of holies at Messrs. Henley Bros. without difficulty. An oleaginous clerk outside informed him that such a thing would be out of the question, but on being requested to guess again and guess quickly he consented to take his name to Mr. Henley, with a result that surprised him.

"My dear Misther Maitland, thith ith a pleasure indeed."

A small, obese Jew almost concealed behind a vast cigar rose at Jim's entrance. He indicated a chair which his visitor took: he proffered an equally vast cigar which his visitor refused. Then sitting back in his chair he contemplated Jim with a watchful look.

"And what can I have the pleasure of doing for you, Misther Maitland?"

"I do not want a thousand pounds, Isaac," said Jim shortly. "Not being a millionaire I couldn't repay you. What I do want is some information."

"What sort of information?"

"Information which even if you can't give me now, you can find out for me. I don't like your trade, Isaac, as you know very well: but you may remember that day in Marseilles when I saved your somewhat worthless life."

Isaac Goldstein remembered it only too well, as the sickly pallor which spread over his face at the mere recollection of the incident testified. It was in the days before he had become Henley Bros., though his method of earning his livelihood had been the same, if on a smaller scale. And some of the inhabitants of Marseilles had suddenly decided that a thousand *per cent* was too much of a good thing. They stand not on the order of their going, do the people of that district: their habits are crude and summary. In short, but for the timely intervention of Jim Maitland who happened to be passing, Isaac Goldstein would not have been sitting in his present position smoking his fat cigar. And being well aware of the fact he had a feeling of gratitude towards this large Englishman with an eyeglass. He would even have gone as far, he told himself, as to reduce his terms for him—than which no more can be said.

"I remember it well, Misther Maitland," he said humbly. "Those sonths of dogs."

"Cut it out, Isaac. You richly deserved all you got. However, you can now do something to repay what I did. Don't turn pale: as I said before it is information, not money, I want. Now in the first place— what do you know of Sir Montague Barnet?"

The Jew stared at him shrewdly.

"I suppoth you don't mean whath written in *Whoth Who?*" he remarked.

"Correct," said Jim.

"Well, I don't know anything perthonally, but. . ."

He waved his hands deprecatingly.

"Precisely," cried Jim. "But. Get on with it, Isaac: I want my dinner. No good pretending to me that you fellows are not all hand in glove with one another."

"Well, in the course of bithineth we do hear things," admitted the other. "And a friend of mine did tell me that he had accommodated Sir Montague two or three timeth."

"As man to man, Isaac, is he in Queer Street?"

And for once the Jew did not beat about the bush.

"Yeth, Misther Maitland: he ith."

"So far, so good. What you've said merely confirms what I've already heard. Now for the next item. Do you know anything about a private gambling den in Oakleigh Avenue up in Hampstead?"

And for the fraction of a second there appeared in the moneylender's eyes a look which Jim found difficult to interpret. Almost it seemed to him there was fear in them: certainly surprise. It went as instantaneously as it appeared, but it did not escape the notice of one of the finest poker players in the world.

"Never heard of it, Misther Maitland," said the Jew.

"You're lying, Isaac," said Jim quietly. "I should have thought a man in your profession would have more control over his face. Now I realise there is no reason why you should answer me: at the same time I did you a good turn once. So once again I ask you the question. What do you know of that gambling den?"

"Why do you ask, Misther Maitland?" said the other at length.

"Why does one generally ask a question?" remarked Jim. "Because, Isaac, I want to hear your answer."

And once again the other hesitated.

"Get on with it, man," said Jim impatiently. "You've admitted now that you know about it: you can either tell me or not as you like. But I don't want to sit here all night."

"There certainly ith a houth in Oakleigh Avenue where they play," said the Jew suddenly. "But I've never been there mythelf."

"Is this man Barnet mixed up with it in any way?"

"He may be, Misther Maitland: he may be."

"And where does a blind dwarf come into the affair?"

The question shot out like a bullet from a gun, and the effect on the moneylender was remarkable. He sat up as if he had been stung by a hornet, and the hand holding his cigar trembled visibly.

"A blind dwarth, Misther Maitland," he muttered. "I don't know what you are talking about."

"Assuredly," said Jim wearily, "you are the world's most indifferent liar. If you don't know what I'm talking about, why did my question bring on an attack of blind staggers? I'm interested in that man, Isaac," he continued gently, "and I would greatly appreciate any information you can give me about him. What, for instance, is his name?"

But the Jew shook his head.

"I know nothing about any blind dwarth, Misther Maitland," he said doggedly. "As I told you I've never been to the houth, and if there ith a blind man there I don't know who it ith. I'm thorry I can't help you."

"Won't, you mean—not can't," said Jim curtly.

He rose, and ignoring the other's proffered hand, went to the door.

"So long, Isaac. I'm not sure it wouldn't have been wiser to have let you fend for yourself in Marseilles that time."

He strolled back to his club, turning the conversation over in his mind. That Isaac Goldstein knew the blind man was obvious, and he regretted now that he had ever been to see him. He had done no good by the interview, and if, as seemed more than likely, the moneylender passed on the fact that he had been to see him it would be definitely disadvantageous. The others would know that he was not going to let the matter drop.

Still the mischief could not be undone. On the spur of the moment he had fired the question at the Jew, and he could only make the best of it. One thing, however, was clear. Not only did the moneylender know the dwarf, but he also stood in fear of him. Nothing else could account for Goldstein's whole manner when speaking. And he found his curiosity with regard to the blind man growing.

Common sense told him that the Isaac Goldsteins of this world are not generally afraid of men of unimpeachable morals. And the point that arose was what niche in the social scheme the dwarf adorned. Was he merely the owner or part owner of a gambling house, or was he something bigger? If the former there was no adequate reason for Goldstein's nervousness: if the latter it seemed possible he was getting into deeper waters than he had anticipated. In which case the sooner he got further information the better. And as he turned in to his club it suddenly struck him that there was another source of obtaining it available. Clement Hargreaves dined there most evenings, and though he was as secretive as an oyster it was possible he might be persuaded to open his mouth. There were few people connected even remotely with the underworld whom Clem did not know, and the dwarf would be an easily recognisable figure.

He found him, as luck would have it, sipping a glass of sherry in the smoking-room, and tackled him forthwith.

"Are you still in your hush-hush job, Clem?" he demanded.

"I still do my poor best to safeguard righteous citizens," answered the other with a grin. "Have a drink, Jim: it's about five years since we met."

"I want you to tell me something, old man, if you will."

"And if I can."

"Ça va sans dire."

He lit a cigarette: he had decided to adopt the same line as he had done with the sergeant at Streatham.

"Last night I went to a house up Hampstead way for a bit of a gamble. Organised place, you know."

"I don't," said the other. "They spring up like mushrooms, those spots. Go on."

"And there I met a gentleman who interested me. He stood about five foot high: he possessed the chest and shoulders of a giant: he was blind. Do you know anything about him?"

Hargreaves finished his drink, and in his turn lit a cigarette.

"In what capacity did you meet him?" he enquired at length.

"I should imagine he had something to do with the place," said Jim.

"And is that the reason of your interest in him?"

"You cautious old devil," laughed Jim. "Are you asking for information, or am I?"

But there was no answering smile on the other's face.

"I know your record better than most men, Jim," he said quietly. "And I know there is no one of my acquaintance more capable of looking after himself than you are. Nevertheless, if you and the man you've described fell foul of one another last night in any way, I can only give you one piece of advice. Do not go near that house again."

"We progress," said Jim. "It is clear that you know the bird. Why this animosity against him?"

"There can't be two men answering to your description," continued Hargreaves. "And I have no hesitation in saying that he is one of the most dangerous swine out of prison at the moment. He passes under the name of Emil Dresler, and he possesses an American passport. His activities are many and varied. At one time he was mixed up in the white slave traffic, but as far as we know he has given that up now. He's a blackmailer, and a drug trafficker. He is a moneylender on a large scale. We are also practically certain that he is responsible for at least two murders."

"Splendid," said Jim mildly. "Would it be indiscreet to ask why this charming individual is out of prison?"

"The reason is simple: we can't get any proof. He's a damned sight too clever. He covers his tracks with such infernal skill that we can't bring anything home to him. He is the brain, and he leaves other people to do the job. And they in their turn pass it on to someone else, till in the end it is impossible to trace his hand in it at all. It's the old question—we know but we can't prove. If we had half a chance we'd deport him like a shot, but so far he hasn't given it to us."

"He seems a cheery lad," laughed Jim. "So you think I'd better cut him off my visiting-list?"

"I can't imagine how he ever got on it. He's a gentleman who keeps himself very much in the background. And if he is running a gambling den, you can bet your bottom dollar there's more behind it than what he makes out of the *cagnotte*. Was the place on the square?"

"Quite, as far as I could see," answered Jim. "But in view of your warning I shall not revisit it."

He turned the conversation: further questions with regard to the place might prove difficult to answer. The last hour had provided him with more information than he had dared hope for, and with a nod to Hargreaves he sauntered off towards the dining-room. On the way he picked up an evening paper. It was the latest edition, but even the Stop Press news contained no mention of the finding of any dead body.

In itself the fact proved nothing. He was more than ever convinced after Hargreaves's remarks that he would find the place closed down. The bigger the man behind it the less would he be disposed to run any risk of trouble with the police. And connection with a gambling den would be quite enough to give the authorities the chance they needed to deport Mr. Emil Dresler. So what really was the object in going there at all?

He pondered the point over the soup: he ruminated on it over the fish. And by the time the Scotch woodcock arrived he had decided—to go. Object or no object he knew that he would have no peace of mind until he had made sure for himself that the body was not there still. What he proposed to do about it he was not sure: sufficient unto the moment would be the decision thereof.

The hall-porter beckoned to him as he left the dining-room: a letter had just arrived for him. It was in a woman's handwriting—one that was unknown to him, and having ordered a brandy with his coffee in the smoking-room he opened it. And the first words that caught his eye were the signature—Judy Draycott. He opened out the sheet and began to read.

Dear Mr. Maitland,

You may remember that we met last night—or was it this morning?—at the beer and bones party. And I then inflicted on you a long and I'm afraid boring story about my brother and hidden treasure in South America. Well, this morning a development has taken place. I told you, didn't I, that Arthur had written to me to say that if anything should happen to him I would find a letter addressed to me at my bank. And though I suppose you think I'm foolish I've been down every morning to see if there was anything. This morning there was. The envelope was a mere scrawl, though I recognised his writing at once: the post mark was London. And inside was a half sheet of paper with a drawing on it and some words. The drawing looks to me like a map—there's a north point marked on it: but the extraordinary thing is that it's not all there. It's sort of like half a map. Some of the words are cut in two, or if not, they don't make sense.

However, I could explain it so much more easily to you than write it. You see apart from whether it may mean anything or not I'm so terribly worried as to whether anything has happened to him. He must have been in London yesterday, so why hasn't he been to see me? Or rung up, or something? Do you think he has had an accident? I've rung up Scotland Yard, and looked in all the papers, but I can't find out anything.

I hate to bother you, but could you possibly come round and see me tomorrow morning some time? I'd suggest this evening, but you may not get this letter in time, and anyway we've got a ghastly dinner party on. I'll stay in until lunch in hopes of your being able to manage it.

I do hope you don't think I'm a terrible nuisance, but I really am most awfully worried.

Yours sincerely,

Judy Draycott.

With a faint smile Jim Maitland folded up the letter and put it in his pocket. Then the smile faded, and he sat staring in front of him. This was an unexpected development, and one that required thought.

It confirmed—if confirmation was necessary—that the dead man was her brother, but it did not make things any easier with regard to telling her. And yet what was he to say when she asked him—as she undoubtedly would—if he thought any accident had happened? He must either tell her the whole thing, or keep it entirely dark.

For the moment he dismissed that side of the problem, and concentrated on the other. A kind of map. It was clear that there was something in this yarn about the treasure, or at any rate that her brother had *thought* there was. Had the boy then had some premonition of danger which had impelled him to send it to her bank? And why did she say like half a map?

There came back to him suddenly the big man's words the night before—"You damned fool—you've wrecked the whole thing." What whole thing? It was a queer remark to make over the murder of a man after a gambling quarrel. It might, of course, allude to the fact that it would be necessary to shut down the house: on the other hand it might not. And the more he thought of it, the more probably did it seem to him that there was something bigger in the whole affair than met the eye at first sight. Or, as he had qualified it before, that there was something which certain people *thought* was bigger. Which came to the same thing at the present moment.

He pressed out his cigarette and rose: there was one thing he could do at once which would not commit him to any particular course of action in the future. He went to the telephone and rang up Grosvenor A123. A man's voice answered and he asked to speak to Miss Draycott. She came almost at once, and her first words were—"Is that you, Arthur?"

"I'm afraid not, Miss Draycott," he said gently. "It's Maitland speaking."

He heard the little sigh of disappointment, and felt horribly guilty. Poor girl! if she only knew the truth.

"I got your note," he went on, "and I'll come round tomorrow about noon. And in the meantime I want you to be sure that that piece of paper is not lost. Is there a safe in the house?"

"No: there isn't," came her voice. "Mr. Maitland, it's most extraordinary that you should have rung up about that. Do you think it's really valuable?"

"Why do you ask?"

"Because I'm certain that while we were at dinner tonight somebody tried to burgle my room."

"Hold hard," said Jim. "Where are you speaking from? Where's the telephone? Wait a minute—don't answer. Only say yes or no to my questions. Is it in the hall?"

"Yes."

"Can you be overheard?"

"Yes."

"Then be careful. Now one more question—are you prepared to trust me implicitly?"

Came a soft laugh. "What can I say but—yes?"

"You haven't known me very long, have you?" he answered. "And what I'm going to ask you to do will entail a lot of faith in a comparative stranger. Now is there a letter-box anywhere near your house? Just say yes or no."

"Yes."

"Could you slip out and post a letter there now at once?"

"Yes: quite easily."

"Then would you put that paper in an envelope, address it to me here at the club, and post it?"

"Well, if you think..."

There was the faintest perceptible pause and her voice sounded a little doubtful.

"I do think," said Jim quietly. "His Majesty's post is the safest thing in the world, Miss Draycott. But put it in the box yourself. I will bring it round with me tomorrow, and we'll discuss the whole thing."

"All right," she said with sudden determination. "I'll do it now."

"Good!" he cried. "And one word more. Do not, if you'll take my advice, talk about it to anyone."

"I see that you do think there is something in it." There was a note of excitement in her voice.

"There may or may not be," he answered guardedly. "If there isn't it doesn't matter: if there is that paper is safer in the post than in your house. Goodnight, Miss Draycott: I'll be round about twelve tomorrow."

He rang off and left the box thoughtfully. So she seemed to think that someone had tried to burgle her room. Was that *another* coincidence? Surely it could not be. And as Jim Maitland re-entered the smoking-room he proposed a silent but hearty vote of thanks to his cousin for having taken him to the Bright Young Thing's entertainment.

CHAPTER 4

"Do you think we'll have any luck, Jim?"

"I haven't a notion, my dear fellow. I'll answer your question in half an hour."

The two men had just turned into Oakleigh Avenue. The car had been left in a garage in Hampstead, as Jim Maitland feared it might prove conspicuous if left standing in the road. Moreover he had no idea how long his visit would take. The road was as deserted as the previous night: save for an occasional taxi homeward bound with a theatre party they saw no one for the first quarter of a mile.

"I think I'll recognise the house," he said at length. "If not we'll go to where you had your party and cast back. I'll get it then for a certainty. Hullo! what's the excitement in front?"

He paused, pulling his cousin into the shadow. A car was drawn up about a hundred yards ahead and some men were standing by it. An altercation of sorts was in progress: their voices—though not the actual words—could be clearly heard. And one, at any rate, seemed very angry.

"We'll saunter on slowly, Percy. For it seems to me they must be fairly adjacent to the house we want."

"I tell you it's a damned scandal." Suddenly the sentence came distinctly. "We'll break the blasted place open. It's a club, isn't it? They've got no right to shut."

They were close now, and by the light of a street lamp, they could see what was happening. There were four men in evening clothes, and three of them were trying to pacify the fourth, and get him back into the car.

"Shut up, you fool," cried one of them, glancing over his shoulder. "The place is closed." And then in a hoarse mutter as he saw Jim and his cousin—"Police."

Still protesting angrily the fourth man allowed himself to be pushed into the car, which drove rapidly away.

"Took us for plain-clothes men," said Jim with a laugh. "And that answers one of our questions. Evidently no gambling tonight. And it also marks down the house."

He inspected it carefully and after a while he nodded.

"Yes: this is the spot. There's the tree I stood behind last night. But they're all so confoundedly alike, these houses up here. Now, Percy, my boy, the fun begins—or let's hope so."

"I suppose you're right, laddie," said his cousin gloomily. "Personally it's not my idea of laughter and games. The bally place gives me the willies."

Jim laughed.

"Cheer up," he cried. "It's much livelier inside."

He took a swift glance up and down the road: then he opened the gate and stepped into the drive. And then for a moment he paused with his eyes fixed on a patch of ground on which the street lamp shone.

"See that," he said quietly. "That deepish track. There has been a heavy vehicle in here today. Probably a *pantechnicon*. The birds have flown all right, or I'm a Dutchman."

"You're quick, Jim," said his cousin. "I'd never have noticed that."

"Because your eyes aren't trained," answered the other. "You see, but you don't observe. Come on—there's no good standing here. Though I'm afraid we're going to have our trouble for nothing."

He led the way swiftly to the back of the house. The window was open, just as he had left it, and without further ado he swung himself into the room.

"Not a sound," he whispered, as his cousin joined him. "Keep your torch handy."

Carefully screening his own from the window behind him, he switched it on. And for the second time he stood very still with his eyes fixed on the ground.

"Do you see that?" he breathed. "I wonder what it means. It's odd—very odd."

The dust still lay thick on the floor, and as he turned his torch from side to side his cousin began to grasp what he was driving at. Across the centre of the room were the imprints of very visible footmarks which went from the window towards the door. In one of them Jim Maitland placed his foot: it fitted exactly. They were his tracks of the previous night. But they were not the only ones. Sometimes crossing one another, but for most of the way as clear and distinct as those made by Jim were other footsteps. And it was at these that he was intently peering.

The foot was small—like a woman's, and the distance between each step was short—so short, in fact, that the tracks might have been made by a child. That they were all the work of one person was obvious, but beyond that Percy's brain failed to advance. Some small girl presumably had been running round the room, and he failed to see why the matter should interest his cousin.

"What do you make of it, Percy?" came in a whisper from Jim.

"Looks as if a girls' school had been having a dancing lesson, old lad. Let's push on: this room gives me the hump."

"You fat-headed blighter. Do you mean to say you can't read those marks? Look at that set of tracks."

Jim focussed his torch on one of them.

"Which way was the person going who made those?"

"From the window to the door," answered his cousin.

"Good boy. And now those?"

"From the door to the window."

"Getting quite bright. Now take the last lot."

"They are from the window to the door."

"Right again. Now think it out. Two lines from the window to the door, and only one from the door to the window. And all the same person."

Percy's brain wrestled with the problem manfully.

"Whoever did it must have been ga-ga," he said at length. "I mean, fancy running about this place for fun."

"And how did the person run? Where did he start from—the door or the window?"

Once again Percy's brain creaked.

"Window to door," he muttered. "Door to window: window to door."

"Not quite right, Percy—but near enough. So where is he now?"

And suddenly the full significance of it sank in.

"Good Lord!" he cried. "He must be in the house."

"Precisely," said Jim. "Therefore don't shout, and keep your wits about you. For it was no small girl who made those tracks. Now—follow me."

They passed up the stairs into the hall. Percy close on his cousin's heels. What had seemed perfectly priceless in the club was not turning out quite such good value as he had expected. From outside came the sound of a passing car: then the same deathly silence settled on the house again.

"Jim," he whispered.

There was no answer, and putting out his hand he encountered air. His cousin was not there.

"Jim." The whisper was louder, and the next instant a hand gripped his arm, so unexpectedly that he almost cried out.

"Shut up, you young idiot. I thought you were behind me. I've been up to the first landing."

"How jolly," remarked Percy. "Are you going up again?"

"To the second floor," whispered Jim. "Had a look at the roulette room: everything dismantled, as I expected."

He was creeping up the stairs as he spoke, and at the top of the flight he paused.

"Do you hear anything?" he breathed in the other's ear.

But Percy could hear nothing save the thumping of his own heart, and was only conscious of a strong desire to flee. If this was the normal manner of a burglar's life he proposed to stick to bigamy in the crime line.

"Perhaps I was mistaken," whispered Jim. "Come on."

They crept up the next flight, and again Jim stopped.

"I'm going to switch on my torch," he muttered. "If we're caught— we're caught."

But the passage was empty, and he flung open the door of the room where the body had been. Then like a flash he stepped back: opening doors can be a dangerous occupation. But nothing happened, and after a while he entered.

The room was as he had left it, save that there was no trace of the dead man. None of the furniture had been moved: papers still littered the top of the desk.

"Stay by the door, Percy," he said quietly. "No—not in the centre, old lad: stand to one side. And keep your ears skinned for any sound."

He flashed his torch over the papers on the desk, but beyond a few bills and receipts there was nothing of any interest. They were made out to Mr. M. Johnson, which might have been genuine or might not: anyway, they did not advance things.

He knelt down on the floor where the body had been, and after a while his attention was attracted by a small piece of paper that was lying just under the bottom of the desk. It was so placed that had he not been on his hands and knees he would never have noticed it, the desk would have hidden it. He picked it up and examined it: then he whistled softly to himself.

It was clearly one corner of a larger piece of paper. It had been torn off violently; the distortion of the paper was obvious. Moreover it was discoloured as if it had been held tightly between a finger and thumb which were warm. Was it possible, he reflected, that this scrap had been in the dead man's hand, and had fallen under the desk when he himself fell?

He held it up to the light and studied it carefully. The two letters WE had been written in indelible pencil, and were presumably part of a longer word. But the main point of interest lay not so much in what it might mean—with such a small clue that was bound to be a closed book to them for the time—but in the fact of its presence at all. Because it seemed to Jim that that scrap of paper justified his line of action. There was something more to it than a mere gambling row, and it was going to be his job to find out what. He put it carefully in his pocket-book, and straightened up. And he was on the point of telling his cousin that they would hook it when he heard the unmistakable sound of a board creaking in the passage outside. He signalled to Percy to stand still: then he waited motionless, his torch focussed on the floor. He knew that in a moment or two he would see again that misshapen figure, and in spite of the element of surprise being absent a queer little thrill ran through him. There came another creak, and the dwarf was standing in the room.

He saw Percy give an uncontrollable start: then for a while the three of them stood without movement. Suddenly the blind man switched on the light, walked to the desk and sat down. He picked up the telephone, and Jim made a sign with his hand towards the door. If possible he wanted to get away without being discovered, and as silently as a cat he crossed the room.

"Is that Exchange? Mr. Johnson, of 95, Oakleigh Avenue, speaking. My call is for rather an unusual purpose. Would you make quite sure you have the name and address correct? Perhaps you would repeat it. Yes: that's quite right. Well, would you make a special note in case a call comes through for him, that a Mr. Jim Maitland is with me at the moment? Yes: Jim Maitland. Thank you so much. I regret having to trouble you."

He put down the receiver and lay back in his chair with a smile, while Jim Maitland stood in the centre of the room staring fascinated at him. As far as he knew he had not made a sound, and yet the little devil had spotted him.

"Good evening, Mr. Maitland." His voice was suave. "Won't you introduce your friend? You can, of course, if you prefer it go away. At the same time, having taken all the trouble you have, a little chat might clear the air."

"How long have you known I was here?" asked Jim curiously.

"Ever since you arrived," replied the other. "You are the most silent mover, Mr. Maitland, that I have ever met, and I congratulate you on it. But I have certain advantages, as you know. I trust your little experience last night has done you no harm."

Jim Maitland lit a cigarette, and pulling up a chair, sat down. The situation was a novel one for him. Not for many years had he found himself similarly placed. On several occasions he had been in tight corners, where only quick shooting and his great strength had saved him. But that had been physical: this was mental. And not since he could remember, did he recall having been up against one man who so definitely threatened him with an inferiority complex.

"Quite right," continued the blind man. "Make yourself comfortable. And your friend too. By the way, you still have not introduced us."

"It would be a little awkward for you if he happened to be connected with the police," remarked Jim.

"A little," agreed the other. "But I happen to know he is not. The police do not as a general rule own Bentleys or belong to the Dorchester club."

"True, Mr. Dresler—very true."

"Did that rat Goldstein tell you my name?" snapped the dwarf.

"Your information with regard to my movements seems fairly complete," remarked Jim. "It is refreshing to find something you don't know. However, for your benefit it was not Goldstein. He disowned all knowledge of you, though I fear he did not do it very well. No, Mr. Dresler, it appears that you are quite a well-known character in the criminal world."

"You flatter me," said the other. "At the same time your use of the word criminal is hardly polite."

"And I was just wondering," continued Jim, "what would be the result if I used your telephone, not for the exchange, but for the police station."

The blind man waved a deprecating hand.

"I admit, Mr. Maitland, that such a course is possible. Though I should hate to think that you would do anything so crude. What, incidentally, would you tell them?"

"The truth," said Jim briefly. "As seen by me last night."

"As I said, such a course is possible," repeated the other. "Nevertheless, there are one or two small points that strike me. In the first place what are you both doing in this house, and how did you get in?"

"You know quite well how I got in."

"My dear sir, of course. But the police would want to know. And to the official eye it looks very like house-breaking. A serious offence, Mr. Maitland. Then there is a further point. Why not tell the police at Streatham this afternoon whatever story you are proposing to tell them now?"

"Agreed," said Jim. "They would probably be very angry with me. But, Mr. Dresler, they would, I think, be even more angry with you."

"I doubt it. After all, your conduct to the official eye has been most reprehensible. You arrived here last night, having broken into the house, in a condition of disgusting drunkenness. So violent did you become that I was on the point of summoning assistance when mercifully you fell asleep. And two friends of mine very kindly laid you out to cool somewhere."

"Do you deny that a man was shot in this room last night?"

"My dear Mr. Maitland—what an absurd delusion. You must have been more drunk even than I thought. It is perfectly true that a man was knocked down. But—shot! Why, where is the body? What has become of it? And if that is the accusation you have to bring—the gravest of all, murder—it was doubly reprehensible of you not to tell the police at once."

In spite of himself Jim laughed.

"You damned little scoundrel," he said. "Where is this conversation leading to?"

"That, my friend, remains to be seen," answered Dresler. "To be quite truthful, Mr. Maitland, I had to assume that you would pass on your strange delusion to the police as soon as you recovered. I therefore made my plans accordingly. When, however, I found that you had said nothing I revised my estimate of your character. I had you shadowed from the time you left the police station, and it soon became clear that you were going to play a lone hand. Your conversation with Goldstein confirmed the fact."

"So he passed it on, did he?" said Jim.

"At once," replied the other. "Now I like people who play lone hands. They belong by unquestioned right to the fellowship of one. Shall we play on the same side, or not? Shall we join forces, or shall we fight?"

"The proposition requires thought," said Jim, with a warning glimpse at his cousin who with his mouth open and his eyes almost falling out of his head had been following the conversation in silence.

"What advantage is it to you," he continued, "if we amalgamate?"

"I will be candid," said the blind man. "From enquiries I have made about you today I have learned several things. You are, I gather, one of those men who like adventure for adventure's sake. You are further an almost legendary figure as far as a scrap is concerned. Last night I managed to control your drunken frenzy, but I am not under any delusions that I should be able to do it a second time. And, while I think of it, may I apologise for that absurd note you received. It was sent when I had no idea as to the manner of man you were."

Jim laughed again.

"I accept your apology," he said gravely.

"Very well, then," continued the other. "It is clear to me that you and I are going to see more of one another in the future. Your presence tonight proves that you are of—shall we say—a curious disposition. And, in brief, I would sooner have you on my side than against me. What do you say?"

"Your side in what?" asked Jim mildly. "Forgive my denseness, but you speak in riddles."

"Is that so, Mr. Maitland?" said the other leaning forward. "Just how much do you know?"

"It would seem," remarked Jim, "that there are one or two things on which you are not omniscient. However, I still await an answer to a very simple question. Your side in what? Running a gambling den?"

The blind man sat silent, motionless: almost it seemed as if he was trying by some form of telepathy to read the other's brain. And his problem was as clear as if he had spoken aloud. Was it merely the sound of the shot that had brought Jim Maitland in the night before? Was it pure coincidence, or was there something more behind it? It was impossible for the dwarf to know of his acquaintance with Judy Draycott: at the same time men of Dresler's kidney are by nature ultra-cautious. And knowing as he did that Jim had recently returned from South America, the reason for his hesitation was obvious.

"No: not that, Mr. Maitland," he said at length. "In fact owing entirely to you our little club below has ceased, as you doubtless observed on your way up. But it is possible that in the near future we might be of great assistance to one another."

"You flatter me," said Jim.

"My strong point, if I may say so, lies more in the planning of schemes, and in their organisation, rather than in actually carrying them out. My infirmity is a great handicap. And as I say, I have great hopes that very shortly I shall be in a position to put a suggestion in front of you which will appeal enormously to a man of your temperament."

"Why this altruism, Mr. Dresler?"

"For the reason I have already stated. I would sooner have you on my side than against me. And from the estimate I have formed of your character it will be impossible to do what I would most prefer—dismiss you altogether."

"Very frank," laughed Jim. "And what is the nature of this suggestion?"

"Should you accept my proposal I will tell you in due course. I may say that it is perfectly legal."

"That must be rather a novelty for you, Mr. Dresler," said Jim rising. "Of course, you will quite understand that it is impossible for me to commit myself in any way until you are more explicit. But at the same time, should your scheme appeal to me, I shall be quite prepared to consider it on its merits."

"Excellent," remarked the dwarf. "And in view of our very amicable chat I can only regret that I took such an unnecessary precaution as to ring up the exchange. I think we understand each other perfectly."

A faint smile crossed Jim's face, which would have caused the dwarf considerable uneasiness had he been able to see it.

"Perfectly," he agreed. "I shall await your suggestion with interest."

"And in the meantime," said the other, "we may dismiss the question of the police, I take it?"

"Assuredly," answered Jim. "A meddlesome body of men. Good night, Mr. Dresler. I have greatly enjoyed our chat."

He signed to his cousin to follow him, and a few moments later they were both in the drive.

"Don't speak," he said quietly. "I don't want to run the slightest risk of him hearing your voice. You may come in very useful later, my lad."

They walked a hundred yards in silence, and then Percy exploded.

"Good Lord! man," he said, "you can't mean to join forces with that little reptile?"

"Just as much," grinned Jim, "as he means to join forces with me. A thoroughly dangerous man, Percy, but unless I'm much mistaken, we've got five to four the better of him. In fact we've done a damned good evening's work."

"He bluffed you good and hearty over the police," said the other.

"Did he? I wonder. A lot that he said was perfectly true. They'd have asked me some very awkward questions."

"Yes, but dash it all, old boy, it's a bit tough on the wretched blighter who was shot. I'd like to see somebody get it in the neck over that."

"You can take it from me, Percy, that someone is going to get it in the neck before I've done with them. There's a good deal I haven't told you as yet: I wanted confirmation before I passed it on. Tonight I've got it."

"Confirmation of what?" demanded the other.

"The fact that there was more in the whole thing than met the eye."

"You mean that last night's shooting was not a mere gambling quarrel."

"Possibly. But a better way of putting it would be that the man who was shot did not go there primarily to gamble. He went in connection with the scheme our friend suggested I should come in on."

"I wonder who the poor devil was. A pity you don't know."

"I do," remarked Jim. "And that, my lad, is where we've got five to four the better of him. He was Miss Draycott's brother."

"Rot," said the other incredulously, stopping dead in his tracks. "How on earth do you know?"

"The likeness of two peas to one another could not be greater," said Jim. "He only landed from South America yesterday—at least that is when the mail boat berthed—and what his movements were after that until he found himself in that gambling den I can't tell you. Who it was who persuaded him to go there I don't know. It may have been the *dago* who finally shot him: it may have been Barnet. The point is immaterial, anyway. What is important is that he had in his possession information which he believed to be of value. And what that little swine was trying to puzzle out tonight was whether I knew that fact or not. So finally he fenced. He alluded to a scheme, but said no word of what it was."

"Have you any idea?"

"I have a very shrewd idea. And I have a further shrewd idea, Percy, that there's going to be a lot of fun in the near future for both of us— that is, if you care to come in."

"You bet I will. I rather enjoy this sort of thing. But isn't it a bit rough on the girl, old lad—little Judy."

"I know what you mean," said Jim. "But I acted with my eyes open. Telling her won't bring him back to life, and would inevitably have brought the police in. It might have resulted in the *dago* swinging, but I doubt it. So in the fullness of time we will take the law into our own hands and shoot him. But not yet."

"Easy over the bricks," cried his cousin. "In my case the condemned man would not eat a hearty breakfast."

"We won't do it here, Percy. I think we shall be going to South America shortly, and it is easy out there."

"South America! What the devil are we going there for?"

"Sea trip with a nice breath of ozone. And in the meantime just remember two things. First we have not been to Hampstead tonight: second and by far the more important, Miss Draycott and I have never met. A still tongue, Percy, and a sharp eye, and you'll be quite a credit to the family before I've done with you."

They drew up at the door of the Dorchester, and Jim got out.

"Night night, old lad. I'll put you wise to everything before long."

CHAPTER 5

It was with real curiosity he awaited the arrival of his letters the next morning. What was this strange document the dead man had sent to his sister? Was the whole thing a mare's nest, or could it be possible that by some strange fluke he had stumbled on something genuine?

He recognised the writing at once, and sitting down in a deserted corner of the smoking-room he opened the envelope. There was a short covering note that he glanced at first, it ran:

Dear Mr. Maitland"
I enclose the map. Am expecting you about twelve.
    Yours sincerely,

       Judy Draycott."

Then he turned his attention to the enclosure. It was as she had said a map, or rather half a map. Evidently the original had been cut in two, and the murdered man's idea was obvious. He had kept one half himself: the other he had sent to his sister.

The drawing was crude: the writing illiterate—just what might have been expected from an uneducated sailor.

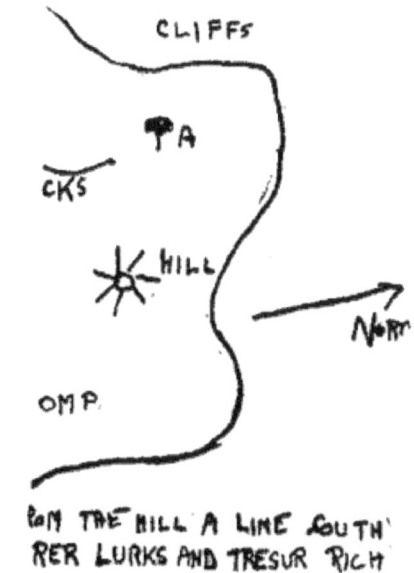

It was clearly meant to represent part of an island: the word CLIFFS proved that. HILL was clear, but what A was struck him as doubtful: possibly a tree. CKS and OMP he gave up. The writing at the bottom was no assistance either. Presumably the first word was FROM, in which case the first line read—FROM THE HILL A LINE SOUTH.

He took out his pocket-book and studied the scrap of paper he had found the night before. From its shape and the position of the letters, it must be the bottom left-hand corner on the other half, and it seemed to him that WE might be the first half of west, so that he got—FROM THE HILL A LINE SOUTH WEST. RER LURKS AND TRESUR RICH was meaningless without the context. In fact the whole thing was useless without the other half. Whether it would prove of any value even with the other half was neither here nor there: without putting the two together no one could get any further.

He leaned back in his chair and lit a cigarette: the main points of the situation were clear. Dresler and his friends had one half—save for the torn-off scrap in the corner: he had the other. But while he knew they had it, they were not in the same position over him. Which was where, as he had said to his cousin, he was five to four the better of them.

That they had intended to kill young Draycott he did not believe for a moment: if they wanted him out of the way it could be done more easily and far more safely by methods other than shooting him in a house in London. But it happened and they had had to make the best of it. They had acted promptly and cleverly: but for the amazing freak of fate which had caused him to meet Judy Draycott just before he heard the shot he would actually have been in the position in which they thought he was—an accidental passer-by who had heard a shot. And had it not been for the fact that the Dago apparently knew his reputation, much of last night's conversation would not have taken place. Dresler feared him because his name was Jim Maitland, with a reputation for looking for trouble, and not because he knew anything of this particular affair.

A new train of thought started. Did the other side know that half the map had been sent to Judy Draycott? Her remark to him over the telephone about her room having been tampered with while she was at dinner pointed to the fact that they did. It also pointed to the fact that they did not think the map was valueless. What proof they had, other than the dead man's word, he had no means of telling, but men like Emil Dresler do not embark on schemes unless they are sure of their facts. And if that was so, the point that arose was how was he to see the half that was in his? Or if possible to do more than see it, and actually get it? He would have not the slightest compunction in stealing it from them if he could—it was Judy Draycott's property, anyway: and then with the complete map in front of him he could use his own judgment as to whether the thing was worth while following up or not. But how to set about it was the problem. That it was a case for guile and not force was obvious, but beyond that main generalisation for the time being he could not get. And it was not until he had sat there for more than an hour that the glimmerings of a scheme began to dawn in his mind.

Once more he studied his half of the map intently, only it was not at the drawing he was looking but at the paper. And the question he was debating in his mind was whether it would be possible to obtain an exactly similar quality and brand in London. It was cheap white paper, with a faint watermark that looked like a crown in the corner, and it had been made in all probability in South America. Could an exact replica be found here? On that point depended the whole idea, which was this.

He could keep the Eastern and Western boundaries of the island exactly where they were: he would keep CKS and OMP in their proper positions; in fact he would alter nothing along the line of the scissor cut. But after that he would draw an entirely new map. The hill could be placed in a totally different place: also the thing marked A. And the wording at the bottom could be changed. As long as the two halves joined when put together, no suspicions would be aroused, provided always the paper matched exactly. And it thus might be possible to get a good look at the genuine other half, whilst only showing a fake of the one he held in his hand.

There were many details to fill in, but he felt instinctively he was working on the right lines. And the first thing to do was to find out about the paper. But before going out he decided to telephone Judy Draycott.

In view of the attention paid him by Dresler the preceding day, he would almost certainly be followed again. And at this stage of the proceedings it was vital to keep the other side in ignorance of the fact that they knew one another. It was too risky to go to her house: the point to be decided was where to meet her.

"Hullo! Jim, how's life?"

Percy had just come in, and Jim drew him on one side.

"I've got a job of work for you, young feller," he said. "I was just going to telephone, but you can take a message instead. It's safer. Go and see Miss Draycott, and tell her that I do not propose to come to her house this morning. Explain to her that for reasons which I'll give her later it would be most unwise for anyone to know that she and I have met, and that since I may be followed I don't want to go to Langham Square. And then, Percy, you will bring her to the ladies' entrance of the club here, and I will join you in due course."

"Right you are, old boy. Presumably no word about last night?"

"No word about anything—yet. And certainly no word about the brother, for she will almost certainly talk to you about him."

He gave his cousin some ten minutes' start before following him into the street. And then he seemed in no great hurry. He stood on the pavement, his stick swinging loosely in his hand apparently enjoying the air. But when Jim Maitland was apparently doing something the betting was largely in favour of the fact that in reality he was doing something else. And in the short space of time he remained there before hailing a taxi his lynx eye had picked up two men whose appearance he mistrusted. They were both loitering there a little too obviously.

He glanced backwards as the car turned into Pall Mall: they had got into another one and were following. And it occurred to him that there might be the possibility of a little fun. So leaning out of the window he told his driver to go slowly round St. James's Square until he told him to stop.

"Round and round," he remarked. "The air there is peculiarly beneficial."

Now, as all the world knows, there are five roads that lead out of St. James's Square, and it put the two gentlemen in a quandary. They dared not stop for fear their quarry would slip them by one of the five: at the same time when Jim had completed the circuit for the sixth time the situation became strained. And it became even more so when he stopped his machine and waved a genial hand at them.

"Good fun, isn't it?" he called out as their car went past him. "Are we going to continue, or are we not?"

The car pulled up and one of the men got out.

"Were you speaking to us?" he demanded.

"No, no, laddie. To the sparrow twittering in yonder tree."

"Cut it out," snarled the other with a quick look round, "or you'll find yourself with a thick ear, my boy."

Jim began to laugh silently.

"You rat-faced excrescence," he said pleasantly, "you couldn't give a thick ear to a baby in arms. But I warn you quite seriously that if you continue to follow me I'll give you in charge to the nearest policeman. Your face and that of your friend are enough to turn the milk sour.... Ah! would you?"

It happened quickly. Enraged by Jim's remarks the other had aimed a definite blow at his eyeglass. It failed to connect by at least a foot, but it was enough for Jim. And a moment later the man was standing helpless with his arm in a grip that felt like a steel vice.

"God! man," he muttered savagely, "you're breaking my elbow."

"No: merely bending it," Jim assured him. "And since you are in this position, I think I will call that policeman who has just entered the square.... Officer," he hailed.

But the other man was not waiting for any policeman. With a

tremendous effort he wriggled free, and ran back to his car which at once drove rapidly away. And Jim was again laughing silently when the majesty of the law approached.

"Did you call, sir?" he said.

"A mistake, officer," he remarked. "My friend who has just left me wanted to know the way somewhere, but I think he's found it."

"Drove off pretty fast, sir."

"Yes," agreed Jim. "He did seem in a bit of a hurry, didn't he? Well, good morning, officer. Sorry to have troubled you."

"Where to, sir?" asked the driver, as the policeman moved on.

"Go to Hyman's in Little Portland Street," he answered. "It's a big paper shop."

"Ugly sort of customer that, sir," went on the driver with a grin.

"A damned fool," said Jim tersely. "I've seen some pretty inefficient efforts at following in my life, but that took the cake. Keep your eyes skinned in case we see them again, but I don't think we shall."

Which proved to be correct: there was no sign of the other car when he paid off his own. Nevertheless he proposed to take no chances, and when one of the assistants asked him what he required he insisted on going to a remote corner of the shop.

"Sorry to appear mysterious," he said with a smile, "but there's a bit of a jest on. And I don't want to be spotted."

He produced the map from his pocket-book.

"I want to know," he went on, "if you can match this paper exactly. Very nearly is no good. The likeness must be so good that when the two halves are side by side anyone looking at them would say they were originally the same bit that had been cut in two."

The assistant took it in his hand and examined it minutely.

"There oughtn't to be much difficulty in that, sir," he pronounced at length. "I'll get a book of samples."

They found what was wanted almost at once—a paper that was literally identical with the original, and Jim ordered half a dozen pieces. Then he started to stroll back towards his club. So far, so good: unfortunately it was not very far. The main part of the problem had still to be solved. To draw a faked substitute was now an easy matter, but how was he going to utilise it to the best advantage when he had done so?

If it could possibly be avoided he did not want the other side to find out that he knew anything about the map. At the same time his whole scheme depended on the fact that the other half of the map should be seen. It was useless merely getting the fake to them by some method: that would give only a negative result to each side. He turned it over from every angle and at length the only possible way out occurred to him. It might fail, but he would have to take the risk. Judy Draycott was the person who must do it.

Whether Dresler and his bunch knew that half had been sent to her or not didn't matter. It would arouse no suspicions in their minds when they found she had it in her possession. And so, somehow or other, she would have to contrive to see the other piece for long enough to memorise it roughly. Presumably it would be as simple and crude as the half he had, and given a minute or so to study it in, she should be able to reproduce it sufficiently accurately for them to have something to go on.

One weak point lay in the fact that they might not let her see the other part. Another was the difficulty of her approaching them, so to speak, out of the blue. Why should she know anything about them at all? He did not even know if she and Barnet were acquaintances. Still those were minor difficulties: he was satisfied that the main idea was right. Judy Draycott was the only person who could do it, without giving things away. And if she did pull it off, and obtained a reasonable mental picture of the other half they would be in the pleasant position of having the truth, whilst the opponents possessed the map of an island, a large portion of which was completely imaginary. At which point in his reflections he turned into his club to find his cousin waiting for him with a worried look on his face.

"She's gone, Jim," he said briefly.

"Come on into the smoking-room," remarked Jim. "Now, then," he continued, after they had found two chairs, "what's this? You say she's gone. Where to?"

"Can't tell you, old lad," answered the other. "The house belongs to an ancient gorgon—Lady Somebody or other, with whom Judy is staying. Well, I blew in and asked for the girl, but the butler pushed me into the presence of the most devastating old ruin you've ever imagined. Shook me badly, laddie, I don't mind admitting."

"'Are you Mr. Maitland?' she boomed.

"I admitted the soft impeachment, and she inspected me through *lorgnettes*.

"'I confess I do not understand present-day mentality,' she went on, 'but Judy's brain must have left her temporarily. She said you were very good-looking and had a magnificent figure.'

"Well, I thought she might have put it a little differently, but the family spirit pulled me through.

"'That's where you scratch the wrong bite,' I said breezily. 'She alluded to my cousin who, I have been told, does bear a slight resemblance to me. He belongs to one of the cadet branches of our family.'"

"You blithering idiot," Jim grinned. "Get on with it."

"Apparently I'd said the wrong thing," continued Percy. "She sat there for quite a while with her mouth opening and shutting, and no noise occurred. I thought she'd slipped her uppers and was wondering what the devil to do if they zoomed into the hearth-rug, when she suddenly gave a harsh, croaking sound which turned after a while into semi-articulate speech.

"'Scratch! Wrong bite! You wretched young man—how dare you?'

"Well, I managed to pacify her: assured her it was a bit of modern slang, and at length, thank God! her breathing became normal again, and the deep magenta look left her face.

"'Now,' I said chattily, 'what about our little Judy? We both, I expect, have to do this and that before worrying the mid-day bone.'

"And little by little I extracted the account of the morning's doings. It appears Judy was giving the once over to the matutinal kipper by herself in the dining-room, when a woman called to see her. She couldn't tell me what sort of a woman as she herself does not shatter the *morale* of the house by appearing at breakfast. At any rate this woman had brought Judy a message from her brother."

"What's that?" cried Jim sitting up. "Her brother?"

"Just how I felt, old lad, when she said it," remarked Percy. "You didn't give anything away, did you?"

"My face remained completely sphinx-like," said his cousin. "To continue. The result of the message was that Judy departed with this female, leaving a message for you to the effect that your proposed party at noon would have to be off."

"Did she say where she was going?" demanded Jim.

"Apparently not. At any rate not to the old trout. And I didn't quite like to ask to see her maid."

"And she said nothing as to when she intended to return?"

"Not a word. So having bowed to the Presence I left the house."

He lit a cigarette, and gave an order to a passing waiter for the necessary.

"So bringing the grey matter to work, Jim," he continued, "one thing becomes obvious. Either you made a mistake, or it is a trap."

"Exactly," agreed his cousin. "And since I did not make a mistake…"

He left the sentence uncompleted: how would this development affect his plan? That they contemplated doing any harm to the girl he dismissed from his mind: no possible object could be served by hurting her. Their object clearly was to get possession of her half of the map, and it therefore proved that they knew she had it. It further proved that they did *not* know she had sent it to him. But how long would they remain in ignorance of that fact? How long would it be before she told him?

He frowned thoughtfully: another point had struck him. What were they going to do about the brother? The girl having been lured away by what she took to be a message from him would naturally expect to see him. Moreover, she would become very suspicious if she did not. And as they could not show her his dead body with a bullet hole through the heart it became a little difficult to see what they were going to do.

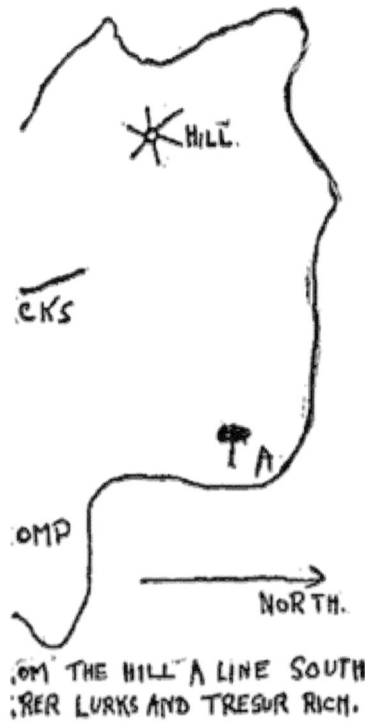

.oɱ THE HILL A LINE SOUTH
ːɤɛɽ LURKS AND TRESUR RICH.

He crossed to one of the writing-tables: the sooner he prepared the faked map the better. Things might eventuate at any moment, and he wanted to be prepared. For a while he again studied the map carefully: then he took one of the sheets of paper he had bought and picked up an indelible pencil.

"That ought to do the trick," he muttered to himself ten minutes later. He put the genuine one in an envelope, and sent it with a covering letter to his lawyer: the fake he put in his pocket-book. Then picking up an illustrated paper he threw himself into an armchair. There was nothing he could do but wait.

Just before lunch Percy returned from what he described as a cocktail date with a hen, and demanded the latest bulletin.

"That's deuced bright of you, Jim," said his cousin admiringly when he had explained his idea. "But now that Judy has actually gone to them it's going to make things a bit harder."

"You're right," agreed Jim. "We can only wait and see what happens. And since they haven't got what they wanted, something is bound to happen soon. She may tell 'em she sent the map to me: she may not. And until we know that, we're left guessing."

"They won't do her any harm, will they?"

"No," said Jim positively. "They'll guard her as the apple of their eye until they get the map And before they do that we step into the picture."

They lunched, and then began an interminable afternoon. Jim did not dare to get out of reach of the telephone: Percy refused to run any risk of missing the fun. And so, sternly dismissing from their minds the fact that Patsy Hendren had been sixty not out at the luncheon interval, they dozed.

The message came through just after five o'clock. A page roused them from their slumbers: Mr. Maitland was wanted on the telephone.

"You go, Percy," said Jim. "If it is Miss Draycott find out where she is speaking from. If it sounds at all risky do the silly-ass stunt. But if she is in London get her round to the ladies' side here, the same as we arranged for lunch."

"Right ho! laddie," cried the other. "You leave it to me."

He came back almost immediately.

"Speaking from Langham Square," he said. "She's coming at once. And, Jim, unless I'm much mistaken, there have been doings. Her voice was rather like that of an agitated hen."

"Good!" cried Jim. "The sooner we get to it the better."

"Do you want me to attend the pow-wow?" asked his cousin.

Jim nodded.

"But say nothing, at any rate at present, about her brother!"

Judy Draycott was as good as her word: she came at once. And it struck Jim as he shook hands that she was even more attractive than he had thought at first. But there was a look of tense anxiety about her that brought him back to business at once.

"What is the trouble, Miss Draycott?" he said as they sat down.

"Mr. Maitland," she answered earnestly, "there's some devilry going on. I'm just worried to death."

"I don't expect it's quite as bad as that," he said with a smile. "Young Percy and I have been having a lot of fun over your affairs too."

"What do you mean?" she said in amazement.

"You shall hear in good time, Miss Draycott," he answered. "Let's get to your doings first. All that we know is that a female of sorts called on you at breakfast this morning, bringing a message from your brother, and you went away with her."

"She had a car waiting outside," began the girl—"and I got in without hesitation. All that she had said in the house was that Arthur wanted me to come, and to bring with me the letter he had sent to my bank. That, of course, I couldn't do without coming round and getting it from you."

"Which you'd have had considerable difficulty in doing," put in Jim quietly. "Did you mention you'd sent it to me?"

"I did not. And really I can't think why I didn't—then. Because at the time I had no suspicions. I did think it a little strange that Arthur should have sent a woman as a messenger, but I was so keen to see him that I didn't bother about it much. I just dashed upstairs, told my aunt, and started off. It was a closed car, and a chauffeur in livery was driving. And after a while it began to strike me that my companion was very uncommunicative. Every question I put to her she answered in monosyllables. So at last I tackled her point blank."

"'Is there anything the matter with my brother?'"

"She tried to evade it for a bit, but I insisted. And to my horror I found he had been involved in a bad accident."

The eyes of the two men met, but the girl was too intent on her story to notice.

"He was in a nursing home, and his eyes had been affected. It was a motor accident, and his face had been badly cut about."

"'Who is looking after him?' I demanded."

"A Doctor Phillips, she told me, was in charge. I asked where the house was. It was on the outskirts of Mayfield in Sussex.'"

"'But what on earth was he doing motoring down there,' I cried in amazement, and she shrugged her shoulders. She had no idea why he had been there: all she could tell me was that the crash had occurred about half a mile from their lodge gates and some workmen had carried him in.

"We arrived at half-past eleven, and when I saw the house my heart sank. It was the most gloomy, depressing spot: anything less suited for a nursing home it would be impossible to imagine. And I think it was as we drove up to the door that suspicion first started in my mind. I caught the woman's eyes fixed on me, and though she immediately glanced away, there had been a funny look in them. And it was then, as I say, that I first began to wonder if all was well.

"The door was opened by a manservant, and as I stepped into the hall suspicion increased. The place was furnished after a fashion but there was a sort of musty smell about everything that you only get in a house that has been empty for some time. However, I said nothing, of course, and a moment later a man came down the stairs.

"'This is Doctor Phillips,' said my companion.

"He shook hands, and led the way into one of the downstair rooms.

"'An unfortunate homecoming for your brother!' he said. 'Our matron has told you, I suppose?'

"'She tells me that Arthur has been badly damaged in a motor accident,' I answered. 'And I should like to see him at once, please.'

"He held up his hand.

"'One moment, my dear young lady,' he remarked—and if there's one thing that drives me to drink it's being called that—'we must have a little chat first. To begin with, your brother is in a very excitable condition just at present—a condition which in view of the injuries to his face and eyes. . .'

"'Eyes!' I cried.

"'Didn't the matron mention that? Yes: I am sorry to say his eyes are involved. It is for that reason that we are keeping him in a dark room. But do not alarm yourself. With care and good nursing I feel confident he will retain his sight unimpaired, if—and this is very important, if—we can keep him calm. Any mental excitement is the worst possible thing for him. Now I naturally have no idea what he is talking about, but the very first moment he began to speak coherently last night he kept asking about some letter he had sent you. He must have it: he must have it at once. In vain for me to point out to the dear fellow that he couldn't read it: that it was safe with you until he had recovered. It was no use. And so I entrusted the matron when she came to get you to be sure and mention it, so that you could bring it. It will pacify him enormously. You have it, of course?'

"And it was then, Mr. Maitland, I did some pretty rapid thinking. I was as convinced as I could be that there was something wrong. I knew that house was no nursing home, and I felt pretty well certain the man talking to me was no doctor. He was too suave and oily. Besides, genuine doctors don't allude to a complete stranger as a dear fellow. But what was I to do? I hadn't got it, and what was going to be the result when I told him so? I was convinced that it was the letter this man was after, and if he found out it wasn't there, he would pull more of his medical jargon out, tell me it would excite Arthur too much if I saw him without the letter, and insist that I should go back to London and get it before I could visit him. And I was determined that that should not happen. I was determined that by hook or by crook I would talk to Arthur before I left the house.

"It's taken a long time to describe what I felt: it actually took a second to decide.

"'Naturally,' I said. 'I'll hand it to him myself.'"

"Well done," remarked Jim quietly. "How did he take that?"

"Not very enthusiastically," she answered, "which merely increased my determination to see Arthur. But short of snatching my bag from me by force he could do nothing, and at last with a very bad grace he rose and left the room mumbling about seeing if Arthur was ready.

"The instant the door was shut I flew to it and listened: he and the woman were having an argument in the hall outside. I couldn't hear what they were saying, but it sounded distinctly acrimonious. And again my suspicions increased: I *knew* the show was crooked.

"The man came back in about five minutes, accompanied this time by the woman. He seemed to have recovered himself, and his smile was more oily than ever.

"'This way, my dear young lady,' he said. 'And you will remember, won't you, that you may find your brother a little strange. The vocal chords—everything has been affected.'

"We went upstairs, and my heart began to thump. Mr. Maitland— the house was empty. No sign of movement: no nurses: nothing at all that you always see in a nursing home. And he seemed to sense what I was feeling.

"'Very slack time just now,' he remarked. 'Which will enable me to give all the more care to your brother.'

"He flung open a door: the room beyond it was pitch dark.

"'Ah! my dear fellow,' he cried, 'good news for you—joyous news. Your charming sister has arrived.'

"I could see a man dimly in the darkness, whose face was covered with bandages.

"'Arthur, old boy,' I cried, 'what rotten luck.'

"'Hullo! Judy,' he said querulously, 'how are you? Have you got the letter? Have you brought it?'"

The girl paused for a moment, and neither man spoke.

"How I didn't scream," she went on, "I don't know. I'd suspected a lot before, but never this. The man with the bandaged face wasn't Arthur at all. It was just conceivable that the voice might have passed muster, but Arthur has never called me Judy."

"'Humour him, please,' whispered the doctor to me, and then turned to the man. 'All right, my dear chap, your sister has got it. She's just going to give it to you.'

"'The letter. I want the letter, Judy.'

"My hands were trembling so much I could hardly open my bag. But one thing I realised—whatever happened I mustn't let them suspect that I knew it wasn't Arthur.

"'Here it is, old boy,' I said, and then turned horror-struck to the doctor. 'Good heavens! Doctor Phillips,' I whispered. 'I forgot to put it in.'

"And just for a moment I thought he was going to murder me.

"'Forgot to put it in?' he snarled, and I saw the woman nudge him in the ribs. He pulled himself together.

"'Forgive me, Miss Draycott,' he said, 'but a shock like that to my patient is very dangerous indeed.'

"He turned back into the room.

"'Now, old fellow,' he said, 'your sister, naughty girl, was so over-joyed at the prospect of seeing you again that she forgot to bring the letter. Don't let it worry you: don't let it excite you: I know she will go back to London at once and get it. Won't you, Miss Draycott?'

"'Of course I will, Arthur,' I said. 'I'm sorry I was so stupid.'

"'Yes, get it, Judy, at once,' he answered. 'It's important.'

"And then the so-called doctor hustled me out of the room and down the stairs.

"'A most unfortunate mistake, Miss Draycott,' he said gravely. 'Had I suspected for a moment that you had not got the letter in your possession, nothing would have induced me to allow you to see your brother. We can only hope that the effect will not be serious. But I must beg of you to remedy it as quickly as possible. The car is there. Fly back to London in it, and return as soon as you can. As you see for yourself, he is in a most excitable condition, and he must not be worried in any way.'

"So I started off alone in the car, and then came a real stroke of luck. The car broke down, and so I got rid of the chauffeur and came back by train. And now, Mr. Maitland, what I want to know is why they are keeping a man who isn't my brother in a nursing home that isn't a nursing home? And where is Arthur? And what does it all mean?"

For a moment or two Jim hesitated. He realised that the time had come when she would have to be told the truth about her brother, and he did not exactly relish the prospect.

"It's pretty clear, I'm afraid, Miss Draycott," he said gravely. "You realise, don't you, that your brother sent you half the map and kept the other half himself? He did it for safety, in case anything happened to him. And I'm very sorry to have to tell you that something has happened to him."

"You mean he's hurt?" she whispered.

"Worse than that, I fear. Miss Draycott, it's going to be the devil of a shock; but your brother is dead."

She gave a little cry, and the two men rose and stood with their backs to her staring out of the window. And for a space there was silence in the room.

"Do you mean he was killed?" she asked at length, and Jim nodded.

"How do you know all this, Mr. Maitland?" she continued steadily.

Briefly he told her the whole story. And when he had finished her eyes were bright and defiant: of the tears he had expected there was no trace.

"Just tell me what you want me to do," she said, and Jim looked at her approvingly.

"Great girl," he cried. "I knew you'd feel that way. Now this is how the land lies. The gang we are up against have in their possession

242

the half of the map that your brother carried. What they are trying to get is the half he sent to your bank, and which you sent on to me. Evidently he must have told them what he had done: hence this elaborate scheme of today. And I think you can be extremely thankful, Miss Draycott, that you kept your head when you realised the man with his face bandaged was an impostor. Our opponents are not people who stick at trifles. Had you given yourself away then, I am more than doubtful if you'd be here now. However, that is by the way. You bluffed it through magnificently, and I want you to carry on the good work."

"I'll do anything you say," she said, and once again he gave her a quick look of admiration.

"You may remember I rather laughed at you when you first told me the hidden treasure story," he went on. "I'm not laughing now at all: I honestly believe there may be something in it. And if that is so you see where we stand: we must get their half. That is where you come in—if you feel like it."

"Of course I feel like it!" she cried.

"You know," he said doubtfully, "I must make it clear that if you care to you can go to the police and tell them what has happened to you."

"What will occur if I do?"

"I should think you would find that the birds have flown," said Jim. "And in addition to that we shall have given ourselves away to the other side. It will be a case of stalemate: each side will have one half of the map. And I want. . . ."

He broke off and lit a cigarette.

"So do I, Mr. Maitland. Let's wash out the police."

Jim grinned.

"Good for you. We'll wash out the police as you say. Now I don't suppose for a moment we'll be able to get their half, but with a little diplomacy we might get a good look at it. Perhaps even..."

He paused, and a sudden gleam of ecstatic joy came into his eyes, a gleam that many men had seen to their cost.

"However, that's my palaver," he continued. "Now I'm gambling on one fact. They expect you to go back there tonight—and you're going. Percy is going to drive you down. And you will take with you—this."

He gave her the faked map, and she stared at it.

"But this is different to what I sent you," she said.

243

"Very different," he agreed. "I drew it myself. The genuine one is at my lawyers. But that one joins on to the other half. Which brings me up to the point I'm gambling on. They are not the sort of gentlemen who leave anything to chance, and I'm banking on them having their half there, to make sure on the spot, that you haven't sold them a pup."

"So that I can get a look at it," she cried. "I see: I'll do it."

"Supposing it doesn't come off we are no worse off than we were before. Leave them that: it's useless to them. They've got an island inspired by my second pink gin. We shall just have to try something else."

"But where do you come in, old lad?" demanded Percy.

"I don't," said Jim happily. "I shall remain outside the nursing home. Unless—I see an opportunity of entering with advantage. In which case I shall enter, and you, Miss Draycott, will exit. So should you hear two short blasts on Percy's klaxon, hop it like blazes in the car and leave me to my own sweet devices."

CHAPTER 6

"You're a damned bungler, Waterlow. The girl isn't an imbecile, and this place looks as much like a nursing home as it does like a night club."

A big man in a light overcoat was the speaker. His face was coarse and dissipated, and suddenly he pulled a flask from his pocket and took a deep drink. The only other occupant of the room shrugged his shoulders.

"You were in such an infernal hurry," he said, "that this was the best I could do in the time."

"But why were you such a fool as to let her go upstairs," snarled the first speaker. "Her twin; and you imagine she won't spot it."

"Dry up, Barnet," answered the other angrily. "I'm getting fed to the back teeth with you. She said she'd got the thing on her, and I believed her. Even if I hadn't, what do you suggest I should have done? Snatched her bag out of her hand to make sure. Of course she wouldn't have suspected anything then, would she? Might have gone further and slogged her over the head with a poker: that's what the doctor in charge of a home generally does to his female visitors."

Sir Montague Barnet took another drink.

"All right: all right," he grunted. "Don't go off the deep end about it. I know you did all you could. That slab of misery who fetched her should have seen that she brought it."

He glanced at his watch.

"She should be here by now if she's coming," he said uneasily. "It's past nine."

"I'll go and see that everything is ready," remarked the other. "And don't smoke that cigar, and have the smell all over the house."

"Perhaps you're right," grunted Barnet, replacing it in his case. "Though once we've got it," he continued with a leer, "she can suspect what she likes."

"Can she?" said the other significantly. "I'm not so sure about that."

He went out of the room, leaving the baronet cursing under his breath. And it was not until the flask had been requisitioned for the third time that he took from his pocket the counterpart of the map sent to Judy Draycott, and put it on the table in front of him.

For the twentieth time he studied it only to give it up as a bad job. Where the deuce was A? Until they could get that point fixed it was useless. And he was just replacing it in his pocket when he swung round in his chair with a strangled cry. For the blind man had entered noiselessly and had touched him on the shoulder.

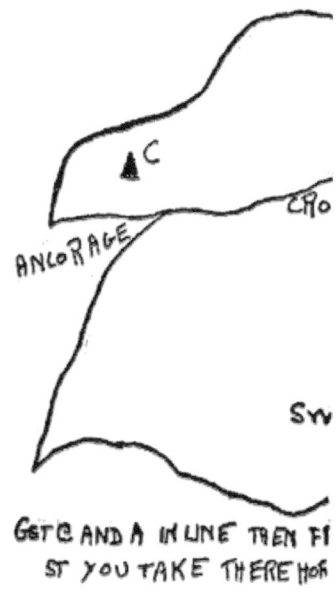

"Good God! Emil, I wish you wouldn't do that," he snarled. "I'd no idea you were here. My nerves are all to hell."

"Judging by the aroma," sneered the dwarf, "you have been doing your best to raise them from the lower regions."

"It isn't you who have had the strain," cried Barnet angrily. "So less of your damned sarcasm, if you don't mind."

Then he pulled himself together.

"Look here, Emil," he said, "there's no good in our quarrelling. What are we going to do supposing this girl goes to the police? I don't see how she can avoid finding out that it isn't her brother."

"Provided she brings the paper—what matter? She has no idea her brother is dead, and even if the worst should happen here, all Waterlow has to do is to say that he made a mistake. It is not a criminal offence to think a man is a girl's brother when he isn't."

"No, but it might prove deuced awkward. Anyway, Emil, if anything should come out: if Maitland, for instance, should give trouble, you and I know it was Ernesto who did it."

An evil smile flickered over the blind man's lips.

"Do we?" he murmured. "My dear Monty, I heard a shot, and you tell me it was Ernesto who fired it. And with my sad affliction I have to take your word."

"You little devil," said the other hoarsely, the veins standing out on his forehead. "You know as well as I do that it was the *dago*."

"As I say, I take your word for it, my dear fellow. In a court of law, however, I fear that that would not count for much. No, no, Monty—please remember that. You understand, of course, that I merely mention it to ensure you taking every precaution against being found out. Of course I am the one person who could not have done it, so it does not really matter to me. I am merely being altruistic."

For a moment it looked as if the baronet was going to strike him. His big hairy fist was raised above his head, and murder was in his eyes. Then with a great effort he pulled himself together, and his hand fell to his side.

"You were present, anyway," he said sullenly.

"True. But a poor blind man is so helpless," said the dwarf gently. "And he had to take precautions to safeguard himself in this harsh world. And that's why I just mentioned it to you, Monty. You would hardly believe it, but there have been times in my life when scoundrels—men I have befriended, men I have been working with—have tried to double-cross me. So just remember won't you? I have no idea who fired the shot, which might prove awkward for you."

For a moment or two the other stared at him, fascinated: then his teeth bared in an evil snarl. But his voice was normal when he answered.

"I'll remember," he said.

"Good! And now it might be well to see if our friend is *compos mentis* again. His snores were reverberating through the house a little while ago."

"I'll go and get him," said Barnet, and the dwarf was left alone. For a while he stood motionless: then feeling his way with an uncanny delicacy of touch he proceeded to explore his unfamiliar surroundings. At length he seemed satisfied, and drawing up a chair, he sat down as the door opened and Barnet came in with an odd-looking character behind him. He was a short, thick-set man dressed in a blue reefer suit, and as he stood there fingering his cap, and staring a little fearfully at the dwarf, it required no Sherlock Holmes to deduce his profession. He was a sailor, and quite clearly he had been celebrating his time ashore in a manner not unusual with his class. He rolled slightly as he took a few steps forward into the room, and as he came under the light a large jagged scar down one side of his face showed up vividly.

"Good evening, Mr. Robinson," said the dwarf gently. "I trust you have recovered from your—er—jag."

"I'm all right, guv'nor, thank you," said the man still twisting his cap nervously in his hand. "I understand as 'ow you wants to ask me summat."

"That is so," agreed Dresler. "I was making some enquiries the other day for a seaman with an intimate knowledge of the east coast of South America, and your name was given to me."

"I reckons I knows every port from Georgetown to the Horn," said the sailor.

"Excellent. I understood that most of your time had been spent in the coasting trade. Now have you, in the course of your wanderings, ever struck a place called by the English, Lone Tree Island?"

"Lone Tree Island! South of Santos. You bet your life I know it, guv'nor; know it well enough to give it a mighty wide berth."

"Most interesting. And may I ask why you would give it a wide berth?"

"Because, guv'nor, the man who doesn't don't have no second chance. There be things on that island wot no man may see—and live.

It be accursed."

"Really: really. You grow more and more interesting, Mr. Robinson. And may I ask how you know this? Is it merely what you've heard from other people, or have you been there yourself to see?"

"Both, guv'nor. I've been there myself: we lay up once for wellnigh a week to the south of the island with a damaged shaft. And I've 'eard from other men too: things wot they've seen. Gawd! I wouldn't spend the night on that island not for a 'undred quid. Straight—I wouldn't."

"What sort of things, Mr. Robinson?"

"Monstrous things, guv'nor: 'orrors. Things that was never made of 'uman parents. Aye! you may laugh, sir"—he turned to Barnet, who was smiling incredulously—"but wot I tells you is the truth. You ask any sailor who knows the coast and 'e'll tell you the same as wot I do."

"I am quite sure that what Mr. Robinson says is correct," said the dwarf. "And we're both very much obliged to him for his information."

"No trouble, gentlemen. Is there anything else I can do for you?"

"If you don't mind waiting a little longer, Mr. Robinson, I hope to be able to show you a map of it. And I should very much like your confirmation that it is the island we've been talking about. Monty, my dear fellow, our friend is probably a little thirsty after all his talking. I have no doubt there is some whiskey in the kitchen."

"Well," he continued, as the baronet returned a few moments later, "the matter becomes increasingly intriguing. 'Things that were never made of 'uman parents: 'orrors.'"

"Do you believe the man, Emil?"

The dwarf shrugged his shoulders.

"Those who go down to the sea in ships are proverbially spinners of tall yarns," he said. "There may be some substratum of truth in it, which has been exaggerated into what we've just been told. And, anyway, I have yet to find the being, whether made by human parents or not, who is proof against a high-velocity rifle."

Sir Montague Barnet started to pace to and fro.

"I wish we knew for certain if it was worth going on with it," he said.

The dwarf smiled contemptuously.

"Life would be a pretty tedious affair," he remarked, "if one always knew for certain. You know the enquiries we've made: you know our sources of information. And even if it should prove to be wrong—what is the cost? A few hundred pounds—a thousand at the most. Which sum, Monty, I am finding, do not forget."

The door was flung open and Waterlow put his head in.

"Car coming up the drive," he said. "Everything is ready."

"Listen, Waterlow," said Dresler quietly. "If it is humanly possible, we do not want the girl to suspect anything. It will save us an infinity of trouble if she doesn't. And so, as soon as she has handed it over, get it down to this room somehow. A minute will be enough for Monty to take a tracing. Then if she wants it—she can have it back."

"I get you," answered the other going into the hall and closing the door.

The car had pulled up at the door, and contrary to the usual custom the driver seemed to be trying to find out how much noise he could make with his engine. He accelerated in bursts, until Barnet swore angrily under his breath.

"He'll wake the whole damned neighbourhood—that fool of a chauffeur," he muttered.

But the chauffeur seemed quite oblivious of his unpopularity: at intervals he raced his engine with an ear-splitting roar—so ear-splitting in fact, that even the blind man's supersensitive hearing was of no avail for any other sound, such as a man might make as he cautiously opened the window a little more and a little more each time. And with the final, full-throttled burst Jim Maitland, who had been reconnoitring the house for the last twenty minutes, found himself with only a blind barring his way to the room. Then silence fell, broken only by Waterlow's voice.

"Really, Miss Draycott, your chauffeur might remember that this is a nursing home."

"So sorry, Doctor Phillips," came her apologetic reply, "but the car is not going very well. That's why I'm so late. How is Arthur?"

A look of relief spread over Barnet's face: evidently she suspected nothing.

"Better now, Miss Draycott. He was very worried and upset this morning after you left but I succeeded in pacifying him. I trust there is no mistake this time, and that you have brought it with you."

"Of course, Doctor, and I shall never forgive myself for being so stupid this morning."

Their voices died away as they mounted the stairs, and the dwarf smiled easily.

"It marches well, Monty," he said. "She would appear to be eating out of our hands. Now get that sailor in."

The blind stirred slightly as the door opened—a natural phenomenon in the faint night breeze—and Jim Maitland's keen eye took in every detail of the room. From above him came the sound of the girl's voice: evidently the interview with the supposed brother had commenced.

He drew back a little as Barnet returned, accompanied by Robinson, though he could still see the whole of the room.

"Now, Mr. Robinson," said the blind man, "we shan't detain you much longer. May I take it that you would recognise a map of the island if you saw one?"

"Well, I ain't much of a hand at maps, gentlemen, but I'll 'ave a shot at it."

"No one can do more," said Dresler genially as the door opened and Waterlow came in.

"Here it is," he said hurriedly. "And get a move on. She knows all about everything, and wants to see the other half."

GET C NO A IN LINE THEN FROM THE HILL A LINE SOUTH ST YOU TAKE, THERE HORRER LURKS AND TRESUR RICH.

"Does she suspect about her brother?" asked the dwarf.

"Doesn't seem to. She's chatting away quite cheerfully."

"Right. Go back. And the sooner you get her away the better. Now, Mr. Robinson," he continued, as the door closed, "perhaps you would have a look."

"We've got it, Emil," said Barnet triumphantly. "The two pieces fit perfectly. Now is that the island?"

He laid them on the table, and the sailor bent over them.

"Aye," he said, "that looks like the place. Anchorage: that's right. That's where we lay: south of the island. And all the eastern part is swampy. Crocks—why, that river is full of them, and other things too."

"Good!" cried Barnet, rapidly adjusting a piece of tracing paper. "Emil—we've got the map complete except for that torn-off bit in the bottom left-hand corner."

"Does it give the location of what we want?" asked the dwarf.

"Yes," said the other laconically. "I'll work that out later."

For a moment Jim hesitated. To knock out Barnet and snatch the map would be easy—a matter of seconds. But he would certainly be recognised, and—what was even more important—Judy Draycott was not yet safely away. He craned forward trying to see, but the baronet's back was between him and the map. And he was on the point of chancing it when once more Waterlow came in.

"She's getting suspicious," he said hurriedly. "Wants to see the other bit. Is it safe?"

"Yes," answered the dwarf quietly. "It's the lesser of two evils. Well, Mr. Robinson, I don't think we need detain you any more. Goodnight, and I'm much obliged to you. Waterlow—show him out. Now, Monty," he went on as the door closed, "have you got that tracing finished?"

"Just finished now," said the other.

"And you have a copy of our half? Good. Put the tracing in your pocket, and we'll have the girl in. You're another doctor, don't forget. And don't get near her: you reek of whiskey even at this range."

There was the sound of voices coming down the stairs, then Judy came in followed by Waterlow.

"Here is Miss Draycott, Professor," he announced.

"It is a pleasure to meet you, Miss Draycott," said the dwarf courteously. "May I introduce my other colleague, Doctor Arbuthnot."

Barnet bowed.

"Your brother is, I think, as well as can be expected under the circumstances," went on Dresler. "It is indeed fortunate that the accident should have taken place so close to my nursing home."

"Very fortunate indeed," said the girl, quietly. "And I am most grateful to you for all your kindness."

"My dear young lady"—the dwarf lifted a deprecating hand—"that is what we are here for. And now that you have brought him the other half of his map, his mind will be at rest."

"Is that it on the table?" she asked innocently. "What is it all about?"

She crossed over and looked at it.

"It all seems nonsense to me."

"I fear you're quite right," said the dwarf. "It *is* nonsense. But so long as he is in his present state he must be humoured."

"He keeps on talking about hidden treasure," she went on. "Where is this supposed to be?"

"I've got no idea," said the dwarf. "He tells me he got it from some sailor in South America. And I fear if the truth be known that it is like so many sailor's stories—complete imagination."

"You don't think this is a real island?" she asked.

"Frankly, Miss Draycott, I do not. And even if it is I'm afraid the chances of there being any treasure on it are remote. Other people would have heard of it long ago, and removed it."

"I suppose so," she said a little sadly. "And the poor boy does seem so keen about it too. However, I have promised him to do all I can, so I suppose I must. But it seems rather a waste of time."

"What are you doing, Miss Draycott?" cried Barnet, and Jim began to shake with silent laughter. For the girl was calmly folding up both parts of the map and putting them in her bag.

"He's just asked me to find out anything I could for him about it in London," she explained, and Jim shook still more. "When you were out of the room, Doctor Phillips. He seemed so keen that I don't like to disappoint him. So I'll just pretend."

Barnet and Waterlow were staring at her in perplexity: their dilemma was clear to the delighted witness outside the window. They both knew that the girl was lying. But they couldn't say so, without giving themselves away. And it was the dwarf who took charge of the situation.

"Quite right, Miss Draycott," he said calmly. "Do anything that will keep his mind at rest. Humour him in every way. And when shall we be seeing you again?"

"Tomorrow, I think, or perhaps the next day," she answered, rising to her feet. "Goodnight, Professor. Thank you again for all you've done for Arthur."

"It is a pleasure, my dear young lady. Goodnight."

"Well, I'm damned," said Barnet, as the door closed. "Why did you let her get away with it, Emil?"

"At times, my friend, I despair of your brain. What else was there to do?"

"But don't you see," fumed the other, "that it is proof positive that she suspects. Johnston never said that to her: she was lying."

From outside came the noise of a self-starter—a splutter, a roar—and as the car swung down the drive Waterlow re-entered.

"The fact had not escaped me," said the dwarf languidly. "Though there is a bare possibility that she herself suggested it to Johnston, and he perforce had to agree."

"That is soon settled," cried Waterlow going into the hall. "Johnston—come down here."

A man of about thirty entered mopping his face.

"Those cursed bandages are the limit on a hot night," he remarked.

"Did that girl make any remark to you about taking the map up to London with her?" said the dwarf.

"Yes. Seemed dead set on it. I didn't know what to say so I left it vague."

"Do you think she suspected you?"

"Didn't seem to. She called me Arthur and patted my hands."

"You see, Monty," said the dwarf quietly, "it was far better to let her take them. What harm can she do? What is the good of that map to anyone unless they know where the island is? And what chance has she got of finding anyone who would be able to tell her? Unless..."

He broke off, and sat brooding.

"Unless what?"

"For the moment I thought of Maitland," remarked the dwarf.

"I wish we'd done the damned fellow in that night," said Barnet savagely. "He knows every inch of South America."

"Hardly that, my dear Monty, though I admit I should feel happier if he was out of the way. And you must remember two things. One—we don't know that he knows the girl: and two—even if he does, it is very improbable that he knows where the island is. Still, I admit

Maitland is a distinct problem, and one that we may have to solve. However, that can wait. The immediate thing is to clear out of here at once. Order my car round, Johnston, and shut this place up. I fear if the lady comes here again she will have a slight shock."

Noiselessly Jim backed away from the window, and keeping on the grass he went down the drive at a steady lope. There was nothing further to be learned, and things had succeeded beyond his wildest expectations, entirely owing to the girl. He had complete faith in his ability to spot where the island was: there were many old pals of his down in Dockland who knew the coast of South America as they did the palms of their hands.

And then suddenly out of the darkness there loomed an immediate solution to the problem—to wit, Mr. Robinson stumping along the road. He could give him the information he needed, but speed was imperative since at any moment the dwarf's car might be on them. Percy was waiting for him a little way ahead, but he wanted no chance of being overtaken.

"Good evening, Mr. Robinson," he said as he came abreast.

"'Oo the 'ell are you?" was the uncompromising answer.

"Someone who is proposing to give you a fiver if you'll run," said Jim with a laugh.

A stationary red light had just come in sight in front of them.

"Run as far as that light with me, Robinson, and I'll give you a lift to London as well, in exchange for a little information," continued Jim.

"Gaw lumme! Fivers seem easy tonight."

He pounded along beside Jim, until they reached the car.

"My friend, Mr. Robinson," cried Jim, "who is coming back to Town with us. Hop in in front, my lad, and Percy, tread on the juice."

He sank down beside the girl in the back seat, and as the car gathered speed he could just see the exquisite profile so close to him.

"Well done," he said quietly. "Well done, indeed."

She made no reply; and merely stared in front of her.

"Miss Draycott! Judy! what's the matter?" he asked gently. "A penny."

She gave a little sigh that was half a sob.

"It's Arthur," she said. "I've had time to think; that's all."

And now the tears were coming unchecked.

"Killed by those brutes the very day he returned. It's wicked. I want them to be punished; I want someone hanged."

A sudden feeling of guilt assailed him: he had actually forgotten all about her brother.

"Listen, Judy," he said gravely, "while I say my little bit. I know exactly how you're feeling: it's only natural. And perhaps I was wrong in not calling in the police at once. But I happen to be one of those blokes that don't instinctively go for the police if anything happens: I suppose I've lived too much in places where there aren't any to go for. And it was the extraordinary coincidence of the whole thing that struck me, coming as it did just after I'd left you. The *dago*, your story about the treasure, everything combined to make me hesitate. And then, as you know, I was outed and it was too late. But what I'm getting at is that now I am glad I acted as I did. Honestly I believe that there is something in this yarn, and the best way of revenging your brother's death is to do those swine down."

The girl did not answer, and gradually her tears ceased. And then somehow it came about that her left hand fell off her lap and encountered Jim's right. Which, of course, was purely accidental, and may be treated as an irrelevant and extraneous detail. Almost as irrelevant in fact as three remarks which were made five minutes later.

"Percy, you blighter, this isn't Brooklands. Ease up, confound you."

And the voice was male.

"Ever so much slower, Percy dear. I'm being blown to bits."

And the voice was female.

"Thank Gawd for that, guv'nor."

And the voice was that of a man in whom some faint hope of life had been rekindled. Mr. Robinson's idea of speed did not coincide with Percy's.

It was past eleven when they drew up finally outside Jim's flat.

"But why the dickens did you want me to go slower, after telling me to tread on the juice?" demanded Percy indignantly.

"One is so much more exposed to things in the back seat, Percy dear," said the girl. "But you drove very nicely."

"Why, we've taken as long to get up as we did going down counting in the twenty minutes we waited while Jim went ahead. Rotten."

"Push inside, and don't talk so much," remarked Jim. "As an ornament to the doorstep I'd prefer a gargoyle. I expect you could do with a drink, Robinson."

"Well, sir, I don't mind if I do," agreed the sailor. "Them machines seem to make one thirsty like."

Jim smiled, and led the way. And as a hardened bachelor he noted with a certain misgiving that installing Judy in his best chair was a very pleasant occupation. Not, of course, that there would ever be anything in it: he had merely held her hand in a comforting, fraternal way. Still—a very pretty girl: very pretty indeed.

"Now, Robinson," he said when they were all settled, "I'd be glad if you'd tell me one or two things. First of all how did you get mixed up in that bunch?"

"That's easy, sir. I was lodging down in Mother Shipwells—she takes in us seafaring men chiefly—when a bloke shoves 'is 'ead round the door at dinner-time today and sings out: "Oo knows South America well?' I says I do. 'E h'asks me a few questions, and then says: 'Would you like to earn a fiver?' I says: 'Stop kidding.' 'E says: 'It's strite.' All I 'ad to do was to go and see some guys in the country that wanted h'information. That's how it 'appened, sir."

"Good," said Jim, "that's clear. Now, from what I heard this evening, you were talking about some island."

"That's right, sir. The first thing that little terror of a dwarf asked me was if I knew Lone Tree Island."

"That was before I got there," said Jim. "And you did know this island?"

"There h'ain't many men, sir, 'oove been in the coastal trade there 'oo don't," answered the sailor. "I knows it all right, as I told them guys down there. Knows it so well, as I says to 'em, that I wouldn't spend a night on it for a 'undred quid."

"But why the deuce not?" cried Percy, staring at him. "I mean, I'd spend a night in a temperance hotel for that."

"Look 'ere, sir," said the sailor to Jim. "A lot of you gentlemen—and you too, Miss—seems h'interested in Lone Tree Island. Now I'm only an h'uneducated man, and maybe you don't pay much count to what I says. But there's a man just 'ome from the West H'Indies 'olding a master's ticket 'oo knows more'n I do about the place. 'E's lodging not far from Mother Shipwells—Cap'n Blackett. . . ."

"Wait a minute," cried Jim. "Big man with a hook nose, and blue eyes, who used to have an old tramp called the *Indus*?"

"That's the man, sir. Do you know 'im?"

"Know Bill Blackett? I should think I do!"

"Well, sir, he'll tell you h'everything, better'n than I can."

Jim put his hand in his pocket.

"Here's some money, Robinson. Get in a taxi, and go and see Captain Blackett. Tell him Jim Maitland wants him, and bring him back with you tonight. And if his memory wants jogging, just say—'The Union Bar, Pernambuco!'"

"Aye, aye, sir. If 'e's there, I'll bring 'im. Evening, mum: evening, gentlemen."

They heard the front door slam, and Jim, his eyes gleaming with excitement, began pacing up and down the room.

"Bill Blackett! A damned good man. We'll get the truth from him, my children, if we can get it from anyone."

And suddenly Judy Draycott understood the reason of Percy's hero worship. Just as a hunter quivers and fidgets at the sound of hounds, so was this man at the thought of adventure. And a little ruefully she realised that in all probability he had completely forgotten that he held her hand in the car.

"A pity that I sent the other half to my lawyers," he went on. "Still, it was safer, I suppose. And we can get to the maps later, after we've heard what Bill has to say."

He came with Robinson an hour later.

"By Jove! Mr. Maitland," he said as he shook hands, "you are the only man in London who could have got me out of bed at this hour."

"Good for you, Bill," cried Jim, and introduced him to the other two. "Take that chair, and you'll find the necessary beside you. I want some information out of you."

"So I gather from Robinson," said the other gravely. "I hear you've been making enquiries about Lone Tree Island."

"That seems to be the name of the spot," agreed Jim.

"Have you got the map of it?"

"Only half: the other is at my lawyers. There it is."

Bill Blackett stared at it for some time.

"Yes—that looks to me like a rough sketch of the southern part of the island. And if it is, Mr. Maitland, or if you—and I know what you are—have any idea of paying it a visit, my advice to you is to tear that up into tiny pieces and forget it."

"But why, Captain Blackett?" cried the girl breathlessly.

"Because, Miss, there are certain things in this world which it is best to leave alone. Mr. Maitland is a match for anything on two legs, as I very well know, but neither he nor any other man is a match for what ever it is that lives on that island. It's accursed: the island is ac-cursed."

"Bill—you're pulling our legs," said Jim banteringly.

257

But there was no answering smile on the other's face.

"Was the case of the *Paquinetta* before your time?" he enquired.

"I don't seem to recall it," said Jim.

"Then if it won't bore you, I'll tell you the story."

"Fire ahead, Bill," cried Jim. "The night is yet young."

CHAPTER 7

"Lone Tree Island," began Blackett, "lies south of Santos. In size it is about five miles north to south, and a little less from east to west. The eastern side has a biggish area of swamp which is practically impassable: the western side is mostly dense tropical forest. The northern part—the map of which isn't here—has one conspicuous conical hill, and west of that hill one even more conspicuous tree standing by itself on high ground."

"That confirms the accuracy of the other part of the map," said Jim.

"The first time I heard of it," went on the other, "was in '06. I was serving then as mate in a small line with its headquarters at Buenos. One day we got sudden orders from the owners to go there, which struck me as being pretty strange, seeing that there was no question of any cargo, and tramps don't generally go on pleasure cruises. And what struck me as even stranger was our old man's manner after we'd sailed. He wasn't a chatty card at the best of times, but that trip I couldn't get a word out of him. What was more, there was something wrong with the men. So at last I took the bull by the horns one morning when he came up on the bridge.

"'What's all the trouble, sir?' I said. 'The crew are as windy as if they were a girls' school.'

"'How long have you been out here, Mr. Blackett?' he answered.

"'About a year,' I told him.

"'You may remember the *Paquinetta* left Buenos six weeks ago sudden like,' he said.

"The *Paquinetta* was another of our line.

"'I do,' I answered. 'Rather mysterious about it too. Nobody knew where she was bound for.'

"'Not only that,' he reminded me, 'but she sailed under a new captain and a specially picked crew.'

"I stared at him hard. He was right—she had, but I'd forgotten it.

"'In your year out here, Mr. Blackett, have you never heard any stories of Lone Tree Island,' he went on.

"Well, I hadn't—not at that time, and I told him so. I hadn't even heard of the island before.

"'Not surprising,' he said, 'it lies well off the beaten track.'

"'What are we going to do there?' I asked him.

"'Find out what's happened to the *Paquinetta*,' he said gravely, and went below.

"Well, Mr. Maitland, you know I'm not a nervy sort of cuss, but I give you my word that that simple remark sent a shiver right down my spine. Don't forget that in those days wireless wasn't fitted to most of the smaller tramps, and the *Paquinetta* had none. At the same time there had been no dirty weather and she was a first-class sea boat. So I told myself not to be a fool—what could have happened to her? But there was the old man with a face a yard long: there was the crew, who somehow or other had got hold of our destination, as nervous as a basketful of monkeys, and there was this mystery about the *Paquinetta*.

"Well, we sighted the island about noon on the third day out. We were steering north-east, and that high ground with the cairn of stones on top, that you can see marked on the map, hid the anchorage until we were close in shore. Then as we rounded the point we suddenly saw her right in front of us, anchored not three cables' length away. So we went hard astern and anchored ourselves."

He paused and took another drink.

"It was obvious," he continued, "at the first glance that something was very wrong. There was no sign of smoke, no sign of life on board her, and when we gave a blast on the siren there was no answer.

"'Lower away a boat,' ordered the skipper. 'I'm going on board.'

"'I'd like to come too, sir,' I said, and the old man looked relieved.

"'I reckon I'll be glad to have you,' he answered. 'There is some devilry afoot.'

"So we rowed over. The companion was down though two of the guys had come adrift, and it wobbled drunkenly as we climbed up. The deck was deserted, and the heat beat up from it as we stood there looking round. Not a sign of a soul: not a sound.

"'We'll go below, Mr. Mate,' said the old man and led the way.

"She was practically the twin of our own packet so we knew our way about. We made for the saloon. It was empty, same as everything else, and on the table were the remains of a meal. Half a cup of tea congealed and rancid, and some meat that was crawling, it was so bad.

259

"'They've been gone some time, sir,' I said, pointing to it.

"'But what manner of man is it, Mr. Mate, who leaves his ship without a soul on board. Tell me that.'

"And I couldn't. The old story of the *Marie Celeste* came to my mind, but she at any rate was found drifting at sea. This was different: the whole lot of them must be ashore. But as the skipper said it pointed to a strange man in their captain.

"'We'll try the chart-room,' said the old man, and even as he spoke there came a sudden chuckle from outside the door. And you can take it from me that we were round in a flash, each of us with a gun in our hands. It was repeated, and there was something in the sound of it that fairly froze my blood. We watched the door opening slowly, and then our revolvers fell to our sides. One of the cook's mates was standing there and it needed but one glance to see that the poor chap was as mad as a hatter.

"He looked at us foolishly, and after a while he began to mumble something.

"'Half men: half beasts. Half men: half beasts.'

"On and on he went saying it, again and again and pointing with a shaking hand through the porthole. We couldn't get anything else out of him, and at length he shambled away again.

"'What the devil does he mean, sir?' I cried. 'Half men: half beasts. Of course, he's plumb crazy.'

"'And what made him crazy, Mr. Mate: what made him crazy?'

"The captain looked at me with sombre eyes.

"'Crazy men aren't signed on, are they, Mr. Mate? And sane men don't go crazy for nothing.'

"He led the way on deck, and for a while he stood there shading his eyes with his hand and staring at the undergrowth that came down almost to the water's edge. Then he turned abruptly and went up on the bridge.

"'Get the log,' he said. 'It may tell us something.'

"So I went to the captain's cabin, and wished I hadn't. For the sight inside was terrible to see. The bunk, the walls, the table, the chairs, the floor—every part of that cabin had great patches of red spattered over it, as if someone with a vast brush had daubed it indiscriminately on anything he saw. And it was blood.

"I turned: the captain was standing beside me and his face was the colour of chalk.

"'God in Heaven!' he muttered, 'there's been butcher's work in here.'

"I went over to the table, on which some papers were lying and picked them up. They, too, were stained with blood, but the writing was still legible. And at last we realised we had some sort of clue, though not one that advanced us much. For the top was evidently part of a rough form of diary kept by the skipper, and the captain pointed to the date—April 26th.

"'18th May now, Blackett,' he said. 'Three weeks ago.'

"'Cannot understand silence of shore party,' ran the entry. 'Three days overdue and no sig——'

"It broke off abruptly in the middle of a word. Signal, perhaps or sign—it didn't matter. But the same thought was in both our minds: what grim tragedy had occurred as he laid down his pencil three weeks before? Whose was the blood that covered everything? The faint sickly reek of it still hung about, and we stumbled back into the fresh air—two badly shaken men.

"'What's it mean, sir?' I cried. 'You knew something before we got here: the crew knew something. What is it?'

"'Rumours,' he said slowly. 'There have always been strange rumours about this island, Mr. Mate. And, by heck! I'm beginning to believe that they're true.'

"He gripped my arm suddenly, and with his other hand he pointed to the shore.

"'Do you see anything moving?' he cried. 'By that tree with the purple flowers, half-way up the hill.'

"I picked out the tree, and stared at it. And after a while it shook, though everything around it was motionless in the stilling mid-day heat. I went on staring: was it my imagination or was there something at the foot of the tree that was moving? We had neither of us brought our glasses, and in the shimmering haze it was difficult to be certain. So at length we gave it up and continued our exploration though we knew from the outset it was hopeless. The ship was empty save for us two and a crazy cook. Where were the rest of the crew?"

He paused, and Jim refilled his glass. And in the silence of the room you could have heard a pin drop.

"The first thing to fix was what to do with the madman, and the skipper decided to leave him where he was for the time.

"'As I see things,' he said to me, 'he has been alone in this boat since April 26th, and it's not going to hurt him to be alone two or three days more. And we'll have trouble with our own men if we take

261

him back with us.'

"'What do you propose to do, sir?' I asked.

"'Explore that river, Mr. Blackett. We've got to try and solve this mystery somehow.'

"So we pulled back to our own ship, and I gave the necessary orders. The men were standing about in bunches talking in low voices, and it wasn't until the old man got going that they bestirred themselves. Of course they'd scented trouble—anyone with half an eye could have seen it after one glance at the *Paquinetta*—but they were not given much time to think about it. We hoisted in the small boat, lowered away the big one, and a marline spike removed any reluctance to man it. The second mate was left in charge, with strict orders to keep a sharp look out, and we started off.

"It had been hot in the creek, but once round the bend of the river out of sight of the open sea it became almost unbearable. Not a breath of wind stirred, and the air seemed to press down on one like a wet blanket. Dense tropical undergrowth hemmed us in on each side: the place reeked of malaria and yellow jack. And crocodiles. I've never seen so many in my life as there were in that river, and the grim thought came to me that they might furnish a possible solution. There would be no traces left of anyone who fell into that water. I said as much in a low voice to the skipper, and he stared at me a moment or two before replying.

"'It's a rum crocodile that can climb the bridge of a ship, Blackett,' he said.

"We rowed on. He and I were sitting side by side in the stern each with a revolver on our knees. Gradually the river narrowed till the blades of the oars were almost touching the banks and the trees met overhead. It was obvious we could not go further, so the skipper gave the order to cease rowing.

"'No good trying to land here,' he remarked. 'We'll try a shout or two. Now then, lads, all together with me.'

"We bellowed 'Ahoy' at the tops of our voices, and then listened. But save for the startled whirr of birds as they rose from the tree near by there was no result—just the same steamy silent heat. We tried again, but it was useless and there was nothing for it but to return to the ship. And it was on the way back that I became conscious of a very peculiar sensation. I mentioned it to the captain afterwards, and found that he had experienced it also, though I think the men were too busy rowing to notice it. And the sensation was one of being watched.

Something was keeping pace with us on one bank, something that I never saw, but yet was acutely aware of. It was not imagination, and the skipper agreed with me.

"Well, that ended our first endeavour to solve the mystery, and the point arose as to what to do next. So we held a council of war, and finally arrived at the conclusion that the best thing would be to steam slowly round the island hooting with the siren at frequent intervals, and looking for a place where we could land a party with safety. For the skipper flatly refused to let anyone go ashore in the wooded part, even if we could have got the men to volunteer, which I doubt.

"So we made the circuit of the island with the siren going every half-minute, and the result was *nil*. No trace of a man did we see, but the time was not wasted since we got the geography of the place in our heads. And it was clear that there was one obvious spot to land—a beach on the north of the island almost at the foot of the conical hill. But it was too late to do anything more that day, so we decided to anchor again, and wait for the next morning.

"Now the *Paquinetta* was lying inside us about two hundred yards from the shore, and a quarter of a mile from us. The night was dead still, and the moon was due to rise about three. And though I was tired when I came off watch at midnight I found I couldn't sleep. I couldn't get this amazing affair out of my head, so I lay down on my bunk and picked up a book. Full sea going, watch was being kept, and I could hear the second mate pacing up and down the bridge.

"Suddenly the footsteps ceased just above my porthole, and I heard him give an exclamation. And the next moment he was in my cabin.

"'There's something going on in the *Paquinetta*, sir,' he cried.

"I was out like a flash, and up on the bridge. Sure enough a light was moving across the deck, but it wasn't an ordinary ship's lantern. It looked more like a smoky torch, such as boys carry on Guy Fawkes's day. We watched it in silence, until it disappeared below.

"'It's that crazy fool of a cook,' I said. 'He'll probably set fire to the ship.'

"And I was on the point of rousing the skipper, when there came across the water a scream of terror so blood-curdling that I felt my hair lifting from my scalp. It was not repeated, and before I had time to decide anything, the captain joined us.

"'Did that scream come from the *Paquinetta*?' he asked.

"'Yes, sir,' I said. 'And there was a light moving on the deck... By Jove! there it is again.'

"The three of us stood there staring at it. As before it moved across the deck, but this time it disappeared over the side. And it seemed to me that it was moving in a curiously jerky fashion.

"Now the gangway was on the far side of the *Paquinetta* and the explanation of the light's movements seemed obvious. Someone had boarded her, gone below, and then left her. And while he was below something had happened to cause that ghastly scream.

"The skipper didn't hesitate, though if it had been me I'm not ashamed to confess that I think I'd have left it till dawn. He ordered a boat to be lowered and called for a couple of volunteers to go aboard the *Paquinetta*. We got 'em readily—a big Swede, and an Englishman. One of them took a crowbar, and the other a pickaxe, whilst the skipper and I carried our revolvers. Then with four lanterns we rowed across. Hit, and hit to kill, were the orders if we met anything.

"We came alongside the gangway, and the first thing we saw by the light of the lanterns was blood on the steps. There was a trail of it the whole way up, a trail right across the deck, a trail of it leading down below. And we followed the trail—the skipper leading and me bringing up the rear. It led past the saloon, and finished in the cook's quarters.

"Ye Gods! the place was a shambles. Just as we had found the captain's cabin, so was this, only now the blood was wet. And the skipper cursed savagely. Somebody or something had battered that poor crazy loon to death, but whatever it was it had disappeared. We searched the ship thoroughly: she was empty. And at last we pulled back to our own.

"And that very nearly brings me to the end. The next day we landed a party and climbed the hill. From it the whole of the island could be seen stretched out like a map at our feet. But of life there was no sign. Dense forest and swamp, and not a thing that moved, save that occasionally a flock of birds would rise from some tree, and then settle down again as if they had been disturbed by something passing below.

"I suggested to the captain that I should take a party of volunteers and try some exploration in the forest, but he absolutely refused to allow it.

"'We've only got three revolvers on board,' he pointed out, 'and very little ammunition. If the crew of the *Paquinetta* were anywhere down there they'd have heard our siren yesterday. They're dead, Mr. Mate—every man jack of them, and I'm not going to risk a similar fate for my own. You'll take command of the *Paquinetta* with an emergency crew, and as soon as you've got steam up—we sail.'

"And that is the story of the *Paquinetta*, from which you can draw your own conclusions. Every sort of theory was put forward at the time, and the one that most people accepted was that a mutiny had taken place. The landing-party which the captain had alluded to in his diary, had come on board, and having killed the skipper and the rest of the crew had gone ashore again leaving only the mad cook. Then when we arrived, fearful that the madman might say something which would give them away, they completed their work by butchering him. They dared not reply to our siren knowing what they'd done, and finally yellow jack broke out and that was the end. For the bald fact remains that from that day to this no word has been heard of any member of that crew."

"And is that your theory, Bill?" asked Jim quietly.

"No, Mr. Maitland, it isn't. Call me a superstitious sailor-man if you like but I believe the solution of the mystery is something far more horrible. And I believe it is to be found in the words of that crazy cook—'half men, half beasts.' I believe that lurking in that dense forest are beings of a certain degree of intelligence—witness the torch, which shows that they understand fire—of inner physical strength—the captain of the *Paquinetta* was a powerful man—and of incredible ferocity. I believe that the landing-party was butchered to a man, and that then, taking advantage of a dark night, these creatures had either swum or rowed out to the ship, and murdered those who remained on board. Why they left the mad cook I don't profess to say: perhaps he managed to hide himself from them. In brief, I believe that the legend of the Guardians of the Treasure is true."

"Now we're coming to it, Bill," said Jim. "Let's hear something about this treasure."

"It was to find it, Mr. Maitland, that the *Paquinetta* was fitted out. The story is that in 1600 or thereabouts one Don Silva Rodriguez, having on board his galleon a fabulous load of gold and precious stones which he had obtained in Brazil, was driven ashore on Lone Tree Island and completely wrecked. He waited and waited, spending each day on the top of the hill scanning the horizon for a sail, but never seeing one. And at length his rage and fury drove him mad. There was he with unlimited riches in his pocket so to speak, condemned to spend the rest of his life on an island where they were useless to him. And in his madness he entered into league with the devil. If the devil would send a ship, he would leave half his treasure hidden on the island where no one could find it, for the exclusive use of the devil. And the devil agreed, provided he could install his own guardians. You smile, Mr. Maitland—and told here in this room I admit the story sounds fantastic. Nevertheless, even if the origin of the yarn is incredible, I still believe that there lurks in that forest a breed of creatures that are neither man nor beast."

"That's right, sir." Robinson, who had been almost forgotten in his corner, suddenly spoke. "The captain's right. 'Orrors: 'orrors that ain't 'uman."

"So you've heard this story too, have you?" said Jim thoughtfully.

"May I ask what causes your interest in the place, Mr. Maitland?" said Blackett.

"You certainly may, Bill. And I can tell you in a few words. We have in our possession a map that purports to show the spot on the island where the treasure is buried."

"How came you by it?"

"It was given to my brother, Captain Blackett, by a sailor he befriended in Monte Video," said Judy Draycott. "And my brother has since been murdered by a gang here in England who want to get it."

The sailor whistled in astonishment.

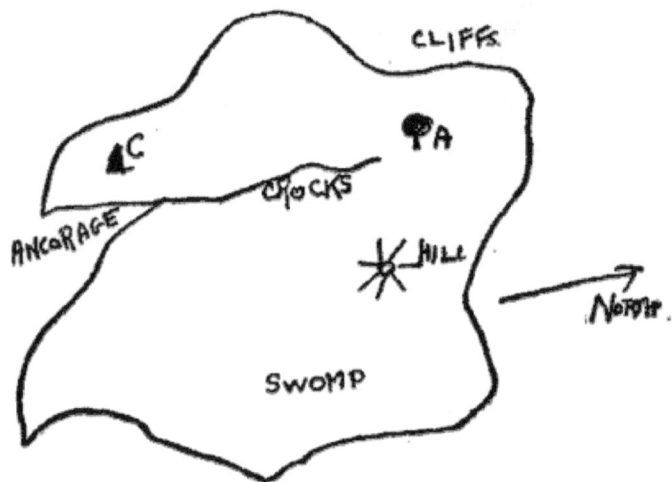

GⓄC AND A INLINE THEN FROM THE HILL A LINE SOUTH
WEST YOU TAKE THERE WARRER LURKS AND TRESUR RICH.

"That's bad luck, Miss," he said awkwardly. "I'm sorry to hear that."

"Now, Bill, the position is this," remarked Jim. "By a subterfuge we have obtained the genuine map as given by the sailor to Miss Draycott's brother. We have also presented the gang with this."

He joined the faked half on to the genuine one and Blackett studied it.

"That, as you will see, Bill, is wrong. The southern half is correct: the northern is not."

"Aye: that's so. The tree and the hill are reversed."

"Well, I'm jiggered," said Robinson. "To think I never spotted that."

"I'm very glad you didn't, Robinson," said Jim. "It would have upset my plans very considerably if you had. To continue, Bill. The other party have no idea that there is anything wrong with the map they've got. It is possible, of course, they may show it to someone like yourself who knows the place, in which case they will discover they've been tricked. But if they don't do that, they won't find their error out till they arrive there."

"Arrive there!" cried Blackett. "Lord save us, you don't mean to say they're going to the island."

"You bet your life, Bill," said Jim. "And so am I."

"You are a fool, Mr. Maitland," said the sailor gravely.

"So are you, Bill," answered Jim, beginning to pace up and down the room. "Because you're coming too. And little Percy."

He paused for a moment with his eyes on the girl.

"Pity—but I'm afraid it's not quite in your line, Miss Draycott. I don't like the sound of that yellow jack."

"Don't you," said the girl, with a sweetness that would have augured danger to him if he had not been so preoccupied.

"Foul thing—yellow jack. Still we're all pretty well pickled against fever, and as far as Percy is concerned he can bite the microbe first. Microbes flee from you, don't they, old lad? Suppose they must draw the line somewhere."

"I had a sort of idea, Mr. Maitland," continued Judy even more sweetly, "that the map of the island was mine."

Jim stared at her.

"By Jove! yes—so it is," he cried. "But it's understood, of course, that when we discover the old tin can buried by Bill's Spanish pal, it's absolutely yours. Bill—when can you start? Fares and all expenses, of

267

course, are mine."

"Are you really serious?" demanded the other.

"Serious as be damned, old lad. And the marvel to me is that I've never heard this perfectly gorgeous yarn before."

And it was just as well for his peace of mind that he did not see the look on the girl's face as she watched him.

"If you don't come," he went on, "I'll have to rope in someone else who can do the sailoring part. But I'd dearly like to have you with me, Bill."

And suddenly the sailor laughed.

"Right you are. I'm with you."

"Great," shouted Jim. "I'll fix details with you tomorrow, Bill, and show you the complete map."

His eyes were gleaming with excitement.

"Speed: speed—that's the order of the day," he continued. "We've got to get there first. And I see no reason why we shouldn't. They suspect nothing, so as far as they are concerned there's no urgent need for hurry."

"Well, we'll have a look at things tomorrow," said Blackett, getting up. "I think you're a fool, Mr. Maitland, and I know I am, but anyway I'm going to bed. Good night, Miss," he added with a grin. "Can't you make him see reason?"

He stumped down the stairs followed by Robinson, and Jim grinned too.

"A priceless fellow," he remarked. "Worth two in a scrap."

"Do you think there's anything in his story about the things in the forest?" said the girl.

"Frankly, I don't," answered Jim. "As he admitted himself sailors are a superstitious bunch, and their stories rarely lose in the telling. But it was a queer yarn, wasn't it, about the *Paquinetta*? I should say myself that the generally accepted theory was correct—mutiny and yellow jack. For all that you'll have to learn to pull a pretty useful trigger, Percy."

But at the moment Percy slept quite shamelessly.

"How will you go?" demanded the girl.

"Either Purple Star or Union Mail as far as Rio. I'll have a look at the list of sailings tomorrow. Then from Rio I'll charter something or other to get to the island in."

"And where will you stay in Rio?" she asked.

"Probably the *Gloria*," said Jim. "Judy—I wish you could see Rio.

It's one of the most divinely beautiful places in the world."

"So I've always heard," she remarked. "You must bring me back some picture postcards of the place."

Jim looked at her suspiciously.

"What are you driving at, Judy?" he said. "The tone of your last remark was very peculiar."

"Sorry about that," she answered. "I was really thinking of something else. What a wonderful judge of character Captain Blackett is."

"Bill! Judge of character! I don't know that I've ever noticed it particularly."

"I mean when he called you a fool. Do give me a match, will you?"

"Not a match do you get until you tell me what you're driving at."

"Well—you must be one. Do you really imagine, Jim Maitland, that I'm going to sit at home here while you and that snoring monstrosity go gallivanting off on a perfectly priceless trip like this which you'd never have heard about but for me. Not so, my lad: you guess again."

"But, Judy," he said feebly. "My dear—think of the fever. And the discomfort. And there may be something in Blackett's story after all," he added as a brilliant afterthought.

"Cut it out," she said calmly. "Where Percy the poop can go—I can go. It's my map, and as a great favour I'll allow you to come with me. Now give me a match."

He still hesitated.

"Judy," he said seriously, "I know it is your map. I know you have every right to take up the position you have. But—honestly, I don't think you quite realise what you're letting yourself in for. The risk of fever is not an imaginary one: that part of the world simply reeks of it. Further there's going to be very real danger from the gentlemen we've been up against tonight. I don't think you ought to come."

"I'm still waiting for that match," she reminded him. "Now, look here, Jim," she went on when her cigarette was alight, "whatever you say, I'm coming. You may remember that conversation we had the first time we met concerning the youth of the present day. Well, now that they've killed Arthur this is my show. And any risks that you run I'm going to run too. Which ultimatum having been delivered the young maiden intimated her intention of retiring. Percy—you horror—wake up."

269

"Did anybody speak to me?" grunted Percy sleepily.

"Wake up, you fat-headed ass. I want to go home."

"All right, my loved one. Have you kissed James goodnight?"

And then occurred an amazing phenomenon. For Judy Draycott, usually one of the most self-possessed of girls, began to blush. Furious with herself, she blushed still more. And Percy howled with joy.

"My invariable present is an order up to five bob on Woolworths," he said dodging rapidly to the door. "Five minutes, my children—and don't forget to turn off the light in the passage when you leave."

"You unspeakable ass—get out," roared Jim, trying not to laugh.

"I go, James. But that is not the way mother taught me to address a chaperon."

"I really must apologise for him, Judy," said Jim, as Percy went down the stairs. "He becomes more of a half-wit daily."

He was holding the door open for her as he spoke, and for a while she looked at him in silence. Then she suddenly smiled.

"Are all your family half-wits?" she said softly, and a moment later he was alone.

Chapter 8

Speed, as Jim Maitland had said, was the vital thing. He had not the heart to try and dissuade Judy Draycott from coming: nor, as he frankly admitted to himself, had he the ability to. But she was going to complicate things. With her as a member of the party, it was essential to avoid a scrap, if it was humanly possible. And as he saw the thing a scrap would inevitably occur as soon as the other people landed on the island, when they would immediately discover that their map was wrong. Therefore it followed that if gun work was to be avoided they must be away before Dresler and his gang got there.

To Bill Blackett's fanciful monsters he attached no importance whatever. He knew sailors and their stories of old: moreover the *Paquinetta* mystery had taken place twenty-four years ago. And in a quarter of a century things grow in the imagination. What was worrying him, and what continued to worry him all the way across to Rio was how long it was going to take them to find the spot where, according to the map, the stuff was buried. It was easy to mark the spot on the map itself—he had already done so and marked it B. But the difficulty was going to be to find that place on the ground. According to Bill Blackett it was right in the middle of the forest, so how were they going to get their compass bearings? Had the place been open country the thing would have been easy. All that would have been necessary would have been to walk along the line from A to C till a point was reached where the hill lay north-east. But in dense forest the matter became much more difficult. And his fear was that it might take a considerable time before they marked it down, and even then they would have to allow for it being only approximately accurate. He felt that a week at least would be necessary to decide whether there was anything there or not. Could he rely on a week?

So far as he knew they had slipped out of England unnoticed. But he was far too old a campaigner to place any reliance on the fact. There had been questions of visas, and visits to consuls for Percy and the girl, and he was under no delusions as to the spying capabilities of the other side. He could only hope for the best, but he took no account of it in his plans. But of one thing he did feel tolerably certain; there was no one actually on board he had to worry about. The boat carried nothing but first-class passengers and was very empty. And with the help of the doctor and the purser he soon had the two or three possibilities satisfactorily accounted for.

His idea was simple, and had been arrived at after talking it over with Bill Blackett. It appeared from what the sailor told him that an eccentric Brazilian had had built to his own design a fifty-ton motorboat. Of amorous disposition he had used her in the past to accommodate a series of lady friends on weekend trips in the vicinity of Rio. Unfortunately, however, the husband of one of them, viewing this innocent pastime with displeasure, had shot the proud owner dead as he disembarked on the Monday morning. With the result that the boat was sold by the executors to a firm of local shipbuilders, who were always prepared to hire her out for any length of time. There was ample room on board for their party, and she was quite big enough for the trip.

On one point, however, Blackett was very insistent.

"Not a word, Mr. Maitland, as to our destination. Apart altogether from the fact that we don't want it talked about, you'll never get a man to work her if it is known where we're bound for. We'll fuel her right up—if necessary we can get some more at Santos—and merely say that we're going a trip along the coast."

The first hitch occurred the day they arrived in Rio—the motorboat was in dry dock being repaired. And when Bill Blackett reported the fact to Jim, for a time he thought of cancelling his plan, and trying to get another craft. But after having inspected her, and realised how ideally suitable she was for the purpose, he adopted the only possible method in South America of getting things done quickly. They said it would take a week, so he offered a thousand *milreis* for every day less than seven that the work was completed in. It cost him four thousand *milreis* but he felt it was money well spent.

And during the three days they stayed at the *Gloria* they did the well-known trips to pass the time. Corcavado, with the gigantic half-completed Christ on the summit: Sugar Loaf Hill by the aerial rope-way: Capacabana with its daily toll of drowned bathers due to the terrific undertow. To Judy Draycott the time passed all too quickly, and had it not been for his anxiety to lose not a second more than was necessary Jim would have felt the same. For the girl, besides possessing an intense love of beauty, had in her the genuine explorer's spirit. It was always the case with her of wanting to know what was on the other side of the mountain. The great blue and green butterflies drifting lazily through the dappled sunshine of trees splashed with scarlet and mauve flowers entranced her: what spoilt it was that just behind them was a large motor-car on a first-class road.

"What a marvellous life you've led, Jim," she said. "Think of this—this breathless beauty—away from towns, away from humans. Your own—not shared by anybody: not spoilt by anybody. And then to go on and find it again and again till you come to the end."

"The end!" He began to quote:—

Have ever you stood where the silences brood,
And vast the horizons begin,
At the dawn of the day to behold far away
The goal you would strive for and win?'

And then, to his delight she took him up:—

Yet, ah! in the night when you gain to the height,
With the vast pool of heaven star-spawned,
Afar and agleam, like a valley of dream
Still mocks you a Land of Beyond.'

"So you like him too, do you?" he said. "I'm glad. He writes the stuff that rings true does Robert Service."

"If you would wish in time for lunch to be, sah, I would suggest ascension of automobile."

The driver's voice, ingratiating, conciliatory, cut in on them, and Jim laughed.

"Marching orders, Judy. His goal is a stomach filled with garlic."

But they were both strangely silent as they drove back.

It was during the afternoon of the last day that they discovered that their hopes of a clear week on the island were not likely to be realised. Bill Blackett, who had spent the morning urging on the work on the boat, arrived when they were half-way through lunch.

"We'll get off tomorrow," he announced, "and its just as well we should."

"Anything happened, Bill?" said the other.

"It may be nothing. Have you ever heard of Bully McIntyre?"

"Can't say I have," said Jim.

"Well, he's heard of you. And he knows you're here. Bully McIntyre has been busy all his life on this coast, and his name is about right. He holds a master's ticket, and there is no denying he's a good seaman. But he's a swine. He doesn't know me, but I once had him pointed out to me, and he's not a man you'll forget in a hurry. Anyway he was down there near the docks this morning having a drink with a couple of *dagos*. And I suddenly heard your name mentioned. So I shifted along a bit and listened as well as I could. I couldn't hear much, but I distinctly caught the word 'Delay.' It may mean nothing, but I thought I'd better mention it."

"Quite right, Bill," said Jim thoughtfully. "When is the next boat in from England?"

"Day after tomorrow," answered the other. "If they come by her, it only gives us one day's start."

"Is this fellow McIntyre the sort of man they might get hold of to run the show for them?"

"Just the sort," said the sailor. "He fears nothing on earth, and he knows this coast backwards. I'll make a few enquiries this afternoon, and find out if he's chartered anything."

"Do," said Jim. "And another thing, too. Put the men, who are working on the boat, wise to the possibility that she may be tampered with, and let them know that whatever the cause may be there's no money unless she's fit to put to sea."

"What are you doing for the rest of the day?"

"I'm going to finish up the grub side. Ordering enough for a fortnight."

"Well, I needn't tell you to keep your eyes skinned," grunted the sailor. "But I'll feel easier when we're away."

"But what could they do?" asked Judy Draycott.

"This ain't London, Miss," said Blackett. "A powerful lot of funny things can happen in these parts. Well, I'll go and find out what I can."

He stumped out of the dining-room, and Jim frowned thoughtfully.

"I always thought Dresler must have someone at this end," he said. "But I wonder how they've got on to me. However there's nothing for it but to keep one's eyes skinned, as Bill said. No trotting round by yourself, young Percy. If they know me, they probably know you. So you stick close to uncle this afternoon."

It was on the way back from the store where they had laid in provisions, that the incident occurred which made Jim realise that there were brains in the opposition. A crude attempt with a knife would not have surprised him, and it was for something of that sort that he was prepared. But the actual ruse when it came was so much more artistic that even he was very nearly caught.

Percy was on the outside of the pavement, with Judy in the middle. And they were just turning into the main boulevard when a girl brushed past them. As she came abreast she seemed to lurch against Percy, and, promptly, with a cry of pain, she collapsed into the gutter. He instinctively turned to help her, and the next moment he found himself almost flung into a passing taxi by Jim.

"Damn it all, old lad," he expostulated feebly as the car drove off, "the wretched filly has hurt herself."

"Sorry, Judy," said Jim as she stared at him in amazement. "They very nearly had me that time. Of course, the whole thing was done on purpose. The girl wasn't hurt at all."

"Even so," remarked Percy, "I don't see why I shouldn't have helped the little darling out of the gutter. She was rather a peach."

"Because then she would have pretended to be hurt. She would have sworn you banged into her and knocked her down. Within two minutes in this town an ambulance would have been on the spot. And if you'd been with her then, you'd have been involved in all sorts of complications. Never touch anybody who has had an accident here: leave them alone, and wait for an ambulance."

"You think the whole thing was done on purpose?" cried Judy.

"I do," said Jim. "Just to cause delay. Percy might have found himself tied up in formalities for days."

They found Blackett waiting for them at the hotel, with a serious look on his face.

"I've found out a good deal," he said gravely. "And we've got to get a move on. You remember that white yacht we noticed as we came in, lying at anchor not far from the old cruiser? Well—that's what we're up against. She belongs to a millionaire here called Miguel, and Bully is getting her ready for sea by the day after tomorrow."

"That means they are coming by the next mail boat," remarked Jim. "A pity: I'd hoped for a bit longer. How's our work going?"

"Practically finished. Get off early tomorrow if the food is all fixed up."

"That's done. Who is this man Miguel, Bill?"

"He rolls in money, and nobody seems to know how he made it. Of course, the whole thing may be a coincidence, but I don't think so."

"No more do I," said Jim grimly, staring at a card a page had just handed him.

DON SILVESTRE MIGUEL

"Here is the gentleman himself."

A swarthy-looking individual, who might have stepped straight off the operatic stage had followed hard on the boy's heels. He bowed magnificently to Judy: then, turning to Jim, he enquired: "Mr. Maitland?"

"My name is Maitland," said Jim curtly.

"It is an honour, Mr. Maitland, to have you again in our country," he declared. "May I be permitted to crave an introduction to your friends?"

Jim complied, even more curtly. Then——

"May I ask to what I owe the pleasure of this visit, Don Miguel?"

"A desire for a little private conversation with you, Mr. Maitland. Could we, perhaps..."

He glanced at the others significantly, and Jim turned to the girl.

"I shan't be long, Judy. Do you mind waiting here with Percy? Don't leave the hotel. Come this way, Don Miguel."

He led him to two chairs in the corner of the lounge.

"It would be waste of time, Mr. Maitland," began the Brazilian, "to pretend that I do not know the object of your visit here. And it is on that subject that I would like a few words with you."

"May I ask how you discovered the supposed object of my visit?"

"Certainly: I propose to put all my cards on the table. Some few months ago it came to my knowledge from a source which I considered reliable, that there was a more reasonable likelihood of the story of the buried treasure in Lone Tree Island being correct. Since you, of course, must know the story I need say no more. I was sufficiently interested to make further enquiries, and what I learned confirmed my opinion. A map was in existence, which was in the possession of a sailor who was rapidly drinking himself to death, and I determined to obtain that map. Then an unexpected thing happened, with the details of which I will not bore you. But to cut a long story short the sailor disappeared. He was in Bahia: then suddenly he vanished.

"I made enquiries, and after a great deal of trouble I traced him to Buenos Aires. There again I lost the trail for a while, though the man was an easy one to get information about. He was a gentleman, I may say, who had come down in the world through drink, and therefore was rather a marked figure in the company he frequented. At last I got on to him again: he was in Monte Video. And he was dying. Moreover I discovered by methods into which we—ah!—need not enter that he was speaking the truth when he told me that he had given the map away, and did not know the name of the man he had given it to."

Don Miguel drew an immense handkerchief from his pocket and mopped his forehead.

"Annoying, Mr. Maitland, as you will agree. To have run the man at last to earth and then find all one's trouble wasted was a bore. But I have sources of information at my disposal, which caused me not to give up hope, even though I left for Uruguay and returned here. And sure enough, some weeks after the man's death I received word that a certain young Englishman had been dining in the Jockey Club in Buenos Aires one evening, and drunk a little freely. Also he had talked a little freely. And again to cut a long story short it was obvious that this young Englishman was the man to whom the sailor had given the map. I, at once, left for the Argentine, only to find that I had again missed my man: he had left a week previously for England. I trust I am not boring you: you possibly know all this already."

"No: I don't," said Jim. "You are filling in one or two gaps very nicely."

"As I said, I am putting all my cards on the table," said the Brazilian. "To continue, I immediately got into communication with some friends of mine in England, giving them the name of the young man, and the boat he was travelling in."

"Thank you," said Jim shortly. "I know what happened then. They killed him."

The Brazilian waved a deprecating hand.

"Deplorable, Mr. Maitland, deplorable. I received a cable in code informing me of the fact. And—er—of other facts too."

"You interest me profoundly," murmured Jim. "What other facts do you allude to?"

Don Miguel lit a cigarette and blew out a cloud of smoke before replying.

"I do not wish to flatter you unduly, Mr. Maitland," he remarked, "but your name is one that is fairly widely known. And when I heard from my friends in London that you had come into the picture it caused me a certain shock. True, they seemed to think that it was purely accidental, and at that I had to leave it. But when I discovered you were actually here, and in addition were with the sister of the young man who was so unfortunately shot, I realised at once that it was not accidental."

"Your reasoning is most profound," Jim assured him.

"And so, Mr. Maitland, we come to the point. What are we going to do about it?"

"Do about what?"

"I will be brief, as one busy man to another. Are we going into this thing together, or against one another?"

Jim, in his turn, lit a cigarette.

"May I ask by what right you come into it at all?" he asked. "The map belonged to young Draycott, and was stolen from him. In addition to that he was killed."

"My dear Mr. Maitland," said the other contemptuously, "are we members of some religious order that we talk about right? And if it comes to that, it was originally stolen by the sailor."

"With that I am not concerned in the slightest," said Jim. "It was given to Arthur Draycott, and further back than that I do not propose to go."

"Am I to take it then that you refuse my offer?"

"I wasn't aware you had made one."

"I suggest to you that you should cancel your proposed trip in the motorboat and come in with us. My friends arrive the day after tomorrow: we leave in the evening. What do you say?"

"Why such altruism, Don Miguel?" asked Jim quietly.

The other shrugged his shoulders.

"If my information is correct there will be plenty for all of us," he remarked. "And since I am quite prepared to admit that Miss Draycott has a right to her share why should we not join forces?"

For a while Jim stared at him as if pondering whether to accept the proposal. Not that he had the slightest intention of doing so—he trusted Don Silvestre Miguel as far as the length of his foot—but he had to decide what line to take with him. The man was wealthy and unscrupulous, and the combination was a formidable one anywhere. In South America, where money means everything, it was doubly so.

"Suppose I fall in with your suggestion," he remarked at length, "what guarantee have I, Don Miguel, that your friends will be agreeable?"

The other leaned forward in his chair.

"I have been in wireless communication with them, Mr. Maitland," he said. "And I may say that it is their idea as much as mine. Come, come: we are men of the world. What is the use of your going in comparative discomfort when I can offer you the luxury of my yacht? We are bound to meet at the island in any case, so why not let us go there together?"

"The only objection to your idea," said Jim, "is the question of Miss Draycott. She knows that your friends were responsible for her brother's death, and somewhat naturally she would not relish being forced to meet them daily."

"Then leave her here, Mr. Maitland. You can look after her interests."

"You don't know the young lady, I'm afraid." remarked Jim, with a smile. "She has a very determined character. See here, Don Miguel,"— he seemed to have arrived at a sudden decision—"I will talk to her about the matter. I have, between ourselves, been trying to find an excuse to prevent her going. From what I hear, the place is most unhealthy, and not at all suitable for a woman. I can say that a hitch has occurred over our own boat, and tell her your alternative."

The Brazilian looked at him searchingly, but Jim Maitland had not played poker in most corners of the globe for nothing.

"Will you do so at once?" he demanded.

"My dear sir, how can I possibly get up straight from a conversation with you, and tell her that our boat has failed?"

Jim gazed at him blandly, and the other nodded his head.

"True," he acknowledged, "true."

"It must be done this evening," continued Jim. "After dinner perhaps."

"And when shall I know your answer?"

"As soon as that incalculable time has elapsed in which it takes a woman to make up her mind," answered Jim, and Don Miguel rose.

"Very good, Mr. Maitland: we will leave it at that."

He picked up the card which Jim had laid on the table and scribbled on it.

"My telephone number," he remarked. "I shall hope to hear from you as soon as possible."

Jim watched him cross the lounge, and leave the hotel, bowing ceremoniously to Judy as he passed. Then he joined his cousin and the girl.

"Where's Bill?" he asked.

"Gone down to the boat again," said Percy. "What did that bandit want?"

He told them briefly.

"But you aren't dreaming of doing it, are you, Jim?" cried the girl.

"I am not," said Jim. "But I had to fob him off with something. If I'd given him a flat refusal we'd never have got off tomorrow. As it is it's not going to be plain sailing, though I think I've fooled him all right."

"Are you afraid he may tinker with the boat?" asked Percy.

"My dear lad, a man with his length of purse in this country can do anything. I wish to heaven we could get away tonight. And here's Bill returning with a face like a boot."

"They're getting at us, Mr. Maitland," cried the sailor as he sat down. "That old rascal Antonio, who is one of the part owners of the boat has just broken it to me. Somebody has spread it around that we're going to Lone Tree Island, and not a man will sail with us. Say they'd rather be sacked than go to such a place."

"Hell!" said Jim. "That just about puts the lid on, Bill. What the devil are we going to do? Can't you find anybody who will volunteer?"

The sailor shrugged his shoulders.

"You know what these dagos are," he said. "I can offer double wages, but I'm doubtful of it being much use."

"What do you want a man for?" demanded Percy.

"To run the motor, you ass," said Jim.

"Less of your natural history references, James," remarked his cousin. "I was about to say that I, in consideration of receiving several blood-red rubies as my share of the swag, will undertake that side of the performance."

"But can you, Percy dear?" cried the girl.

"Can I run that darned motor?" snorted Percy. "Great heavens, woman, what do you take me for? I could run it in my sleep."

"By Jove! old boy," said Jim quietly, "one up to you. I'd forgotten you were a motor fan. That's settled that, Bill. Now they're still carrying on with the work, aren't they?"

The sailor nodded.

"Yes. I told them to finish it."

"And now the point that arises is how to slip away. That blighter Miguel is bound to be keeping the boat under observation."

"We've got to chance that," said Blackett. "And my suggestion is this. Instead of waiting till dawn tomorrow, we'll get away as soon after midnight as possible. There is a night watchman on the yard who's a pal of mine, and there will be no trouble about getting in. I'll let Antonio think that we're giving up the trip as we can't get a mechanic, and we'll just have to trust to luck."

Jim shook his head.

"Not good enough, Bill. I agree over getting her away under cover of darkness, but we've got to plant 'em on a false trail. Otherwise there's going to be knife work. You and young Percy will have to get her ready, while Miss Draycott and I draw them off. Let's all go down there now, and we'll start the good work. You perceive, don't you, one of our friends—that sallow-looking swab in the corner. He's been watching us like a lynx."

He ordered the concierge in a loud tone to obtain a taxi, and with no effort at concealment told the driver to go to the boat yard.

"That," he remarked as he got in, "will save our friend following too close on our heels. Though I don't suppose he's the only one."

Having arrived he sent for Antonio and, in fluent Brazilian, he told him exactly what he thought of his firm, himself, and his workmen. And during the telling a couple of men drew closer and closer.

"However," he wound up, "since your hands are too cowardly to come with us there is nothing more to be said. I shall not require your boat, having found another method of getting to my destination— Don Miguel's yacht. Bill," he ordered, "get on board. And you too, Percy. And stay there," he added in an undertone.

"All the kit and stores," he relapsed into angry Brazilian, "have to be packed up, just because there isn't a man with guts in the place."

"I shall chance it about eleven o'clock, Bill," he muttered. "Be ready for us. You can leave the boat for a bit, if they seem to be getting suspicious, but get everything fixed by then. I'm going back to the hotel to continue the good work."

Still fuming he helped Judy into the taxi, and gave the address.

"Your *rôle*, Judy," he said, as they drove off, "is a flat refusal to go by the yacht. You're going to remain here in Rio until our return. Don't forget your part for an instant: anyone may be a spy. But with a little bit of luck we may bluff 'em."

"Do you think he really intended to take us in his yacht?" said the girl.

"Not a hope," laughed Jim. "We should have been left high and dry here. You can bet they haven't taken all this trouble in order to share anything that may be there with a single unnecessary person."

"Won't it be marvellous if we do find something."

"Don't build on it, Judy," he warned. "Though I honestly am quite hopeful. Neither Miguel nor Dresler strike me as gentlemen who waste time or money. Here's the hotel: play up for all you're worth."

And play up she did to the vast edification of the sallow-faced gentleman who reappeared mysteriously from nowhere. No power on earth would induce her to go on Don Miguel's yacht, and if Jim was unable to get anyone to man the boat she would remain in Rio. And finally with a shrug of his shoulders he strolled away to the bar, calling high heaven to witness on the unreasonableness of woman. Then he instructed the hall porter to get Don Miguel on the telephone for him, and to him he spoke at length. He wondered who could have given his destination away: so did Don Miguel. Anyway it settled things, and he would accompany Don Miguel in his yacht, at which the Brazilian professed himself overjoyed. And finally he left the box with the comforting reflection that if the bluff had failed it was not for want of lying.

They had dinner, after which there was nothing to do but sit and wait. The sallow-faced man had gone, but there were several men in the lounge any one of whom might have been his successor. They had decided on their plan, and time seemed to drag interminably. At ten o'clock Judy rose from her chair.

"Jim," she said irritably, "it's insufferably hot. Can't we take a car and go somewhere before going to bed?"

He stifled a yawn.

"Bit late, Judy, isn't it?" he remarked doubtfully.

"I can't help it: I'll never sleep. Let's drive out to that place where they bathe."

"Capacabana!" His expression was resigned. "All right."

He beckoned to a page.

"Tell the hall porter to get me a taxi. I want to go for a run to Capacabana."

The boy gave the message, and returned shortly after to say the car was waiting.

And it was not until they were halfway to their destination that Jim turned to the girl.

"A little bit too clever, Judy," he said in a low voice, "or rather, not quite clever enough. But it's going to complicate things. This driver is one of them."

"How do you know?"

"At about a quarter to ten I had a look at the taxi rank opposite the hotel. This car was in front. Two taxis were ordered between then and ten o'clock when we got this one. Why did he let two other men take the jobs?"

"What are you going to do?"

"You'll see in a moment," he said. "But it's a lucky thing all taxis here are open cars."

He gave an order in Brazilian to the driver.

"I've told him to drive right out to the end beyond the hotel," he told the girl. "And when we get there I will show you a little trick of my own."

The lights grew fewer and farther between, and at length ceased altogether. And suddenly Jim told the man to stop. In his hand he held a short bar which he was balancing carefully. She watched him fascinated, as, all in a single movement, he rose and hit the driver one blow on the nape of the neck. And the driver collapsed like a log on the floor of the car.

"Not everybody's weapon," said Jim calmly, as he rummaged under the seat for some rope. "It's very easy to kill a man with it unless you're careful. Now this sportsman will sleep peacefully for about four hours, but in case he wakes sooner we may just as well truss him up."

He pulled out a length of cord evidently used for baggage, and tied the unconscious driver up deftly. Then he placed him gently in the ditch, and put a hundred *milreis* note in his pocket. After which he jumped into the driving-seat.

"It's neck or nothing, Judy," he said, as he turned the car round. "We'd never have got away with that lad at the wheel. And now I think we may, if luck is with us."

They swung back towards Rio, with Jim crouching over the wheel to conceal his height. To reach the docks they had to go through the main street, and it was there that the danger lay, for the police in the Avenida Rio Branco are an extremely capable body of men. But fortune was with them: nobody held up the car, and at a few minutes to eleven he pulled up outside Antonio's boat yard.

The place looked dark and deserted, but not until he had taken a careful look round did Jim allow the girl to get out of the car. Piles of wood and barrels afforded admirable hiding-places for would-be watchers, and he dared take no risks with Judy. At last he was satisfied, and taking her by the arm he rushed her across to the entrance.

Bill Blackett had been as good as his word: it was open. And still holding her arm he piloted her inside. The boat lay some twenty yards ahead of them and he was making straight for it when his eye caught a movement near a big coil of rope on his right. Instantly he thrust Judy behind him, and, in a low voice called out something in Brazilian.

It was the only chance, and he took it. If the mover was Bill or Percy it did not matter: if he was one of the opposition he might, in the darkness, think Jim was one of his friends. And the ruse succeeded: a figure rose and came towards him. He waited tensely: on the look-out at any moment for a knife to be thrown.

He spoke again, and the man answered.

"Is that you, Pedro?"

And a fraction of a second too late he realised it was not. He opened his mouth to shout, but no sound came. Jim's vice-like grip closed on his throat, and he felt himself picked up like a child.

"Run, Judy, run for the boat," Jim muttered. "There are others about."

He dragged the man with him, and hauled him on board gurgling and spluttering. Out of the corner of his eye he saw a light in an adjoining shed, and heard the sound of voices: the rest of the bunch were playing cards. And then from in front of him he heard the girl give a little cry. She was in the saloon which was lit by a solitary candle. And trussed up in two chairs like a pair of gagged mummies were Percy and Bill Blackett.

"Not a sound," whispered Jim imperatively. "It's our only hope. Get a knife out of the drawer and cut 'em loose. Bill first."

He dared not relax his grip for an instant on his own man for fear he would shout, and in a fever of impatience he watched the girl slashing at the rope until Bill Blackett was free.

"Cast her off, Bill," he ordered, "from the boat. It doesn't matter if we lose the ropes. Then fend her off from the side."

"I get you," grunted the sailor, sprinting on deck.

"Percy—stand by the motor. But for the love of Allah don't start it until I tell you."

His cousin nodded and he turned to the girl.

"Quick, Judy—I must go and help Bill. Take my handkerchief from my pocket and cram it into this swab's mouth with the handle of the knife. Mind your fingers, for he'll bite. Good. Now some of that rope. Can you make a running noose? Splendid girl. Slip it round that elbow. That's right: I can manage now."

He hauled the rope tight, lashing the man's arms behind his back: then he attended to his knees. And finally he wound the table-cloth round his head, and threw him into one of the off shore cabins.

"Stay here, Judy. On no account come on deck."

He vanished silently, almost colliding with Bill Blackett.

"She's cast off," said the sailor, "and if you can take one boat hook aft I'll go forrard with the other."

"We want to get her out just far enough for them not to be able to jump, Bill," he said, and the other nodded.

The card game was apparently still in progress, as they got on deck, and an angry altercation was taking place, which was all to the good. But the motor was bound to make too much noise for any quarrel to drown, and Jim realised, only too clearly, that it was touch and go. At length they got her out about six feet, so that she had a clear run for the open water. It was then or never, and he beckoned to Bill.

"Tell Percy to start up," he ordered, "and slip her into half-speed at once, without waiting for any signal. I'll steer."

He waited tensely at the wheel, and suddenly, with a snort, the motor hummed into life. Came instant silence from the shed: then a rush of cursing men to the side of the wharf. Ten yards: twenty, and a knife quivered in the deck at his feet. Thirty: forty—they'd done it, and he grinned happily.

"How did they get you, Bill?" he sung out to Blackett, who was fixing the lights.

"About a dozen of 'em swarmed on board, and caught us napping," answered the other.

And it was at that moment that Percy popped his head up.

"I say, dear old lad," he remarked, "everything is fearfully jolly and all that, but I suppose you know it's my cabin you have bunged little bright eyes into."

"Good Lord!" cried Jim, "I'd forgotten all about him. Unlash the blighter, and send him up on deck."

"Now, you swab," he said, as the man appeared shaking with fright. "Can you swim?"

Not a yard, he protested, with chattering teeth. Since childhood he had had a horror of water.

"What the devil are we to do with him, Bill?" said Jim.

"Let him do the washing up," answered the sailor. "There's a cubby-hole aft he can doss down in."

"Take him with us? Yes: I suppose we must. If the man can't swim, we can hardly throw him overboard."

He turned to him and spoke in Brazilian.

"You're coming with us, do you understand. And you'll have to make yourself generally useful. For if I have the smallest trouble with you I'll trail you astern at the end of a rope as bait for sharks."

CHAPTER 9

They sighted Lone Tree Island at dawn on the second day, and as they drew nearer Blackett searched the shore anxiously with his glasses. It was the northern end they were approaching, and his memory of the place was a little rusty. The beach which lay at the foot of the hill was guarded by a reef of rocks, and the line of surf looked unbroken. But somewhere there was a gap, and it was for that he was making. They had decided that it would be fatal to use the southern anchorage: they would see quite enough of the opposition without lying alongside them. And from what he remembered the gap was wide enough to let their boat through but would prove impossible for the yacht.

At last they saw it, and Jim looked at him doubtfully. It was about ten yards across, and at each edge the swell broke lazily on vicious black rocks. Beyond it, some two hundred yards away, was the shore, and the intervening water was as calm as a lake. An ideal harbour; anything but an ideal entrance.

They nosed in closer going dead slow, and the nearer they got the nastier it looked. Blackett was at the wheel: Jim was up in the bows peering into the water ahead.

"If we bump, go all out, Percy," he said. "We'll have to beach her."

And to this day Bill Blackett swears the boat must have had an india-rubber bottom.

"She bounced twice and then skidded," he affirms, "but she got through."

After which the crew had breakfast, and discussed the plan of campaign.

"We can presumably rely on having today undisturbed," said Jim. "And there is a possibility of tomorrow also. They can't arrive until tonight, and they won't know until it's light that they've got a useless map. Then they've got to find us. So that if we're away from here by dawn tomorrow we may get an extra twelve hours. But that is the absolute maximum. Wherefore, chaps, we've got to get a move on."

And so, a quarter of an hour later they rowed ashore in the dinghy leaving the Brazilian to amuse himself on board. Each of them carried a revolver and a heavy stick, and Jim had a rucksack strapped on his shoulders, in which was the food for lunch. And having beached the dinghy they started the climb.

The northern side of the hill was practically bare of any vegetation. For the first two or three hundred feet a few stunted shrubs grew sparsely: above that a thin brown weed, which might by courtesy have been called grass, stretched up to the summit. The slope was steep, but easy, and since the sun as yet had but little heat they made the top without difficulty.

"Seems rum to be back here after all these years," said the sailor. "If anyone had offered me a hundred pounds to sixpence against it I wouldn't have taken it."

Below them lay the swampy half of the island. A thick mist covered it eddying sluggishly into the giant trees which came down to the edge of the marsh land and there stopped abruptly. A faint southerly breeze was blowing, and it carried to their nostrils that strange unmistakable scent of rotting vegetation which sends the man who knows to his medicine-chest for quinine twice daily. Fever—the place stank of it, as Bill Blackett had said in London.

Surrounding the swamp on three sides was higher ground: on the fourth lay the sea. Their own vantage point was the highest in the island, rising from the low foothills that formed the northern end. And due west, some two miles away there stood the Lone Tree. It seemed to have escaped from the forest which comprised the western half, and to be standing like a solitary sentinel in front of an army that had halted a few hundred yards away. And Jim, as he looked at that dense jungle, felt his heart sink. He alone of the party knew from past experience the difficulties of cutting a path through undergrowth of that sort, and keeping any sort of direction. However he said nothing and produced his compass.

"We'll take a bearing due south-west from here," he explained, "and see if it passes through any conspicuous spot which we can remember when we get to the Lone Tree. Then when we get the line between C and A from there, we may get an approximate position."

He let the compass settle, and then prolonged the line by laying his stick on the ground.

"It's pointing straight at that huge mass of scarlet flowers," cried Judy.

"Come on," he said abruptly. "Let's get to the Lone Tree."

The mist was slowly clearing from the swamp, showing glimpses of vivid green interspersed with dull brown ground.

"Lord! what a death trap," he exclaimed involuntarily, and at that moment Bill Blackett clutched his arm.

"Look," he muttered, "at that bit of green half-left of you."

He was staring through his glasses, and Jim focussed his own. The mist was still swirling in thin wisps over the marsh, but it suddenly lifted for a few seconds from the spot which the sailor had pointed to. And, quite distinctly, he saw something heaving and struggling in the green slime. Then all was still: whatever it was had gone under. But still he kept his glasses fixed. What was that moving on the brown ground which flanked the green? There were two, three, half a dozen. . . . And then the mist came down again, blotting out everything.

"Is that what happened to the crew of the *Paquinetta*?" said Blackett sombrely. "Anyway, what was it, Mr. Maitland?"

Jim glanced at him quickly: evidently he had not seen the others.

"Some animal caught in the bog," he said shortly. "It often happens, even on Dartmoor, or in the New Forest. Let's get a move on."

But half-way to the Lone Tree he paused and adjusted his glasses once again. The mist had completely gone: the swamp lay open below them. But though he scanned it from end to end no living thing stirred. Only the faint reek of it rose poisonous to heaven.

It was getting hot when they reached the Lone Tree, and a haze was already shimmering over the forest. But it was not enough to prevent them picking up the cairn of stones on the high ground at the south of the island. And having done so for a moment or two they all stood silent staring at one another. For the line to the cairn passed directly through the centre of the great patch of scarlet flowers they had picked up from the hill.

"Why we've only got to walk till we find it," cried Judy, "and we've got the spot."

"Not quite so easy as it sounds, Judy," said Jim. "In the first place we've got to keep our direction going through the undergrowth, when we shan't be able to see the flowers; and in the second place the flowers look very different when looked at from where we are now, to what they will when we're standing underneath them. What's up, Bill?"

The sailor drew him on one side.

"For God's sake, Mr. Maitland," he said in a low voice, "chuck it. It's not worth it. Those flowers never grew there naturally: why, there's not another patch that you can see. They have been planted, I tell you—planted as an ornament, as a decoration."

"Decoration! For what?"

"For what is underneath them. There, in the forest."

"You're talking rot, Bill," said Jim curtly, though the strangeness of that one flaming splash of colour had not escaped him. And yet the thing was absurd: the sailor was a superstitious ass. The flower looked like the ordinary scarlet hibiscus, as common in the tropics as the daisy is at home. It was just coincidence, and lucky coincidence that this great square of them should mark the spot they wanted. So he argued to himself, cursing Bill mentally for having made such an argument necessary.

He took the compass bearing on the cairn of stones, and found it was south-south-west: then he gave the order to march.

"I'll lead," he said. "Then Judy after me. Bill—you bring up the rear. And watch for snakes every step you take."

He calculated that the distance was about three miles, and it soon became obvious that they would never do it that day. The heat once they left the open became well-nigh unbearable: the undergrowth in places seemed like a solid wall. Huge lianas—the size of a ship's cable—hung in great festoons from the trees; rank weeds and tropical ferns with tendrils the size of a man's arm blocked the way, and had to be slashed at with knives to afford a passage. In places they were almost in darkness, so thick was the foliage above: then they would stumble into a patch of sunlight where gorgeous humming birds flitted like exquisite coloured jewels above their heads.

The sweat poured off them, and at the end of an hour Jim made out that they had blazed a trail for about half a mile. But the exertion had been terrific, and the girl, though she made no complaint, was obviously exhausted. Moreover the going was becoming worse as they got deeper in, and reluctantly he called a halt.

"We must take a breather," he said, "or we'll all be cooked. Anyway, Bill," he added with a laugh, "your boy friends you told us about in London haven't used this route."

But there was no answering smile on the sailor's face.

"Maybe not, Mr. Maitland, but that isn't to say they're not here."

"You're a darned old optimist, aren't you?" said Jim, lighting a cigarette. "But if they are, I wish we could rope 'em in to do a job of work."

For half an hour they sat there in the steamy heat. Save for the hum of a myriad insects the silence was complete. Once in the distance they heard the raucous screech of a parrot, but, save for that, everything was still. And then quite suddenly there came a sound which brought them all to their feet listening intently.

It seemed to come from a long way off, and yet, though faint, it was quite distinct. *Clang: clang: clang*: it went on monotonously for more than a minute. Then it ceased, and silence settled on them once again.

"It sounded like a bell," said Jim.

"Like a ship's bell," agreed Blackett gravely. "I forget if I told you that the *Paquinetta's* bell was missing."

"Look here, old sailor," put in Percy, "you're enough to give one the woodle-ums, you know. This darned wood ain't my idea of fun and laughter at the best of times, without having the ghost of a bell chucked in."

Jim was staring thoughtfully in front of him. There was no possibility of a mistake: they had all heard it. Whether it was the *Paquinetta's* bell or not was immaterial: the vital fact remained that some bell had sounded. Who had rung it? It had pealed methodically, at fixed intervals of time. What agency had been at work?

He began to pace up and down the little clearing. What were those things he had seen in the swamp that morning? Could it be possible that there was something in Blackett's fantastic theory? And if so— what about Judy? He and the two men could take their chance, but the bare idea of the girl falling into the hands of some primitive race of savages made him shudder to contemplate.

There was another point too, which had to be taken into consideration. In this dense forest they were at a terrible disadvantage. The value of a revolver was reduced to nothing, if the target was invisible.

At any moment they might be surrounded by things that knew their way about the undergrowth, and though they might account for a few of them the risk was too great while Judy was with them. There was nothing else for it: they must go back. And the fact that, in any event, at their present rate of progress they could not hope to reach their objective that day, afforded Jim an admirable excuse without mentioning his fears.

"We've got to think of some other way of doing this job," he remarked at length. "This is impracticable, especially in this heat. Let's go back to the boat and have a *powwow.*"

"But what other way can there be, Jim?" cried the girl.

"That's what we've got to talk over," he said. "But this is no go, Judy. About turn, Bill: you lead the way."

They halted for a time at the top of the hill to get the benefit of the faint breeze that was blowing, and to search the island more thoroughly with glasses. But nothing moved, save the shimmering heat haze which lay like a blanket over the whole place. At last they descended to the beach and pulled out in the dinghy to the boat.

"Think of an iced Pilsener," said Percy, "pouring gently down your throat with two more on the table to follow."

"I hope that ass Lopez has remembered to keep the drinking water in the sea," remarked Jim. "And where is the blighter, anyway."

They tied up the dinghy and climbed on board: the deck was deserted.

"Lopez!" he called: there was no answer.

"Probably asleep," said Percy. "Iced Pilsener," he repeated dreamily: "in long, long glasses. Lovely light yellow beer. And instead of that— tepid water in enamel mugs. Who would be an explorer? James, you would appear to be perturbed. What ails your manly spirit?"

"Lopez is not in the boat," said Jim quietly.

"He's probably gone a little ta-ta ashore," said his cousin. "Got tired of playing alone here, and thought he'd be an explorer too."

"How did he get ashore?" remarked Jim even more quietly.

"In the dinghy," said his cousin, and then paused abruptly. "By Jove! old lad, your meaning penetrates the grey matter. We left the dinghy ashore."

"Exactly," said Jim.

"Are you perfectly certain he's not on board?" cried the girl.

"Perfectly. Bill and I have looked everywhere."

"He must have swum," said Percy.

"He can't swim," answered Jim.

"He *said* he couldn't, Mr. Maitland," said the sailor. "Maybe he lied. Maybe he didn't relish the thought of meeting his pals at Rio just after he'd let 'em down."

"That's true, Bill," said Jim thoughtfully. "But what about his clothes?"

"In the absence of all our lady passengers he probably dispensed with them," answered Percy.

"I can't say I saw many signs of a naked man rushing wildly about the hillside," said Jim, "but perhaps you're right."

"Well, dash it all, old boy," remarked his cousin, "the blighter can't have jumped two hundred yards, and since, so far as I know, he didn't possess wings he bally well must have swum if he's not here. And personally I'm going to get into my little paddling drawers and do the same. Come on, Judy: let us brave the octopi together."

"You're worried, Jim," said the girl quietly.

"Not a bit, bless you," he cried. "Probably Percy is right. You go and hit the water and I'll join you in a few minutes. Then we'll decide on a plan of campaign."

He watched them go below: then he lit a cigarette thoughtfully. And he had barely taken a puff when Bill Blackett who had gone aft called him.

"What is it, Bill?" he said, joining him.

In silence the sailor pointed to the little sink where the washing up was done. In it lay the fragments of half a dozen broken plates which had been dropped in a pile.

"Well!" said Jim. "What about it?"

"What made him drop them, Mr. Maitland?" remarked the sailor gravely.

"Ask me another, Bill," answered Jim. "Such things have been known to happen before."

"Aye! that's true, and I'm not saying it may not have been an accident." He was stuffing his pipe from a weather-beaten pouch, and Jim waited. "Mr. Maitland," went on the sailor, "clothes or no clothes, the dago was not on shore or we should have seen him from the top of the hill."

"He may have been in the forest, like us," said Jim.

"In the forest," snorted the other. "Not he! I can sling enough of his lingo to have talked with him once or twice. And the Hounds of Hell would not have even got him ashore here, much less into the forest. He was scared stiff of the place."

"Then where the devil is he?" demanded Jim, and Blackett pointed downwards with his thumb.

"Drowned," he said tersely. "That was no accident—the smashing of those plates. He dropped them because he was frightened to death. Something came round the corner of the cuddy, Mr. Maitland, that drove him mad with terror—so mad that it didn't matter whether he could swim or whether he couldn't. He sprang overboard sooner than face it."

Jim stared at the sailor thoughtfully: was it possible he had hit on the right solution? He agreed with him—though he had appeared to differ—that the Brazilian would not have gone ashore of his own free will. And if he had remained in the boat something of the sort must have happened. But what manner of thing could it have been that drove a non-swimmer so crazy with fear that he jumped overboard to certain death by drowning?

The dinghy had not been moved: they had found it in exactly the same spot as they had left it. Therefore this thing must have swum to the boat. And suddenly he noticed a damp patch on the deck just in front of him, which might have been caused by wet feet. Outside the sun would have removed all traces, but this was in the shade. And he pictured to himself the wretched Lopez turning round as a shadow fell on him: the plates falling from his nerveless hands, his scream of fear as he dashed away from the thing that had entered. And then the splash as he hurled himself overboard. Or maybe he had been thrown.

"Well, my dear Watson, I trust you have solved the trifling problem of the Missing Brazilian, remarked Holmes, injecting cocaine into his left ankle."

Percy had joined them in his bathing kit.

"He seems to have been a bit prodigal with the crockery," he went on as he saw the broken plates.

"Look here, Percy," said Jim, "Bill has got a theory. And, 'pon my soul, I'm not certain he isn't right."

"We are prepared to listen, remarked Holmes courteously, injecting cocaine into the right ankle. But I pray you—be brief. I would fain bathe."

He seated himself on the table and lit a cigarette, while Jim told him the sailor's idea.

"And as I said before," he concluded, "I'm not certain he isn't right."

"Well," said his cousin, who had become serious as he listened, "granted for the moment that he is, what do we do next?"

"If you take my advice, gentlemen," remarked the sailor gravely, "you'll up anchor and leave at once. You know the other name for the island, don't you? I forget the native words, but translated it means the island of no return."

"Seems a bit fatuous to come all this way, and then go all the way back again just because a *dago* disappears," said Percy.

"It's not because he disappeared," said the sailor stubbornly, "it's because of what made him disappear."

"Steady on, Bill," put in Jim. "We mustn't fall into the error of taking your theory as a proven fact, you know. There are at least two others which would account for things. He might have lied when he said he couldn't swim, and in spite of our not seeing him, he may be on shore now. Or he might suddenly have been taken ill, dropped the plates, rushed to the side and fallen overboard."

"Come on, you lazy blighters: it's glorious in the water."

Judy's voice hailed them from outside.

"*Avaunt*, child," answered Percy. "A council of state is in session."

"Not a word to her, Percy," muttered Jim, "of this idea of Bill's," and his cousin nodded.

"Naturally not," he said, as the girl poked her head round the corner.

"What are you sitting in this frowsty hole for?" she demanded.

"We'll be along in a minute," said Jim. "We're just having a bit of a *powwow*. Now look here, you fellows," he continued as she disappeared, "I figure it out this way. Let us assume for the moment that you're correct, Bill. Let us assume that something made its way on board that was so terrifying to Lopez that he shot overboard. Now he was unarmed: moreover he was down here. So he was taken by surprise. But we know this something that we are assuming came on board, must have swum. Even if it had come in the dinghy it had to cover two hundred yards of open water. What chance then would it have had if there had been a look-out on deck with a rifle?"

"Not an earthly," agreed Percy, and Bill grunted assent.

"Now two facts stick out a yard," continued Jim. "The first is that under no conceivable circumstances must we run the slightest risk of Judy being put in the same position as Lopez."

He paused and a faint smile came to his lips.

"And the second?" demanded the sailor.

"The second, Bill, is that I am of an inordinately curious disposition. I just wouldn't sleep o' nights for the rest of my life if I didn't find out who rang that bell and why: what lies under the patch of scarlet hibiscus: and a lot of other things."

"You're mad and foolhardy, Mr. Maitland," said the sailor. "How do you propose to do it?"

"Go and have a look," answered Jim with a grin, "leaving you, Bill, armed with the express rifle on guard over Miss Draycott here. Percy can please himself. He can either stop here with you, or he can come with me."

"It's madness," said the sailor once again. "Utter madness."

"Can't help it, old lad: I've always been mad. Well, Percy, what about you? For the shore after lunch, or not?"

"You bet your life I'm for the shore," said his cousin. "But what exactly are you intending to do? Carry on from where we left off this morning?"

Jim shook his head.

"No," he answered. "We started off on a false trail there. I propose that we wander along the edge of the swamp, and see if we can't find some track that will lead us into the forest without the necessity of hacking our way through the undergrowth. We may fail: if so we can only return."

"And you'll be back before dark," said the sailor.

"That's the idea, Bill," agreed Jim.

"And supposing you're not," continued the other.

"Why then, Bill, we'll be back after dark," laughed Jim. "Cheer up, you old croaker: Percy will be there to look after me."

The sailor shrugged his shoulders.

"All right, Mr. Maitland. You're the captain of this outfit, and what you say goes. But I still think you're a damned fool who is asking for trouble. And if you get it don't blame me."

With which Parthian shot he stumped off to his cabin.

"I say, Jim, do you *really* think there is anything in his idea?" said Percy.

"That, old lad, is what we propose to find out," answered his cousin. "And in the meantime let's join Judy in the water."

Jim had chosen the edge of the swamp as the line of advance for two reasons. Firstly, it struck him that by sticking to the brown tracks which flanked the green patches they would get good going in the open: and secondly he hoped that if there were any paths leading into the forest they would find some of them there. He had not forgotten the things he had seen through the mist that morning, and he argued that they would probably have had some line of approach, since the only place they could have disappeared into was the forest itself.

At the same time he fully realised that if there were tracks, and Percy and he used them, their chances of an encounter would be much greater than if they tried to again force a way through the undergrowth. And he was under no delusions as to the possibility of danger. They would be tackling them on their own ground, and under the most unfavourable conditions, especially as Percy, though he had practised assiduously on the way out was still a positive menace with a revolver.

What he wanted to do if it proved feasible was to see one of them without being seen himself. Then they could arrive at a decision as to whether they would carry on or not.

"You see, old lad," he remarked to Percy, as they beached the dinghy and proceeded once more to climb the hill, "we know the forest is inhabited, possibly by the most harmless creatures in the world, possibly not. And in the latter event, treasure or no treasure, we hop it. There aren't enough of us for Judy to be safe. But if they're harmless it's a different matter altogether."

Away to the north a smudge of smoke lay low on the horizon, but the island itself seemed lifeless in the intense heat. They scanned the open ground, searching for Lopez: there was no sign of him. Nothing moved, nothing stirred: the only sound was the lazy beat of the surf. And with a final glance backwards at the motor-boat, and Bill sitting grimly in a deck chair with his rifle across his knees they began the descent to the swamp.

It was two o'clock which gave them a good four hours in which to explore and be clear of the forest before it was dark. What Jim had surmised proved correct: there was a fringe of firm soil skirting the edge of the undergrowth which gave them easy walking. In places it was several yards wide, in others only a few inches, and lapping it on the other side, save where branches of it forked out and meandered across the marsh, lay the deadly green slime.

They pushed on steadily but cautiously, and it soon became obvious to Jim that the track was often used. There were places where the vegetation had been deliberately forced back to give greater width. And it was in one such place that they came on their first clue. Up till then the ground had been as hard as a rock: here they suddenly came on a stretch of some ten yards where a stream oozed sluggishly over the path. It had practically dried up, leaving the soil soft and muddy, and for a while Jim stared at it, with his face growing more and more grave.

"Look at the footprints, Percy," he said at length. "Poor devil."

His cousin looked at him sharply.

"What do you mean by 'poor devil'?" he asked.

But Jim did not reply: he was down on his knees studying the ground more closely. The marks were perfectly clear cut, and had obviously been made very recently. They were of two distinct sorts, and he examined them both in turn.

The first were those of a naked human foot. The imprints of the five toes were deep, and very wide apart: the mark of the heel was even deeper showing the great weight of its owner. But it was the size and the length of stride that staggered him. His own feet were not small, but he could comfortably have got both of them inside one of these. And the distance between them was over five feet.

The second were very different. They had been made by the toe of a pointed shoe, and the distance between them was four feet.

"So Bill was on the right track after all," he said straightening up. "Poor devil!"

"Look here," remarked Percy, "you might remember that I am not as well versed in reading mud as you. I assume you are alluding to Lopez, but you might explain your sympathy."

"You spot, don't you," said Jim, "that that is made by the toe of a shoe." He pointed to a second trail. "You can see the alternate feet— right and left. You remember also the very pointed shoes he used to wear. So the betting is a hundred to one that that trail was made by him. Now how did he make it? How would you make a mark like that with your shoe?"

"By standing on tip-toe," said his cousin.

"And then hopping four feet like a ballet dancer!" Jim laughed shortly. "No, my lad, you can take it from me that those marks were not made by him trying to imitate Pavlova. He was a short man, and look at the length of his stride. He was running for his life, pursued by the thing that made those other marks."

"How do you know he was being pursued?"

"Because in two places the thing has obliterated his footprint. Therefore it was pursuing him. And it was not running: you can see the mark of its heel every time. Though in all conscience with a stride like that it would have no need to."

"Good Lord! it's a bit grim," said Percy shakily. "What do you think happened, Jim?"

"My dear man, I know no more than you do. Perhaps the thing went on board, as Bill said, and forcibly seized Lopez. Perhaps Lopez swam ashore, and came walking down here. All that I can tell you for certain is what is written there in the soft ground. And that is that at this actual spot the Brazilian was fleeing for his life pursued by something, the like of which I have never come across before."

"And which must certainly have caught him," said his cousin.

"Unless a miracle occurred."

"And then?"

Jim pointed to the bog.

"That would seem at any rate one solution," he remarked quietly. "Though they may, of course, be keeping him as a prisoner. And now to get down to the present situation, young feller. You may remember I mentioned the possibility of these things being harmless. Well, you can wash that out."

"Carry on," said Percy.

"It's up to you to decide. Do you want to go on, or do you want to go back? I tell you candidly that I think we may at any moment bump into a position of very grave danger."

"What are you going to do yourself?" demanded his cousin.

"In view of the fact that that poor devil may still be alive, I'm going on," said Jim.

"Then I'm darned well coming too," cried Percy. "In fact your question, my dear James, seems to be of the fatuous order that I have so often noted with pain over the rest of your conversation."

"Stout fellow," grinned Jim. "Let's push."

They skirted round the sodden patch, and twenty yards beyond it came to what Jim had been searching for. Stretching into the forest till it disappeared in the gloom ran a path: they had found at any rate one of the tracks that might lead them to the solution of the mystery.

They stood for a time getting their eyes accustomed to the semi-darkness after the blinding sunshine: then Jim took his revolver from its holster.

"Take yours out too, Percy," he said, "but for the love of *Allah* don't point it anywhere near me. And keep your eyes skinned over the back of your shoulder. You don't want to be surprised from behind."

The going was good: evidently the path was one in frequent use.

To start with it ran quite straight: then it began to twist and jink though the general direction remained the same. And after a while even the sound of the surf died away: the silence seemed to press on them like a blanket.

At length they reached a small clearing from which four other tracks led out like the spokes of a wheel, and Jim paused. None of them seemed to be a direct continuation of the one they had come along, and it was a toss-up which to take. The compass was well-nigh useless, as they had only the vaguest idea of their present position, but Jim finally selected one that ran a little south of west. Then having placed a conspicuous fern to mark the path they had come by they started along the new one.

The pace Jim set was as fast as he dared, consistent with safety. He had not exaggerated when he spoke of very grave danger, and he realised that it would be graver still if darkness overtook them while they were still in the forest. And so, whilst he scouted with the utmost caution whenever he came to a bend, he almost ran along the straight stretches. The reassuring thing was the continued silence, which seemed to indicate that the other occupants of the forest were asleep. And he was sufficiently confident of his powers of stalking to hope that, if that were so, he would be able, if they had the luck to find them, to get near enough to see what manner of thing it was they were up against, and then get away again in safety. There might even be a bare possibility of rescuing the Brazilian if he was still alive, but that could only be decided later.

Such was the general plan he decided on as they pressed forward, when there came a sudden startling interruption. From away to the left a ship's siren blared three times. They halted abruptly, and Jim stared at his cousin.

"I wonder who that is," he said thoughtfully.

"Probably that ship we saw from the top of the hill," answered Percy.

The siren wailed again, and Jim frowned.

"What are they making that infernal din for?" he cried. "Sounds to me as if they were signalling. Percy, I wonder if that is Miguel's yacht come earlier than we expected. If so. . ."

He did not complete the sentence, for a further interruption occurred, this time much nearer at hand. The bell they had heard that morning began to toll, and with it the sleeping forest awakened to life. From all around them came the sounds of movement, and Jim seized his cousin by the arm.

"In here, for your life," he muttered, forcing his way off the track into the undergrowth. "We're right in the middle of them."

The bell went on tolling, though its sound was almost drowned by the noises around them. And once or twice a hoarse bellow, that was half roar, half grunt, rang out.

They cowered down behind some giant ferns: some of the things were close to them. But so dense was the vegetation that they could see nothing. And after a while the sounds grew fainter and fainter until they died away in the distance. The bell ceased tolling: silence settled once again.

At length Jim straightened up and stepped out into the path.

"That was rather nearer than I liked," he remarked. "It is a damned lucky thing for us, old lad, that they were asleep when we arrived."

"What do you make of it, Jim?" said his cousin.

"The bell was obviously a warning signal," he answered, "which was rung when the siren was heard. And now they have gone off to investigate."

"But what are they?" cried Percy.

"You can take it from me," said Jim gravely, "that whatever they are, it is a question of running no risks. But since we are here, and the owners of the place appear to have gone, we may as well explore a little further."

They moved on cautiously: it was more than likely that all of them had not gone, and that a guard had been left. And then, quite unexpectedly the track opened out into a big clearing.

"Good God!" muttered Jim, "look at that."

The space was some thirty yards square, with several openings similar to the one they stood in. Above them the trees met, seemingly a solid ceiling of scarlet, splashed here and there with the vivid blues and yellows of gaudily coloured parrots. Shafts of sunlight shone through, dappling the sides with every shade of green: it was a riot of colour that would have made an artist rave. But the two men who stood motionless at the entrance hardly noticed it: they had eyes only for what stood in the centre of the ground.

Hanging from a frame was a brass bell, which was still swinging gently though no sound came from it. And chased on the bell in black lettering they could read the words—S.S. *Paquinetta*. Underneath it, between the two uprights a man was sitting, a man who did not stir. His knees, lashed together with some fibrous stuff, were drawn up: his hands were stretched out in front of him. His head lolled sideways: his face, so distorted with agony and terror, that the features were almost unrecognisable, stared at them. It was Lopez, the Brazilian, and he was dead.

"Poor devil," muttered Percy shakily. "How did they do it?"

"Ask me another," said Jim grimly, as he bent over the dead man. "They've murdered him somehow, and yet there's not a sign of any violence nor a trace of any blood."

"Perhaps he died of fright."

"Fright may send a man mad, but I've never yet heard of it killing anybody."

He again bent over the Brazilian, and suddenly he gave an exclamation.

"Look at his right hand," he said. "Do you see how terribly swollen it is? He's been poisoned, Percy. That's how they killed the poor blighter."

He straightened up thoughtfully.

"And if they used poison," he continued, "and lashed his legs, it proves they have a certain measure of human brain. No mere animal would do such a thing."

He stared round doubtfully: what was the best thing to do? Never again would they have such an opportunity for exploration. A number of paths similar to the one they had come by led out of the clearing: it seemed too good a chance to miss. And selecting one at random he started along it.

It led to another clearing, and they had barely gone ten yards along it when he stopped short with a sudden gasp.

"Great Heavens!" he muttered. "It can't be true."

In the centre of the second space there stood a mysterious object. It was about four feet high and fashioned into the representation of a grotesque little man. The thing was a monstrosity with a huge paunch and tiny legs. In colour it was dull yellow, and in the centre of the forehead there glittered a blood-red pool of light. And after a while the usually imperturbable Jim began to shake with uncontrollable excitement: he had seen that dull yellow before in smaller images, and knew what it meant.

"Gold, Percy: gold or I'll eat my hat," he cried. "And if that's a ruby in its forehead it is worth a king's ransom."

The thing stood on a little island with a circular strip of water some five feet wide all round it. Between its base and the water there was undergrowth also to a width of about five feet.

"It's the temple of their image," went on Jim. "Gosh! old lad, what about having a dart for that ruby. If it's gold, as I'm sure it is, there will be no difficulty in working it loose."

"I'm with you," cried Percy, "but we'd better get a move on."

They went towards it, and suddenly with a cry of warning Jim tried to spring back. For the ground in front seemed to rise towards them, and they felt themselves falling through space. So intent had they been on the idol that they had paid no attention to the path. And they had trodden on one end of some baulks of wood roughly joined together which pivoted seesaw fashion on a central hinge.

It was not a long fall, and they picked themselves up shaken but otherwise unhurt, as the thing creaked back into position again leaving them in darkness.

"One of the oldest native animal traps there is," cried Jim bitterly. "My God! Percy, we've let ourselves in for it now. Thank heavens! there were no spikes at the bottom. What a foul stench," he added.

And then he paused abruptly and gripped his cousin's arm.

"There's something here," he muttered. "I can hear it moving."

They crouched motionless staring into the darkness, and quite distinctly they could hear its heavy breathing. Then came a slow movement, as if some big body was gradually changing its position. The smell seemed to increase, and they waited tensely, conscious only of the loud beating of their own hearts.

Came a grunt and a shuffling noise: the thing was coming towards them. And suddenly they saw two gleaming eyes not a yard away. The thing was on them, and at that moment Jim's revolver roared out, sounding deafening in the shut in space.

The eyes disappeared: he had fired straight between them. There was a thud which shook the ground, one or two convulsive movements, then silence. The thing was dead.

"That's going to bring them about our heels," muttered Jim, "if they're anywhere in the neighbourhood."

And then he gave a sudden exclamation.

"By Jove!" he cried, "I believe this is a passage, and not merely a trap. It's lighter along there."

"Are you going to have a look and see what you've killed?" said his cousin.

"I'm going to beat it while the going is good," answered Jim grimly. "If we're found here, my lad, we shan't be needing our return tickets from Rio."

He led the way, and his surmise was correct. They were in an underground tunnel, and on coming to the bend where it had seemed to Jim to be less dark they could see the entrance ahead of them. They raced towards it, up the rising ground; and found that it opened into a corner of the original clearing. And for a while they stood there listening. Had the sound of the shot brought the others back? But nothing stirred: save for the motionless figure of the dead Brazilian the place was deserted.

Suddenly Percy gripped his cousin's arm again.

"Look down that track," he muttered. "I saw something move. Something dark. It swung itself across. Man, it was the size of an elephant."

"I don't see anything," said Jim. "Are you sure?"

"It was gone in a flash," cried Percy. "But I know I saw it."

"Then let's go," remarked the other. "Probably our hosts are returning. You lead the way this time."

And with a final glance at the dead man, and the bell from the ill-fated *Paquinetta* he followed his cousin out of the clearing.

CHAPTER 10

"I say, Jim, oughtn't we to have come to that junction of the paths by now?"

They had been walking rapidly for over a quarter of an hour, and so far there had been no sign of anything following them. Whatever it was that Percy had seen, apparently it had not seen them. And as the significance of the question sank into his mind Jim cursed himself for a fool. He had followed his cousin blindly out of the clearing, his mind preoccupied with other things, and he realised now that Percy had taken the wrong path. They should have reached the junction long since.

"You're right, Percy," he said. "We're on a different track."

"I'm damned sorry, old boy," said his cousin apologetically. "I was so flustered by that thing I saw that I forgot what I was doing."

"My fault as much as yours," cried Jim. "However we can't go back, so we must go on. It will probably lead us into the open somewhere. The devil of it is that we haven't got much more daylight."

They pushed on faster, and after a while Jim began to grow uneasy. For the track kept turning right handed, and the ground was becoming appreciably softer.

"We're getting near the river, Percy," he said. "And that's about the last spot we want. Unless we find a path going away to the left we're in the soup."

Suddenly the track forked, and Percy paused.

"Which one, Jim?"

"Left, of course, but where on earth is this foul stench of musk coming from?"

They went on a few yards and soon discovered. The track had forked in order to pass on each side of a large, stagnant pool. Rotting vegetation hung in festoons round the banks, but by craning forward carefully they could see the water. And floating motionless in it, their evil-looking snouts just above the surface, were scores of crocodiles. Others were lying on the slimy ooze round the banks, and one huge one occupied the post of honour on a half-submerged tree trunk.

"Repulsive looking brutes," said Jim. "We must be nearer the river than I thought."

And a further few paces brought them to it. Their path turned abruptly left-handed following the bank, and they were just turning along it when from the distance there came a steady creaking noise and they paused listening.

"The rowlocks of a boat," remarked Jim. "Now we may find out something."

Only a thin screen of undergrowth separated them from the water, and with infinite caution they peered through. In front of them was the river; to their right the stinking crocodile pool. And by leaning forward a little they could see down stream for about fifty yards.

Suddenly a boat hove in sight, and in the stern sat Don Miguel. By his side was a bloated looking red-faced man who held the tiller ropes, and Jim put his lips to his cousin's ear.

"Bully McIntyre," he whispered. "So it was the yacht."

He was evidently having some argument with Don Miguel and at length the latter shrugged his shoulders. The sailor gave an order, the men ceased rowing, and McIntyre ran the nose of the boat into the bank.

"Get ashore, Mr. Murdoch," he ordered, "and see what it's like."

An officer who had been sitting in the bows seized some over-hanging branches and hoisted himself out. He was on the opposite side of the pool to Jim and Percy, but they could see the glint of his white ducks through the undergrowth.

"There's a regular path here," he sang out, "which seems to lead into the forest. Shall I go along and explore it a bit?"

"Yes—but don't get lost."

And even as McIntyre spoke a scream of fear rang out. They had a fleeting glimpse of a white-clad figure falling through the air, followed by a splash. And the motionless logs were motionless no longer. The water in the pool swirled angrily, and before their eyes the wretched man was torn to pieces.

"What's the matter?" shouted McIntyre, as the boat moved away from the bank, and came upstream a few strokes till it was abreast of the pool.

"Good God!" he went on, "he fell in that damned pool and the crocs have got him. You filthy brutes," he roared picking up a rifle and taking aim at the big one on the tree. He shot it through the eye, and with its tail lashing furiously the great reptile rolled over and sank in the water.

"I guess we'll come back tomorrow morning," said Don Miguel, "when we've got the day in front of us." And the other nodded assent.

The boat went about, and after a while the noise of the oars died away in the distance.

"Why did that poor devil scream, Percy?" said Jim with a queer look in his eyes.

"Dash it all, old lad, most people would give tongue if they found themselves in a crocodile pool."

"Yes—but not until they found themselves there. He yelled before he knew there were any crocodiles."

Percy stared at Jim.

"You mean. . ."

"I mean that he never fell in: he was thrown or pushed in. And it was what he saw in that fleeting second that terrified him, and nothing to do with the crocodiles. Didn't you see the undergrowth moving on the other side of the river as something went through it, keeping pace with the boat? Well, there was something this side as well."

"Following Miguel's party."

"Exactly. And for that reason, at any rate, we can be thankful the yacht has arrived earlier than we expected. It's distracted the attention of these brutes away from us. Otherwise, I don't mind telling you that I think our chances of getting through alive were pretty minute."

"I'd like to have seen that thing you shot."

"So would I. And in due course you shall—or one like it. But not this trip, Percy."

"You are coming back?"

"Of course. Once Judy is safely on her way back to England I return here."

"And what about the other bunch?"

"They haven't got the map, and if we can get away tonight we've got 'em stung. Moreover, seeing that almost all the crew are dagos, one or two more regrettable incidents such as we've just witnessed are going to shake 'em badly. Let's get a move on."

They turned along the track going up stream, and found that it soon left the bank and turned back into the forest. And now time was vital: at the most half an hour of daylight remained to them. The track jinked, then jinked again, and Jim gave a sigh of relief as he glanced at his compass: they were heading for the open. But there was still at least two miles to cover, and the going was getting worse. Evidently the track they were on was not much used: tendrils of vegetation met across the clearing through which they had to force their way. And dusk was beginning to fall when the first faint reek of the swamp came to their nostrils.

At last they saw it in front of them, and Jim's face was grave. A thin white vapour was already rising, and only too well did he realise the danger that that portended. In the walk that lay before them a single false step might mean death in the green bog, and to have mist as well as darkness to contend against would double their difficulty. And he was just debating in his mind whether it would not be better to spend the night where they were and wait for the dawn, when they saw stealing out from behind the hill that stood outlined against the darkening sky, the lights of a ship.

"Don Miguel's yacht," he muttered. "What the deuce has she been doing there? I don't like it, Percy. When we heard her siren she was away south of us. What has taken her round to the north of the island?"

"Probably looking for us," said his cousin.

"Exactly," remarked Jim. "And they couldn't avoid finding us."

"I don't see that they can do any harm," said Percy. "They are probably peeved over the map, but as you've got that in your pocket it doesn't matter much."

"Damn the map: they can have that for shaving paper. It's Judy I'm thinking of."

"Surely they wouldn't touch her."

"That swine of a dwarf would murder his mother for sixpence," grunted Jim. "Still, Bill was there. Anyway, that settles it: we must push on. I suppose one party went away to explore the river, while Dresler went round in the yacht to find us. Hullo! what's that?"

Clear and distinct through the still air had come the sharp crack of a rifle. They paused instinctively, and the next moment even Jim felt the hair on his head begin to rise. Yell after yell of frenzied terror rang out: then sudden, abrupt silence.

They peered ahead, but could see nothing in the fading light.

"Heaven send it wasn't Bill coming to find us," cried Jim.

"What was it, Jim?" muttered his cousin.

"It *was* a man," he answered grimly. "I wouldn't like to say what it is now."

"Somebody fallen into the bog perhaps."

"Possibly. But you don't let off your gun at a bog. And as I say, Heaven send it wasn't Bill."

"He'd never have left Judy."

"I agree. But supposing Judy left him."

He pointed at the yacht which was now abreast of them.

"That's what I'm afraid of, Percy."

"You mean they may have kidnapped her."

"Exactly. As a lever to make us give up the map. And then Bill came along to meet us."

"He'd never have let them take her."

"How could he prevent them? He would have shot anything he saw coming off from the shore, but he couldn't shoot a boat-load of men coming from a yacht. Damn it! if it isn't Bill who can it be?"

"And you think one of the things got him?"

"I do," said Jim gravely. "The poor old lad fired and missed. And what we've got to watch out for is that we don't do the same. It may have been a chance encounter, or they may post sentinels out at night."

They pressed on as fast as they dared. Luckily the mist was getting no denser, but the light had almost gone. And it was about five minutes after they had heard the shot that Jim rounded a projecting bush and stopped abruptly with his hand held up in warning to his cousin.

"Look at that," he muttered as Percy joined him. "It was here that it happened."

The undergrowth was trampled and beaten down, showing every sign of a desperate struggle. But of the combatants there was no trace.

They listened intently: nothing stirred in the forest. And at length Jim crept cautiously forward.

Suddenly his foot met something hard, and he stooped and picked it up. And the next moment he cursed savagely.

"My gun, Percy," he said. "The one I gave Bill."

A spasm of rage shook him.

"By God!" he cried, "these things—whatever they are—will regret this. Once I've got Judy safely away, I'll come back here with a proper expedition and exterminate the lot. What's the matter?"

His cousin had bent forward excitedly, and was staring at something on the ground.

"It's a hat, Jim," he cried. "And it's not Bill's."

"What's that? Let me see it."

He picked up the hat: it was wet and sticky. And glancing at his fingers he saw they were red. He looked inside the hat, and then with a feeling of uncontrollable repulsion he flung it far out into the swamp. For its late owner's head had been literally battered to pieces.

"Poor devil," he muttered. "You're sure it's not Bill's, Percy?"

"Absolutely certain."

"Then how did my gun get here?"

But his cousin did not answer: he was standing by a big tree that grew on one side of the beaten-down patch.

"Jim," he cried shakily, "this tree is all wet."

It was true, and for a moment Jim stared at it incredulously. At first he had assumed that the deed had been done with a club or even possibly the butt of the gun. But the blood on the tree told a different tale, and one that was well-nigh inconceivable. For it proved that the man had been killed by having his head bashed against the trunk, and the strength necessary to do such a thing was unbelievable. And in his imagination he visualised the scene. The shot, fired in a panic at the monstrous thing that had suddenly appeared out of the dusk: the brief hopeless struggle when the bullet missed, and then the ghastly ending with the lifeless body flung into the bog.

But who was it? Surely Bill would not have handed over the only long range weapon they had with them to somebody else, unless he had been compelled to. At the best of times he was a very bad shot with a revolver, so it was hard to believe that he would have lent the rifle to anyone willingly. And if that was so what had happened on board the motorboat?

The forest was silent as they started off again. Twice during the next hour they heard from far off that strange grunting roar answered from three or four different places which showed that the denizens were on the prowl. But their luck held good: the track along the edge of the swamp was deserted. And at last they were clear of it, and able to increase their pace as they began to climb the hill.

They reached the top: the lagoon below them was in darkness. No light came from the place where the boat had been anchored. And sick with anxiety they half ran, half slid down towards the beach. The dinghy was still where they had left her, and it was while they were getting her afloat that a large stone came bounding down the hill and crashed into the water a few yards away.

For a moment Jim paused, staring up at the sky line behind them. Was it they who had loosened it as they came down, or had something else started it? But he could see nothing, and jumping into the dinghy they pulled feverishly for the boat.

"Bill," he shouted. "Ahoy! there, Bill."

There was no answer, and leaving Percy to make the dinghy fast, he scrambled on board.

"Bill," he cried again. "Judy. Where are you?"

He dashed into the little saloon, and this time there was an answer.

"Good evening, my dear Mr. Maitland," came a well-known voice. "You are, if I may say so, a little later than I expected."

He lit the lamp: seated at the table was the dwarf with a malignant smile on his lips.

"You little devil," roared Jim. "What have you done with Miss Draycott?"

The blind man held up a deprecating hand.

"Really, Mr. Maitland," he protested, "the space here is very confined. Would it be too much if I asked you to moderate your voice?"

"Where is Miss Draycott, Dresler?" said Jim controlling himself with an immense effort. "Because I warn you quite quietly that I am not in a mood to be trifled with tonight, and if anything has happened to her I shall blow out your brains without the smallest compunction."

"It is extraordinary," remarked the other, "with what unerring accuracy I have read your character. I actually said to Monty—you remember Sir Montague Barnet, of course—when he went ashore that I was sure you would say something bright and original like that."

Jim glanced at Percy who had come into the saloon.

"So Barnet went ashore, did he? From here?"

"Yes. I thought perhaps you might meet him, but in the darkness you must have missed one another. However he is sure to be back soon."

"May I ask if he was wearing a Homburg hat?"

"My dear sir, you know my affliction. I'm afraid I didn't ask him. But if you saw a man with a Homburg hat it must have been Monty."

"I didn't," said Jim tersely. "I only saw the hat."

"You speak in riddles," murmured the dwarf.

"You'll get the solution soon," remarked Jim. "To return to Miss Draycott. I assume she is on board the yacht."

"Correct. And with her is the admirable guardian you left whose name I fear I do not know. He was most abusive, and had to be hit over the head with a belaying-pin, but I don't think his condition is dangerous."

"And your object in this abduction?"

"My dear fellow, you pain me. You know as well as I do. Now where is the correct map?"

"In my pocket," said Jim.

"Excellent. By the way I congratulate you on the idea, Mr. Maitland. It appealed to me immensely when I gathered from Monty's blasphemy what had happened."

"Cut it out," remarked Jim curtly. "I assume that you want it."

"That is the notion. And fearing you might prove difficult about it, I took the precaution of removing the lady. She is quite safe at present, and her quarters are far more comfortable. But I do not need to remind you, do I, that my friend Don Miguel has a keen eye for a pretty girl, and that his reputation is not perhaps all that it should be. And so I earnestly advise you not to play any more tricks this time, either over the map, or with me. Because if you do I cannot guarantee Miss Draycott's continued safety."

"And what is your proposal?" said Jim.

"A simple one. As soon as Monty returns, you will start up the motor and take your boat round to the other side of the island where the yacht is now anchored. We will all go on board her, and then when you have satisfied us that the map is what we want—well, my dear Maitland, as far as I am concerned you can go to the devil."

"Very interesting," said Jim with a laugh. "Extraordinary what bloomers you always seem to make in your schemes Dresler, isn't it?"

"What do you mean?" remarked the blind man softly.

"I mean that if we wait here till Barnet returns we shall wait a considerable time. It was very unwise of him to go ashore alone."

"Have you killed him?" said the dwarf even more softly.

"No: but he's dead. This island is a funny place, my friend, and if you take my advice you'll do what I'm going to do—leave it."

"How did Barnet die?"

"His brains were bashed out against a tree, if you want to know."

"Who by?"

"I think *what* by would be a better way of putting it."

"I don't believe you," snarled the other. "You murdered him because he'd found the treasure. He told me he thought he might be able to."

"With the map he'd got?"

"Yes. You may be clever, Mr. Maitland, but other people aren't fools. You'd altered the position of the hill and the tree, but the writing at the bottom remained."

"Except for the little bit that was missing in the left-hand corner," said Jim.

"That either had to be east or west," sneered the dwarf.

"It was west to be exact. I found it that night we had our little chat in your house at Hampstead. I fear Barnet may have thought it was east: that might account for us finding his hat where we did."

"His hat! Where was Barnet himself?"

"His body had evidently been flung into the bog. There was no trace of it."

"A likely story, Mr. Maitland. You tell me that a man of Barnet's size and weight had his brains bashed out against a tree and expect me to believe it!"

"It's a matter of complete indifference to me whether you believe it or whether you don't," drawled Jim. "I'm sorry the poor devil met the end he did, but he wasn't a gentleman whose habits I liked, and I'm not going into mourning for him."

"Don't be too sure about that," said the other thickly. "I would point out that there are some forty of us against you two. And justice can be summary."

"Do you suggest making Percy and me walk the plank," laughed Jim. "Come, come, Dresler—I don't think the old brain is working very well. Do you seriously imagine that I am going to barge straight into the lion's den, and deliver myself bound hand and foot to a bunch of damned stiffs like you?"

"And if you don't what about Miss Draycott?"

"Go a little further, my friend: what about you? You seem to forget that it is fifty-fifty. Until Miss Draycott and Bill Blackett are delivered over to me safe and sound, you stay on board here. You can't catch me in a row boat, and if your pal Don Miguel tries any monkey tricks like ramming me with the yacht I'll hang you over the side to act as a fender."

For a while the dwarf was silent: then he shrugged his shoulders.

"There is no reason why we should lose our tempers, Mr. Maitland, is there? I feel sure that matters can be settled amicably."

"Then go on feeling sure," remarked Jim. "It may help. But all I'm sure about is that if a hair of Miss Draycott's head has been injured you'll pray for death before I'm through with you. And you'd better make them understand the fact on board the yacht, when we get there tomorrow morning."

"Why tomorrow morning? Why not tonight?"

"Your second error, Dresler. The passage through the reef here is bad enough even when it's light. To do it in the darkness would be literally impossible."

"You know best," said the dwarf uneasily. "I would have preferred to reach the yacht tonight."

Jim stared at him grimly.

"You don't suppose that I want to remain here, do you, you rotten little sweep? But when I say it is impossible, I mean it's impossible. There would not be one chance in a thousand of our getting through without stoving in our bottom. And though I have not the slightest objection to your drowning, I have the very gravest to losing the boat and being compelled to leave Miss Draycott on board the yacht."

Once again the dwarf shrugged his shoulders.

"Very good, Mr. Maitland. As I said before, you know best. Might I ask what the time is now?"

"Ten o'clock," said Jim curtly. "Eight hours before we can start."

He began pacing up and down the tiny saloon, his mind on the rack with anxiety. The thought of Judy alone in the yacht, with Bill possibly still unconscious, drove him almost insane. But there was nothing to be done: to attempt to navigate the entrance would be the act of a madman. For a while he even thought of the possibility of trying to make his way on foot over the island, but even if he succeeded there would be no way of getting on board the yacht save

311

by swimming. And the chances of a swimmer in those shark infested waters were negligible. As far as he himself was concerned he would have been prepared to risk it, but the vital consideration was Judy. And if anything happened to him what was going to become of her?

"Well since there is all that time before us," remarked the dwarf cutting into his thoughts, "it might be interesting to exchange views on the matter that has brought us both here. Have you had any luck in locating this hypothetical treasure, Mr. Maitland?"

"I have not," said Jim tersely. "The only luck that my cousin and I have had today is getting off the island alive!"

"Are you really serious?" said the other with an incredulous smile.

"I have already told you what happened to Barnet," answered Jim. "And as you yourself remarked he was a big heavy man."

The smile became more incredulous.

"I quite appreciate, of course, your natural wish to keep the pitch for yourself," said the dwarf gently. "But I fear you will have to get a rather better one than that, Mr. Maitland."

"Look here, Dresler," remarked Jim wearily, "I'm getting a little tired of you. What do you imagine can be my object in telling a lie over a thing that can easily be proved or disproved? Anyway you can now go along to Blackett's cabin, and I'll pull you out in the morning. I want a respite from your face. Show him the way, Percy."

The dwarf got down off his chair, and stood for a moment or two in the centre of the saloon. Jim was rummaging in a cupboard for the whisky: Percy was lighting a cigarette. And so there was no one to notice a head that suddenly appeared in the fan-light, with a pair of bestial eyes fixed on the short misshapen figure of the blind man. Amazement followed incredulity in their expression: gloating anticipation followed amazement. Then as Jim straightened up the head was abruptly withdrawn.

"Good night," said the dwarf as Percy took him by the arm.

"Between half-past five and six," grunted Jim.

"I shall be ready," remarked the other.

"It's the devil, Percy," said Jim when his cousin returned. "I tried to bluff it out in front of that little swine, but they've got six to four the better of us. And anyone who is not bughouse can see they have."

"You don't think they'll hurt Judy, do you?"

"No," said Jim thoughtfully. "At any rate not tonight. Their only idea is to get the correct map. And they're not going to do anything which would jeopardise their chances of obtaining it. But the fact remains that we shall have to give it to them. We must get Judy off that yacht, and they won't let her come without it. It's a pity, but it can't be helped."

"You meant to come back here?"

"Of course I did. Once we'd got Judy safe in Rio, we could have fitted out a properly armed expedition. And even if we'd found no treasure we should have had a lot of fun. But now that swab Miguel will know as much as we do. He may or may not decide to carry on now, when he finds the island is not uninhabited. And if he doesn't the same idea will strike him—go back and refit. Which is where he will score. He's got a yacht ready to hand: we haven't."

He rose and stretched himself.

"Ah! well. Absolutely nothing matters beyond getting Judy safely out of it. Hullo! what the devil do you want?"

He swung round and stared at the dwarf who was standing in the entrance white faced and shaking.

"Was it either of you," he quavered, "who passed his hand over my face?"

"It was not. What happened?"

"A hand—a huge hairy hand—touched me. I could feel the fingers pressing on me gently."

"Stay here," snapped Jim. "Percy, get your gun, and come with me."

He picked up his own revolver, and started along the corridor out of which the cabins led.

"Is there a light inside?" he muttered.

"No," said Percy. "I didn't bother as he's blind."

"Go back and get my electric torch. It's in the small locker." And suddenly his voice rose to a shout. "God! look at that."

They had left the dwarf standing in the centre of the saloon. He was still there, but just above his head were two great brown hands, that, even as they watched, shot down and clutched him by the throat. Then, before their eyes, he was drawn up, screaming like a pig, and disappeared.

For a moment or two they stood motionless, rooted to the spot: then simultaneously they dashed back into the saloon. The fan-light was wide open: he had been lifted through it. They could still hear him screaming, but as they darted up on deck there came a heavy splash, and silence.

"The dinghy," roared Jim. "Pull it alongside, while I get the rifle."

313

They jumped into the little boat, and rowed feverishly for the shore. And having beached her they stood listening. Not a sound could they hear, save the monotonous roar of the breakers on the reef. And then from some way off the piteous shrieks of the dwarf began again. They raced along the beach, but the cries grew fainter and fainter. Some stones came rattling down beside them: the thing was climbing the hill. And after a while silence settled once again.

They made their way slowly back to the dinghy: any idea of pursuit was impossible. By day Jim would not have hesitated to fire, trusting to his marvellous eye not to hit Dresler. But in the darkness he was helpless.

"This is getting beyond a joke," he said quietly, as they rowed back. "Not that I care a damn what happens to that little brute, but it's going to make it the devil for us."

"In what way?" cried his cousin.

"He was our guarantee for Judy. And now tomorrow morning we've got to tackle the yacht with neither him nor Barnet. Of course they won't believe us. Damn it! Percy, I wouldn't believe it myself if I hadn't seen it with my own eyes."

They tied up the boat, and went on board. And at that moment the moon rose from behind the hill. Silhouetted on the sky line was an enormous figure, and instinctively Jim threw up his rifle. Then he lowered it again.

"Too long a range," he said regretfully. "But look at the size of the thing."

A bellowing roar of defiance, twice repeated, came across the water: then the sky line was clear once more.

"I hold no brief for Dresler," he went on gravely, "but he's going to pay for his sins this night. Look at the marks of the brute on the deck."

In the brilliant light of the tropical moon the wet footprints showed up clearly: marks just like those they had seen in the mud that afternoon.

"Probably the same one that took the wretched Lopez," muttered Jim. "Gad! Percy, I'll be glad to get Judy out of this."

"Why don't we push off now?" said his cousin. "This light is almost as bright as day."

"You're right, old lad. We will. I'd forgotten about the moon when I said tomorrow morning. Go and get the engines started."

Percy went below, and Jim sat down on a coil of rope thinking.

How to get Judy off the yacht—that was the problem. He had no idea which her cabin would be, and even if he could find out it would be impossible to approach the yacht unseen in the moonlight. There was certain to be some form of watch kept, however slack discipline might be. And then there was Bill too: it was out of the question to leave him behind. Still it was a good idea to go now: anything was better than this enforced idleness. And he would feel easier in his mind if he was on board the yacht himself.

He glanced at the opening in the rocks with anxious eyes. If only Bill had been still with them it would have made it so much easier. They wanted someone in the bows badly, to help con the boat.

"All ready when you are," shouted Percy, and he rose to his feet. The sooner they were through the better, and if they were going to pile up there was no good putting it off. But their luck was in. Twice did a wet jagged pinnacle of rock show out of the swell within a foot of them: once quite distinctly they felt her graze. And then came Jim's cheerful shout of "Full speed ahead"; they were through, and steering for the open sea.

"What did you make of that thing, Jim?" said his cousin, joining him at the wheel. "Have you ever seen anything like it before?"

"No, I haven't," answered the other thoughtfully. "But we've seen what happened to Lopez. And there is no doubt at all in my mind that he never went ashore of his own free will. They got him just as they got Dresler. Which shows pretty conclusively that they do not remain merely on the defensive, but are prepared to be the aggressors. Incredible though it may seem, Percy, my own belief is that very few people have ever got away from this island—that what Bill told us was true. And it's that, far more than any harm Judy may come to from Don Miguel, that is making me so desperately uneasy."

"You think they may attack the yacht?"

"I think it is a certainty. But my hope is that they may wait till a party goes ashore, as they did in the case of the *Paquinetta*. They evidently possess a certain low cunning, and then they may hesitate to board the yacht when she is fully manned. In which case it will be tomorrow night, because they won't land anyone till they've got the map. That's what I'm banking on."

He paused abruptly, staring ahead. They were steering parallel with the edge of the swamp, over which the mist now lay like a blanket of cotton wool.

"Listen," he cried. "My God! there's another. Race her, Percy: take

315

the bottom out of her. There is firing going on in front of us."

His cousin sprang below, and the next moment the boat was quivering from bow to stern like a mad thing. But even above the sound of the engine came the ominous crack, crack, of firearms, followed after a time by an even more ominous silence. And sick with anxiety Jim stood at the wheel staring over the glittering silver water ahead. Did that abrupt cessation of firing mean that the things had been repulsed, or did it mean. . .? Not even to himself could he complete the alternative.

They rounded the point, and saw the yacht lying at anchor a mile away. Lights were shining through some of the portholes, but they could see no sign of any movement, though in the moonlight the deck and bridge were clearly visible. She was about a quarter of a mile from the shore, and the first thing they noticed as they drew alongside was that the steps of the gangway were sopping wet.

They made fast, and dashed up on deck. And the sight that confronted them was so incredible that for a moment or two they stood there unable to move. The yacht was a shambles. Just in front of them lay Bully McIntyre, a blood-spattered crowbar still gripped in his hands. His head was bent back, and round his throat were great red weals. His neck had been broken from behind. Others of the crew lay about with their heads battered in: the sickly smell of blood was everywhere. It was a ghastly scene in the cold white light at any time, but one that was calculated to make them numb with horror when they thought of Judy.

They rushed below; all the cabins were open. And inside the first one they entered they came on what was left of Don Miguel. But it was not on the crushed remnants that Jim's eyes were fixed, but on the chair that stood by the bed. On it lay a little revolver, and he picked it up.

"Judy's," he muttered hoarsely. "The one I gave her. Oh! my God."

"Jim: come here."

A hoarse shaking voice which he dimly recognised as Percy's came from outside, and like a man walking in his sleep he joined him in the corridor.

"Look at that."

The door of the next cabin had been splintered to match wood, and on the bed lay Judy's hat. For a while they stood looking at it, not daring to meet one another's eyes. The situation was beyond speech:

beyond thought. Judy was in the hands of these monstrous horrors, without even a revolver to protect herself with.

"What are we going to do, Jim: what can we do?"

"Do," answered the other tensely, "do. Go after her, of course. And if there's no other way out—shoot her. But there's going to be another way out, Percy."

His voice rose to a savage shout. "We'll beat the brutes yet."

<h2 style="text-align:center">Chapter 11</h2>

Judy Draycott bolted the door of her cabin in Don Miguel's yacht, and tried to think coherently. Her brain was whirling: the events of the last few hours seemed like some hideous nightmare. She had been asleep when Jim and Percy went ashore, and had only awakened two hours afterwards to find Bill Blackett mounting guard and looking worried.

"Where are the others?" she asked and he told her.

"Madness, miss," he remarked gloomily, "but there's no use arguing with Mr. Maitland. And what makes it worse is that the *dago's* yacht has arrived. She passed some way out, and she hasn't seen us yet, but if she comes to look for us there's no way of hiding. And then we're between the devil and the deep sea."

He scanned the side of the hill through his telescope, but nothing stirred.

The afternoon dragged slowly on, and at four-thirty she went below to make some tea. To while away the time the sailor had been telling her some of Jim's exploits, but she noticed that he never let five minutes elapse without searching the hill with his glass. And when she returned with the cups he was pacing up and down the deck looking anxiously at the sun.

"Another hour and a half, two hours at the most, and it'll be dark," he said. "Blast! here's the yacht."

She turned round: steaming slowly round the headland came the boat whose graceful lines she had last seen in Rio harbour.

"They've spotted us," said Bill, shutting up his telescope. "Now what are they going to do?"

They were not left long in doubt: having arrived opposite the opening in the rocks the yacht's engines stopped, and she remained there rolling lazily in the swell while a boat was lowered.

"Eight of 'em," muttered Bill. "That dwarf I've heard you talk about is one of them, and a great red-faced fellow who looks English."

The boat was being rowed towards them rapidly.

"Don't let them come on board, Bill," cried Judy.

"How can I stop 'em, Miss?" he said gravely. "I can't shoot the lot. Maybe they've only come to ask questions, and mean us no harm."

"Is Maitland there?" sung out the red-faced man whom Judy at once recognised as Barnet, as the boat came alongside.

"He is not," said Bill. "He's ashore. What are you wanting?"

"You'll see soon enough," grunted the other. "Up you get, Emil."

He helped the dwarf on board, and came up after him followed by four of the boat's crew.

"We don't want the whole Brazilian Navy on deck," cried Bill angrily.

"It doesn't matter what you want. You'll damned well take what you get. Now then where's that map?"

"Mr. Maitland has got it on him."

Barnet stared at him suspiciously, and whispered something to the dwarf who shrugged his shoulders.

"When will he be back?"

"I know no more than you do," answered Bill. "He went ashore three or four hours ago."

And once again the two of them whispered together, evidently deciding to adopt a different line.

"My dear Miss Draycott," began the dwarf ingratiatingly, "I feel sure we shall be able to arrange matters amicably. I must say that I have the greatest admiration for the way you have scored off us up to date, but I feel certain that you will be the first to admit that matters cannot go on as they are any longer."

"I prefer to have no discussion at all with men who were responsible for my brother's murder," said Judy passionately.

"Come, come," said Dresler, "I can assure you that was an accident. No one regretted it more than Sir Montague Barnet and myself. Anyway it is over and done with: it belongs to the past, and we are concerned with the present. Now then, are we going to work together or not?"

"Nothing would induce me to have anything to do with you," cried the girl.

"But I fear you will have to," said the dwarf suavely. "I don't want to waste time pointing out obvious facts but we outnumber you by more than ten to one. And only my abhorrence of violence makes me discuss the matter at all. The position is this, Miss Draycott. Mr.

Maitland has the map: we want the map. Moreover we intend to have the map. Now if you will give me your solemn promise that you will persuade Mr. Maitland to hand it over to us, then I, in my turn, will give you my promise that a fair share of the treasure, should we discover any, will be handed over to you."

"And if I won't promise," said Judy.

Once again the dwarf shrugged his shoulders.

"Need we go into such an eventuality," he said softly. "I will leave it to your imagination."

"Then I will give you my answer, Mr. Dresler. Rather than see that map in your hands, I shall ask Mr. Maitland to tear it up and throw it in the sea. Oh! you brutes!"

She gave a sudden cry, as the four men, obeying a quick gesture from Barnet, hurled themselves on Bill Blackett. For a few moments he fought like a demon, and one of his assailants went overboard with a broken jaw. But it could only end one way when Barnet, with a loaded stick in his hand joined in as well. There came a dull thud, and Bill crashed forward on the deck unconscious.

"There's no good wasting time, Emil," grunted the baronet. "That fellow Maitland may be back at any moment. Put him in the boat."

They lowered the motionless sailor into the boat alongside, and Barnet picked up his rifle.

"Now, Miss Draycott," he said curtly, "will you kindly follow your friend or have we got to lift you in too."

"What are you going to do with us?" said Judy.

"Exchange your quarters for more comfortable ones on board the yacht. Emil, I'm going ashore: I will return with Maitland."

And so having landed him she found herself being rowed to the yacht, with Bill still lying unconscious in the bottom of the boat. And though she tried not to notice it, a feeling of sick fear began to come over her as she saw the way the sailors looked at her. They were talking to one another in Brazilian and every now and then they laughed evilly, as if enjoying some secret joke. What a fool she had been to speak so precipitately: why hadn't she temporised till Jim got back? But when she stared at the hill, the only moving thing she could see was the figure of Barnet slowly climbing.

An officer received her as she mounted the gangway, and she hated him even more than the sailors.

"In ze regretted absence of Don Miguel," he leered in broken English, "it is to me much pleasure to receive you. Will you please to come: I show you ze saloon."

She watched Bill being hoisted on board; then sick at heart she followed the officer.

"It is pretty, is it not?" remarked her guide, and as she glanced indifferently round the room, he suddenly seized her in his arms and kissed her.

It was just what Judy wanted to rouse her from her despondency. With a smack like the shot of a pistol she got him with her open hand on the cheek, and he staggered back snarling. Then muttering something in Brazilian he came towards her again, only to find himself looking down the wrong end of a small business-like automatic.

"Another step, you little swine," said Judy, "and I'll kill you."

For a moment they stared at one another: then with an ugly laugh he turned away.

"You wait, you English mees," he remarked, "till Don Miguel come on board again. You have lovely time then."

"Get out," cried Judy, and with another glance at the automatic, he went.

After a time she relaxed, and going to one of the portholes looked out. The throb of the engine had already told her they were under way, and she saw they were going back to the south of the island. In the distance she could still see the motor-boat, with a squat figure of the dwarf on the deck: then the hill hid it from sight.

No one else came to disturb her, and she remained at the porthole watching the island listlessly. Where were Jim and Percy? It was getting almost dark: even if they were in the open it would have been impossible to see them. And at last with a feeling of utter despair in her heart she sat down at the table in the centre of the saloon.

After a while a steward came in and turned on the light, and at the same time the engine ceased. She rose and peered out again, as the rattle of the chain told her they had anchored, but it was too dark to see more than the bare outline of the land. They were lying close in, but beyond seeing that it was wooded she could make out nothing.

The door opened, and she turned round. Two men were standing there: one she had never seen before, the other was Don Miguel.

"Welcome, my dear young lady, to my yacht," said the millionaire. "And allow me to introduce Captain McIntyre."

"How is Captain Blackett?" she cried.

"As well as can be expected under the circumstances," he remarked. "I can assure you his life is in no danger. Did he prove intractable or what?"

"He was the victim of an unprovoked assault," she said angrily.

"Dear me!" he laughed. "It's lucky for him that his head is hard. So I hear Mr. Maitland is carrying out a little private exploration. I wonder if he was more fortunate than we were. We rowed all the way up the river, and all the way back again and found nothing at all, except a pool containing crocodiles."

He pressed the bell, and ordered a bottle of wine and some whisky.

"Sit down, McIntyre," he said, "and help yourself. You will join us, Miss Draycott?"

"No, thank you," she answered coldly.

"A pity. This is an excellent vintage."

His eyes were fixed on her gloatingly, and involuntarily she shivered.

"Not cold, I trust. Or perhaps a touch of fever. May I get you some quinine?"

"How long are we to be kept prisoners?" she burst out.

"What an ugly word," said the Brazilian. "Let us put it that I hope you will enjoy my hospitality for a considerable period. Let us also hope that Mr. Maitland does nothing foolish with the map. It will prolong matters if he should, and this island is not a spot that I would select as a health resort."

"It's a stinking fever-soaked hole," grunted McIntyre.

"But doubtless our lady guest will enliven the tedium of it," murmured the other.

"Will you kindly show me where my cabin is?" she said icily, and Don Miguel again rang the bell.

"Show Miss Draycott to her cabin," he ordered as the steward entered. "The large one—next to mine."

The man grinned and led the way. And in the last glimpse she had of the two men, they were shaking with silent laughter.

She bolted the door, and sat down on the bed to try and get things straight in her mind. She was afraid, desperately afraid. And the more she thought about it, the more hopeless did it seem. Even if Jim gave them the map, what guarantee was there that they would be allowed to go? And he and Percy could do nothing with the numbers they had against them. Anyway as a last resource she had her revolver, and even as she comforted herself with that reflection she remembered that she had left her bag with it inside in the saloon.

She went back at once: the two men were sitting where she had left them. Her bag was still on the table, but the instant she picked it up she realised by the weight that the revolver was no longer inside. She looked at the Brazilian: he was balancing it in his hand.

"Give my revolver back to me," she cried furiously. "How dare you touch my bag."

"Just to see that no dangerous lethal weapons were being carried, my dear young lady," he grinned. "You've no idea what a lot of damage one of these little toys can do. Captain McIntyre was terribly nervous when he saw it."

"Sure," said the sailor with mock gravity. "I told the boss I wouldn't be able to sleep a wink if I knew anyone on board had a gun."

"You cowardly brutes."

She faced them defiantly, though in truth she felt very near tears.

"You wouldn't dare do a thing like that if Mr. Maitland was here."

"But since he isn't here the point does not arise, does it," said Don Miguel softly. "And since it is more than doubtful if he ever will be here the point will never arise either."

"What do you mean?" She stared at him with dilated eyes.

"I have my own methods of dealing with people who try to double cross me," remarked the Brazilian. "I warned Mr. Maitland in Rio, and he decided not to heed my warning. I fear he may regret it."

His eyes narrowed as he looked at her.

"Whereas you, my pretty one, will I trust have no cause to regret your visit to South America."

She fought down the sick fear that was gripping her.

"If you do anything to Mr. Maitland," she said, "you won't get the map."

"In which case our stay here is likely to be much more prolonged," he remarked. "But with you on board to comfort me I shall view the prospect with equanimity."

He rose suddenly and came towards her, and she cowered back. There was something so utterly repulsive about this swarthy looking brute that she felt almost hypnotised with loathing. And the next moment he had caught her in his arms.

"Jewels shall be yours, my pretty," he whispered thickly, "and money. You shall have all your desires granted."

His face was coming closer to hers, until, making a desperate effort, she broke away from him and fled like a wild thing to her cabin. And not till the door was bolted once more did she feel safe.

She sat down panting for breath. What was she going to do? It was only a temporary respite: sooner or later she would have to eat and drink. And that would mean meeting Miguel again. What, too, about Jim? They intended treachery: the Brazilian had admitted it himself. They would get the map by means of specious promises, and then knife him or something from behind.

A knock came on the door, and the steward enquired what she would like for dinner.

"Nothing," she cried, "nothing at all," and the man went away. Eating was a physical impossibility, but after a while she rose and gulped down some water from the carafe. It was luke warm but she felt better for it. And for a time she stood staring out of the porthole.

Nine o'clock: surely Jim should be there by now. But no sound broke the stillness of the night except a gramophone which was being played by some member of the crew. And as the hours went on her anxiety increased. Why didn't he come? Had some accident happened to him on the island which had prevented him?

The gramophone ceased: the yacht grew silent. Once her door handle was softly tried, and Don Miguel's voice came from the other side. But she did not answer him, and after a while he went away and she heard the door of the next cabin shut. And at length, still sitting in the chair she fell into an uneasy doze.

A sudden sound awakened her, and she sat up with a start. The moonlight was flooding her cabin, and for a moment or two she sat trembling in her chair. And then to her horror she saw a slowly widening crack in the partition wall of the cabin. A panel was sliding back, and it had been the click as it started that had aroused her.

She watched it with dilated eyes: on the other side of it was Don Miguel's cabin. And at length his head was poked cautiously through. He looked round until he saw her, and for a while they stared at one another in silence. Then with a leer he pushed the panel right back, and stood in the opening.

"Have you changed your mind, my pretty," he whispered.

"Get out, you unspeakable cur," she said tensely.

"But I've only just come," he remarked. "Wasn't it thoughtful of me to give you the cabin next mine? All specially prepared as you see. Now are we going to be wise, or are we going to give trouble?"

The leer grew more pronounced, and he took a step forward. And at that moment she heard him give a strange gurgling noise: saw something brown round his throat, and watched him being dragged back through the opening. He disappeared, and with no thought in her mind save the incredible fact that he'd gone, she sprang to the sliding panel and slammed it to. And as she did so there came from the other side of the wall a blood-curdling scream, followed by a series of bumps as if a heavy sack was being thrown about.

She cowered back terrified: the noise was like nothing she had ever heard. And even as she listened to it pandemonium broke loose in the ship. Shots, oaths, yells of terror came from every direction, and every now and then a loud splash indicated that somebody had fallen overboard. She forced herself to go to the porthole, but there was nothing to be seen though the din had now become indescribable. And mingled with it came a succession of strange snarling grunts.

She crossed to the little window that opened into the corridor, and drew back the curtains. Pressed against the glass was a face, and as she stared at it every drop of blood seemed to freeze in her veins. It was human, and yet it was animal. Its teeth were bared like those of an angry dog: its flattened nostrils were distended. And in its eyes was a look of bestial savagery.

Suddenly it put its hand straight through the glass, and tried to clutch her, but she fell back half fainting on the bed. For a while the great hairy arm continued groping: then it was withdrawn, and she could hear it snarling angrily, evidently furious at having cut itself. And then to her unspeakable horror the door handle rattled violently. The thing was trying to get in.

The door creaked and groaned: she could see the panels bulging inwards. And in those few moments Judy experienced the supreme acme of human terror. *For she knew the door handle would not hold.* Already the wood was beginning to splinter, and in one last desperate throw for safety she tried to clamber through the porthole. But it was too small, and with a pitiful little moan she cowered back on the bed just as the door, with a final crash, was burst open, and the thing came in. And it was then that something snapped in her brain, and Judy fainted.

When she opened her eyes again she found herself in darkness. She was lying on the ground, and for a while her mind refused to act. Then little by little it came back to her, and she bit her lip to prevent herself screaming. It wasn't some hideous nightmare: it was the truth. Something had come into her cabin, something that she dimly remembered as being of vast size, and unspeakably horrible. And it must have carried her off the yacht.

Where was she? She felt the ground with her hand and found it was hard earth. And suddenly the full horror of her position dawned on her: she was in the power of these awful creatures. From close beside her there came a movement, and involuntarily she gave a little cry. And then with a feeling of unutterable relief she heard a well-known voice.

"How are you feeling, miss?"

"Bill," she cried, "where are we? What's happened?"

"The same as happened in the *Paquinetta*," he answered grimly. "They've slaughtered or taken prisoner every soul in the yacht, and now we're in their power."

Some voices started jabbering Brazilian near by, and she asked Bill who they were.

"Some of the crew, miss. There are about ten of us altogether. The rest are dead."

"Thank God, they didn't kill you, Bill."

"It was that crack on the head in the motor-boat saved me, miss. I'd come to, and was lying dazed and sick in the bunk where they'd thrown me, when I heard the fight start. So I staggered up on deck unarmed as I was and ran right into two of them. It was so unexpected I didn't show any fight, and they just carted me off."

She forced herself to ask the question, though she dreaded the answer.

"Have they got Mr. Maitland too?"

"I haven't seen him, miss, or his cousin either."

"He may be able to do something," she said, hope springing up in her mind.

The sailor said nothing. In the first place he doubted if Jim could ever find them, and if he did what could he possibly do? There were scores of these hideous monsters, and even if he succeeded in shooting a few of them, it would only make the others more savage.

"By the way, miss," he said at length, "have you got your revolver with you?"

"I haven't, Bill," she answered. "That brute Don Miguel took it from me."

And the sailor almost groaned aloud. No good now alarming her more than she was already, by telling her to blow out her brains in certain eventualities: they could only wait in agonising suspense.

"What will they do to us, Bill?" she asked tremulously.

"God knows, miss," he said gravely. "We've just got to keep our spirits up and hope for the best."

"But, Bill, are they human?"

"Half man, half beast, miss. You remember I told you. They've got a sort of language for I heard them talking, but to look at they're more like gorillas."

"I suppose," she said quietly, "they'll kill us."

And he dared make no reply. All that he could pray for was that they would kill her and that nothing worse should happen. He was unarmed himself: he was powerless to help her in any way. And the realisation of the girl's peril made him well-nigh sick with fear. He had tried to take note of the direction in which he had been brought, but it had proved hopeless. It had seemed a veritable maze of paths, and since for long stretches of the journey the moonlight had not penetrated into the forest, most of it had been done in darkness. All that he knew was that they were in some form of underground cave.

Two of the sailors near by were talking, and he understood sufficient Brazilian to get the gist of their remarks.

"Do you hear what those blokes are saying, miss," he said, when they had finished. "According to them some of the words these things use are a sort of Brazilian *patois*. And from what they heard the reason for the attack on the yacht was that their chief or king or something like that was killed this afternoon."

"Doesn't seem to help us much, does it?" she said with a pitiful little laugh. "Bill, wouldn't it be possible to escape? There must be a way out."

"First thing I thought of, miss. But the brutes have blocked the entrance of the tunnel we came in by."

"So that our only hope is Jim," she whispered under her breath.

They fell silent: and Judy's thoughts went back to that night in Hampstead when she had first met Jim and asked his advice about the treasure. Who, by the wildest stretch of imagination could have dreamed that it would have ended as it had? It was all so inconceivable that even now she had a feeling that she would wake up soon and find it was some fantastic nightmare. And suddenly she cried out almost hysterically.

"It can't be true, Bill. It is just like Alice in *Alice in Wonderland*. We'll find it's all a dream and these things are just a pack of cards."

And the sailor who had come on deck just in time to see Bully McIntyre's neck broken with a flick of the wrists could think of nothing to say. In fact he found himself praying that her reason might give:

then at any rate she would be spared the mental horror that lay in front of her.

For the twentieth time he asked himself what was going to happen. How long were they going to be kept in this underground hole, and what was their fate going to be when they were taken out? Presumably the brutes were asleep resting after the fight: in which case it might be many hours before they knew.

Suddenly the silence was broken by the most extraordinary uproar from above them. The bell began clanging furiously: a chorus of bellowing grunts that increased in intensity as more and more of the brutes joined in almost drowned it. The ground over their heads shook violently: they could hear the lumbering footsteps passing backwards and forwards.

Gradually the clamour died away and the bell ceased, though a kind of deep chattering which still continued showed that their captors were very wide awake. It sounded as if something had excited them greatly, something which they were now discussing at length. And then clear above everything came an anguished cry.

"Help! For God's sake—help!"

Bill Blackett sat up with a jerk.

"That's not Mr. Maitland," he said positively, "though I know the voice."

"It was the dwarf," cried the girl. "I'd know his voice anywhere."

"The dwarf," said the sailor slowly. "And he was blind. That means they've been on board our motorboat."

"And it means," said the girl excitedly, "that they haven't got Jim or Percy. He was left there alone."

Bill Blackett said nothing. Did it mean that of necessity? Or did it mean that Jim and his cousin had put up a fight and been killed, and that the dwarf being helpless had merely been captured?

The excitement above continued, though it was more controlled. One of the monsters seemed to be holding forth to the others, and when he'd finished his audience emitted a series of bellows that seemed to betoken approval. And almost immediately after there came, from the entrance to their prison, the sound of the barrier being removed, and the soft padding of bare feet on the ground. One of the brutes was with them.

They could hear its heavy breathing as it stumbled about, and suddenly there came a yell from one of the sailors—an Englishman.

"It's got me," he screamed. "Save me, boys."

His voice died away: the barrier crashed back, and Bill Blackett wiped the sweat from his forehead. One of them had been taken: whose turn was it going to be next? Impossible to help the poor devil: impossible to do anything except sit in the darkness and wait.

Above them the noise had again increased, and mingled with it came the shouts of the dwarf and the sailor. And then once again the bell began tolling, whilst the rest of the uproar ceased abruptly.

There was something almost solemn in the monotonous clanging: it sounded as if it might have been the accompaniment of some religious ceremony. It continued for about five minutes: then in the silence that followed one deep grunting voice could be heard. And suddenly one of the Brazilians near them cried out in horror and said something to one of his companions, something which once again Bill Blackett could understand roughly, and which caused him to stare into the darkness with haggard eyes. Sacrifice: human sacrifice to some god: that was what was going on above their heads.

"Help me, you little swine. Don't sit there doing nothing."

The voice of the sailor who had been taken came to them faintly, and Bill cursed under his breath. The poor devil was English anyhow, and it was intolerable to have to sit there helpless while he was being killed, perhaps tortured.

"Help me. For God's sake, say something to these brutes."

A frenzy of fear rang in the man's voice: evidently the end, whatever it was, was drawing near. And then it came.

"One of them has got me. One of them has got me."

The scream was almost inarticulate, and subsided into a meaningless babble of words which was drowned in the triumphant outburst of noise from the spectators. And after a while that too, subsided, and all was silent once more.

"What does it mean, Bill," said Judy in a trembling voice.

"It means, miss, that now we're one hand short," he answered quietly.

"You mean he's dead."

"That's it, miss, I'm afraid. They've killed him."

"And that's what is going to happen to us," she went on steadily.

"It looks like it, miss," he said.

"How do you think they did it?"

"I haven't an idea," he answered. "From what he called out he seemed to be appealing to that dwarf to help him."

"He said, 'One of them has got me.' Oh! my God, Bill," her voice rose to a scream, "can't you strangle me now?"

"Steady on, miss," said the sailor gently, though his heart was sick within him. "Don't let's give up hope yet. Maybe Mr. Maitland will find some way of escape for us."

But his voice lacked conviction and he knew it.

"Don't try and deceive me, Bill." With an effort she pulled herself together. "Things have gone too far for that. Do you think we've got a chance?"

"Yes," he cried stoutly. "I do. Provided Mr. Maitland is still free."

"And if he isn't?"

"Then our number is up, miss."

There was no good beating about the bush, he reflected: the girl was thoroughbred and had better know the truth.

"That's what I wanted to find out," she said. "Now, Bill, we've neither of us got a revolver, so I want you to do something for me. These sailors have all got knives. Will you please borrow one?"

"I have a knife myself, miss," he said quietly.

"Good. Then if the end comes, Bill: if we have to give up hope will you give me your solemn word of honour that you will kill me."

The sailor swallowed hard for a few moments, and then he answered her in a husky voice.

"If there's no hope left, miss, I give you my word of honour that I will kill you."

And with a little sigh of relief Judy Draycott stretched out her hand to him in the darkness. She knew he would not fail her.

"Will it be long, Bill, do you think?"

"Heaven knows, miss," he said, and even as he spoke there came the sound of the barrier being removed from the end of the tunnel, and a flickering light danced on the walls of their prison. One of the monsters carrying a torch which threw out great volumes of black smoke was coming towards them. Others were following, and the girl crept closer to him.

"Now, Bill—now. Quick—you promised."

He drew his clasp knife, and opened the big blade. The sweat was pouring off his forehead: his hand was shaking like that of a man with the ague. And he was just nerving himself for the supreme effort, when suddenly, clear and distinct there came a sound that made him pause. It was faint but unmistakable: it was the siren of the yacht. And who could be blowing it?

The monsters paused: the prisoners dimly outlined in the smoky light sat up listening. Steadily it went on blaring: long, long, long: long, short, long. Over and over again, until the meaning dawned on Bill. The Morse code: O.K. Someone was sending those two letters into the night; who could it be but Jim Maitland? And with almost a sob of relief he replaced his knife in his pocket. In view of that message there was still hope.

CHAPTER 12

All around them the sailors were muttering excitedly. Even though they knew nothing of the existence of Jim Maitland, they realised that some human agency must be at work, and that therefore there was at any rate somebody who was not a prisoner.

And the monsters themselves seemed to realise it too. The one in front who appeared to be the leader was conferring with two others, stopping every now and then to listen to the siren which still went on monotonously, whilst the smoke from the torches made Judy's eyes smart and caught her in the throat.

At last they came to a decision, and the leader gave a gruff roar which was evidently an order. It was answered from the other side of the smoke, and the prisoners heard the sounds of hurried movements which quickly died away in the distance.

"Some of the brutes have gone to investigate," muttered Bill to the girl. "I wonder what is going to happen now?"

But what he wondered far more, though he did not say so, was how Jim, assuming it was him, was going to get from the yacht in time to be of any help. The sacrifice that had already taken place had not been a long affair.

"Bill, they're coming nearer."

The girl clutched his hand terrified, as the three torch bearers advanced into the centre of the circle of prisoners, their faces looking, if possible, more incredibly evil in the flickering yellow light. And then they knelt down in a row and remained motionless, their gleaming eyes fixed on the entrance of the tunnel. Something was coming along the passage towards them.

Fascinated in spite of their terror the captives stared into the darkness. What new horror was going to reveal itself? At last they saw it, dimly outlined in the smoke, moving slowly forward a step at a time. It was another of the monsters and it was carrying something in its arms. Foot by foot it advanced, and then bending forward it deposited its burden on the floor, so that the light of the torches shone on it clearly.

And even Bill Blackett gasped in amazement: the burden was nothing less than the blind dwarf.

"Merciful Heavens! miss," he whispered, "they're worshipping him. They think he's some sort of god."

Over and over again the three torch bearers prostrated themselves so that their foreheads touched the ground, whilst from the darkness behind there commenced a deep chanting noise which grew in volume till they were almost deafened. Then, abruptly, it ceased: the three torch bearers straightened up: silence reigned. The only sign of movement came from the dwarf whose head was turning from side to side in a frenzy of fear.

Suddenly one of the monsters began what seemed to be an address. Sounds which were clearly meant to be words were strung together in sentences; and, whenever he paused, his companions, unseen in the smoke, answered with grunts of approval.

To Bill the whole thing was complete gibberish: he could make neither head nor tail of what the brute was saying. Once or twice he caught a word that seemed to have a Spanish ring about it, but except for that it was merely a jumble of meaningless sounds, which, coupled with the stifling fumes from the torches tended to make him half conscious. He still held Judy's hand in his, and he knew by the pressure of her head on his shoulder and her heavy breathing that it was affecting her in the same way. All the better, he reflected stupidly: pray heaven she remained in that condition till Jim Maitland came—if he ever did.

And then suddenly one of the sailors opposite burst into a wild torrent of Brazilian, to which Bill forced himself to listen. He only got the bare gist of it, but that was sufficient to make his mouth go dry, and tighten the grip of his arm round the girl's waist. Sacrifice— he'd guessed that already, but he had hoped for time. Now from what this man was screaming out, it was to be at once, unless... He listened intently: then he too began to shout.

"Shut up, you lily-livered swine," he roared furiously. "By God! if I could get at you I'd cut your throat."

The monsters had ceased as if surprised at this unexpected interruption, and Bill scrambled to his feet.

"Hi! you blind man," he cried, "I don't know your name, but you listen to me."

The dwarf turned his agonised face in Bill's direction.

"These things that have got us think you're a god. Do you get me?

331

What you say goes. It's up to you to decide what is going to happen. Now there's a lady here—just a young slip of a girl. And somebody has got to be sacrificed to you. At once. Now we've got to gain time, do you see. There's a chance of our being rescued. And according to that spawn of Satan opposite what these monsters have been saying is that it's either got to be Miss Draycott or six of us. Now I'll be one of the six, but as there's a God above unless you say that you wish her spared, I'll get at you and kill you."

"How can I say anything," quavered the dwarf, "I don't know how to speak to them."

"Leave it to me," howled the Brazilian sailor in broken English. "I tell all right. I make understand. Why six of us—for one girl—you damned Englishman."

And then breaking into Brazilian, a torrent of words came pouring from his mouth to which Bill could only listen impotently. The three torch bearers had turned their heads and were looking at him: the one that had carried in the dwarf seemed to be listening also.

Suddenly Judy clutched Bill's arm.

"Listen," she whispered tensely. "Didn't you hear something?"

"Nothing except that damned *dago*," he answered. "What was it, miss?"

"There: there: again." She was shaking with excitement. "Bill: it was a voice: it was Jim's voice."

"Steady on, miss. Mr. Maitland can't have got here from the yacht yet."

"I don't care: it was his voice. Oh! Listen, Bill: listen."

The sailor craned his ears, and at that moment there came a momentary pause from the sailor opposite. And in that pause, quite distinctly from somewhere above their heads, there came a low voice:

"Worship the dwarf."

And the voice was the voice of Jim Maitland. Apparently the others had not heard it, and Bill turned to the girl, by this time as excited as she was.

"You're right, miss," he muttered. "It's Mr. Maitland. Come on: let's do what he says."

The Brazilian was off again, as Bill, taking Judy by the hand advanced into the circle of light. And then with the utmost solemnity they prostrated themselves on the ground in front of Dresler. The sailor, surprised by this new development ceased talking: the monsters watched in silence. And the dwarf, sensing that something strange was happening called out in a terrified voice.

"What is it!" he cried. "Tell me for God's sake. I'm going mad."

"Keep it going, miss," muttered Bill. "It's our only hope. Good Lord! what's happening now."

There had come a sudden stir amongst the ape-men, and out of the corner of his eye Bill saw that a beam of light was flickering round the walls. They jibbered and chattered to themselves as they watched it: then with one accord they threw themselves on their faces. It was a message from their god. At times it shone on the clouds of smoke: then finding an opening it would pierce through them and light up one of the beast faces. But always it moved on until at length it rested on the sailor who had begun speaking again. And there it remained motionless, till his voice died away and he stood there staring upwards stupidly.

There came a triumphant shout from one of the monsters, and the three torch bearers sprang on the Brazilian who screamed like a wounded hare. The one who had carried Dresler in seized the dwarf and pulled him up, and a few seconds later all the ape-men had gone. So had the Brazilian sailor. The prisoners were alone again in the darkness, with only the reeking fumes left by the torches to remind them of the incredible scene they had just witnessed.

But to Judy everything was different: Jim was there. How he had reached them: what he was going to do next: how he had done what he had done she did not stop to ask. The mere fact that he was on the spot was good enough for her: somehow or other he was going to save them.

Suddenly she realised Bill was speaking.

"I can't make it out, miss," he was saying. "There must be a hole in the roof somewhere through which he shone an electric torch. And then he worked on the superstitions of these things. But how did he get here: how did he know where we were? And how is he going to escape them now?"

From above was coming a repetition of the sounds of the former sacrifice: the Brazilian sailor was following in the steps of the Englishman. And Judy covered her ears with her hands in her endeavour not to hear the poor wretch's screams of terror. At last they ceased: the second victim had paid the penalty, and for a while there was silence.

She had kept casting feverish glances in the direction of the passage, hoping against hope that the flicker of Jim's torch might suddenly appear, or that she might hear his voice close to her. But the darkness had remained unbroken, and the only voice she had heard had been that of the poor brute yelling above them.

And now as the silence continued she began to try and get some order into the chaos of her mind. Bill was right of course: for some reason or other these horrible creatures regarded the blind dwarf as a god. And in him it seemed to her lay their best chance of safety. The trouble was that, not unnaturally he was more terrified than any of them. They, at any rate, could see what they were up against: whereas to him the situation must appear doubly awful. To be utterly helpless in their hands: to be picked up and carried by them would be enough to send him off his head. And if that happened—what then? He would be useless as far as helping any of them to escape was concerned.

Time dragged on; still no sign of Jim. And after a while she began to lose heart. What could one man do, even a man like him, against a horde of these foul monsters. Strong though he was she realised that he would be like a child in the hands of one of them: what then could he hope to do against fifty? Had he just postponed the inevitable for a short time? Would it have been better if Bill had not shut up his knife?

And then another ghastly thought struck her: supposing they had already got him. And killed him. Some of those yells might have come from Jim. And if that was so she realised that she didn't mind what happened to her.

At length nature asserted herself and she began to doze. Around her all the others were fast asleep, except Bill who forced himself to keep awake on the chance of getting another message from Jim. And it was his sudden grip on her arm that awoke her, as much as the noise of a dull boom accompanied by a distinct earth tremor.

"What is it, Bill?" she cried.

"Sounded to me like an explosion, miss," he answered. "And it came from a long way off. Seems to have woken the brutes again, too."

Above them they could hear the ape-men moving about and talking to one another excitedly. And then from a great distance there came faintly a roar. It was caught up and repeated from closer at hand: then again from quite near by. A signal of warning was being communicated through the forest, and the effect on the monsters above was instantaneous. Pandemonium broke loose: the ground over their heads shook so much that lumps of earth were dislodged and fell on them.

"Can't have been a big gun," said Bill thoughtfully. "There couldn't be a warship here, and if there was she wouldn't fire. Besides we'd have heard the shell burst."

He struck a match and looked at his watch: two hours now before daylight. And he was just blowing it out when his eyes fell on a twisted piece of paper lying at his feet. He snatched it up, and opened it out: it was a note from Jim.

"It's from Mr. Maitland, miss," he cried excitedly. "He must have dropped it through when he spoke to us that time. You read it while I light some more matches."

With their heads together they pored over it.

"Do not be alarmed whatever happens," it ran. "Obey me implicitly, and we'll do it yet. As a last resource I have a revolver. The crucial time will be after the explosion. Then keep your heads close together."

"That's now, miss," muttered Bill. "And here come the brutes back again."

The torch bearers were returning along the passage: the others came crowding behind them. And it was clear that they were in a furious passion. Angry, snarling grunts came from all sides and the prisoners cowered back against the walls. The dwarf instead of being placed reverently on the ground was thrown down with such force that he lay there half stunned: evidently his period of godhead was over. And the leader of the monsters, its face convulsed with bestial rage shambled round the circle peering at each victim in turn.

Suddenly it paused, and a hush fell on them. Once again that mysterious circle of light was playing round on their upturned faces, and Judy clutched Bill's hand. Jim was there once more. The light danced here and there, until it finally centred on the dwarf where it remained steady. And with a bellow of rage one of the ape-men picked him up.

Instantly the light began to move again, and the great brutes paused. What further victim did their god desire save this false imposter? Round the waiting circle the beam moved, lighting up each face in turn and then on to the next. And suddenly Bill remembered the letter.

"Then keep your heads close together."

He leaned over till his cheek touched Judy's.

"Orders, miss," he whispered. "It's us this time, or I'm a Dutchman."

He could feel her body quivering against his; the light was only two away. Once more it moved: and then again. Their two faces showed up clear in the beam, and the beam remained steady.

An ape-man dashed at them: the light went out, and the monster paused. Once more it shone out, and from above them came the order "Get up." Bill helped her up, the light shining on their faces as they moved. And once more two of the monsters came at them. Instantly the light went out again, and the brutes halted, evidently puzzled. Their god clearly did not wish these two victims to be touched.

"Move."

Another laconic order, and with the light again illuminating their heads they walked towards the entrance tunnel. The ape-men thronged round them till Judy thought she was going to faint with horror. But they did not touch her, and with Bill's arm supporting her she stumbled along the narrow passage.

The beam from above had ceased: only the flickering yellow light from the three torches showed the way. In front of her she could see the agonised face of the dwarf, as he was carried along by one of the monsters, and in spite of all he had done, she could not help feeling sorry for him. He could be no help to them now: he was just a fellow victim more helpless far than they were.

At length they reached the open air, and she drew great gulps of it into her lungs until she felt steadier on her feet. Then still clinging to Bill's arm she peered round half hoping to see Jim. It was dark, but not with the overpowering blackness of the underground prison they had left. And as her eyes grew accustomed to it she realised they were standing in a big clearing. The shadowy forms of the ape-men were moving about: close by them stood two of the hideous monsters. And one of them suddenly put out its hand and touched her on the shoulder.

She gave a little scream, and shrank closer to Bill. But the pressure continued and she found herself being forced forward, while the sailor kept close by her side. The clearing narrowed into a track, then widened out again into another open space. And the ape-man's grip tightened so that she stood still.

The monsters were curiously silent: there was a feeling of tension in the air. By the light of the torches she could see their eyes shining as they crouched in a semi-circle round her. In front of her stood the one carrying the dwarf, and at its feet there gleamed a streak of something on the ground. Water: the smoky flames were reflected in it as by a mirror. And beyond the water—nothing.

Suddenly a sound that was half a gasp ran round the motionless watchers, and Bill clutched her arm. The darkness beyond the water was becoming faintly luminous. The monster holding the dwarf put his burden on the ground and fell flat on its face: the others prostrated themselves likewise, as the luminosity increased. And with curiosity overcoming her terror Judy stared at this extraordinary phenomenon.

The centre of the light seemed to be about six feet from the ground, and as it grew stronger and stronger the ape-men began to manifest signs of increasing terror. The torch bearers had dropped their burdens, which lay smoking on the ground, and had thrown themselves on their faces also. Only Judy and Bill still stood up, with the misshapen figure of Dresler just in front of them moving restlessly about on his stunted legs.

At last the light focussed itself into a definite nucleus: a circle some three inches in diameter that shone steadily. Around the circle it grew fainter till it faded into the general darkness. Gradually the nucleus increased in size, and as it did so the agitation of the monsters became extreme. A low wailing noise came from them, and the leader began to beat its great chest with its hands. And then with startling sudden-ness the nucleus of light expanded and grew until it took the form of a luminous face hanging in mid air.

"It's a trick, miss," muttered Bill, though his voice was shaking a little. "It must be a trick of Mr. Maitland's."

She stared at it fascinated, and though she knew Bill was right her mouth felt a little dry, and her knees were inclined to shake. There was something inconceivably ghostly about the dismembered head float-ing in the air in front of her, with its reflection glinting in the water. Its features were Mongolian and evil, and in its forehead was a black patch from which no light shone.

The monsters were beside themselves with fright, though none of them seemed to be able to pluck up enough courage to go. And she was just wondering what was going to happen next when there came a scream from the dwarf. The leading ape-man had risen to his feet and was holding Dresler high above his head. It gave a heave with its mighty shoulders, and flung the dwarf clean over the water towards the shining head. Then once again it threw itself on its face.

They heard the dwarf land with a crash in some undergrowth: then silence, broken only by a faint rustling noise. A further sacrifice had been offered—but how? The fall could not have killed him. Motion-less the monsters waited, their eyes fixed on the spot. And then came a shout from the dwarf.

"Help me! They're all round me. Ah-h———"

The shriek died away in his throat, and Judy gave a little moan. There was something too horrible in this unknown terror of the darkness. What were all round him? They could hear him stumbling about on the other side of the water moaning pitifully. And then again he shrieked.

"I can't stand this," muttered Bill. "The poor brute is blind."

He took a step forward, and then occurred a thing so unexpected that he stopped, rooted to the spot. There came a hissing noise, and leaving a trail of sparks behind it, a rocket soared up from behind the luminous face. It burst above them, and for a space the clearing was lit up as brightly as if it was day.

With yells of terror the ape-men scattered in every direction, until Bill and Judy were left standing alone in the centre. And as if turned to stone they stared fascinated at the sight in front of them. The head was the head of an idol, its luminosity no longer showing in the brilliant light that flooded the place. But it was not at the idol they were looking.

Standing below it, in some low undergrowth was the dwarf. And even as they watched him a deadly yellow-brown head raised itself to a level with his face, and struck twice. They looked at the edge of the water: the coarse grass was moving. Another swaying head raised itself and hissed angrily: another and yet another. They watched them writhing in every direction as the dwarf blundered about: they saw him bitten twice more before the light died out. The place was a heaving mass of snakes.

Then as the head once more grew luminous, and the smoking torches still guttered on the floor, there came a sudden splash. The dwarf by chance had found the water and came blundering through it. His face was distorted with agony: twelve times had he been bitten. And he barely reached the edge before he gave one final moan, fell on his face and with a last dreadful convulsion lay still. Emil Dresler, blackmailer, white slave trafficker and arch-scoundrel was dead.

All round them the ape-men moved restlessly in the dense growth that formed the sides of the clearing. Occasionally they saw two gleaming eyes staring at them, but the brutes themselves did not dare to venture into the open. And then the movement ceased: eyes were watching from everywhere, as if waiting for something.

Judy turned round: what was happening now? The leading ape-man was just behind her: its hands were coming out to seize her. And with a pitiful scream—"Bill save me," she felt herself picked up as if she was a child above the brute's head, and carried towards the edge of the water. She was the next sacrifice.

Bill had sprung forward fumbling madly with his knife, when suddenly she found herself deposited once more on the ground. And forcing herself to look at the monstrous thing towering above her she saw that it was staring at the idol with a puzzled expression in its eyes. She looked herself, and to her amazement saw that the luminous head had disappeared. And yet there was still a diffused light which came from the direction of the idol.

Two of the torches had died out: the third gave but a feeble flicker, so that the darkness was almost complete. And gradually there rose from behind the idol two shining hands followed once more by the face. The idol itself was moving, and with a bellow of fear the ape-man flung himself down. Upwards rose the hands, but Judy with every nerve tingling had her eyes riveted on the face. For now the features were not evil and Mongolian: the features were the features of Jim Maitland. What he had done, what trick he was playing she neither knew nor cared: Jim was there and nothing else mattered.

Fascinated she watched him: what was he going to do next? Very steadily the face rose till it seemed an incredible height in the air. Then it came rushing through the air towards her, and she realised Jim had jumped. From all around her came roars of terror, and the sounds of heavy bodies stampeding through the undergrowth. Their god had come to life.

Jim landed in the water, and then with measured step he approached the one prostrate ape-man who remained. It rose to its feet and backed away whimpering, followed by those terrible shining hands, and face. And as Jim passed Judy he muttered "Follow me."

It forced the monster to the entrance of the clearing; then with a sudden bound he sprang at it, and placed both his hands on its chest. And there marked in fire on the brute's body were the imprints of his fingers. They remained there glowing in the darkness, and as the ape-man looked down and saw the marks of its god gleaming on its own chest its nerve broke completely. It gave one gigantic bound, and disappeared into the forest: the three of them were alone.

"Come," said Jim quietly, "We've got no time to lose. The effect of my *ju-ju* may not last long."

"But how did you do it, Jim?" cried the girl breathlessly.

"That will keep, Judy," he answered. "What we've got to do now is to make tracks for the motorboat and Percy."

"What about the others, Mr. Maitland?" said Bill.

"We'll open the barrier for them," said Jim, "but after that they must fend for themselves. There will be no room for them on board the boat."

"What about the yacht?"

"Unless I'm very much mistaken there is no longer a yacht," answered the other gravely. "Percy has done his work passing well. Now then—heave on this, Bill: again so—and again."

The heavy barrier slid back: the way to the tunnel was open.

"You are free," shouted Jim down it. "Make your way to the north end of the island, and we'll try and rescue you later. Quick now, you two: we can't have them following us."

He darted across the main clearing the other two at his heels. A luminous patch glowed faintly on a tree, which marked the entrance to one of the paths, and a moment later they were running down the track. They came to a fork: another luminous spot showed them the direction. And at every point where there might be any doubt the same sign was found.

"I marked the places where we might go wrong on my way," explained Jim. "Lord! but it's been touch and go."

He slowed up to a walk: then stopped to listen. From behind them still came the sounds of the ape-men calling to one another, and once they heard a shrill human scream.

"I don't give much for the chances of those other poor devils," said Jim gravely. "But it would have had to be all or none, and we couldn't have taken more than two at the utmost."

He pushed on again, with the luminosity gradually fading from his face and hands, until at length he came to the alligator pool where he forked right down stream. And after about a quarter of a mile he let out a hail which was answered from in front of them. Percy was there in the motor-boat.

"Yes, dear," he said quietly as he lifted her on board, "it was touch and go."

For a second they were alone, and she put her arms round his neck.

"I don't know how you did it, Jim," she whispered, "but I think you're the most wonderful man on earth."

Which was the moment that Percy would choose to appear.

"Welcome, wench," he remarked. "Dear me! how very strange. I'd no idea that phosphorus travelled aerially so to speak."

"What are you blathering about, you unspeakable mess," demanded Jim, and then happening to glance at Judy's face he made a dive for his cousin. For her lips were luminous, and the method by which they had become so was not hard to guess.

"I just can't believe I'm back here," said the girl a few minutes later. "Can you, Bill?"

The boat was nosing down the river towards the open sea.

"I can't, miss," he said solemnly. "How did you manage it, Mr. Maitland?"

"Well, Bill, one thing stood out a mile."

The first streaks of dawn were beginning to show in the east, and the three of them were sprawling on the deck with Percy at the wheel.

"The only possible hope was to frighten those brutes by something which they would regard as supernatural. Gun work was useless: there were far too many of them. And it was then that I remembered that I'd stowed a pot of luminous paint amongst our kit for the very purpose I used it for in the forest—marking a trail by night.

"Now Percy and I had been to the spot where we found you yesterday afternoon, and while there we had fallen through an ancient type of trap into the very place where you were imprisoned. And there we killed one of the monsters. But the barrier was open at the end of the tunnel so we escaped all right. The point however is that I knew where you would be taken to, which was a very great advantage.

"Then came the second discovery—made by Percy. For what purpose they brought it I don't know—probably in case blasting was necessary—but there was a large quantity of dynamite on board the yacht. So we concocted a plan. By the way—what happened to her, Percy?"

"All in good time, Jim: you carry on."

"Percy was to land me complete with phosphorus paint, and then return to the yacht. Three quarters of an hour later, so as to give me time to get to you he was to let drive on the siren. I told him to send O.K. to cheer you up, but the real object was to draw as many of the monsters away from you and back to the yacht as possible. It succeeded admirably: at least thirty of them went crashing past me in the forest."

"And thirty of them came on board the yacht," put in Percy. "When I heard 'em down there by the water's edge, I laid a ten minute fuse to the dynamite, and hooked it in the motorboat. She split open like a rotten apple, Jim, and sank at once, and I think the little pretties were all in her at the time."

They had reached the open sea, and all around them the water was strewn with wreckage.

"Pity," said Jim. "She was a nice boat. However so much for that. To go back to you and Judy. I had no idea, of course, what was going to happen, or how those brutes proposed to deal with you. I'd heard the screams of a man as I went through the forest."

"That was the Englishman they sacrificed first," said Bill.

"Also shouts from someone else whose voice seemed familiar. And you can guess my amazement when I realised as I got nearer that that someone else was none other than Dresler, who had been abducted from the motor-boat earlier. Moreover they were obviously making a god of him, and the reason suddenly dawned on me. The golden idol which they worship is made in the form of a misshapen dwarf, and they probably thought that Dresler was this idol come to life.

"However all those who hadn't gone to the yacht were below with you, and by peering through a chink in the booby trap, which apparently is not set when they are there I could see you quite distinctly. And I could also hear that unpleasant Brazilian sailor. So since it was essential to find out the way they went to work, I thought he would be an admirable person to start on.

"Well the trick with the electric torch succeeded, and they brought him up whilst I hid in the undergrowth. They lashed his feet and his hands—just as we found Lopez, Percy—and threw him over the water towards the idol. And there they left him to be bitten to death by *fer de lance* and poisonous adders—just about as deadly a combination as you could get. Moreover a complication on which I had not reckoned.

"You see I'd already made up my mind that the only hope lay in playing the fool with their idol. But the point that now arose was how the devil I was going to get to it. A *fer de lance* is no respecter of persons, and as you saw for yourselves that ground was alive with the brutes, which were imprisoned there by the water. However I knew it had got to be chanced, but I had to wait till the explosion took place. I guessed that would rouse them, and it was essential to get you and Bill up from below while it was still dark, or else my luminous paint fell flat.

"It all worked according to plan except that for some reason or other they turned on Dresler. However that didn't matter: he richly deserved all he got. I got through the snake belt by wrapping my coat round my legs; then I stood behind the idol on a sort of pedestal place. And the rest you know. First I rubbed its face with the paint: then I hoped that the rocket would finish them. But it didn't. So I covered the idol's head with my coat and decorated my own hands and face keeping hidden behind it while I did so. And that's that."

"Not bad for you either, James," remarked Percy kindly. "Sorry I wasn't in at the death but I quite enjoyed myself this end. Great fun seeing that yacht blow up. Hullo! do my eyes deceive me, or are those some of the little pets on the edge of the swamp?"

Jim snatched up the field-glasses. The sun had risen: the mist had lifted from the bog which stretched away to their left. And as he watched a peculiar smile flickered round his lips. There were more than a dozen of the ape-men, and they were clustering round a small squat object that lay on the ground. Then with a great effort they lifted it, and flung it into the swamp. For a while they stood there: then they vanished into the forest.

"Half a million gone west," he remarked. "Assuredly I damaged that god's reputation. And I guess it's just as well that I spent some of my spare time removing this while I stood behind it."

From his pocket he drew a huge red stone the size of a hen's egg. It lay in his hand like a ball of crimson fire; then he held it out to Judy.

"That's for you, bless you," he said. "And you richly deserve it after all you've gone through."

She looked at it quietly for a moment or two: then she glanced up at Jim.

"It's a ruby, isn't it?" she asked.

"It certainly is," he answered. "Moreover I should say that it literally is priceless."

"And you give it to me?"

"That," he remarked, "is the idea."

She stared at him steadily, a strange look in her eyes. Then with a quick movement she flung it overboard, and with that streak of glittering red light there vanished for ever the last of the treasure.

"I couldn't bear it, Jim," she cried. "It's haunted. We would never have a moment's peace while we had it."

"We?" he said, taking both her hands in his.

The others had gone below: they were alone.

"That," she repeated softly, "is the idea."

★★★★★★

Thus ended the strange adventure of Lone Tree Island. No trace was ever found of the members of the yacht's crew, who perforce had been left behind: in fact the island was reported to be uninhabited. But sometimes o' nights an expression comes over Jim's face which makes Judy look at him suspiciously. Is there still treasure hidden somewhere in that forest guarded by the survivors of the ape-men? Is there perchance another god of solid gold in some undiscovered clearing? Who knows? And as far as Judy is concerned there is one person who certainly never will—her husband.

LEONAUR

ALSO FROM LEONAUR
AVAILABLE IN SOFTCOVER OR HARDCOVER WITH DUST JACKET

THE COLLECTED SCIENCE FICTION AND FANTASY OF STANLEY G. WEINBAUM 1—INTERPLANETARY ODYSSEYS *by Stanley G. Weinbaum*—Classic Tales of Interplanetary Adventure Including: A Martian Odyssey, its Sequel Valley of Dreams, the Complete 'Ham' Hammond Stories and Others.

THE COLLECTED SCIENCE FICTION AND FANTASY OF STANLEY G. WEINBAUM 2—OTHER EARTHS *by Stanley G. Weinbaum*—Classic Futuristic Tales Including: *Dawn of Flame* & its Sequel The Black Flame, plus The Revolution of 1960 & Others.

THE COLLECTED SCIENCE FICTION AND FANTASY OF STANLEY G. WEINBAUM 3—STRANGE GENIUS *by Stanley G. Weinbaum*—Classic Tales of the Human Mind at Work Including the Complete Novel The New Adam, the 'van Manderpootz' Stories and Others.

THE COLLECTED SCIENCE FICTION AND FANTASY OF STANLEY G. WEINBAUM 4—THE BLACK HEART *by Stanley G. Weinbaum*—Classic Strange Tales Including: the Complete Novel The Dark Other, Plus Proteus Island and Others.

THE COLLECTED SCIENCE FICTION & FANTASY OF JACK LONDON 1—BEFORE ADAM & OTHER STORIES *by Jack London*—included in this Volume Before Adam The Scarlet Plague A Relic of the Pliocene When the World Was Young The Red One Planchette A Thousand Deaths Goliah A Curious Fragment The Rejuvenation of Major Rathbone.

THE COLLECTED SCIENCE FICTION & FANTASY OF JACK LONDON 2—THE IRON HEEL & OTHER STORIES *by Jack London*—included in this Volume The Iron Heel The Enemy of All the World The Shadow and the Flash The Strength of the Strong The Unparalleled Invasion The Dream of Debs.

THE COLLECTED SCIENCE FICTION & FANTASY OF JACK LONDON 3—THE STAR ROVER & OTHER STORIES *by Jack London*—included in this Volume The Star Rover The Minions of Midas The Eternity of Forms The Man With the Gash.

THE CRETAN TEAT *by Brian Aldiss*—The Cretan Teat is a wry and comic novel that interweaves its own fiction with an inner fiction about the discovery of a Byzantine painting of the Mother of the Blessed Virgin Mary suckling the infant Jesus and a fake ikon that becomes an instrument of Nemesis.